For Dan

Thank you for all the years of shared stories,
both great and small.

By Andrew J. Luther

Tales of the Undying Empire

Undying Empire: Rebellion

Acknowledgements: As always, there are a few people I want to thank for helping me with this novel.

My wife, Pam, for continuing to support my obsession with telling stories.

Dan and Bev for all their fantastic feedback. A couple of the better chapters in this book are the direct result of their comments and questions.

And of course I want to thank everyone who continues to buy and read my novels. Your comments and feedback are inspirational.

TALES OF THE UNDYING EMPIRE

The Witch's Path

ANDREW J. LUTHER

VANISHING GOBLIN

www.vanishing-goblin.com

The Witch's Path

© 2014 by Andrew J. Luther

ISBN: 9780993650208

Vanishing Goblin Inc.
www.vanishing-goblin.com

Prologue

F IRE!"

The call went up as flames billowed out from the windows of an abandoned tenement on the very edge of the Warren, the poorest district in Ythis filled with the destitute, the desperate, the downtrodden, and the dangerous. Within minutes, the whole structure was ablaze, and the flames had spread to adjoining buildings. The clouds that blanketed the night sky reflected the flickering light back down over the city.

In this part of Ythis, the construction was mostly wood, with the occasional stone or brick edifice providing support to the ragged and unstable homes that leaned on one another like the drunken beggars who crawled through the Warren's streets. A fire could easily consume this entire section of the Empire's capitol city, killing thousands and leaving many more homeless.

The Fire Brigade responded quickly, though by the time they had gathered around the spreading blaze, they knew they would be fighting a determined battle to stop the hungry flames. Desperate, pain-filled screams from those trapped inside the burning structures told of horrific deaths that would haunt the onlookers' dreams for many nights to come.

Near the docks, the Brigade made a frenzied effort to turn the massive pumps that would send water from the Bay of Ythis up through buried channels to stations situated across the city. By the time the nearest spigots began spraying water into the line of waiting buckets, an entire city block was roaring with the enormous conflagration.

The workers did not waste effort on trying to save any structures that were already ablaze, but instead turned their attention to the surrounding buildings in an attempt to keep the fire from spreading. In this, they found themselves more successful than expected. Despite the glowing embers floating through the air and touching down on roofs for many blocks in every direction, no new fires sprang up.

One small home—little more than a shack made from a collection of wooden planks nailed to each other and to the wall of a burning tenement—seemed resistant to the flames. Had it caught fire, it would have acted as a bridge to a larger structure. But for no reason the workers could determine, the wood blackened from the nearby heat yet did not ignite.

On all sides of the raging inferno, those fighting the fire noticed such strange occurrences, as if the fire was somehow choosing which buildings to attack and which to ignore. After the first hour, as they continued to douse the walls and roofs around the perimeter of the blaze, it became clear the fire was no longer spreading and had not made the jump to any new structures for some time.

The area continued to burn throughout the night, throwing flames up into the dark sky and the red glow making the clouds resemble demonic faces leering out over the citizens of Ythis. The streets were thronged with people, many fleeing the devastation and just as many coming to watch the desperate battle to save the city from burning to the ground. Some joined in to help, but most just watched and shivered at the sight of such destruction.

In the shadows beside a doorway, beyond the perimeter of where the Fire Brigade workers continued to douse the nearby buildings, a lone figure stood watching the pillar of flames. Despite the combined heat of the summer night and the huge fire, the figure wore a heavy cloak, the hood pulled up to conceal his or her face. A few onlookers noticed the figure, but none approached or otherwise tried to discern the identity of the person.

It was rarely wise to pry into another's business in Ythis unless you had no other choice.

The figure stood watching while the fires burned, hour after hour, until the night had passed.

Shortly before dawn, the roar of the flames was replaced with a rising groan, combined with creaking and snapping, and the workers quickly retreated from the edge of the conflagration. The sound rose in volume until, with a resounding crash, the original tenement, the neighboring buildings, and every structure within the circle of flames collapsed inwards.

An enormous cloud of sparks and embers rose up into the sky as a wall of smoke billowed outwards from the site of the fire. Onlookers ran from the growing fog, coughing and choking, though the cloaked figure remained motionless and seemed unaffected by the ash filling the air.

Without warning, as the sparks in the sky winked out, the flames below dwindled and died, leaving an impenetrable darkness that was unexpected and unsettling after the bright light of the flames. A few Fire Brigade workers stumbled toward the edge of the burned area, but the smoke was too thick to see the extent of the devastation wrought by the inferno. They backed off and waited for the sun to rise and illuminate the damage.

As the sky lightened above Ythis, it became clear to anyone observing that the smoke was dissipating. A large shadow within the billowing clouds of ash and steam seemed to indicate a building was still standing, despite the collapse that had seemed to put out the fire. They waited still, none wanting to approach the edge of the burnt ground.

Finally, the smoke cleared enough for those still gathered to see what had replaced the block of homes, tenements, and small shops that had been consumed by the flames. As a gust of wind scattered a rising plume of smoke, the remaining workers collectively gasped at the sight.

The wreckage of the destroyed buildings lay scattered across the ground, though it appeared there was a clear path through the smoking remains. The path led to the base of a tower, perhaps five stories in height, made of what appeared to be blackened rock. Wisps of smoke continued to curl and eddy around the entire height of the tower, and a chimney at the top poured a thick column of ash into the air.

Though none knew to whom the tower belonged, everyone understood what it was. Five other towers stood over Ythis, each home to a powerful sorcerer. The Five were advisors to the Emperor, and rivals of the Church. And as the cloaked figure turned and walked away from the scene of the fire, the onlookers on the streets around the charred remains suddenly understood what the tower's presence meant.

The Five had just become the Six.

Chapter One

JADIR DROPPED A COIN INTO THE WAITING PALM OF THE merchant and tucked the half-loaf under his arm. The man eyed him with a suspicious frown, but Jadir ignored the look as he turned and walked away from the stall. Though he had purchased bread from this merchant many times in the past year, he was always watched with a disapproving glare.

He didn't take it personally—Jadir knew his size was intimidating. Not only that, but some of Jadir's acquaintances stole produce and other goods from the market almost daily, and truth be told, he wasn't above pilfering a bit of food himself when money was short. As a young man in his late teens he was lucky to have a job, but it wasn't always enough to make ends meet.

He left the market as the sun peeked above the horizon to the east of the city. The area was not yet crowded, but would shortly fill with buyers and sellers, thieves and Watchmen, hagglers and guards. Jadir wanted none of that crowd. He wanted to get back to his room before Marilsa woke.

His young sister always slept in later than Jadir, and it gave him the chance to go out, get enough food for the two of them to break their fast, and return before she was aware he had gone. While he didn't really like leaving her alone in the single room they rented together in the tenement just up the hill from the sprawling expanse of warehouses that hugged the docks, he felt he had little choice. Time was always limited, and he wanted Marilsa to get as much rest as she could.

He walked the short distance back to the tenement and scaled the rickety wooden stairs to their room on the third floor. As he passed the doors of other rooms, Jadir could hear his neighbors stirring and preparing themselves for what would likely be a day of hard labor. He arrived at his own door and was about to reach for the latch when he heard sobbing coming from the other side.

Fear stabbed him in the belly as he fumbled with the large metal key and unlocked the door. Had something happened to his little sister? Had someone broken into their room and was even now....

Jadir shoved the door open and stepped inside, looking around wildly, but nothing appeared out of the ordinary. Marilsa lay on her side on her sleeping pallet, facing away from him. She was no longer making any noise, but he knew she only pretended to still be asleep. He closed the door and put the bread on the small table in the corner of their room.

"Marilsa?" he whispered to her.

She stirred, shifting slightly on her pallet but not turning to face him. He waited while she pretended to slowly awaken. Still turned away, she spoke softly.

"Good morning, Jadir."

He could hear the tears in her voice, though she tried to hide it. He moved to her side, knelt and placed his hand on her shoulder.

"Marilsa, are you okay? Is something wrong?"

She hesitated before answering.

"No, I'm okay. It was just a bad dream."

Her words didn't comfort him. She had already told him about the nightmares she had been having, more and more often.

"Was it another like the others?"

She nodded her head, still not looking at him. He reached up and gently rubbed her head, pulling her hair back from her face, though he could not see her expression. His palm nearly covered the entire top of her head, and he knew she liked that—it made her feel safe. He wished he could do something more to help her, to stop these terrifying dreams from coming back, again and again.

It had started just over a month ago, with Marilsa bolting upright in the middle of the night, screaming. Jadir had trouble calming her down, and it took several minutes before she had realized where she was. Their neighbors had been rather annoyed by the commotion.

The subsequent dreams didn't cause her to wake screaming, but they were no less disturbing. They didn't come every night, and there was no pattern that Jadir could discern, but the nightmares returned often enough to affect Marilsa's sleep. She wasn't getting enough rest, not after working hard each day as a servant in the house of a rich and demanding merchant.

Jadir worried about her. He had questioned her about these dreams, and she claimed she barely remembered them once she was awake. All that remained with her was the face of a man with long, black hair and bright yellow cat eyes.

At first, Jadir had wondered if the merchant—or someone in his home—was doing something to Marilsa. But she declared she was safe enough in her servant's job. They certainly weren't the nicest of employers, but they didn't abuse her or otherwise harm her in any way. Marilsa's confidence in her job convinced Jadir it wasn't the source of the nightmares.

Regardless of the frightening nature of the dreams, however, she had never reacted like this before. He didn't know if it was exhaustion that had caused her sobs or something new in the dream. But she was only thirteen years old, and he cared too much about her to ignore the problem.

"Marilsa, we need to talk about this. You're not sleeping enough, and the dreams seem to be getting worse. Something is causing these nightmares, and we have to figure out what is scaring you so much that it comes into your dreams."

She lay there and said nothing for a full minute. Jadir waited for her to think it over and decide what to tell him. He knew she trusted him—he had taken care of her as long as she could remember, since back when they were in the orphanage together. He loved her with all his heart, and she knew that too.

Finally, she took a deep breath and let it out slowly.

"Jadir, I'm scared. I don't know what to do."

He continued to rub her head as he talked.

"It's okay. We'll find out what's scaring you and we'll fix it. And then these dreams will go away."

"No, that's not going to work. He won't go away, Jadir. I've tried to run away from him, and I've tried to push him away from me. But he won't leave me alone. He's drawn to me, and I don't know if I'm strong enough to resist him."

A chill ran up Jadir's spine. The way she spoke about the man with the yellow cat eyes, as if he was a real person....

"He's just a dream, Marilsa. Or is there someone in real life who frightens you so much you've turned them into this man in your dreams?"

She finally rolled over and faced Jadir, and he was shocked to see her bloodshot eyes and pale face. His sister looked as if she hadn't slept in *days*.

"Oh, Marilsa—" he began, but she interrupted him.

"He isn't a dream," she said, and there was something urgent and desperate in her voice. "He comes *into* my dreams—it's how he speaks to me. He wants me, Jadir, he wants to...."

She trailed off, embarrassed, and Jadir realized what she had been about to say. The man in her dreams wanted to have to sex with her. But she was still just a girl. She would probably become a woman soon, and Jadir was acutely aware of how little he knew about what would happen, except in broad terms. For now, though, she was just his little sister.

Jadir could see she was terrified. He wanted to convince her that the man wasn't real, just her imagination, but he also could tell it was the wrong approach. She needed her big brother to understand what she felt. She needed his support.

But before he could say anything, she pulled her arms out from under the blanket that covered her. With fear in her eyes, she pulled back the sleeves of her shift and bared her forearms. A cold fear gripped Jadir as she showed him the truth.

"He's coming through, Jadir," she said as Jadir stared at the bruises on her arms in the shape of large hands. "I can't push him away, and he's gotten so close he can touch me now."

Tears leaked from the sides of her eyes and dripped onto her pillow.

"He's coming through," she repeated. "He's coming for *me*."

Jadir sat back, stunned. There was no mistaking the bruises on her arms—someone had taken her in a crushing grip and left hand-prints in her skin. He wanted to ask her who had done that to her, who had grabbed her this way, but when he opened his mouth, no sound came out.

She had already told him who had done it. But that couldn't be true. It *had* to be someone at the merchant's home, or someone in this building.

Or Jadir himself.

The thought struck him with enough force that he threw himself to his feet and backed away from her. Had he done this himself? Had he been sleepwalking and attacking his sister in the night without being aware of it? Was that possible?

He saw the look in her eyes as he backed away, and she began to cry harder.

"Please," she whispered. "Please don't be afraid of me."

She thought he was backing away because *he* was frightened to be near *her*. She needed him, and he was terrified he was the cause of her pain.

"Marilsa," he began, and had to clear his throat before continuing. "Marilsa, you need to tell me, you need to be honest with me. Did I do this?"

She frowned at his question, confused.

"Did you do what?" she asked.

"Have I been causing your nightmares? Did I leave the bruises on your arms? Have I been doing…things…in my sleep? If I have hurt you, I need to know. I won't get angry with you, or abandon you. But I need to know if I'm the one doing this."

He saw the meaning of his questions hit her and she began crying even harder. He wanted to go over to comfort her, but he was afraid he was right, and that she'd pull away from him. Marilsa was all the family he had. The thought of losing her was too much to consider.

Finally, she managed to calm herself down enough to answer him.

"It's not you, Jadir. The man in my dreams is…something else. He's not human. Jadir, I need you—you're the only one who cares about me. You couldn't ever hurt me."

Jadir's vision went blurry as he returned to embrace Marilsa, and he felt tears running down his own cheeks. His relief was overwhelming, but mixed with a dread that what she was saying was true. Some being was invading her dreams, and it was no longer content to just frighten her.

Jadir was not a violent person, but he wanted to get his hands on whatever that man was who had harmed his sister. Jadir worked in a warehouse every day, lifting heavy crates, barrels, and sacks. He was large for his age, bigger than most of the fully-gown men in the warehouse, and easily the strongest of all of them. And while he wasn't one to get into fights if he could help it, he had faced his share of challengers and had learned what it took to win most confrontations.

He could feel anger welling up inside him. He would defend his little sister from whatever was trying to hurt her. He would do whatever was necessary to keep her safe. No one would harm Marilsa as long as he was alive and able to fight.

But he knew, deep down, that his physical strength wasn't the answer. A creature who could invade a person's dreams, that was something beyond his knowledge, and he doubted it would appear in a physical form to give Jadir the advantage. They needed help.

From where, though? This was clearly something supernatural, and there wasn't a lot of help out there for people who found themselves in situations like this. He wasn't exactly going to go to one of the Five—or was that now the Six—and ask a sorcerer to protect his sister.

The Church was an option, but not one he could fully trust. They were supposed to protect the people of the Empire from supernatural threats, and it was true that they had driven off that creature in the Bay of Ythis a few months ago. But the priesthood was almost as frightening as the sorcerers.

The youngest and newest priests were known to help people from time to time, to tend to their "flock" as they called the people of the Empire. The only problem was that all priests were mad, a result of regular contact with their god. If they thought you were a threat, they had the right to take you inside the Great Temple, by force if necessary.

And no one but priests ever left that place once they were taken inside.

It was a risk Jadir wasn't willing to take, not with Marilsa's life at stake. No, there had to be another way to get help.

Marilsa pulled away from Jadir and wiped her eyes. She looked up at his face, saw that he had been crying as well, and giggled at him. The sound made him smile back at her.

"We have to hurry, big brother. They'll fire me if I'm late, and we can't afford that."

Jadir nodded and stepped back to let her get up. He turned his back as she dressed herself, and then they both stuffed hunks of bread into their mouths while they prepared to leave for the day.

"Marilsa, what are we going to do about tonight?"

She looked down at her feet and shrugged.

"Maybe I can stay awake, and then he can't come."

"You can't stay awake forever. Besides, you're tired enough as it is. Any less sleep and you'll start making mistakes at work. And then they *will* fire you."

She looked Jadir in the eyes.

"I can't face him again. I don't think I can stop him from...doing whatever he wants to me."

Jadir realized he had clenched his fists, and he forced himself to calm down.

"I have an idea that may help. I'll speak to Phana today."

Marilsa smiled despite herself, and Jadir regretted mentioning the name. Phana was a member of a local gang, and she liked to tease Jadir. The fact she was pretty made it even worse for him. Marilsa had met Phana once, and they had immediately hit it off. Marilsa loved to bug Jadir about his "girlfriend."

Jadir preferred to avoid thinking about the situation. It made him too uncomfortable.

"Not a word about Phana. We don't have time. And besides, this isn't something to joke about. She might know someone who could help you. Or at least make a few suggestions."

Marilsa nodded, but kept smiling. At least she was distracted from thinking about the man in her dreams.

They locked up and went down to the street together. Once outside, Jadir gave his little sister a final hug, and then she turned north and walked up the street toward High Town.

Jadir turned in the opposite direction and headed down toward the docks. He had a feeling it was going to be a long day, and he knew he would worry about Marilsa constantly until he saw her again tonight. But at least by then he might have some help for her.

He just hoped he wasn't wrong about that.

Chapter Two

THE ORPHANAGE WAS SMALL, AND SURVIVED SOLELY ON the charity of others, which meant there was barely enough money to feed the children who lived there. Jadir's first memory was of Mother Adari, a spindly, wrinkled woman who worked with a quiet efficiency, only the slightest hint of compassion breaking through her business-like veneer on rare occasions.

It was Mother Adari who told Jadir how old he was—seven—and that Marilsa was his little sister. She explained his role as big brother, and that he needed to protect the baby girl and take care of her. The two of them would not be able to stay in the orphanage forever, and it would be too easy to fall into the hands of slavers, or worse.

Over the next few years, Jadir helped Mother Adari as best he could, while Marilsa grew into a quiet child who was always content to be near her big brother. In ones and twos, the other dozen children left the orphanage, to various fates. Some joined the gangs as lookouts and runners, others learned the skills of begging. Almost half were taken as slaves, or had their lives ended early by violence, disease, or starvation.

By his twelfth birthday, Jadir was not only the oldest child left in the orphanage, but the largest as well. He continued to help Mother Adari with her charges, took care of Marilsa as best he could, and eventually took a job helping carry packages for a local merchant. His meager earnings went right back to Mother Adari and was used to help support the children.

He watched Marilsa turn into a beautiful young girl with a generous spirit and a calming influence on the other children. She was only six, yet she often led the children in song, or knew when some-one desperately needed a hug. The younger children adored her, and the older loved having her around.

Their lives were simple, yet they were happy enough. Of the remaining children, only Jadir had a sense of what the world outside the orphanage was like. In his job, he often witnessed some of the darkest aspects of a city like Ythis. The streets were hardly safe, and only his size and ability to talk his way out of danger saved him from beatings or worse on many occasions.

The year that Jadir became fourteen, everything they had came crumbling down. Mother Adari's health had been declining for some time, and one morning Jadir awoke to find her sprawled face-down on the floor of the common room. He touched her hand and found it cold, and he knew she was dead.

One of the other children, Haidai, a boy of about ten, declared that they needed to tell "somebody," and he bolted out of the or-phanage before Jadir could stop him. Jadir looked around the room at the other dozen children and his heart sank. He felt responsible for them, wanted to help them. But he knew he would have enough trouble saving himself and Marilsa from what was coming.

"We have to go," he told his sister.

"Why?" she asked. At eight years of age, Marilsa was still the heart of the orphanage, and he knew she would have great difficulty leaving the other children.

Jadir grabbed a change of clothes for them both, and then raided the pantry for some stale bread and crusty cheese, the best of the food currently stocked.

Some of the younger children asked where he was going, and tears ran down his cheeks as he told them he needed to do some things and would be back soon. The two other older children, both a couple of years away from their teens, gave him a look and departed.

Marilsa was standing in the middle of the room beside the body of Mother Adari, looking at each child's face, one-by-one. Jadir hated himself for what he was doing, but his only thought was for the safety of his little sister. That was more important than anything else.

Finally, he took her hand and led her out into the street.

To their left, he saw Haidai returning followed by two Watchmen and a third man. Though Jadir did not know the man, he knew from the man's clothing what he represented. The man was a slaver. A few coins to the Watchmen, and the slaver would take possession of the children still inside.

"This way," he said to Marilsa, and led her across the street into the shadows of an alley mouth. Haidai frowned and looked his way, but the other boy seemed to be unsure if he had seen Jadir or not. He led the Watchmen and the slaver into the orphanage.

As soon as they were out of sight, Jadir turned to Marilsa.

"I'm sorry, Mar. I wanted to save them, but I can't. Please forgive me."

Marilsa looked at him solemnly and then stepped close to him and wrapped her arms around his middle. She sobbed as she hugged him.

"I love you, Jadir. Thank you for taking care of me. I don't know what I'd do without you."

Jadir put his hand on her head and stroked her hair. From that point on, the two of them were truly on their own.

*   *   *

JADIR LIFTED THE BUNDLE OF *NOLÉ* WOOD FROM THE BACK OF the wagon and carried it into the warehouse. Carefully setting it down beside the others, he wrinkled his nose at the pungent smell coming from the pale, yellow wood. He turned away and sneezed twice, and the other workers gave him a wide berth.

The *nolé* was one of the most valuable goods in the warehouse, though he hated it when those shipments came in. The odor always seemed to set off a sneezing fit, and he would inevitably end up with a headache at the end of the day. He couldn't imagine why anyone would burn it and inhale the fumes, though apparently it was a current fashion among nobles and the wealthy to do exactly that.

Jadir knew how expensive this was—it had to be shipped all the way from the kingdoms in the far south, and even there it was rare. Each of the bundles he carried was worth a small fortune. A half-dozen guards stood watch around the wagon and inside the warehouse, making sure that no one attempted to steal a length of the *nolé* wood. A trio of guards would stay here over the next few nights until the wood was shipped out to the noble estates and merchant houses in and around Ythis.

When Jadir stepped back outside, he moved off away from the doors and took a few deep breaths to clear his head. The foreman, Chayesh, saw him and came over. Jadir hoped the man didn't think he was being lazy. He was one of the best workers in the warehouse.

"You sick?" Chayesh asked him as he approached.

Jadir shook his head and let out another sneeze.

"No, sir. Something about the *nolé* makes me sneeze. It always happens when I carry it."

Chayesh gave him a searching look, as if trying to decide if Jadir was lying.

"I just need a couple of breaths of air, sir, and then I'll get right back to it."

The foreman nodded.

"Yah, you will. Listen, I wanna talk to you for a minute. Come over here."

He led Jadir further away from the main doors, to where none of the other workers could overhear.

"You're a good worker, Jadir. You don't complain and you don't slack off. You got any family?"

Jadir was taken aback by the man's words. Praise wasn't something the foreman handed out, to anyone, ever. He wasn't the worst of men to work for, but he wasn't friendly with his employees either. Chayesh expected a solid day's work out of you before he'd hand over your pay, and he had been known to fire men for missing a day or two of work, regardless of the reason.

"Uh, yes, sir. A sister. She's younger—"

"Yah, listen. I see you don't really hang much with the other guys. You know how to keep your mouth shut?"

That question made Jadir uncomfortable. He knew enough to

know when someone asked you if you could keep your mouth shut, they were about to tell you something that could bring trouble if anyone else found out. Jadir went out of his way to avoid trouble whenever he could.

At the same time, there wasn't an easy way to answer the foreman's question. Even though the foreman hadn't told him anything yet, there was obviously something else going on. If Jadir replied that he *couldn't* keep his mouth shut, Chayesh would wonder if he would repeat this conversation to everyone else and raise the other workers' curiosity.

Either way, he was now in a difficult spot. He knew he would have to tread carefully.

"I know enough not to talk about things that are none of my business, sir."

Chayesh nodded at him.

"Yah, good. I thought so. You wanna make some extra money?"

This was another dangerous question. Jadir's size and strength had attracted others who were interested in using him to intimidate or hurt people on their behalf. He had never accepted such work—it went against his nature. He had a feeling that whatever the foreman wanted from him, it wasn't going to be legal.

"Well, sir, I'm willing to do some extra work for extra pay, if you need me to carry or move other heavy crates or barrels or such."

Chayesh smiled, and Jadir didn't like the look in his eyes.

"Good. That's what I'm talkin' about. Don't worry, it's nothin' dangerous or illegal, if that's what you think."

Jadir waited for more detail before he would allow himself to feel relieved.

"Listen, the owner wants to sell off some of the wood to someone other than their usual customers. But that deal must remain private, you know? The fewer who know about it, the better. So they're sending one man to come pick it up, but he'll need help loading the wagon. You're my strongest guy. It'll be just you, me, the owner, and him. You interested?"

Despite what Chayesh had said about it being legal, Jadir knew there was more to this than the foreman was telling him. However, it didn't sound dangerous, and if all he was doing was loading some bundles of wood into a wagon, he figured the extra money was worth it.

"If that's all there is to it, then I'm interested in the extra work, sir."

Chayesh smiled again.

"Yah, good. Listen, there is one more thing—you can't ever tell anyone you got the extra work or what you did. That's important. Once you're done, you forget about it. Can you do that?"

Jadir nodded.

"Okay, do your regular workday here, but hang back when everyone else leaves. The guy will be here about an hour after we close up for the day."

Shit, thought Jadir. *He wants me to do this* tonight.

That would make it more difficult for Jadir to meet up with Phana. He knew where she could be found in the early evening, but as the night wore on, she might be anywhere in Ythis. Jadir needed to see her if he was going to help his sister.

"Sir, do you know how long this will take?"

Chayesh's smile disappeared.

"Listen, it'll take as long as it takes. You said you wanted some extra work. I'm givin' it to you."

"Yes, sir. It's just that I need to take care of something tonight for my little sister—"

"Yah, you'll have to do that after we're done here."

Chayesh looked around.

"We've talked long enough. The others will get suspicious. Go back to work and say nothin' to anyone."

He walked back toward the open door and Jadir forced himself to follow. Now he was stuck. The truth was he *did* need the extra money. But tonight of all nights was the worst time to have to stay late. He would have to bolt the instant they were done tonight and go looking for Phana. Hopefully, he would find her without too much difficulty.

The thought of Marilsa going to sleep while he was still out and unable to protect her filled him with dread. Then again, she might not let herself fall asleep until he returned. Tired as she was, Marilsa was terrified of the man in her dreams.

Jadir wished there was some way to get a message to her, but his options were limited.

He moved up to the wagon, grabbed another bundle of *nolé* wood, and wrinkled his nose at the smell.

Chapter Three

JADIR HAD BEEN WORKING FOR CHAYESH FOR NEARLY A year when he first bumped into *her*. He was walking back one evening to the tiny room above a shop that he and Marilsa rented from an old spice merchant when he noticed a wagon stopped up ahead. The wagon was heaped with boxes covered by a tarp, the bed of the wagon tilted toward one corner.

He heard her voice before he saw her. She was standing behind the wagon, swearing a blue streak in a barely audible growl. Jadir noted that the front wheel of the wagon had come off. It appeared to be unbroken, but unattached.

As he reached the horses, she stepped out from behind the wagon and gave a start. She had apparently not heard him approach, and before he could say something, she drew a long knife and dropped into a fighting stance.

"Beat it," she said to him in a flat voice. "This one's mine."

She was dressed in black tunic and trousers, with a thick leather vest and high black boots. If they had not been near a streetlamp, Jadir would have had trouble picking her out of the darkness of the night. Her hair was short and dark, framing a rather pretty face.

Jadir took a step backward and held up his hands.

"Whoa, I was just coming over to see if I could help," he said.

"Help yourself to my stuff, more like it."

"Okay," Jadir said, continuing to back up. "I don't want any trouble, so I'm just going to leave you to your wagon."

He stayed facing her for another dozen backward paces before turning around to walk away.

"Wait," she called. He turned back to face her, but didn't say anything.

"Actually, I *could* use some help."

Jadir marveled at her audacity. She still held the long knife in her fist.

"I think it's best if I leave," he replied. "No offense, but you're a bit too handy with that blade."

She looked down at the knife in her hand, but didn't sheath it.

"Please," she said. "I'm stuck out here, and I really could use some muscle power to help get that wheel back on. You wouldn't leave a helpless female out in the street late at night all alone, would you?"

Jadir couldn't help but laugh at the suddenly innocent look she put on her face. She smiled back at him.

"You don't look so helpless to me."

This time, she did sheath the blade.

"I don't have any money," he told her.

"What?"

"If you're trying to get me to lift the edge of the wagon so that you can put a knife to my back and steal my coins, you're out of luck. I'm the poorest guy you're likely to meet tonight, and I don't have any coins."

"I really just want to get this wheel back on and get out of here," she said earnestly. Despite her clothing and weaponry, she didn't look like a hardened criminal. As much as Jadir wanted to be careful, he didn't really believe she would stab him in the back.

He stepped up and examined the wagon. It appeared the metal pin that held the wagon wheel in place had snapped.

"There's no point in putting the wheel back on—it'll just fall right off again as soon as you start moving."

She reached into a pouch and pulled out a short iron spike.

"Will this work?" she asked.

Jadir took it from her and examined it.

"It might. I'll have to pound it into place, and you should avoid going too fast until you can get it properly repaired, but it should get you where you need to go tonight."

She nodded and walked past him to pick up the wagon wheel.

"If you can lift that corner of the wagon high enough, I'll push the wheel back into place."

Jadir got a good grip on the edge of the wagon and heaved. Using his legs, he slowly managed to lift the corner of the wagon up a few handspans, and she shoved the wheel into place. Though the weight was immense, and he strained to hold up the fully laden wagon, he waited until she was finished and had stepped back before he gently lowered it back to the ground.

Taking the iron spike from her, he shoved it as far into the hole on the axle as it would go. Then he stepped to the side of the road and grabbed a loose cobblestone. When he struck the head of the spike, it rang out through the night like a bell.

"Uh, can't you do that any quieter?" she asked.

"Not really. What's the problem?"

He struck the spike again and drove it farther into the hole. As he paused to examine the spike, he heard someone shouting in the distance and the sound of booted feet on cobblestones.

"Time to go," she said, and climbed up onto the wagon. Jadir turned and looked up the street to see a group of five or six figures running towards them. The rivets on their leather breastplates glinted in the light as they passed a streetlamp.

"Climb up, and let's go," she said hurriedly.

"What's going on?" he asked her, and she glanced back over her shoulder.

"That's trouble coming for us," she explained. "And there's no such thing as an innocent bystander. I suggest you get in the wagon now and we'll get out of here before they reach us."

Jadir took a second to consider the situation. She was right—if those men were after her, they wouldn't bother asking Jadir what part he had played in tonight's events. He climbed up into the wagon beside her.

"Remember, don't go too—"

She whipped the horses and yelled, and the beasts took off as quickly as they could with the heavy wagon attached to them. In seconds, they were moving faster than the running men. Jadir looked back and recognized the designs on the armor as that of the City Watch. The men chasing the wagon gave up as the horses gained speed.

"I'm Phana," she said to him, laughing, as she steered the wagon through the city streets.

"Jadir," he replied. "That was the Watch. You don't own this wagon, do you?"

"You catch on quick. I thought I had lost them until you started hammering on the wagon wheel. Where can I drop you?"

Jadir blinked at her, and then couldn't help but chuckle at her wild energy and joy at escaping from the Watchmen.

"I can get off anywhere. I'll walk the rest of the way home," he said as he watched her face.

Phana pulled on the reigns and the wagon rolled to a stop. Jadir jumped down and turned to face her.

"Thanks for your help," she said to him. "I couldn't have done it without you."

"Yeah, well, I didn't realize this wasn't your wagon."

"Oh, please. Don't try to tell me that wasn't fun. Besides, now I owe you a favor."

She winked at him, and Jadir felt his face heat up. He was glad the darkness hid his blush.

"I mean it," she said seriously. "If you ever need anything, just come see me. I'll be glad to help you out."

"And how would I possibly find you? Walk the streets looking for broken carriages?"

She frowned at him in mock anger. "Just come to where I work. It should be easy to remember."

She flicked the reigns, and the horses started up again.

"It's called the Iron Spike," she shouted over her shoulder, and Jadir stood there watching her ride off into the night.

*   *   *

JADIR SWORE UNDER HIS BREATH AS HE MARCHED UP THE STREET that ran along the north edge of the Dock District. It was just past midnight, much later than he had wanted before he managed to get away from the warehouse. It had been delay after delay, and now he just wanted this night to be over.

The owner had arrived shortly after the rest of the workers had gone home. Jadir had waited in the main warehouse area while Chayesh met with the owner in the small office. The merchant had completely ignored Jadir, and Chayesh had fawned over the man.

The new "customer" was late arriving, and had shown up accompanied by a second man, a guard of some sort. The guard was only a bit older than Jadir, but looked dangerous. Jadir had noticed he was missing the bottom half of one ear—probably the result of a fight.

The presence of the extra man had caused quite a bit of discussion between the merchant and the driver of the wagon, but the second man had stepped up and spoke to the merchant in a low voice that Jadir could not overhear. It became apparent the "guard" was really in charge, and the driver was merely there to handle the wagon.

The merchant and the younger man went into the office, leaving Chayesh, Jadir, and the driver to stand waiting in the warehouse again. More than another hour had passed before they finally emerged and Jadir was ordered to load twenty bundles of *nolé* wood on the wagon. When he was done, the wagon and its passengers left, and then the merchant had addressed Jadir directly, repeating his foreman's instructions to forget everything that had just happened.

Now, Jadir saw the familiar sign of the Iron Spike up ahead and made a silent wish he would find Phana inside the tavern. He was worried sick about Marilsa, but knew there was no point in returning home until he had what he needed. He would do whatever he could to help his sister.

A tough-looking man lounged outside the tavern, as if waiting for someone. He saw Jadir marching toward the door wearing a determined look on his face, and the man let out a low whistle and stepped into Jadir's path. From the alley to one side of the Iron Spike, two more men emerged.

"There something I can help you with?" the thug asked. Jadir pulled up short in front of the man and shook his head.

"I'm just looking for someone."

"What for?"

Jadir didn't have time for this. He needed to see Phana. But the other two men were slowly approaching, spreading out and drifting around behind him. He realized he looked like he was going to cause trouble. These men were here to make sure the trouble stayed outside.

Jadir raised his hands, palms out, and the man in front of him almost flinched.

"I'm sorry; I've been here a few times before. I just need to see Phana. She's a friend. I'm angry at myself for being late, not at anyone inside."

The man looked him over.

"What's your name?"

"Jadir. Is Phana around?"

"I don't know anyone by that name. But I'll do you a favor and save you the trouble of going in there yourself. Wait here and I'll see if anyone named Phana is inside."

Jadir knew the man was lying about not knowing Phana—he was a member of her gang. In fact, Jadir had seen this man in the Iron Spike on other occasions when he visited Phana. Something was obviously different tonight, like the gang was expecting trouble of some kind. Jadir didn't want any part of that trouble, so he nodded and forced himself to relax as the man turned and went inside the tavern. The other men stood on either side of Jadir, just out of his reach. They said nothing, just watched him. He didn't bother trying to engage them in conversation.

A moment later, the man came back out and jerked his head at the two men.

"Jadir, you can go in. Turns out I do know Phana after all. She's inside."

Jadir entered the tavern as the other men retreated back into the alley. It was dark inside, and smoke wreathed the air, making it hard to see the inhabitants clearly. He stepped away from the door and peered around, but didn't see Phana.

He felt a hand touch his back and slide up onto his shoulder.

"What a great surprise, Jadir."

He turned to see Phana standing behind him. As he faced her, she slid her hand up around the back of his neck and stepped up to him, her face inches from his. He was acutely aware of how attractive she was. She pressed herself against him, and something deep in his belly made it difficult to breath.

"I was just thinking it had been a while since I last saw you," she said in a low voice, her breath caressing his mouth. He suddenly realized his body was starting to react to her, and he couldn't handle the embarrassment tonight. He put his hands on her hips and gently moved her back a couple of steps.

"Please, Phana, this is serious. I really need your help. It's about Marilsa."

Her expression changed immediately. The teasing look disappeared, to be replaced by concern.

"What's wrong, Jadir. Is Marilsa all right?"

"Can we sit down somewhere quiet and talk?"

Phana nodded and led him over to a quiet corner. Jadir felt a little light-headed, but he wasn't sure if it was her close presence that was causing it or the smoke he couldn't avoid inhaling as he moved through the room.

Phana's gang dealt in all kinds of narcotics, both legal and not, and its members were frequent users of their own products. He was pretty sure not everyone currently in the Iron Spike was a member of her gang, but he expected most of the inhabitants were probably under the influence of one drug or another. In a few cases, probably two or three.

Jadir himself didn't generally partake. For one thing, it was an added expense he could ill afford. For another, he took his responsibility for Marilsa seriously, and thus did very little socializing. So while he had nothing personally against the idea of such drugs, his experience was very limited.

Phana sat him at a small table and pulled her chair around beside his. She sat down and curled an arm through his own. There was no teasing look, however. She wasn't trying to make him uncomfortable, and he had to admit there was something wonderful about this simple human contact.

"Tell me everything."

Jadir didn't know where to start. How could he explain that a man was visiting Marilsa in her dreams, had started hurting her physically? He couldn't make sense of it himself.

"Phana, I'm going to tell you something that sounds crazy, but I assure you it's true. Marilsa has been having trouble sleeping for the last month or so. At first it was just nightmares. She kept dreaming about a man chasing her. The nightmares have been getting worse, and she's afraid to fall asleep."

Phana frowned.

"Has she...has anyone...?"

Jadir shook his head.

"No. I'd take care of it myself if it was something like that. Last night, the man in Marilsa's dreams caught her. She struggled with him before she woke up. He left bruises on her arms where he grabbed her."

"Bruises? In her dreams she has bruises?"

"No. When she woke up, her arms had bruises on them. I saw them myself."

Phana leaned back and made the sign to ward against evil. Jadir nodded again.

"Yeah, some*thing* is attacking my sister through her dreams. She told me this morning that he is trying to come through, into this world, using her."

Phana's arm dropped away from his, and Jadir felt the urge to take her hands in his own. He needed that contact right now. And he was afraid Phana would pull away completely, avoid him and Marilsa. But he needed her help.

"Phana, I don't know what to do. I'm afraid to go to the Church and ask for their help; the risk is too great. But I don't know anyone else who can tell me what's happening and what I can do about it."

She looked down at the floor and considered it.

"I don't know of anyone else myself. But I can ask around. I've heard there are others who might be able to do something. Maybe a witch?"

Jadir shrugged.

"Sure, if I lived in some tiny village out on the edge of the Empire,

I might consider that as an option. But this is Ythis. There aren't going to be any witches here, not near the Great Temple, not in the same city where the Fi—*Six* have their towers. But if you can help me find someone who can help Marilsa, I'd do anything to pay you back."

He realized as he said it that he knew what she might ask. Phana had approached him before about joining her gang, as had others. He had declined, and she hadn't pressed the issue, but she made the suggestion every so often in case he changed his mind.

"But that might take a while, and I need to do something for Marilsa right away. She can't stay awake every night, and once she falls asleep, he's waiting for her in her dreams. So, I was wondering if you know of something she could…take…that would stop her from dreaming at all."

Phana's eyes widened in surprise. He was asking to buy drugs for his sister. This was something he knew she never would have expected from him. Phana took a moment to think about his question.

"There might be something that can help. Stay here. I'll be right back."

Phana left him at the table and went through the door behind the bar, into the kitchen area of the tavern. Somewhere back there would be the gang's stash of drugs. If there was anything that could prevent Marilsa from dreaming, there was a good chance Phana's gang might have it.

He silently willed Phana to hurry. Every minute that passed was another minute his little sister was alone at home, trying to stay awake.

Chapter Four

WHEN JADIR RETURNED TO THEIR ROOM, MARILSA was sitting on the floor beside her sleeping pallet, her back against the rough, wooden wall. Dark circles under her eyes stood out like bruises against her pale face. She looked up at Jadir with a mixture of exhaustion, relief at his arrival, and fear of what was waiting for her if she should sleep.

Jadir felt his heart ache at his sister's appearance. She was trying to be brave for him, but he could see what the dreams were doing to her. He came over and knelt beside her. Marilsa wrapped her thin arms around his waist and buried her face in his chest.

They stayed like that, saying nothing, as Jadir gently stroked her hair. Minutes passed, and he began to worry that she was drifting into unconsciousness, so he carefully shifted away from her. He was relieved to see she was still fully awake.

"You were gone so long," said in a low voice, though there was no hint of accusation there, only worry.

"I was held late at work, and then I went to get something for you. Something that may help."

She looked up at him and his heart lurched again at the hope in her face. He was worried his idea might not work, and he couldn't bear the thought of her despair if it proved ineffective. He stood and pulled out the small package Phana had given him.

He pulled open the wrapping to find a handful of small, purple leaves with rounded edges. He didn't recognize the plant, though having spent his entire life in Ythis, he was hardly familiar with different types of vegetation. Marilsa also stood to see what he had, and he took one of the leaves and placed it in Marilsa's palm.

"Phana told me to give you only one. It's called yirresh. You're supposed to chew it until it turns mushy in your mouth, and then swallow it down with some water."

Marilsa frowned at the little leaf in her hand.

"What will it do to me?"

"It will stop your dreams. At least, that's what it's supposed to do. I've never taken anything like this before."

Marilsa looked back up into Jadir's face.

"Phana gave it to you?"

He nodded. She apparently trusted Phana, as she took the leaf in two fingers and delicately placed it on her tongue. She paused for a moment, and he was about to remind her that she had to chew it up when she closed her mouth and began to crush the leaf with her teeth.

It took some effort, but eventually she picked up the jug of water, poured some into her wooden cup, and drank it down.

"Marilsa…," Jadir began, and then stopped. He didn't want to worry her—she seemed so content thinking this small plant would solve her problem. But she heard the tone in his voice and raised her eyebrows at him.

"Marilsa, I don't know if the yirresh will help. I mean, I figure the man comes to you in your dreams, and so if you're not dreaming, he can't come, right? But it still might not work. We don't even know what he *is*."

She stepped forward and gave him another hug.

"It will help," she said, and he realized she was trying to reassure *him*. "I'm going to have a real sleep tonight because you took care of it."

He wrapped his big arms around her and gave a squeeze, and then she climbed onto her pallet and pulled the thin blanket over her.

"I'll watch over you tonight," he said.

"No, Jadir. You need your sleep more than I need mine."

"One night won't really make a difference to me, and I need to know you're okay. Go to sleep. I'll be fine."

She gave him a look that said she disapproved, but her exhaustion was too strong for her to put up a real fight. He wondered if the drug was also making her extra sleepy, but Phana hadn't mentioned anything about that. Jadir sat on his own pallet and watched as Marilsa's eyes slowly closed and within a couple of minutes, she was fast asleep.

Jadir leaned against the wall at the head of his own sleeping pallet and sighed. He was also tired—it had been a long day. But he had promised her he would watch over her while she slept, and there was no way he'd break his vow.

Marilsa's sleep seemed peaceful. She didn't twitch or move, and made no sound except for her deep and regular breathing. In order to remain conscious, Jadir was forced to stand up and pace around their room every half hour or so. His movements didn't seem to disturb Marilsa.

Hours passed, and Jadir figured dawn couldn't be far off when he felt his resolve slipping. He realized his head had drooped down and his eyes were closed, and he fought to regain his composure. Blinking rapidly, he looked over at Marilsa, who had rolled onto her back.

She still seemed to be sleeping peacefully. Jadir considered standing again, though he was sure it had only been a few minutes since he had last sat down. But he didn't want to fall asleep, and willed himself to move. Only his body didn't want to respond, and he thought about standing up to wake himself up, over and over, but nothing seemed to happen.

And then his eyes snapped open and he yanked his head up, slamming it into the wall behind him. He had been asleep, and his thoughts about standing were only echoes in his dreams. He turned to look at Marilsa and a cold chill ran down his spine.

The lone candle on the table had burned down and gone out, and the room was in shadows. A figure crouched over Marilsa, a patch of deeper darkness in the murk. Jadir couldn't make out any features on the figure, but it leaned down closer to his sister.

Jadir felt rage take him, and he yelled as he pushed himself off the pallet—a primal growl at this *thing* that was attempting to harm his sister. He leaped over her sleeping form and drove into the figure, but met no resistance and crashed into the wall on the far side.

Jadir spun and saw the figure float over Marilsa's body and reach down to touch her head. She didn't react in any way, but continued to breathe regularly as if she was deeply asleep. Jadir swung his fists through the creature's head, again and again, but he couldn't feel it and seemed to have no effect.

The figure reached down and cradled Marilsa's head between its hands. As she exhaled, Marilsa let out a low moan and her brow wrinkled in a frown.

"Iathephos help me," Jadir whispered. He wasn't in the habit of invoking the God of Ythis—it wasn't the kind of god people turned to when in need—but the phrase came to his lips before he could consider it.

But his words had an immediate effect.

For the first time, the figure noticed Jadir standing there in the darkness. It straightened up, still floating in the air. Jadir could see the figure was that of a naked, muscled man. It opened its eyes, and its yellow pupils glowed in the darkness.

Jadir let out a breath, and a cloud rose in front of his face. The temperature in the room had plummeted, and frost was starting to form on the table and other surfaces. The figure clenched its fists, and Jadir heard what sounded like a snarl come as if from the other end of a long tunnel.

"By the Abyss, get away from my sister!" Jadir yelled at the figure. It raised one arm and pointed at Jadir, and he could see frost begin to form on the smoky surface of its skin. Suddenly, the creature lunged at Jadir and he raised his arms to protect himself.

But as it shot forward, the figure dissolved into nothing. Jadir gasped as the temperature suddenly snapped back to the normal heat of a late summer evening. In seconds, all the frost melted and left only moisture in its place.

Jadir knelt and checked on Marilsa. Her face was peaceful, and she seemed to be sleeping normally once more. The drug had helped her resist the presence of the dream-man, and Jadir's invocation of Iathephos had seemed to cause the creature some discomfort, and had apparently driven it away.

A tiny thought in the back of his mind told him that it was never a good idea to call the attention of the God of Ythis, but in this case he was glad he had done it. For the first time in a long time, Marilsa was going to sleep safely.

*   *   *

QUDOVO FLUNG THE CHAIR INTO THE CORNER, WHERE IT BOUNCED off the wall and fell over. He turned and eyed Phana as if he was trying to decide whether or not to lash out at her, too. She stood impassively, meeting his gaze without any indication of fear or remorse.

"The cost of the yirresh is coming out of your cut," he announced.

She wasn't surprised and didn't bother to argue or agree.

Let him have his tantrum, she thought. *He needs to get it out of his system, or it'll fester for days.*

Phana wasn't afraid of Qudovo, though many others were. She knew him better than most, and understood his moods. He was strong, tough, and could be suddenly violent, though he knew better than to try anything with her. That was not a mistake she would let him make twice.

No, Qudovo would rant and take money from her cut of the gang's profits to save face, but nothing serious would happen to her. She was in a position of power and knew it.

"You have a job to do, but instead you give him drugs and let him leave. What game are you playing?"

He waited and she realized he truly wanted an answer.

"No game. He came to me for help, and I gave it to him. And now—"

"He needed something from you, and you didn't use it to get what *we* want from him. No, you gave him what he wanted and let him leave. No promises, no bargains, nothing!"

Qudovo turned and kicked the chair back against the wall. One of the legs cracked off and skittered across the floor.

"And *now*," Phana continued, "he owes me. He was here to take care of his sister, and if I had used that to try to drag some concession from him, he'd have left the Spike and never spoken to me again. And that would ruin things for good."

Qudovo clenched his fists but let her keep talking.

"Jadir is not one to leave his debts unpaid. So I'm going to ask him for a small favor in return—nothing big, nothing to do with gang business," she finished.

"I don't believe this!" shouted Qudovo. The vein on one side of his forehead pulsed, and his shaved scalp turned red. "He owes you and you're going to waste it on what? Get him to fuck you?"

Phana raised one eyebrow at him.

"That's what you want, isn't it?" he continued. "You're obvious enough about it. You're thinking with *that*—" Qudovo pointed at her crotch, "instead of with your head."

She could see he was getting himself all riled up. Then he'd say— or do—something stupid and she'd be forced to react. This wasn't how she wanted it to go, but before she could say anything to calm him down, he continued.

"Come to think of it, why *haven't* you fucked him yet? Think maybe that would be enough to convince him to join us? Seems like a fair trade to *me*."

And here it was—he had pushed her to the point where now she was angry.

"Are you suggesting I whore myself out for you?"

Her voice was mild, but Qudovo saw the look in her eyes as she asked the question, and something warned him that perhaps he had gone too far. Leader or not, big man or not, Phana had already taught him once not to cross certain lines with her. His next words might make things turn ugly very fast.

Qudovo stopped for a second, and then waved her off.

"Of course not, you know better than that."

"Then what *were* you suggesting?"

He took a deep breath and shook his head at her.

"By the Abyss, Phana, no one thinks you should be a whore. But I'm pissed off at you right now. You do what you want, when you want, as if you're not even one of us. At the very least you should have come to me before giving him the yirresh for free."

He grabbed the chair and righted it, but it immediately toppled over again. She almost laughed out loud at the look on his face.

"I wonder if you belong in this gang at all."

That drained the amusement from her like blood draining from a gutted pig. He *could* kick her out of the gang. It would cause him some trouble, but nothing he wouldn't come out of pretty much unscathed. There was only so much leeway he could give her, and she knew she pushed him to his limits far too often.

"Listen," she said to him, trying to keep any annoyance out of her voice. "You've had others trying to recruit him for, what, a year? And how successful has that been? He's no more interested now than when you started. You're not going to trap him, you're not going to intimidate him, and you're not going to force him."

Qudovo looked over her shoulder at the closed door. He was obviously concerned about others overhearing their argument. A leader was supposed to be in control, but everyone else already knew Phana followed her own path regardless of what Qudovo ordered.

She tried to be respectful of his position when others were around, tried not to give him a reason to force the issue. The fact was that this gang was her family, even Qudovo. She didn't want to be in charge, and didn't think the others would follow her anyway. Phana was no leader. She was too rebellious, too independent.

So she walked a careful path, trying to respect the structure of the gang even while she often took matters into her own hands. Phana was not good at following orders. That was something that would never change.

"Fine," he answered. "You want to let me in on your little plan so that I can pretend I know what you're doing? In case anyone asks me what you're up to?"

His words dripped with sarcasm, but she didn't care.

"I'm going to ask him to do something small, because if I push too hard, too quickly, he'll never trust me. But the truth is that his sister is going to need more help. And I'm going to *keep* helping, because that's the only way he'll come to see us as more than just a gang that wants to recruit him. Nothing else has worked, Qudovo. So let me do it my way, at *my* pace, and maybe you'll get what you want."

Qudovo stood there, looking at her, thinking it over. Finally, he gave a quick nod.

"But don't take too long. We don't have forever."

She shrugged.

"It'll take as long as it takes. You know, it would be helpful if you told me why we want him to join us so much. I mean, sure, he's big and strong and that's always good, but there's got to be something else, right?"

Qudovo opened his mouth, but paused, and she realized he didn't really have an answer and was trying to make something up on the spot. He saw the look in her eye and gave up.

"Phana, I might tell you, if I knew. But I wasn't told the reason either. The order came from straight from the Den. That's all I know."

Phana nodded and left the room. As she returned to the common area of the Iron Spike, she thought about what that meant. The Wolf himself was interested in Jadir and had told Qudovo to recruit him into their gang. But what was so special about Jadir that Ythis' most powerful—and infamous—head of organized crime would get personally involved?

It was a mystery Phana knew would bother her until she had an answer.

Chapter Five

I MEAN IT, FOUTEP. WHAT I'M ABOUT TO TELL YOU STAYS between us."

Jadir stood pacing in the alley behind the warehouse, while his friend leaned against the rough, wooden wall. They only had a few minutes to eat before they were expected to get back to work, and Jadir was hoping Foutep might be able to help him with Marilsa's problem. His friend had gotten him this job in the first place, and Jadir trusted him to keep their secret.

Foutep nodded, looking concerned.

"Is this about why you stayed late last night?"

Jadir paused. So his friend had noticed, which made Jadir wonder if any of the other workers knew something had happened here after they had all left for the day. Foutep saw the look on Jadir's face and held up his hands.

"You don't have to tell me any details if you don't want to. I'm really just curious."

Jadir heaved a sigh.

"No, it's nothing to do with last night. It's about my sister. Do you know of someone who might be able to help with a problem...uh, someone who can give me charms or potions? I mean, *real* charms, ones that have actual power."

Foutep's eyes went wide and he looked around to make sure no one was listening.

"You know that stuff is outlawed in the Empire, right?"

"Of course I know that. But I need something real—the fake stuff in the marketplace won't help me."

"Jadir," Foutep said slowly. "What's going on?"

Jadir looked down at the ground. He really didn't want to go into any detail. It wasn't that he thought Foutep might betray him. But Jadir had already told Phana, and he was starting to worry that it might have been a mistake to let anyone else know about Marilsa's problem. It was their secret—an incredibly dangerous secret—and every extra person who knew about it increased the risk.

"I don't think I should tell you the whole thing."

He saw the hurt look on Foutep's face. The older man looked on Jadir as a younger brother, and he obviously thought Jadir didn't trust him.

"No, it's not that I don't want to tell you. But I think it's better that you don't know too much. I can't even guess what's going to happen, or how this is going to end. It's possible Marilsa and I...," and Jadir dropped his voice to a whisper, "...it's possible the Church might come for us if they find out what's happening."

Jadir couldn't stop thinking about what had occurred earlier this morning. About how he had called upon Iathephos and it had seemed to affect the creature attacking his sister. Did the priests know he had done that? Was there some way for them to find out? Jadir had never attended one of the services that took place each day in the small temples scattered across the city. He didn't know enough about the God of Ythis and the Church to guess what they could do.

The blood drained from Foutep's face as he considered Jadir's words.

"I...uh, I don't know what I can do. Are...are you sure about...whatever it is?"

Jadir was disappointed to see that this was too much for Foutep to handle. The fear coming off the man was almost physical. It had been a mistake asking him for help, and now Jadir wondered if his friend would be able to get control of himself well enough to not make the other workers in the warehouse curious or suspicious.

"Foutep, it's okay," Jadir replied, trying to comfort his friend and downplay the danger. "The chance that the Church would notice us is almost nothing. Not really any more dangerous than walking the streets of Ythis and catching the attention of a priest. I'm just trying to protect you from any risk, even if it's tiny."

He could see his words were not reassuring his friend.

"I just think someone is trying something, and maybe they found a charm or talisman that is letting them cause us some trouble. All I need is something to break their connection to us, that's all. I know it's illegal, but it's not like there aren't lots of illegal things going on in this city every day."

Foutep looked around again, and then nodded at Jadir. He still looked unsettled, but he was calming down.

"I'll find something, Foutep. Don't worry about me. Thanks for listening."

He put his hand on Foutep's shoulder and began to lead the other man back around to the front of the warehouse, but Foutep stopped.

"Wait," he said.

Jadir lowered his hand, dreading the thought that Foutep was going to question him about Marilsa, or let his fear overtake him again. He stood there, waiting for the other man to speak.

"I...think I might know something that could help you."

It took a couple of seconds for Jadir to register what Foutep had said.

"You do?"

Foutep shrugged.

"Maybe," he replied, lowering his voice to a whisper just as Jadir had done a few moments before. "I know a few people who live in the Warren. I've heard there is a...witch...who lives there. The word is that she tells fortunes, sells charms, casts hexes...you know, that kind of thing."

Jadir's heart leapt at the thought of finding someone who might be able to help.

"How do I find her?"

Foutep shook his head and took a step back from Jadir.

"I don't know. My friends have never said, and I never asked. Really, it's just a rumor—she might not even exist at all."

Jadir could see how nervous Foutep was at the thought of connecting him with such a person. He wanted to ask his friend if he could find out more about the witch, but knew it was the wrong idea. Even if Foutep agreed—and Jadir had his doubts about that—the man would be too nervous to remain discrete. Jadir needed secrecy.

"Thank you for telling me. You're right, she probably doesn't exist, and I'd have no way to find her even if she did. I'll find another way to deal with my problem. Thank you for listening, my friend."

Foutep looked Jadir in the eye, but couldn't hold his gaze and dropped his head.

"You...you're welcome. I wish I could help more...but this is too...."

"It's okay. You did help."

He put his hand on his friend's shoulder again and Foutep let Jadir guide him out of the alley. By the time they had walked back around the front of the warehouse, Foutep had composed himself and no longer looked terrified.

Chayesh was standing by the main doors when they returned, and he eyed Foutep and then Jadir carefully. He also looked Jadir in the eye, but unlike Foutep, there was no nervousness there. Chayesh held Jadir's gaze, and the challenge was clear. The foreman was wondering if Jadir had told his friend about last night's business. Jadir kept his face expressionless and met his boss' look with confidence. The last thing he needed was for Chayesh to think Jadir was unable to keep secrets.

As he went back to work, Jadir thought about the witch who lived in the Warren. Though he and Marilsa lived near the edge of that neighborhood, neither of them was familiar with it. And the witch wouldn't exactly be easy to find—her life would depend on her remaining hidden from the Church and the Six.

Foutep would be no more help, but Jadir knew Phana might be able to find out how to get in contact with the witch. He was concerned about returning to her for another favor, but she was the best resource he had.

And—he admitted to himself—he was starting to trust her.

*　　　　*　　　　*

RELAEL OCHALLUM STEPPED INTO THE NARROW COURTYARD and pushed the metal gate closed behind him. He turned and locked it before proceeding up the short path to the small house. The cobblestones on the path were uneven and many were broken. Weeds sprouted between the cracks, partially hiding the stones and forcing Relael to step carefully to avoid twisting an ankle.

The gardens on either side of the path were also untended and overgrown. Relael looked up at the dilapidated house as he approached and smiled wryly. The effect was perfect—no one would give this property a second glance.

He stepped up to the door and tried the latch, but it, too, was locked. He inserted the key and gave it a twist, and the lock turned smoothly and without sound. Relael gave a last glance around— it paid to make sure one was not being watched or followed—and slipped inside. He closed and locked the door behind him, and then sneezed violently.

The interior of the house was similar to the outside—untidy and apparently unused. Dust covered most surfaces, though the floor was swept just well enough to hide any footprints that might be left by visitors. Thick curtains covered the tall but narrow windows, and in the gloom Relael could make out the sitting room to his left, furniture scattered haphazardly as if it had simply been moved in and abandoned quite some time ago.

He moved to a nondescript door near the base of the staircase that led to the second floor and found this latch unlocked. The doorway led into a slim stairwell lit by a single candle in a wall sconce about halfway down. Relael carefully picked his way down the stairs and entered a damp basement with dirt walls. He could smell mildew and felt his nose tingle with the beginning of another sneeze.

Covering his lower face with a sleeve, Relael stepped behind the staircase and found a short section of wooden wall, with a door in the center. He opened the door and stepped into a clean, well-kept room with wooden paneling covering the walls and floor. A simple square table sat in the center of the room, holding a lantern that fully illuminated the small space.

Seated at the table, facing the door, was the person Relael had come to meet. The man gestured for Relael to close the door and join him at the table.

"Master Eudain," Relael said, giving a short bow to the other man before taking a seat. "I trust you are well?"

The other man nodded once and gave a small smile.

"As well as can be expected," he replied in a low, gravelly voice. "And how are you keeping?"

Relael smiled back and clasped his hands on the table in front of him.

"Always the same, my friend. Always the same. Thank you for making the time to meet with me, Tyath. I know you must be very busy."

The other man shrugged.

"Your request to meet was neither surprising nor unwelcome. With all that has happened recently, I also felt it best to talk directly."

Relael looked Tyath over carefully, looking for any changes in appearance that might give him information on the other man's current health and wellbeing. The last thing Relael needed was for his colleague to disappear and be replaced—it had taken him years to cultivate this relationship with the Imperial Spymaster, and he had no intention of letting it slip away now.

Though it had been several months since they had last met, and perhaps Tyath had a little more gray hair, a few extra wrinkles, the man otherwise looked healthy. He had always been a small man, but he sat straight and his gaze was clear, and he projected the impression of someone larger than he was.

Relael waited for Tyath to continue, but the other man said nothing further. Relael knew they would sit here in silence for quite some time if he didn't take the lead, and so spoke the words that they both knew would be their main topic of discussion.

"The new tower," he said. "I admit it was something of a surprise to us to see it raised. From what we knew, none of the apprentices were quite ready to assume the mantle of sorcerer. And you?"

"It was only a matter of time," Tyath replied. While he didn't admit it had come as a surprise to the Spymaster's organization as well, the look on Tyath's face told Relael it had not been expected.

"They are calling it the Tower of Ash," continued the smaller man. "You no doubt know more details about it now than I do."

This was a common tactic of Tyath's. He rarely admitted having any information on any subject, the better to draw out what others knew. Relael was not one to fall for such an obvious trick—braggarts simply did not make it into his sect of the Church. But he knew Tyath's habits were hard to break.

Still, their relationship required a bit of give and take, and it cost nothing for Relael to confirm what he knew about the newest sorcerer of Ythis.

"She is known as the Burning Crone, a recent apprentice of the sorcerer Veylar Dust. Her ascension was rapid—she bypassed the most senior of Dust's apprentices, a man named Delash Wiar."

Tyath raised his eyebrows slightly at this news, and Relael knew he had shared a new piece of information.

"That explains why we were caught unprepared. My information says that Apprentice Wiar is nowhere near being ready to assume the mantle of sorcerer."

Relael nodded.

"So the Five have become the Six. The balance of power in Ythis has shifted. No doubt you will see the new sorcerer at the next Great Council. One has to wonder how this will affect their influence on the Emperor."

Tyath shrugged, but Relael could see it was mostly for show.

"The Emperor has dealt with new sorcerers before. Remember, he was ruling the Empire back when there were only the Three."

"The Church acts as a counterbalance to the Five," replied Relael. "We have been the Emperor's staunchest allies since the founding of the Empire. But the growing power of the sorcerers cannot be ignored."

Tyath's brows drew down into a frown, and this time, it wasn't just for show.

"Is there some reason the Church cannot continue to fulfill its role as opposition to the Six?"

Relael knew he was never supposed to admit to any weakness in the Church. While he and Tyath generally worked toward a common purpose, he could never fully trust this man. But he also knew the Emperor couldn't let either the sorcerers or the Church become too powerful. If one side or the other came to dominate Ythis, even the Emperor himself could see his own power waning.

"Of course we will continue to oppose the sorcerers of Ythis," Relael reassured him. "But our current High Priest is new to his role, and recent events in this city have, shall we say, *stretched* our resources fairly thin. Let's be honest, my friend. The Emperor has used the power of the Five to keep us in check. And now we are ill prepared when the Five has suddenly increased their own power."

Tyath considered Relael's words silently, and then nodded slowly.

"Fair enough. I won't deny the Emperor is concerned about letting your brethren run rampant throughout the streets of Ythis. He doesn't want a return to the early days."

"No one does," replied Relael.

"Okay, but where does that leave us? I know you better than to think you requested this meeting just to exchange a few tidbits of information. You want something."

"Yes, Tyath, I do. The people of Ythis are nervous about the new tower and what it might portend. A new sorcerer is a danger to everyone—who knows what she might do before she fully understands the political situation here and the role she must play? The other sorcerers won't rein her in unless the Emperor orders it. They'll let her revel in her new power to excess and wait to see where the Emperor draws the line."

"And you're worried the Emperor will wait too long. That he'll accept some 'excess' as you put it before acting, and that will shift even more power toward the Six."

"Yes, that is exactly my concern."

"So, I'll ask again," said Tyath. "What is it you came here to ask me *for*?"

"I think it's important to Ythis that this Burning Crone does something visibly dangerous right away, something the Emperor cannot ignore. He needs to come down on the Six immediately, to reestablish his dominance as quickly as possible."

"But how can you guarantee the Crone will do what you want?"

"I will take care of that. My concern lies with the Imperial Guard. Some of the investigators can be overzealous at times. When an obvious, public display of the Crone's danger happens in Ythis, the Church will bring their concerns directly to the Emperor. I need the Imperial Guard to back up the Church. And I need you to make sure no one in the Guard investigates the matter too closely, just in case there are any loose ends that might be picked up."

"You play a dangerous game," replied Tyath. "If you make any mistakes, it will turn around to bite you. You're trying to frame a sorcerer and manipulate the Emperor."

"No, *we* are trying to provide the Emperor with the perfect opportunity to rebalance the situation in Ythis. Do we have an agreement?"

Tyath leaned back in his chair and considered Relael's plan. He said nothing for several minutes as he turned it over in his mind. Relael let him ponder the risks and rewards in peace. Without Tyath and his own influence, none of this would work.

Finally, the Imperial Spymaster let out a sigh and clasped his hands on the table in front of him, mirroring Relael's own posture.

"You have my support, Relael. I agree drastic action is necessary, and I know what you're capable of doing. But I'll be completely honest with you here. I will help cover things with the Imperial Guard, and will use what influence I have to encourage the Emperor to act. But if you mishandle this, if it goes so far off the path so that we cannot recover, my support will dissolve, and you will be left alone to deal with the consequences. I will not give up everything I have to save you."

Relael smiled a cold smile.

"I wouldn't expect it any other way, Tyath. I agree to your terms. Together, we will save Ythis."

Chapter Six

THE LOOK OF SURPRISE ON PHANA'S FACE SEEMED genuine as Jadir entered the common room of the Iron Spike for the second night in a row. Her expression quickly changed to worry, but Jadir gave her a small smile as he weaved between the tables toward her, and she seemed to relax. He grabbed the chair beside her, and she waved off the two other women who had been sitting with her.

"I'm glad to see you again, Jadir, but was there anything wrong with what I gave you last night?" she asked, unable to hide the concern in her voice.

"No, it worked exactly as I needed. Marilsa was able to sleep and wasn't...bothered...by any dreams."

Phana looked into his face and could tell he was holding something back.

"What happened? You look exhausted."

He looked down at the table, still not sure if he should tell her everything. But he needed her help, needed to find the witch who lived in the Warren.

"I tried to stay up all night and watch over Marilsa. Early this morning, the man from her dreams came back."

"I thought you said she didn't have any dreams—"

"She didn't. I saw him myself."

"In *your* dreams?"

"No, Phana. I was awake. He...the man or whatever he is...appeared in our room, and I *saw* him, crouching over Marilsa. He was just a shadow, but I knew who he was. I tried to tackle him, but I just went right through him. He was trying to get to Marilsa, but the drugs you gave me were blocking him from getting into her head."

"By the Abyss," Phana whispered. "How did you...?"

This was the part Jadir didn't think it was wise to tell Phana, how he had invoked the name of Iathephos, and it seemed to drive away the man. He was worried she might pull away from him if she thought he had attracted the attention of the God of Ythis, and he didn't know where else he could turn if she didn't help him.

"I...I got his attention. But he couldn't do anything to Marilsa, and I guess he can't do anything to me when I'm awake, so he disappeared."

Jadir looked down and realized his hands were shaking, so he put them on his thighs and hoped the table would hide them from Phana.

"I need your help again, Phana, and this time I don't care what it costs me. I've heard there is a witch who lives in the Warren. It's just a rumor, and it may not even be true, but if she does live there, I need to find her. I can't go to the Church yet—it's too risky for Marilsa. But I know that witches are supposed to help people who can pay what they ask. Is there any way you can find out where she is? How I can contact her?"

Phana sat there, stunned by what he had told her, what he was asking her. This was well beyond getting some drugs to help Marilsa sleep. She blinked at him and then reached over and laid her hand on his.

"I think I can help you. I don't know anything about any witch, personally. But I know someone who would, if she's really there. I'd like you to meet him. He's rather well connected in Ythis and I think he'd be happy to help you."

Jadir felt the slightest pang of something—jealousy?—at Phana's mention of this other man. Something in her voice spoke of admiration and maybe something more, and Jadir wasn't sure he liked that.

Of course, it was clear that Phana liked Jadir, too. She had made enough suggestive remarks over the last year that even Jadir understood what she was insinuating. But he had no idea how to respond to such attention—he was too inexperienced with women to flirt back with Phana. And he was worried about how any involvement with a woman would affect his ability to take care of Marilsa.

He realized Phana was waiting for a response from him. In his exhaustion his mind was wandering.

"I don't think it's a good idea to tell too many people about this, Phana. If word gets back to the Church—"

"I know," she replied. "Remember who you're talking to, here. It's not like the people I associate with are the types to talk out of turn— that kind of habit gets you killed. The person I'm talking about can keep secrets. I will personally vouch for him when it comes to that."

Jadir hesitated.

"Listen," she said. "You're worried about Marilsa, and so am I. You can't fight this thing, whatever it is. Marilsa can't take the drug forever, either. Eventually she's going to build up a tolerance for it and it'll stop working. And besides, it's not good for her to suppress her dreams. People who take that drug for too long start to have other problems."

A cold dread filled Jadir's gut. What had Phana given him? What had he given Marilsa?

"What problems? What didn't you tell me?"

Phana gripped his hand tighter.

"Nothing, Jadir. It's not dangerous for Marilsa, not for a while. But if you're not having any dreams, then you're not really sleeping fully. She may be fine for a week or two, but she'll get more and more tired. Eventually, it'll exhaust her to the point where she'll be too weak to do anything."

Jadir could tell from the look in Phana's eyes that there was more.

"What are you not telling me?"

"I'm no expert on this, but I've heard what's happened to people who took that drug for long periods of time. It seems that you can't stop dreams from coming forever. After a while, your dreams *will* come, and it won't matter if you're asleep or not. You'll have them, even if you're walking around out on the street. But if you start dreaming when you're awake, you won't be able to tell what's real and what's part of your dream."

"So you're saying this will eventually drive Marilsa crazy."

"I'm saying that after a while, and I'm talking about many weeks at least, she'll start having dreams during the daytime, when she's working or walking home after she's finished for the day. And other people may *think* she's crazy."

Jadir considered her words. He had known the drug would only be a temporary solution. And this morning he saw that the drug would not fully protect Marilsa from the man who came to her in her dreams.

Phana saw his hesitation and tried to reassure him.

"Jadir, last night you trusted me enough to tell me what was happening to Marilsa. And I helped you. I haven't told anyone what's going on with you, not even Qudovo, and believe me he wanted to know."

Jadir didn't like the leader of Phana's gang. Qudovo had tried to convince Jadir to work for him, and didn't respond well to Jadir's answer. He had stopped just short of threatening Jadir—which had been a surprise. Jadir didn't know why he had attracted such attention, but he knew working for Qudovo would be a mistake.

"Jadir, the man I'm talking about is not like Qudovo. He'll help you. If a witch really lives in the Warren, he'll find her. I'm not going to contact him unless you agree to it, but I'm trying to help Marilsa, too. Please, trust me on this."

Jadir was torn between his desire to protect Marilsa and his fear that the wrong person would hear about her problem and bring in the Church. But, ultimately, he couldn't save her from this man by himself. He didn't know anything about this kind of stuff. He needed help.

"Okay," he said to Phana. "You can tell this man about Marilsa. You set up a meeting and I'll come."

Phana smiled and Jadir couldn't help but smile back at her. She really was a very pretty woman.

"Great," she replied. "I just know Koral Creyss will be able to help."

*   *   *

"THAT'S ENOUGH," KORAL SAID IN A LOW VOICE. DESPITE THE FACT the others were shouting at each other, his words cut through their argument and brought them all up short. Koral had learned long ago that shouting got you nowhere, that it showed people you had no real power.

He never raised his voice anymore. He never needed to.

He looked from one gang leader to the other, making sure he had their full attention.

"I brought you here to discuss the problem between you, and to find a resolution you both can live with. Despite that, you persist in arguing and throwing threats at each other."

One of the other men opened his mouth to speak and Koral glared at him until he closed his mouth again.

"The Wolf has had enough with your little war on each other. You both work for *him*. He sent me here to solve this, *today*, and that's what I'm going to do. Is that clear?"

He waited until both men had nodded in agreement and then turned to Gaitu, who led a gang in the neighborhood where West River entered the Market District.

"Gaitu, as far as I can tell, this was started by your man, Eodai. He went into another gang's territory in order to meet a woman who he knew was involved with a man belonging to that gang."

"But—"

"And yes, he's dead now because of it. So no further punishment is coming your way."

Koral turned to the other gang leader.

"Bejral, your man Lotou pushed things too far by killing Eodai. A beating would have sufficed, but he pulled a knife and deliberately murdered a member of another gang. Where is Lotou now?"

Bejral shrugged, but Koral could tell from the look in his eye that he knew where the murderer was hiding.

"Let me make something clear to you, Bejral. You're responsible for the men and woman under you. Someone must take the punishment for his actions. Is it going to be him, or you?"

Koral's voice was mild, but there was an edge in there. Both gang leaders knew neither of them could beat Koral in a fight. And both also knew that, even if they did manage to take Koral down, it would only be a matter of days before the Wolf would have them hanging for it.

"He...he's at a tavern near the docks."

Koral nodded.

"Good. You're going to give him to Gaitu."

Bejral knew what would happen to Lotou once he was in the hands of the other gang.

"You can't—"

"Yes, I can. This was started by Eodai and Lotou, and now it ends with them. I don't care about any of the other fights, or who else was killed or injured in the skirmishes that came afterward. Lotou gets handed over, and that's the end of it. If I hear about a single other fight between your two gangs, whether it results in someone's death or not, you will both be removed from your positions."

Once again, he looked both men in the eye, one at a time.

"Am I clear?"

Gaitu nodded, and Koral could see the man was not happy, but could accept and be satisfied by his decision. Bejral, on the other hand, was furious. He held his temper in check and nodded at Koral, but it was obvious there would be more trouble there in the future.

I'll never understand why these guys want to bring such grief on themselves, he thought.

"Good," he said out loud. "Bejral, you have two days to deliver Lotou. Now go your separate ways."

The two gang leaders left the room and Koral heaved a sigh. He expected Bejral to comply with the order to hand Lotou over—he was angry but not ready for mutiny. But Koral could see it was building and he expected Bejral's gang would do something stupid within a week or two. Koral would have to set a couple of his own men to watch the situation and intervene before too much damage was done.

He left the small room and reentered the tavern's common room. He saw that both gang members had already departed, and no more than a handful of patrons sat at the tables.

"Koral?" said a woman's voice to his left. He turned and saw Phana seated at a small table, and Koral couldn't help but smile at her. Koral was always glad to see her—he was greatly attracted to her, and she seemed to like him as well.

"Phana," he said as he joined her at her table. "It's good to see you. It's very late...were you waiting for me?"

Phana nodded and Koral hoped it was pleasure instead of business.

"I need your help, Koral." His heart sank at her words. So it was business after all.

"Whatever I can do, you know you just have to ask."

She smiled at him and he smiled back. Phana was a couple of years older than he was, and was under the protection of the Wolf. Koral didn't know the story there—just that she was given a position in one of the gangs that operated in the south of the city where the Trades District, the Dock District, and the Warren all met, and that anyone who harmed her would be crossing the Wolf.

Koral knew that, as the Wolf's primary hand in the direct workings of the criminal elements of the city, he would be the one to mete out the punishment should anyone do anything to Phana. As such, he felt protective of her as well. He wondered if that would cause problems if they were to become involved with each other.

"Koral, it's about Jadir, the man we've been trying to recruit."

Jadir was another mystery. The Wolf had made it clear that Jadir was also under his protection, though Koral was pretty sure the two men had never met. The Wolf wanted Jadir to join the same gang where Phana was a member, but Jadir had no interest and had refused. Koral didn't know why the Wolf was interested in Jadir, but was confident his boss would tell Koral what he needed to know if it became important for him to do his job properly.

In the meantime, it was his duty to render assistance when and where he could.

Koral motioned Phana to come into the back room with him, where they could speak without danger of being overheard. She followed him in, and he closed the door.

"Okay, tell me everything."

Phana quickly explained the situation with Jadir's sister, Marilsa, and the strange man who visited her in her dreams.

"So Jadir thinks a witch might be able to drive off this spirit or whatever it is," she finished. "He heard a rumor that a witch lives in the Warren, but I don't know anything about that."

Koral considered what Phana had just told him. He wondered if there was something special about Jadir and his sister that the Wolf knew about. But he reminded himself that speculating was pointless until the Wolf decided to share the truth about the young man.

At least Koral would be able to help Jadir find the witch.

"Her name is Undilsa, and yes, she lives in the Warren."

Phana's eyes went wide and Koral had to fight the urge to put his arms around her.

"I can arrange for Jadir to meet Undilsa. But he has to be able to pay her price himself to get her help."

"Jadir doesn't have much money," Phana said, frowning.

"Undilsa doesn't ask for money. She asks for...unusual things. I can help Jadir find whatever Undilsa demands, but he'll have to get it himself. She'll know if I just give it to him."

"And then what?"

"And then, Jadir and his sister will go see the witch and hopefully she can help them with their spirit problem."

Phana grabbed Koral and gave him a hug. He wrapped his own arms about her waist as she pressed into him, and she seemed in no hurry to let go. Finally, she lowered her arms and stepped back. He looked into her eyes, and their faces were only inches apart.

"I...I'd better go," she finally said. "I should tell Jadir I was right about you. I knew you could help."

Koral nodded and stepped back.

"I will contact the witch and find out what her price is for Jadir. I'll meet you at the Iron Spike tomorrow night."

Phana gave him a shy smile as she let herself out of the room and closed the door behind her. Koral's own smile lasted for quite some time.

Chapter Seven

MARILSA PLACED THE SMALL LEAF IN HER MOUTH AND began to chew. Jadir waited patiently until she swallowed and then handed her the cup of water. He knew he wouldn't be able to watch over her again all night—he was exhausted from his lack of sleep last night and two full days of work.

Instead, he pulled his sleeping pallet over next to Marilsa's. He hadn't told her about what had happened last night. He was worried she would panic if she knew the man was able to manifest to the point Jadir could see him.

"I have to sleep tonight, Marilsa. But I'm right beside you if anything happens."

She looked at him and frowned.

"What do you think will happen?" she asked.

"Nothing. I'm just making sure, that's all."

She lay down on her pallet and pulled the blanket over her.

"Marilsa, this drug…you won't be able to use it forever. But I'm working on a way to get rid of that—thing—that's scaring you."

She looked up at him. He could see she was still frightened, but she also had total faith in him. Marilsa knew he would not fail her.

I wish I was as confident as she is, he thought.

"I love you, Jadir."

He leaned down and hugged her.

"I love you, too, Mar. Now go to sleep."

She turned on her side and drifted off in less than a minute.

As much as Jadir wanted—no, needed—to get some rest himself, he was hesitant to lie down. He worried that as soon as he drifted off, the man would return. Would Jadir wake up if Marilsa started to moan in her sleep? If he didn't, the drug might not be enough to protect her.

Worse, what if the man did return? Last night Jadir had called upon Iathephos in his panic to protect his sister, but to do so again was folly. And yet, he knew of no other way to drive off the spirit that was attacking Marilsa.

And there was something else Jadir didn't want to acknowledge, but which was true, nonetheless. Last night, the creature had become aware of Jadir, had obviously seen him as a threat. Could the man do something to Jadir when he was asleep? Jadir just didn't know enough to guess whether he was safe or not.

He briefly considered consuming one of the leaves Phana had given him, but quickly dismissed that thought. If the creature tried to attack Jadir, it seemed unlikely he would try to invade Jadir's dreams. It seemed like a more direct threat.

Jadir sat on the edge of his pallet and clenched his fists. There was no path that seemed safer than any other. He needed rest, and yet giving in might put him in terrible danger. And if anything happened to him, Marilsa would be left defenseless.

It occurred to him he should have gotten someone else to come sit up through the night. Phana would probably have agreed if he had asked, though he was also starting to worry about how many favors he owed her. Still, it would have been a help having a third person.

But it was too late now. Jadir couldn't leave the room while Marilsa was asleep, in case the creature came back while he was gone. He had no way to contact anyone else who might agree to help.

Jadir sat there, his exhaustion weighing down on him like a dozen heavy blankets draped over his head and shoulders. He couldn't imagine staying awake all night and still being able to work tomorrow. He would make a mistake, possibly injure himself, and then he and his sister both would be in a much worse situation.

There was nothing else he could do at this point. He had to let go and get some sleep. He kicked off his shoes and lay down on the bed, fully clothed. He figured not being too comfortable might keep him from sleeping too deeply, so that he would be able to respond if

Marilsa found herself in distress during the night.

At first, as he lay there, he realized his chaotic thoughts might keep him awake anyway...

...and then he was at work again, only none of the others had come in. Several fully laden wagons waited at the doors, and Chayesh was yelling at him to get them unloaded right away or he would lose his job.

Jadir grabbed a heavy crate from the back of the first wagon and pulled it off, and the weight of it nearly made him fall over. He dragged his feet as he carried it into the warehouse and placed it in the right spot. The heat inside the building was oppressive, and Jadir found it difficult to breathe.

He returned to the wagon and grabbed a second crate and began to carry it inside, but Chayesh knocked it out of his hands and when it hit the dirt floor, it shattered into nothing but dust.

"Too slow!" Chayesh screamed in Jadir's face. "You're going too slow! That's coming out of your pay! You've run out of time!"

Jadir turned back to the wagon and saw the driver was the dark figure of the man who was harming Marilsa. His sister sat in the back of the wagon, looking at him with wide, frightened eyes. As Jadir stepped toward the wagon, the man flicked the reigns and the horses began to gallop, taking his sister away from him down an endless street.

Jadir tried to chase the wagon, but another wagon rolled up in front of him, and the wall of crates on the back cut off the sight of Marilsa. Jadir gasped for breath, not able to get enough air into his lungs.

He grabbed another crate and carried it into the warehouse. Flies buzzed around his head, their noise loud in his ears. Jadir placed the crate on the floor and turned back to the wagon, but the door was gone, replaced by stacks and stacks of wooden crates.

Jadir tried to find his way back to the door, but every turn brought him to another alley made of crates stacked to the ceiling high above his head. He couldn't get enough air to think clearly—in fact, he could no longer breathe at all. The flies buzzing around his face forced him to close his eyes.

Jadir clutched his throat and tried to call out to Chayesh, but no sound came out. He felt...something...around his throat, tightening, tightening, cutting off all air. He sank to his knees and knew he was going to suffocate here, alone on the rough, dirt floor of the warehouse, in the middle of endless stacks of wooden crates, and no one would ever find his body.

The hands around his throat tightened again and the thought came drifting through his mind that someone was choking him. He raised his head and forced his eyes open to see the man, the spirit creature, standing in front of him with its hands around Jadir's throat. The yellow eyes bore into his, though Jadir could make out no other features.

Jadir grabbed the creature's wrists and tried to pull them away from his neck, but he was too weak from lack of air and the grip tightened further.

This can't be real!

The thought came to him as he realized the man was solid, and was able to harm Jadir directly.

This can't be real. This must be a nightmare. The man is attacking me in my dreams!

With a sudden clarity, Jadir knew he was asleep and that he had to wake up or he would die. His vision was dimming from the lack of air, but he willed himself to wake up. He fought his exhaustion with everything he had and forced himself to escape from this deadly nightmare.

With a start, he was suddenly awake. His eyes snapped open, though the pressure on his throat had not eased. He looked up and would have screamed if he could have gotten any sound out.

Marilsa was straddling his shoulders, her hands pressed down on his throat with all her weight. She was looking down at his face, her lips pulled back and her teeth bared in a horrific smile. She appeared to be fully awake.

And her open eyes glowed with a deep yellow flame.

*   *   *

BROTHER RELAEL OCHALLUM STOPPED OUTSIDE THE HEAVY, iron-bound door deep in the bowels of the Temple. Many levels further down lay the vast chamber where dwelt Iathephos, the God of Ythis. Despite the layers of rock separating Relael from that mind-chilling space, he could still feel his God shifting and turning below him. He shuddered and tried to block out those sensations, as of snakes slithering through his mind.

He had once been closed off to such feelings, blocked from such a connection to his God. The very act of communion with such an entity inevitably drove human beings insane. To be a priest and to serve Iathephos was to begin an inescapable and irreversible spiral down into madness. The hierarchy of the Church was full of such men and women.

This fact had led to the creation of a special sect with the Church known as the Hidden. These priests did not commune with Iathephos, and in fact underwent rituals to fortify their minds against the lunacy that came with such proximity to their God. As long as they avoided direct contact, they would retain their sanity.

The Hidden acted as a guiding hand for the leadership of the Church, the most powerful of the priesthood. For even the High Priest of Iathephos himself was twisted and riddled with mental disorders. The Hidden understood what was needed to keep the Church healthy and strong, even when their leadership was at the mercy of demented impulses and ideas.

For Relael, his surety in the stability of his own mind had crumbled the day he was forced to work side-by-side with the sorcerer Veylar Dust. Their task had been to drive off a huge, violent creature—a being alien to this world—that had come to reside in the Bay of Ythis and was destroying ships trying to enter or leave the city's harbor. Relael had been present when a ritual was conducted to communicate with the creature and use the power of his God to drive it away from the city.

Relael had witnessed the creature rise from the waters of the Bay, and his reality had turned to ashes around him. The rituals fortifying Relael's own mind melted away in the direct presence of such alien and overwhelming power. On that day, Relael knew a seed of madness had been planted in his mind. And now, proximity to Iathephos watered that seed, gave it sustenance so that it could grow into a tree whose branches would spread throughout Relael's brain.

He knew he would be removed from the Hidden should his superiors discover that tiny flicker of madness within him. Worse, he knew a great deal about the inner workings of his sect, and could not be trusted not to betray his fellows as his own mind became unstable. So Relael kept his thoughts to himself, lest his brethren decide to give him to Iathephos as a sacrifice to the power of his God.

Relael realized he had been standing beside the door for some moments, lost in his own reverie. He shuddered again and withdrew a key from a pocket in his robes. He unlocked and opened the door and stepped inside.

A small, stone chamber sat on the other side of the door. Three priests reclined in comfortable chairs set against the other three walls of the room. In the floor, a round iron plate covered the hole leading to the Chamber of Eyes.

One of the priests—the most senior—stood as Relael entered the room. Relael bowed to the senior priest.

"Brother Relael Ochallum, here to visit the oracles." He handed a rolled-up parchment to the priest.

The other man scanned the document and examined the seal at the bottom. Only a rare few were allowed to see the three oracles—distractions were always kept to a minimum—but Relael's superior in the Hidden had the authority to grant permission for short visits. The priest motioned for the other two men, who pulled out their own keys and unlocked the large gears holding the plate in place.

One man operated a crank that turned the gears while the other stood at the edge of the pit and ensured no one was attempting to come up. When the door was fully open, Relael lowered himself onto the iron rungs set into the side of the long, stone tube that led down to the Chamber. As soon as his head lowered below the edge of the floor, the priests cranked the metal plate back into place.

Relael climbed down to the bottom of the tube and faced the last door that stood between him and the oracles. He took a deep breath and then twisted the large latch that withdrew the silver bolts holding the door in place and warding this doorway against any attempted escape by the oracles.

Upon opening the door, he was assaulted by ear-piercing screams that echoed off the stone walls of the Chamber before him. The voices—for the screams came from more than one throat—were filled with agony and madness. Relael hesitated on the threshold, for the first time unsure if he wished to continue. Steeling himself, he stepped in and pulled the door closed behind him. He heard the silver bolts automatically slide back into place. He was now locked in here until the priests above let him leave.

The Chamber of Eyes was a vast, circular room, at least a hundred paces across at its widest point. Ornately carved pillars—covered in bas reliefs of thousands of eyes—were scattered haphazardly across the Chamber, though Relael knew they were precisely positioned in a specific pattern that amplified the eldritch energies coursing through the room. At the very center of the Chamber hung a lone lantern, illuminating three small wooden desks where hunched and cloaked figures sat scrawling in thick ledgers with ragged quills.

Relael approached the three desks and, looking down at the ledgers, noted the writing was in no language he understood. The hands holding the quills were all wrinkled and spotted with age. Leaning down to peer under the hood of one cloak, Relael saw an ancient face, papery skin creased and crumpled, gender indeterminate. Where the writer's eyes should have been, there was only blank skin.

With the shrieks and wails echoing off the circular stone walls, it was impossible for Relael to tell precisely where they were coming from. He turned his back on the wizened writers and peered into the gloom around him. To his left, he could just make out some movement in the shadows. Relael took a deep breath and strode in that direction.

At first, he wasn't sure what he was seeing, but as he came closer, he realized a body was hanging from the high ceiling. Though the light of the lone lantern in the center of the chamber did not penetrate quite this far, Relael's eyes slowly adjusted to the lowered light levels and he could discern the naked body of a man, hanging perpendicular to the floor. The man was on his back, his front to the ceiling, though his head hung back to nearly face Relael. This man was the source of one of the voices howling his torture into the room.

Metal hooks were embedded in the flesh of his arms, legs, groin, belly and chest, attached to chains that hung from the ceiling. His body was covered in cuts, bruises, punctures and other—uniden-tifiable—wounds. Relael couldn't imagine how someone in such a state could still be alive, and yet the man's voice was strong as he howled his torment.

From behind a pillar a few paces away, a woman stepped out of the shadows. At first, Relael thought she wore heavily decorated skin-tight leather, but as she came closer, he realized she was nude. The skin of her body was covered in intricate tattoos of hundreds of eyes. Even her bald head was decorated, leaving only her face to remain unblemished.

When she spoke, her voice was merely a whisper, though Relael heard it clearly over the screams of the man hanging before him.

"Your thoughts are chaotic, Relael Ochallum. You are filled with fear, anger, and...ambition. It is a sweet mixture."

She smiled, revealing a mouth filled with hundreds of thin, needle-sharp teeth. Relael forced himself not to recoil from her. It would only encourage her to toy with him instead of answering his questions. A few of the eyes tattooed on her skin blinked randomly.

"I-I have questions for you...about the Burning Crone. She is the new sorcerer—"

"I know why you are here," she whispered turning to the hang-ing man. "Don't I, lover?" She reached up and Relael saw the nail of her index finger was long and serrated. The woman dragged it slowly across the man's shoulder, and the skin parted with a rush of blood. The man's screams continued unabated, though somewhere in those howls Relael could tell the tone had changed slightly.

"Ah," the woman continued, as if she could hear his thoughts. "You are so near to understanding the language of agony and mad-ness, Relael Ochallum. You need only a little push. But there's no hurry, is there? It is a push you will give yourself—you need no help from others."

Relael didn't want to hear this, and he wasn't sure if she was playing a game with him or was predicting his future. He held himself back from responding to her taunt and focused on the task at hand.

"I need to know if the Burning Crone will inflict any damage on the people of Ythis, something more than is allowed by her status as one of the Fi—uh, the Six. Something I can use for my own purpose."

He didn't elaborate further, sure that she already knew his plan. He watched as an expression of mock sadness crept across her face.

"No," she replied. "The Burning Crone will disappoint you. She is too clever to revel in her newfound status and power. She knows what her position means, and will do nothing to threaten it. She surpassed them all because she always understood the true meaning of power better than the other apprentices of Veylar Dust."

Relael couldn't hide his disappointment. It would have been so easy if the Crone had caused the problems herself.

"Then I must create the disturbance myself," he said aloud to the woman before him. She leaned over and kissed the wound on the man's shoulder. The skin blackened at the touch of her lips as if burnt, but the wound had closed. Again, the tenor of the man's shrieks changed slightly.

"You want an opportunity," the woman continued. "Something you can use for your own ends. From the smallest mistake comes the chance you need. A simple error in a moment of fear, and Iathephos hears his name uttered by a young man protecting his sweet little sister."

"Who is this young man? How can I use him?"

The woman smiled again and something black and scaly slithered behind the line of those teeth like some horrid serpent living in her mouth.

"I will tell you how to find them, but the rest is up to you. The young man is your key. It is his sister who is the doorway."

Chapter Eight

JADIR WAS ON THE EDGE OF BLACKING OUT, AND KNEW IF he did he would never wake up. He was no longer strong enough to pull Marilsa's hands from his throat, but he also didn't want to hurt her. These thoughts rushed through his mind but his body reacted without thought.

His fist caught Marilsa on the side of her head and slammed her off balance. She fell to one side and Jadir gasped as the pressure on his throat disappeared. He gulped a lungful of air and rolled himself away from her, pushing himself up into a sitting position.

Her full weight landed on his back and her arm snaked around his neck before he could fully recover. Once again, the pressure on his throat cut off his supply of air. Her own breathing, ragged and uneven, sounded in his ear as she tried to choke him once more.

Jadir was in a panic and couldn't think clearly. All he knew was that Marilsa was trying to kill him, and that she had almost succeeded and still might. He had to stop her, one way or another.

He curled his arm and hooked his fist up over his shoulder into another punch that connected with Marilsa's forehead. Her head snapped back and her arm around his neck loosened. He grabbed her wrist and twisted it away before yanking her sideways onto her back. She tried to claw at his eyes, and he grabbed her other wrist and pinned her arms to the sleeping pallet.

In an instant, as he crouched above her—coughing and gasping, his lungs heaving—the light vanished from her eyes and Marilsa fully woke up. Her scream pierced his eardrums and Jadir recoiled, letting go of her wrists.

Marilsa threw herself away from him and scrambled toward the door.

"Marilsa, no!" he yelled and lunged after her. If she ran off into the street, thinking Jadir had attacked her, he might never find her again. She reached for the latch just as he hit the door, blocking it from opening. She looked up at him and screamed again, backpedaling away from him toward the small window.

"Stop! Just stop! It's me...Jadir. I'm not going to hurt you, Marilsa!"

A red welt rising on her forehead put lie to his words. His voice was rough and ragged, and he didn't sound like himself. He could see the fear in Marilsa's eyes, and she was nowhere close to calming down. Jadir dropped to his knees and pleaded with her.

"I'm not going to hurt you, Marilsa. It was the man—he came back and...attacked us both. Please, just calm down. Please. I won't hurt you," he repeated. "I would never hurt you."

She remained huddled against the far wall of their room and watched him as he tried to regain his breath. He sat down on the floor with his back to the door and coughed over and over.

A fist hammered on the door behind him and Marilsa screamed again.

"Open up in there!" called a man's voice, and Jadir thought it might be one of their neighbors who lived in the tenement.

"Okay," he tried to call out, but his voice came out in a whisper. He pulled himself to his feet as he heard other voices in the hallway outside the door. He unlatched the door and pulled it open to see his guess had been right—Hib was standing in front of the door, ready for a fight.

His neighbor wasn't nearly as large as Jadir, but the man was older and more experienced, and had been a brawler for most of his life. Jadir held no illusions how he would fare if the man attacked him.

Jadir held up both hands in a surrendering gesture and stepped back into his room to let Hib enter. Three other neighbors stood in the hallway and watched, though Jadir didn't know any of their names.

"What in the Abyss is going on in here?" Hib asked as he looked

3343

332

32333

Andrew J. Luther

from Jadir to Marilsa and back. "Are you beating her?"

"No," whispered Jadir. "It was…a nightmare. She was having a nightmare and…in her sleep she thought I was…she attacked me, and I lashed out before I was fully awake."

There was no way Jadir was going to tell the truth to Hib. He didn't know the man well enough to trust him with this. Hib looked to Marilsa.

"He tellin' the truth? Don't be afraid to speak up—his size don't mean a thing to me if he's doing something bad to you." Hib looked at the sleeping pallets pushed together, and he eyed Jadir with a disgusted look.

Jadir grabbed their one chair and sank into it. He looked up at Hib wearily.

"It's not like that, Hib—"

"I asked your sister a question," he interrupted and turned back to Marilsa. "Well, is what he said true or not? You don't have to let him do anything he wants to you, you know."

Marilsa looked at Jadir and something in her gaze told him she was frightened of something more than just how she had woken up. She was afraid of *him*. But Hib didn't know her well enough to see what she was thinking.

She nodded at Hib.

"Yeah, it was a nightmare. I have bad dreams sometimes and I asked Jadir to sleep beside me."

Hib was obviously skeptical of her words, but chose not to argue. He turned to Jadir.

"You always seemed like a decent guy. But if I find out you're beating this young lady, or doin' anything else you shouldn't be doin' with her, you'll be in for more than a beating yourself. You understand?"

Jadir wanted to argue with him, but knew it would only make things worse. He nodded at Hib.

"I understand. And thank you."

Hib gave him a confused look.

"For what?"

"For looking out for Marilsa. I'm glad you're around, even if it's me you're threatening right now."

Hib shook his head and walked out of the room, and the others in the hallway pulled back as he left. He pulled the door shut behind him, and Jadir could hear him talking in a low voice to the other neighbors, but he couldn't make out what was being said.

He looked at Marilsa, and knew the mark on her forehead was going to turn into a large bruise. He felt a pang of grief at causing her harm, even though he knew he'd had little choice.

"Do...do you know what happened?" he asked her. He watched as a single tear ran down her cheek.

"The drug didn't keep my dreams away. I had a nightmare...about you...."

She trailed off but Jadir waited for her to say more. He needed to know what was going on in her mind. She took a deep breath, wiped the tear away, and continued.

"You were trying to...hurt me. You said it was my time to...you wanted to be my first, said it was your right for taking care of me. I was running away from you, but I was so tired, and you kept chasing me."

More tears joined the first and Marilsa had trouble keeping her voice steady.

"You caught me and hit me, and then threw me on the ground. You were holding me down, and...."

Jadir knew what was coming even before she said it.

"And then you woke up," he finished for her.

She nodded at him and covered her face with her hands as she began to sob quietly.

He wanted to tell her what had really happened, why she had woken up like that, but he hesitated. The man had broken through the protection of the drug. He had somehow caused a nightmare that made Marilsa think she might not be able to trust Jadir.

The man had possessed her, had used her body to attack Jadir directly while he was sleeping.

Could Jadir really tell her the truth? How would she take it, knowing that she had been a puppet, completely unaware she was trying to murder her brother?

Would she believe him? Her own nightmare had planted a seed of doubt in her mind about Jadir, and waking up as she had only reinforced the terrible feelings from her dream. What could he say that would comfort her? He wasn't sure the truth was the best thing for her, but he also didn't want to lie to her, either.

He sat there in silence, while Marilsa quietly wept.

*   *   *

"Jadir, I'd like to introduce you to Koral Creyss."

Phana watched as Jadir held out his hand to the other man and Koral gave a firm shake. The three of them stood in the same back room of the Crown and Coin, where Phana had asked for Koral's help last night. Looking at the two men, Phana realized how different they were.

Jadir was tall, with broad shoulders and thick arms. Though his dark hair was cut short like Koral's, his face was open and honest. Koral appeared to be perhaps a year or two older, but carried himself with an air of someone with much greater life experience. He was shorter than Jadir—barely taller than Phana herself—and wiry. He moved like a stalking panther, all smooth grace, and he rarely expressed any visible emotions on his face.

"Koral, this is Jadir," she finished as both men stood and stared at one another. She had unconsciously moved to stand at one side, positioned equally apart from the pair of them.

"Small world, isn't it?" Koral said to Jadir.

"It seems to be," Jadir answered.

Phana glanced from one man to the other.

"You know each other?"

Koral grinned at her.

"We weren't formally introduced," he said. "But we recently happened to be in the same place at the same time."

He turned back to Jadir.

"Did they pay you for your extra time?"

Jadir nodded again.

"Phana says you agreed to help me," he said, getting right to the point. "What is it going to cost me?"

"The witch has decided you must bring her three live snakes. The breed doesn't matter."

Jadir shook his head.

"No, I meant your help—what will *that* cost me?"

Koral looked at Phana as if wanting her to explain. She wasn't sure what to say. It wouldn't exactly be a good idea to reveal to Jadir the help was coming directly from the Wolf. He was likely to start asking questions for which neither Phana nor Koral had answers.

"It won't cost you anything, Jadir," she lied. "Koral owes me a few favors, and I'm cashing one of them in for you."

Jadir looked her in the eyes and she saw something in his gaze that unsettled her. He was angry, and worried, and desperate. He had told her the drugs hadn't worked last night, but wouldn't tell her anything else. Things seemed to be spiraling out of his control and he was obviously concerned that he was getting himself deeply in debt to her.

As much as they were friends, she ran in the kind of circles he tried to avoid. She believed he was worried that she would drag him into her world as payback for everything she was doing to help him. And that was exactly what she had in mind, but not until Marilsa was safe and he was no longer terrified of losing his sister.

"I-I'm not sure I want that," he replied to her. She saw Koral raise his eyebrows but Jadir didn't notice.

"Jadir, this isn't about you owing me anything. Marilsa needs our help. She's a sweet girl and doesn't deserve whatever is happening to her. So I'm going to do whatever needs to be done. And right now, Koral can get you the help you need."

Jadir held her gaze for a few more seconds and then nodded once at her. He turned back to Koral.

"I'm sorry; this has been a very difficult day."

"Don't worry about it," Koral replied. "I know family's impor-tant."

Jadir stood there and said nothing. Koral waited, and the silence stretched out. Phana was uncomfortable and spoke up just to break the tension.

"Jadir, you won't be able to see the witch until tomorrow, but Koral will help you get the snakes tonight."

She put her hand on Jadir's arm and Phana thought Koral narrowed his eyes ever so slightly, but when she looked directly at him, she wasn't sure if she had imagined it. She dropped her hand and then silently cursed herself for letting a man's look affect her behavior. She had an urge to hook her arm through Jadir's, but she knew that would be petty.

"How am I going to get three live snakes?" asked Jadir. "We're in the middle of Ythis—I've never seen a live snake in my life."

Phana knew some of the vendors in the vast market sold snake meat and snakeskin, but she didn't know of anyone who kept live snakes. There was at least one shop that sold exotic animals to the nobility and merchant princes of Ythis, but she was pretty sure they didn't keep the animals on hand. And Jadir wouldn't have been able to afford them anyway.

Koral shrugged at Jadir.

"There are a couple of places in the city where you can get them. But the thing is, I can take you to where you might find some snakes, but I can't get them for you. I can't even directly help you get them. When the witch gives someone a price, they must pay it themselves. And she knows when someone tries to cheat."

Jadir nodded, but it was obvious he was too far out of his element.

"So, these places sell live snakes?"

Koral grinned at him, but there was no humor in it.

"Sort of. The issue is convincing the owners to sell them to *you*."

"Why?" asked Jadir, confused. "If the snakes are for sale, why wouldn't they sell them to me?"

"I can explain on the way. I have other things I have to do tonight, so let's get this moving."

Koral moved to the door and Phana asked "Where are we going?"

Koral stopped and turned to her.

"You're not coming."

"What? Why? I'm Jadir's friend and I want to help."

Koral met her gaze evenly and she could feel a powerful attraction pulling her to him. But it dissolved as soon as he spoke.

"That's the problem, Phana. You can't help Jadir, or you'll mess it all up. I'm taking him to get the snakes, but he must do it all himself. But this isn't an expedition—it's just Jadir and me."

Phana could feel her anger rising and opened her mouth to argue, but she forced herself to pause. Jadir didn't need her to tag along, and Koral was taking his job seriously. She admitted to herself that she just wanted to come to see what would happen.

But this wasn't about her—it was about Marilsa and Jadir. And her presence would likely complicate things between the two men.

That's their *problem*, she told herself, but she knew she would let them do what they needed to do without her interference.

"Okay, I won't try to insert myself where I'm not wanted."

Jadir looked at her as if he was going to try to reassure her that he had no issue with her presence. He was sweet, but incredibly stupid when it came to women. She would have to fix that.

"Jadir, I'm going to keep Marilsa company while you two are out tonight. You look exhausted, and you said someone needs to watch over her. I can stay up all night and make sure she doesn't start having nightmares again."

This time, she was sure there was an expression of disapproval on Koral's face, despite his effort to remain impassive. Jadir blushed, which only made things worse.

"You need to sleep," she told him. "We don't both have to stay awake. Besides, I'm more a night-person, anyway."

Jadir opened his mouth to speak, but it took him a couple of tries.

"Um, thanks. Marilsa will be happy to see you again. And I could...I could use a real sleep."

Phana stepped forward and gave Jadir a quick hug and was away before he realized what she was doing and could wrap his arms around her. He really was nearly dead on his feet.

She turned to Koral, grinned and winked, and pushed past him out the door. As she walked the length of the common room, she could almost feel his gaze on her. She wondered what was going through his mind as she left without looking back.

Chapter Nine

JADIR WALKED SILENTLY BESIDE KORAL TOWARD THE DOCKS. He seemed lost in his thoughts and Koral didn't really feel like interrupting with small talk. He wasn't terribly interested in getting to know the other man, who seemed to be a year or two younger than Koral himself. Koral's job was to get Jadir to where he could complete his task, and make sure nothing bad happened to him.

Finally, Jadir broke the silence.

"So where are we going?"

"It's a...tavern, of sorts. Called the Black Door."

"And they serve snake there?" asked Jadir.

Koral nodded and didn't elaborate, but Jadir thought it through and seemed determined to ask more questions.

"But they keep live snakes? Why don't they buy snake meat the same way other places do?"

"The patrons of the Black Door prefer to eat snakes while they're still slithering."

"What? Who would do that?"

"Don't ask," replied Koral. "Not everything that lives in Ythis is human."

Jadir stopped and Koral was forced to stop and turn around to face him.

"Koral, what am I going to be dealing with?"

"You're going to be dealing with the man who prepares food at the Black Door. He *is* human. You won't need to see the patrons of that place, and you don't want to."

Jadir looked at Koral and his distrust was obvious.

"Look, Jadir, I'm not setting you up or doing anything that'll cause more trouble for you. You asked to see the witch, and she sets her price, not me. If you don't want to go through with this, say the word and we'll call it all off."

"What happened to your ear?"

The question took Koral off guard. No one ever asked him about the missing half of his left ear. Of course most people who knew who he was were too afraid to ask him rude questions like that. But Jadir wasn't really being rude—he was asking to see how Koral reacted, which would tell him what kind of person Koral was.

"The blade of a spear," he answered. "Someone was trying to kill me, after they had killed my parents and siblings."

Koral said it as if he was talking about a distant past that no longer had any power to hurt him. But he saw pity in Jadir's eyes and was immediately angry. He opened his mouth, unsure of what he was going to say, but Jadir interrupted him.

"I never knew my parents. It's always been just Marilsa and me. Sometimes," he paused and looked up at the dark sky, "sometimes I think it would have been better to just have myself to look after."

He looked down and met Koral's eyes.

"Would it?"

Koral realized Jadir hadn't been showing pity. Jadir was feeling *guilty* over wanting to be free of his little sister. He was beyond tired, frightened of what was happening to her, worried about how they were going to get out of it, and he wished it all would go away. But he was the kind of person who couldn't accept those thoughts for what they really were. So now guilt had been added to the mix.

"For some of us," Koral replied, "being alone was the best thing that could have happened to us. I just met you, Jadir, but I'm willing to bet you're not one of those people. If you were, you wouldn't be here, doing what you're doing."

Jadir's eyes narrowed.

"And why, exactly, are *you* here, doing what you're doing?"

"I believe Phana already answered that question."

Jadir said nothing, just stood there looking at Koral. Finally, he muttered "Let's go," and started walking again.

Koral joined him and led him to the alley where the back entrance of the Black Door was located. Jadir checked the sack tucked in his belt that he had purchased at a shop back near the tavern where they first met up.

"Ask for Deiru," Koral instructed Jadir. "He is responsible for the food here. Offer to buy the three snakes and give him something extra for his trouble."

Koral turned and moved back to the mouth of the alley as Jadir turned to the door. He watched Jadir hammer his fist on it a couple of times and wait. A minute passed, and the door was yanked open.

"I-I need to speak to Deiru," Koral heard Jadir say.

"He's busy. What do you want?" The voice coming from the doorway was rough and Koral could tell it was an older man.

"I need to buy something from Deiru. It's...I have money, and he'll want to see me."

Don't lie, thought Koral. *It'll just make things more difficult.*

"Who are you?"

Jadir turned and looked up the alley at Koral. It was all the excuse the man needed, the thought that there were others hiding out of sight. He grabbed the door and tried to shove it closed.

But Jadir, moving faster than Koral expected of him, lunged forward and blocked the door from closing fully. He heaved at the door and it crashed inward. Koral couldn't believe Jadir was doing this. There was no way they'd sell him anything now. He saw Jadir dart into the hallway on the other side of the door.

Koral drew his short sword and ran back down the alley to the door. A very fat man lay on the floor just inside the threshold, barely conscious, his forehead bleeding. The heavy wooden panel must have caught him in the face as Jadir shoved it open.

Koral stopped at the threshold, not sure what to do. His orders were to protect Jadir from danger, and this certainly qualified. There would be hired guards in there, and Jadir was no warrior. But if he entered and helped Jadir, the witch would decline the meeting. And Jadir really needed her help.

A crash and a yelp from inside sent Koral leaping nimbly over the fat man on the floor, but he had only taken a few paces when another door at the far end of the hallway was roughly shoved open and Deiru tumbled out to sprawl on the floor. Jadir followed him, clutching three snakes by their tails.

Jadir saw Koral in the hallway, looked back over his shoulder, and shouted "run!" He came barreling down the hallway as Koral spun and flung himself back out into the alley. He had time to see three guards, long knives drawn, chasing Jadir down the hallway. As Jadir passed the door, he reached out with his free hand and yanked it shut behind him.

Koral and Jadir bolted up the alley as the first of the three guards smashed into the suddenly closed door. With the fat man's body partially blocking the hallway, it would take the guards a few extra seconds to wrench the door back open and give chase. It was all the time Koral and Jadir needed to lose pursuit.

As Koral led Jadir through twists and turns in the alleys, he glanced back at the snakes in the other man's hand.

"Jadir!" he yelled. "They're vipers!"

The snakes were swinging back and forth, trying to twist in Jadir's grip and bite him, but were unable to reach his bare hands.

"By the Abyss!" Jadir shouted, still running. "What do I do?"

"The bag—you need to get them in the bag before they bite you."

The sack was still tucked in Jadir's belt and he grabbed it with his free hand. He flicked it open and flung the snakes at the hole. Two of the snakes went in head-first, but the third missed the opening and landed on the ground.

Jadir stopped and dropped the sack with the opening beside the one loose viper before it could find a crack or hole to slither into. He raised his foot and brought his boot down hard on the cobblestones right beside the snake's head. The serpent recoiled and slid right into the sack.

Jadir quickly grabbed the edge of the sack and yanked it upright and the three snakes fell to the bottom. He twisted the opening and tied the cord in a knot to prevent their escape.

Koral stood there, dumbfounded at how easily Jadir had handled the poisonous viper. Jadir looked up at him, his own eyes wide and his breathing ragged, and Koral realized it had been pure dumb luck that had saved Jadir's life. He stepped over to the wall, leaned against it, and started laughing.

Jadir looked at Koral and then at the bag in his hand, and a grin broke over his face. He started laughing too, and it was some minutes before either of the two men could speak. Finally, Jadir turned to Koral.

"I can honestly say I never want to do that again."

"I seriously doubt you'll ever have to. Tomorrow night you give those snakes to the witch, and she'll take care of your problem."

Jadir started walking down the alley and Koral paced beside him.

"Just one thing," said Koral as they walked back in the direction of Jadir's tenement. "You should tell the witch that you've got vipers in that bag before she opens it."

Jadir chuckled and kept walking.

*　　　　*　　　　*

KORAL'S FATHER, BUDIL, HAD BEEN A THUG. HIS BRUTE STRENGTH, combined with a hair-trigger temper, made him a perfect candidate for the roughest of the city's gangs. He was an enforcer, beating and murdering anyone who posed a threat to—or who just got in the way of—the gang to which he belonged.

His own family was hardly spared his wrath. From his earliest age, Koral remembered his father beating him, his two older brothers, and his mother for any transgression, real or imagined. They lived in a squalid building in the Warren, and the boys were expected to spend their days near the docks, begging or stealing so the family would be able to eat.

Budil always had money. His gang would often break into warehouses in the Dock District, or waylay anyone foolish enough to be out on the streets of Ythis after dark without an armed escort. But that money was for his own comforts, and his family was expected to fend for themselves.

Koral hated his father, hated his life. He often dreamed of sneaking aboard a ship and stowing away in order to escape Ythis. Only his fear of the sea—and the thought that he might just be dumped overboard when found—kept him from acting on his thoughts. He was also concerned that Budil might sell the boys into slavery for some extra coin if they didn't earn enough during their daytime "jobs," which resulted in many sleepless nights.

But for all his strength, his temper, his street smarts, Budil remained a thug, and a not terribly bright one at that. And, in what Koral later considered an inevitability, his father's gang eventually crossed the wrong person. Naturally, it wasn't just Budil who paid the price.

Koral was on the docks the day the ship from distant Charnai arrived, its translucent orange sails billowing despite the lack of wind as it entered the harbor. Cries went up along the dock as work crews noticed the ship and its distinctive red-stained hull, the promise of Charnai gold bringing rivalries to the fore.

Koral had never seen a Charnai ship before, but he had heard stories about them. The Charnai were tall, dark-skinned people with a regal bearing and an advanced civilization far to the southeast, across some of the most dangerous seas known to the people of the Empire. They rarely visited Ythis, and their arrival was always noteworthy.

Rumor was that the Charnai were all sorcerers or conjurers of some sort, and stories told of Charnai emissaries visiting the Five whenever they came to the city. They often brought expensive and wondrous items for sale to the Emperor and the noble families of the Empire, and even the lowliest of their coins was made of gold.

Koral watched the Charnai ship pull up to the docks, towering over the other ships at berth, and the crew worked feverishly to unload its vast cargo. The ship's passengers disembarked, surrounded by fierce-looking Charnai warriors in black leather armor, bearing short spears and shields shaped like upside-down teardrops.

The cargo was unloaded and filled up three warehouses rented by the Charnai merchants who owned the goods. Within hours, nearly everyone in Ythis had heard of the arrival of the ship. Unfortunately, that included Koral's father.

Despite the reputation of the Charnai guards, Budil and his gang decided that Charnai goods sitting in an Ythis warehouse was too good an opportunity to pass up. If they could steal a few choice items, they would have money for liquor and whores to last them a year. It apparently never occurred to them that they might not be alive to spend it.

From what Koral was later able to puzzle out, his father and the rest of the gang attempted to break into the warehouse that night and beat the guards into unconsciousness before taking whatever they could carry. The Charnai warriors had not cooperated with this brilliant plan, and most of the gang were dead within the first minute.

The rest of the gang, including Budil, abandoned the plan and fled, chased by additional warriors who had appeared out of the shadows of the streets around the warehouse. Budil had made it back to the room where his family was sleeping, hoping to hide out until the Charnai ship left Ythis.

Koral woke as a pair of Charnai warriors smashed their way into the room. He screamed and flung himself at the back wall, where a small hole would allow him an escape route. In the darkness, Budil howled as a spear point was thrust through his belly, while the second warrior impaled Koral's brothers as they jumped up and tried to run out the door.

Koral made it into the next room—thankfully empty—and from there out a window into the alley behind the building. One of the Charnai warriors smashed through the thin, wooden wall and, seeing Koral climbing out the window, flung the spear at his head.

Koral threw himself out the window as the spear's blade brushed the side of his head. He took off down the alley, terror giving his legs the strength they needed to keep running even when he felt the blood running down his neck from his severed ear.

Though he didn't know it, he was three weeks shy of his eighth birthday.

For the rest of those three weeks, Koral hid from the Charnai warriors. He later realized that no one was hunting him, but his terror of those spears kept him almost completely off the streets, coming out only to steal food when his hunger became too great to bear.

Koral was almost relieved when he was finally caught. He didn't want to die, but neither was he able to take any more of the running and hiding. He had snuck into an inn and was about to steal some food from the kitchen when a hand clamped down on his arm. Koral yelped and tried to pull away, but the grip was too firm.

The man holding him wasn't the cook, nor did he work at the inn. He was short and wiry, with long dark hair tied back with a short leather cord. Short whiskers surrounded his mouth, and his eyes were as dark as his hair.

"Hold still, boy," the man said in a smooth voice. "You're not going anywhere."

Koral stopped struggling and waited for a beating, or worse.

"You're not very good at this, are you?" the man asked.

Koral was too shocked at the man's question to answer. Why was this man talking to him?

"How long has it been since you've eaten anything?"

Koral thought about it and then answered, "A couple of days, I think."

The man nodded. He reached out and grabbed the hunk of bread that Koral had been trying to steal, and then handed it to Koral. His other hand never relaxed its grip on Koral's arm. Koral took the bread and tore into it. He didn't know why the man was giving him the bread, but he was going to take advantage of it while he could.

"You're on the run from something, aren't you?" the man asked. Koral gaped at him, and the man chuckled.

"I can see it in your face. I'm good at that sort of thing. What's chasing you?"

"Char...Charnai warriors," Koral blurted out. His first instinct was to lie, but his own mouth somehow betrayed him.

"I see. And what did you do to earn their attention?"

"My father...he tried to...."

The man nodded before Koral could finish.

"So he was one of the men who tried to rob the Charnai, hm?"

Koral nodded back at him.

"You the only one who escaped?"

"Yeah. They killed my brothers."

The man stood there, holding Koral's arm, while Koral finished the hunk of bread. The man grabbed a piece of cheese and handed that over as well. Koral began to think he wasn't going to be killed.

"Listen, kid. The Charnai aren't hunting you. They feel enough justice was done already to make up for the attack on the warehouse. Especially since not one of their warriors was even wounded."

"Why are you helping me?" Koral asked, dreading the answer. The thought that this man was a slaver rose to the front of his mind.

"That's a good question. A few reasons. One, you look like you need some help. Two, I can easily afford to pay for some bread and cheese. Maybe even a bowl of stew. Three, I'm looking for friends, and I know better than to discount an opportunity when one comes up. And four, I can see the potential in a person long before it's visible to anyone else."

The man let go of Koral's arm, and Koral almost bolted out of the inn. But something about his man was different from anyone else he had ever known.

"You've got potential kid, and I'm on a mission. It won't be easy, and it won't necessarily be fun. But the rewards are more than worth the effort. So, Koral, how would you like a job?"

The man smiled at him and for an instant Koral was reminded of a tapestry he had seen once, of a forest scene with a large wolf looking out of the tapestry at the viewer. This man's face resembled that wolf. But Koral wasn't frightened—rather, he felt protected.

It never occurred to him until much later to wonder how the man had known his name.

Chapter Ten

JADIR OPENED THE DOOR TO SEE MARILSA AND PHANA sitting side-by-side on Marilsa's sleeping pallet, talking quietly. Marilsa looked up at Jadir and something in her eyes told him she was thinking about her dreams of last night, and the incident this morning. Jadir wondered if she had told Phana everything that had happened.

The bruise on Marilsa's forehead had formed throughout the day, and was now a dark splotch calling attention to where he had struck her. Another pang of guilt hit him—he couldn't believe he had harmed his little sister, after trying so hard to protect her for so long. He wondered if she would ever forgive him.

Phana met his gaze and gave him a very slight smile, and he took that to mean things were not quite as bad as he might think. He felt a small sense of relief and stepped into the room, closing the door behind him. He placed the bag with the snakes on the table and checked the knot around the opening once more to ensure they could not escape.

"I take it you were successful?" asked Phana.

"Yes. But whatever you do, don't open this bag. It's full of vipers."

He almost laughed as both Phana and Marilsa gaped at him, their eyes round and their mouths open. Phana recovered first.

"Why in the Abyss did you get vipers?"

Jadir hesitated. How much did he want Marilsa to know?

"They were the only snakes available, and we were in a hurry."

Phana gave him a look that said she was sure there would be more to the story, and that she expected to hear it.

"Where's Koral?" she asked, her voice mild. Jadir couldn't help his frown, but she merely raised her eyebrows, as if challenging him to explain the problem to her. He wasn't ready to do that, so he shrugged and told her.

"Once I had the snakes, he left. He said he had other things to do tonight."

She nodded and looked down, and Jadir realized she was disappointed that Koral had not come back here with him. Had she wanted Koral to keep her company while Jadir and Marilsa slept?

Jadir turned back to the table and closed his eyes, taking a deep breath. This was getting ridiculous. He liked Phana, but there was nothing going on between them, and he couldn't let himself get distracted by this nonsense while he was trying to solve a very real, very dangerous problem. He turned back to face Phana and his sister.

"Marilsa, I want to tell you...," he said and then paused to swallow past a lump in his throat. "I want to say I'm so sorry for hitting you this morning. I...I was trying to stop you from hurting...yourself...and it got out of my control."

He got down on his knees beside Marilsa, and she looked up at him with eyes that were filling with tears.

"I love you so much, and I would never willingly hurt you, Mar. This will be over soon—we're going to see the witch tomorrow night, and she'll help us get rid of this spirit, and then we can put this behind us."

A single tear ran down her cheek, and he reached out to wipe it away, and Marilsa flinched slightly as he raised his hand. He stopped, shocked at her reaction, but then she flung herself into his arms and hugged him tightly.

"It's all my fault!" she cried, and he squeezed her to his chest and shook his head, though she couldn't see his face.

"No! It's not your fault. You've done nothing wrong. I promise we'll get through this okay. I promise."

He looked up to see Phana wiping her own eyes. She glared at him, daring him to say anything about her tears, and he knew enough to keep his mouth shut.

Finally, Marilsa drew back and gave a great yawn.

"Mar, you've got to get some sleep. Phana is staying here tonight to help me watch over you. One of us will be awake through the night, so you'll be safe."

"Do I have to eat that leaf again?"

Jadir shook his head and said, "It didn't seem to work after the first night, so it's not worth it. Try to get some real sleep. You need it."

Marilsa was obviously apprehensive about sleeping, but she lay down and Jadir placed the blanket over her. Phana stood and moved over to the table to give Marilsa enough room to get comfortable. Jadir sat beside Marilsa, and she lay there, her eyes open, trying to fight her own exhaustion. But it was a battle she could not win, and her eyes began drooping almost as soon as she was settled in. Within a few minutes, she was sound asleep.

Jadir stood and moved over to Phana.

"You also need to get some sleep," she whispered to him.

"Yeah, I will," he whispered back. "Listen, I want to thank you for coming over tonight. It obviously means a lot to Marilsa to have you here."

"Just Marilsa?"

Jadir could feel himself blushing, and was glad only a single candle dimly illuminated the room.

"No I—I'm also glad you're here. Thank you for helping us. I couldn't really fix this on my own, and I owe you a huge debt."

Phana stepped closer to him, her face only inches away from his, and looked into his eyes. He almost took a step back, but something in her gaze stopped him.

"Not everything I do is to collect favors and debts, you know," she said. "Maybe I'm helping you because I truly care about the two of you."

"I—"

But Jadir was interrupted as Phana leaned in and kissed him. He found his arms sliding around her waist, and she pressed herself against him as he kissed her back. Her mouth opened and he felt her tongue sliding against his. Without warning, his body started to react to her closeness, and he pulled back and gasped for breath.

"I'm sorry, but I've never—"

Phana grinned and moved close to him again, pushing him back against the wall. The sensation of her body pressed against his was incredible, and his embarrassment melted away.

"I know," she whispered into his ear. "Do I look like I care?"

Jadir had no idea how long they stood there, his back to the wall and Phana pressed against his front. All he knew was that he had wasted so much time keeping her at arm's length, and now he regretted all those missed opportunities. He knew that kissing her would be the limit of what would happen tonight—they were here to watch over Marilsa, after all—but the thought of being alone with Phana sent his brain into a whirlwind.

Jadir's own fatigue had melted away, and though he knew he should be getting some rest himself, there was no way he would stop what was happening just to sleep. The night moved on, and he didn't care.

Until Marilsa's whimper brought him back to the present.

His eyes opened and he pulled his face away from Phana. Cold dread settled in his stomach, shoving out all other feelings. Phana looked over her shoulder and gasped, her grip on his shoulders tightening from fear rather than passion.

The man was floating over Marilsa's body, his arms stretched out to either side and his legs parted. In the dim light, Jadir could see the man's engorged penis. Marilsa had turned her face away from the creature above her, her brow furrowed as it invaded her dreams.

But despite her fear and discomfort, her hands were slowly pushing the blanket off her body.

Jadir moved to Marilsa's side and grabbed her shoulders.

"Marilsa! You have to wake up!" He shook her, but it seemed to do nothing.

He was about to pull her away from the creature, pick her up and run out of the room, when she turned her face to him.

Her eyes opened and she smiled at him, a lascivious look horribly out of place on her young face.

"No, Jadir," she said in a slow, thick voice. "Leave us alone. I *want* him."

*   *   *

RELAEL SHIFTED IN HIS SEAT, UNABLE TO GET COMFORTABLE ON the carriage's wooden bench. His two companions appeared to have no such difficulty, as neither had moved so much as a muscle for the last hour. They both had their eyes closed, and he had wondered if either or both had fallen asleep, but their rigid postures and tightly clenched fists had not relaxed, and he knew they were both concentrating on the task at hand.

Once again, Relael reflected on all he had learned from the oracles. This was an opportunity too good to pass up. If all went according to plan, the new sorcerer would see her power curtailed before she could bring any of it to bear.

The street outside the tenement was quiet, and the brother—Jadir—had gone inside a couple of hours before. A grunt from the priestess across from him brought Relael out of his reverie. He could see her eyes flicking back and forth under their lids, and her breath had quickened. The priest beside him—Brother Ontherim—slowly opened his eyes and glanced sideways at Relael.

"There's something out there," he said in a half-whisper. "Sister Zera can feel it moving about."

"What is it?" Relael asked, leaning forward toward the priestess, though she still hadn't opened her eyes.

"It is…gone," replied the priest, and Sister Zera let out a breath and visibly relaxed. Her hands unclenched and she opened her eyes to focus on Relael. He would have preferred for her to keep them closed—there was madness behind those eyes, a wildfire of chaos and strange urges that Relael was sure he would not want to witness.

"What was it?" he asked again.

Sister Zera opened her small mouth and licked her lips before speaking.

"I do not yet know, Brother Relael. It came and was quick, like a zephyr. It seemed drawn to the building, but was hesitant. It fled before I could bring my sight to bear on it fully."

"Did it sense you?" If the spirit, or creature, knew Relael and his companions were stationed outside the tenement, it might not return to the girl this night.

"No," replied Brother Ontherim. "We were not detected. It will return before the night is through."

Relael looked at the man sitting beside him and tried to suppress a shudder. Brother Ontherim Worestald was very nearly a walking corpse. His addiction to hyatherin—a painfully addictive drug that gave powerful visions—was rotting his body from within. The man's skin hung slack over his skeletal frame, and he gave off a sickly-sweet smell, as of overripe fruit.

By contrast, Sister Zera Xodoc was intensely... *alive*. There was a strange vibrancy to her, as if she existed in dimensions beyond one's vision. She was a bottled storm, full of barely contained lightning and smelling of copper. Her white skin was stretched too tight over her tall frame, topped by a ragged patch of short, black hair that stuck out in all directions.

In general, Relael preferred to work alone, or with other members of the Hidden, but tonight he needed the abilities of fully ordained men and women of the Church. There was always a risk, working in the open with those who could manifest their derangements at any time, but nothing of value came without some risk. And he had worked with these two before.

Sister Zera ran her fingers through her hair and took in a deep breath, letting it out slowly. Then she placed her hands in her lap, clenched her fists, and closed her eyes. Brother Ontherim let his own eyes drift closed and Relael was alone in the carriage once more. He could only hope the creature would return so they could discover what it was. The spirit and the girl were both key elements of Relael's plan.

"It has returned," murmured the priest beside Relael. Across the carriage, Sister Zera's closed eyes were darting back and forth once more.

"It nears the girl, and...."

The priest hesitated and Relael felt himself holding his breath. He forced himself to let go, to relax his body. He could not make this happen any faster than it would. He was not in control tonight. His part was to listen, to learn, and to remember.

"There is something else there, in the room."

Relael wanted to ask what, but dared not disrupt their concentration.

"The room is filled with lust," said Sister Zera, and she sounded intense, hungry. "It distracts the spirit from his goal. He watches...."

The priestess was grinning, her teeth bared in a way that spoke of a predator getting ready to pounce on its prey.

Brother Ontherim spoke up again. "The other entity, I cannot see it fully. It hides, but its brightness is too powerful, it leaks through and announces its presence."

Relael was confused. Were there two spirits? The oracles had said nothing about a second entity.

"Ah, the lust has aroused it, and now it focuses on the girl." The priestess' voice was almost a purr, and Relael found it disturbing. "It has established a connection, and...."

"No," whispered the priest, and Relael heard fear in his voice. "We cannot let...."

Sister Zera grunted, as if in pain, and Relael watched as she arched her back, her face lifting toward the carriage's ceiling. They had come here to watch, to gather information before moving forward with his plan. But he could see they were both in some kind of struggle.

Sister Zera began chanting in the language of the Gods, a horrific, twisted utterance that human throats were not meant to make. A thin trickle of blood came out of her left nostril and left a red scar down her face.

"Do not destroy it!" shouted Relael, and to the Abyss with their concentration—he needed that spirit for his plans. Sister Zera's chanting stopped and she coughed up a bright bubble of blood that burst and left flecks of red around her mouth. Relael opened his own mouth to give more orders, but Brother Ontherim understood what needed to be done.

"We must...block the link...to drive it away...tonight. The girl...has opened...to it."

Sister Zera shook her head, her eyes still closed. "I cannot hold it—it twists and turns and tries to slip past me."

Relael realized his own fists were clenched in frustration. He didn't really know what was happening up there in that room—only that something had gone wrong and his companions were trying to stop the spirit from doing whatever it had intended to do to the girl tonight. Relael felt helpless, and he hated it.

Brother Ontherim muttered under his breath, a prayer to Iathephos, it sounded like.

"The emotions in that room...I am siphoning away the desire, the lust...the creature loosens its hold on the girl."

Sister Zera shuddered and clasped her hands to the sides of her head, as if blocking out a loud noise. "It is trying to flee the room...what do we do?"

"Let it go," answered Relael. "It's drawn to the girl, so it'll be back. Let it go. Chaining it will not help us."

The priestess gave another grunt and sat back against the wall of the carriage. She slowly let her hands fall to her sides as she opened her eyes and focused on Relael again.

"The girl," said Brother Ontherim in a low voice, "is...unharmed."

"What happened up there?" asked Relael.

"That room became a center of power, of sex magic," said Sister Zera, and the predatory smile came back to her face. "The girl nearly let herself be taken by the creature, and we would have had to slay them all."

"Why? What is it that comes to her?"

"An *incubo*," whispered the other priest.

Relael knew his own smile likely mirrored the one on the face of the priestess sitting across from him in the small carriage. He now knew exactly what to do.

Chapter Eleven

MARILSA LOOKED AROUND WORRIEDLY AT THE shadowy figures in darkened doorways and alley mouths, and Jadir put his arm around her shoulders. On her other side, Koral walked confidently, directing them through the twisted streets of the Warren.

Jadir had rarely been in this part of Ythis, and then only on the edges of the neighborhood, and he had certainly never brought Marilsa here before. Koral, however, seemed to know this area like he lived here. Jadir was glad to have him as their guide. He couldn't help liking the man, despite the fact he was a rival for Phana's attention.

Once again, Jadir's thoughts drifted back to Phana. His time with her last night had been fantastic, though there was something…strange…about it he couldn't quite identify. He had been lost in the moment until the spirit had come for his little sister.

Jadir still didn't know what had happened. Marilsa hadn't been controlled by the creature the way she was when she attacked him. No, last night she had been herself and yet…she had wanted to let the spirit do what it…it just didn't make sense. And then the "man" had started twisting and struggling as he floated above her, as if he was being grabbed or attacked by some unseen hand.

Jadir had managed to drag Marilsa away from the apparition as it fought its invisible attacker, though she had struggled to stay near the spirit. Phana had just stood there, transfixed by the sight of the creature, and the sight of her face had almost made Jadir let Marilsa go so that he could tear Phana's clothes off and take her right there against the wall.

And then Jadir's desire had just drained out of him and he had nearly lost consciousness as exhaustion hit him like a sledgehammer. Phana had sunk to her knees with her back to the wall, and Marilsa had stopped struggling. An instant later, the spirit broke free and flew away through the outer wall.

What had the creature been fighting? How had it been driven off? Jadir feared the answer lay in his inadvertent prayer to Iathephos two nights before. Perhaps the god was now watching over the two of them? That thought was horrifying, for Jadir knew they would pay a terrible price for calling such attention to themselves.

Koral led them around a corner and stopped at a small wooden door set into a stone wall. Jadir looked up and noted that this structure was solidly built, a block of fitted stone that seemed to hold up several leaning wooden buildings clustered around it. Jadir hadn't been sure what to think, but certainly hadn't expected *this*.

Koral knocked on the door, and it opened almost immediately. A young girl of less than ten summers stood framed in the dark doorway. She gave Koral a cursory glance and then looked at Jadir and Marilsa. Jadir felt naked in that gaze, as if the girl could read his every secret thought. He felt heat rush to his face as he blushed.

The girl gave no outward sign she was aware of his discomfort, and simply turned and walked into the darkness. Koral stepped up to Jadir and spoke in a low voice.

"I can't come in, just you and Marilsa. Remember to warn the witch about the vipers when you give her the bag. Be polite and don't do anything stupid, and she'll give you the help you need."

Jadir nodded and dropped his arm from Marilsa's shoulder so that he could take her hand. Koral stepped to one side and Jadir led Marilsa through the door into a dark hallway. Another door at the far end stood open and a light shone inside what appeared to be a small room. The girl stood framed in the far doorway, and then she stepped around the corner and was lost to sight.

Jadir proceeded down the hallway, Marilsa clutching his hand. He reached the door and looked into the room, seeing a simple wooden table and three chairs. An old woman sat in one of the chairs at the far side of the table, her head bowed and her wrinkled and gnarled hands resting flat on the table's surface. A single, fat candle sat in the middle of the table, giving off the only light in the room.

There were no other visible exits from the room, neither door nor window, but the young girl was not here. Behind Marilsa, Jadir heard the door to the street close softly. Marilsa turned to look, but Jadir knew the hallway would be too dark to see anything.

He stepped into the room and pulled Marilsa in to stand beside him. The old woman raised her head and he saw her eyes were nothing but white orbs. Marilsa gave a little squeak, and the old woman turned in her direction.

"Afraid of the blind, are you? You've got bigger things to worry your little head." Her voice was like rough wood, with grooves and dirt and hidden catches along its surface. She raised one hand and motioned for them to sit in the chairs.

Marilsa sat, and Jadir followed suit, to find the chair was barely big enough to hold him. He was worried it might break if he stayed seated, but didn't want to disobey the witch.

"Um, I'm sorry, but I think I might be too heavy for your chair. I don't want to break it."

The old woman—the witch—gave a sharp laugh.

"You'll break before it does, boy. Where's my price?"

Jadir placed the bag on the table beside the candle. The witch immediately grabbed the knot—it made Jadir wonder if she was entirely blind—and began to undo the cord.

"They-they're vipers," he said. "I got you three vipers, so be careful opening the bag."

The witch paused for an instant, her empty eyes aimed in his direction. And then she yanked the cord off the bag and shoved her arm inside. Marilsa gasped and Jadir almost yanked the bag away.

But the old woman withdrew her arm from the bag and the three vipers were coiled around her thin limb, their faces turned to hers. She lifted her arm to her face and gave each serpent a small kiss on its nose. The snakes didn't react, their gazes as unreadable as hers.

Jadir could feel Marilsa trembling beside him as the witch put her arm back in the bag, and then withdrew it. The snakes stayed in the sack, and she slid it to one side before resting her palms on the table again.

"So what do you want from me?"

Jadir opened his mouth, but it was Marilsa who answered.

"A man comes to me in my dreams. He wants...he wants to have...sex...with me. It's getting hard to resist him—"

"Because you want him just as much as he wants you, is that it, girl?"

Marilsa closed her mouth, but Jadir was shocked to see her nod.

"That's because you're not just a girl anymore, are you?"

Blood rushed to Marilsa's cheeks and she looked down at the table. Jadir wasn't sure what the witch meant...had his little sister already had sex with someone?

"Wait, Marilsa...did you...?"

"Oh, hush, boy," snapped the witch. "This isn't about you—you've got your own issues to deal with, and they might just be more than you can handle. But you're here for Marilsa, so let her speak or you can wait outside."

Jadir wanted to tell the witch to mind her own business, but Marilsa needed her help and so he kept quiet.

"It started a few months ago," Marilsa said, and she raised her head to look directly at the witch as she spoke. "I knew about it beforehand, so I wasn't afraid."

"And the man began entering your dreams before your menses started, didn't he?"

Jadir suddenly realized what they were talking about and he was glad he hadn't asked Marilsa whether she was still a maiden.

"Yes, he would appear in my dreams sometimes, but once I started having...he showed up every night."

The witch sat there, saying nothing, and Marilsa waited. Jadir wasn't so patient. He wanted to ask the witch if she could help, he wanted her to tell them what was happening, he wanted answers. Finally, he couldn't wait any longer.

"Who is this man?" he asked the witch. "What does he want with Marilsa? Can you help us; can you send him away for good?"

The witch turned to Jadir and he felt sure she was looking at him with those blank, white eyes. When she spoke, he could almost feel her voice rubbing his skin raw.

"No, I can't send him away. It wouldn't do any good if I did, another would take his place."

She turned to Marilsa.

"That man is a spirit called an *incubo*. It wants to impregnate you, so that it can take physical form by inhabiting the body of your baby. If you let that happen, you will die a painful, horrid death."

Marilsa flinched at the witch's words, but the old woman went on without pausing.

"But the *incubo* is also a boon. It is a source of power for you as well, if you learn how to resist the lure of his desire."

The witch smiled, but there was no humor in it, no comfort.

"And you will learn that from me."

"I don't understand," said Jadir. "Marilsa doesn't want any power from this spirit. She just wants it gone. Why do you want to teach her this stuff?"

"Because, boy," answered the witch. "Marilsa is a beacon to the *incubo*, and if not this one, then another. She has to learn to control it, or she'll be overpowered and give in to him, and then she dies."

"But why did this spirit pick Marilsa? Why her?"

"By the Abyss, you're dense!" the old woman shouted at him. "The *incubo* is the spirit that gives a witch her knowledge, her power."

She turned back to Marilsa.

"You were born with the blood of a witch, young lady. You've been picked by your *incubo*. And now you've got to learn to handle the power that goes with it."

Marilsa sat, staring at the witch with wide eyes, unable to say anything. Jadir couldn't believe what the old woman was saying. It must be some kind of mistake—she *couldn't* be right about Marilsa.

Never had his sister shown any strange abilities, never had she been attracted to the unknown, the magical. Marilsa was a normal young woman in every way he knew. He thought back to their childhood together, as far back as he could remember, but there was nothing to foreshadow a revelation like this.

It had to be a mistake.

This kind of thing didn't happen to people like them. Neither of them was important nor powerful. They were orphans, who had grown up together, had taken care of each other. They had learned what they could, and then had gotten simple jobs that allowed them to survive in Ythis.

It had to be mistake.

Marilsa couldn't be a witch. She couldn't live on the edge of society, distrusted and feared by everyone around her, even while those same people wanted her to use her abilities for their own advantage. Marilsa couldn't live her life under the threat of death at the hands of the Church, or the Five...or Six, or however many sorcerers there might be.

It *was* a mistake.

"That...that can't be right," he said to the old woman. "Marilsa can't be a witch."

Those sightless eyes turned to Jadir and he could feel the power in her gaze. She may not be able to see him directly, but there was no question she was looking into him, into his real self.

And then she flinched.

The old woman raised her hands in a warding gesture at him, and Jadir had a moment of panic as he thought she was going to cast some kind of curse on him. But she turned away from Jadir and Marilsa and brought her hands to her face. She said nothing, and neither he nor his sister spoke up. He had no idea what to make of her behavior.

Finally, she slowly lowered her hands and turned back to them. She didn't raise her head to face them, and there was something in her voice when she spoke...fear?

"Young...man. You know what I'm telling this is girl is true." She paused. "Or perhaps you don't know, but you feel it. She has this power in her blood, and there's no stopping it. You know what she must do, what she must become, or she will die. And you cannot let that happen, can you?"

Jadir was taken aback—what kind of question was that? Of course he couldn't just let Marilsa die. But something in her words...he felt some stirring deep down in him. He pondered the witch's statement and then looked at his sister. Marilsa turned her head to face him and when his eyes met hers, he *did* feel it.

For the first time, he saw something in her gaze that was more than just the sister he had known all his life. He could feel his own heartbeat quickening as he started to feel an energy, a power contained within her. As he looked into her face, he once more had the overwhelming urge to protect his little sister from all of this, the same urge he had felt over and over during his life with her.

But this time it was different. This time, Marilsa was the one in control.

Jadir realized the witch's words were true. He didn't know how he knew, but there was no mistake. Marilsa had the blood of a witch.

He could tell Marilsa felt it, too, the connection between them. Their blood sang with it, because even though Jadir could never have the power of a witch, he was family, they shared the same mother. The same blood ran in their veins.

Marilsa's expression changed slightly. She almost smiled, and Jadir saw her start to realize the power she might have. She wasn't seeing a life of loneliness spread before her. She was seeing opportunity.

Marilsa turned back to the old woman.

"Does...does this mean my mother was a witch?" Marilsa asked. The old woman didn't raise her head, only shook it slightly.

"I do not know. There is...no way to tell. Once you come fully into your power, you may spend the time to find out—there are ways for you to follow the trail of your own bloodline, trace your lineage. But for now, you have more pressing concerns."

That brought Jadir's thoughts back to the present. The *incubo* was waiting for Marilsa. It wanted to take control of her before she had the skill to turn the tables.

"You will spend the night here, young lady, and I will teach you the basics of what you need to know. The rest will be up to you."

"You'll teach her everything in one night?" Jadir asked. It seemed the old woman was purposely avoiding turning in Jadir's direction as she answered him.

"I will show her what I can. Every witch is different, and a witch's path is unique to her. She needs to figure out her own path, for to follow mine would lead her to her doom. What I will show you to-night, young lady, will let you hold off your *incubo* long enough to negotiate your own pact with him. Everything else must come from you."

Marilsa turned to Jadir. "If I stay here all night...."

"You'll be in no shape to work tomorrow," he finished.

"Work? She will have no more time for a job. She needs to spend her waking hours practicing what I teach her, and developing her path. Time is not on your side—you cannot put this off while you go to your job each day."

Jadir had known this would happen, but was hoping he was wrong. If Marilsa could no longer work, then they could not afford to live where they were, not if they wanted to eat. The two of them together barely had enough money to survive as it was.

He knew what the answer was, though he had been trying to avoid it. But he no longer had any choice. Marilsa's life was at stake, and he would do whatever it took to protect her. He could not imagine losing his little sister; he could not imagine life without her.

Jadir smiled at her.

"It's okay," he said. "I can take care of us both. I have another job I can take that pays more. We'll be okay."

He could see Marilsa knew what he was saying. Jadir would final-ly agree to work for Qudovo, the man who led Phana's gang. Marilsa was worried about him, that he was going to do something he had not wanted to do, all for her. But he put his arm around her and gave her a squeeze, and she relaxed.

As much as she had a frightening and difficult path ahead of her, she wasn't alone. They would face it together, and she would be okay. They had come this far, and they wouldn't let something like this pull them apart.

Jadir could tell she was not afraid anymore. She was...eager...to get started.

"You must leave us," the old woman said to Jadir. "Come back at dawn to collect Marilsa, but what I have to say is for her ears alone."

Jadir noticed the old woman had called his sister by name for the first time since they had arrived. He gave Marilsa a last quick hug and then stepped into the dark hallway. As he felt his way along its length toward the door, he could hear the old woman speaking, but her voice was muffled and unintelligible and he did not know what she said to Marilsa.

He reached the door, pulled it open, and stepped back out onto the streets of the Warren.

Chapter Twelve

YANAN QUANTEF STARED AT THE PRIESTESS, ALMOST afraid to believe what she had just told him.

"Are you absolutely sure?" he asked her slowly. "There cannot be any mistake."

"Of course I'm sure!" Sister Zera Xodoc snapped at him. "I've seen her myself."

Yanan took a deep breath and slowly let it out. He couldn't quite believe it was almost over—twelve years of searching for the brat and now she had just fallen into his lap.

"Tell me the rest," he said.

The priestess' eyes gleamed in the shadows of the hall. Her smile showed too many teeth, as if she was getting ready to eat something that wasn't dead yet.

"Brother Ochallum wants to use this young witch for his own ends. And we're tasked with manipulating the *incubo*, to direct it where he wants."

Yanan almost asked where that was, but he stopped himself. The truth was, he didn't want to get involved in any political maneuverings among the priests, and he'd prefer the option to plead ignorance if anything bad happened. The Sister was betraying one of her own by passing this information on to a Witch Hunter, but Yanan cared only about the girl.

It had all started in Jh'tira, hunting the witch Ineir. He had discovered she was pregnant, and knew her line would continue if she gave birth to a girl. It had been a race between them, Ineir trying to stay alive long enough to give birth, Yanan trying to catch and kill her before that could happen.

In the end, though Ineir was dead, Yanan had failed. And he had continued to fail for the next twelve years, as the baby girl had disappeared along with Ineir's servant. He had managed to follow the trail as far as Ythis, and that's where it ended.

But Yanan had never forgotten his vow to end Ineir and her abomination.

And now this priestess was telling him she had found the girl. Of course the priestess didn't know the girl's complete history. But the information she and her companions had uncovered—the timeline, the orphanage, the brother, and now the *incubo*. There could be no question.

Marilsa was the girl he had hunted. And now she would die.

"I suppose you want to accompany me to slay the witch," he said aloud.

The priestess narrowed her eyes at him.

"Why would I want that? Then he'd know I told you about her. No, do what you must, and take full credit for it. He cannot touch you for slaying the witch, not when he hasn't gotten the blessing of your High Counsellor for his little scheme."

Yanan considered the situation.

"Can I expect interference in my work, then?"

"I will be there, in the black carriage in front of her building. Brother Worestald will be with me. But we will remain in the carriage while you do your work."

"And Brother Ochallum?"

"He will not be with us tomorrow night," she explained. "So you do not have to worry about him."

"Then the girl and her brother die tomorrow," he said.

The priestess left the hall, and Yanan paced among the tall stone pillars, considering the preparations he must make. Then, his plan mapped out in his mind, he strode out of the hall and left the Temple.

Within the hour, the Witch Hunter was seated at the table in a common tavern near the Market District of Ythis. Across from him sat Anral and Heuko, two mercenaries he'd worked with before.

Yanan outlined the plan to take down the young witch. The priestess had told him that the boy, Jadir, worked until mid-evening at a local warehouse. When he was away, there were no other protectors around her.

Yanan knew she was too young and inexperienced to have formed a coven yet. The boy would no doubt be her first coven member, but he needed to earn money to pay for food and shelter, and so couldn't be around to protect her at all times. And she hadn't had a chance to attract more followers.

Yanan was committed to seeing her dead before she started down that road.

The only question was her *incubo*. The priestess said she couldn't help Yanan without the other priest in the carriage knowing what she was doing. That meant Yanan had to drive off the *incubo* himself.

But in this case, the witch's inexperience gave Yanan the edge. She wasn't ready to feed power to the spirit and use it to protect herself against attackers. And she hadn't yet figured out how to draw the spirit's power into herself to perform her own tricks. He reached up and absently touched the amulet that hung around his neck.

"Heuko, you'll stay outside the building and make sure there's no interference. There's always a chance the brother will return while we're there. He's big, but from what my contact in the Church has said, he's not much of a fighter. If he comes back, you kill him right in the street."

Yanan gave Heuko a description of Jadir and turned to the other mercenary.

"Anral, you'll accompany me. When we come into the room, I'll have to make sure she can't use her witchcraft to affect us. If it turns out there is anyone in the room with the witch, you kill them and then guard the door, just in case."

He looked back and forth at the two men and smiled.

"Both of you are professionals, so I probably don't need to say this to you, but I'll say it anyway. We've done this kind of assault together many times in the past, and always been successful. That doesn't mean something isn't going to go wrong tomorrow. Don't get complacent, don't make assumptions. Stay focused and do what you know how to do."

Heuko leaned forward and looked Yanan in the eye.

"We may have done this before," he said, "But I've never seen you so…excited about it. If I didn't know you any better, I'd say you were nervous. That means you know something we don't, and I don't like that."

Yanan paused, and then decided he needed to reassure them.

"You're right, Heuko. This one is different. I've been hunting this girl since before she was born. I thought I had lost her, years ago. And now she turns up right under my nose."

"This is personal for you?" Anral asked. Yanan shook his head.

"Not in the way you mean. You're worried that if things go bad, I'm not going to retreat—that I'll risk all our lives to finally succeed. But that's the opposite of what I'm thinking. I feel…refreshed. My failure to kill the girl has bothered me all this time, but now I re-alize that it doesn't matter how much time has passed. I will find her and end her life no matter what. If it doesn't happen tomorrow night, it'll happen soon after."

He leaned back in his chair and projected an image of outward calm.

"I'm just looking forward to getting started," he said.

The other men looked at each other, and then Heuko shrugged. Anral visibly relaxed and Yanan knew they accepted his explana-tion. It didn't matter that he was lying to them. Tomorrow night he would finally succeed, no matter the cost.

*   *   *

KORAL WAS WAITING ON THE STREET OUTSIDE THE WITCH'S HOME. He turned as Jadir stepped out and pulled the door closed.

"I need to see Qudovo."

Koral raised his eyebrows. "Why? Is your sister all right?"

Jadir nodded and debated how much he should tell the other man. He didn't really know Koral, didn't know who he worked for, didn't know exactly why he had been such help. Jadir didn't really believe it was just a favor for Phana.

On the other hand, the old witch seemed to trust Koral with the knowledge of how she could be found. She obviously believed he wouldn't betray her to the authorities, and she had much more experience than Jadir in matters like these. Still, it seemed risky to give away information about Marilsa when he didn't know if he could fully trust this man.

"Marilsa will be okay, but she won't be able to work for a while. And my job doesn't pay enough for us to live on my wages alone."

"You're going to ask Qudovo for a job?"

Jadir nodded. "Marilsa will be here all night, so I'm going to the Iron Spike. Qudovo asked me to join his gang a couple of times before. Hopefully, he's still interested."

Jadir began to walk back toward the docks, and Koral fell into step beside him.

"Are you coming to the Iron Spike?"

"Yeah," Koral said. "I know Qudovo well. Maybe I can put in a good word for you."

That brought Jadir up short.

"Why would you do that?"

Koral shrugged. "You and your sister seem like decent people who need some help."

"Koral, I'm not asking you to help me. I'm already in debt enough to Phana—I can't afford to owe money or favors to a bunch of different people."

"I don't expect to get paid for every little thing I do, you know," Koral replied. "Sometimes I help because it costs me nothing and I can." His voice was mild, but Jadir could tell he was insulted.

"Sorry," replied Jadir. "I didn't mean it like that. I'm just used to having to pay for everything, one way or another. People don't usually help others in this city unless there's something in it for them."

"Don't worry about it," said Koral as he started walking, and Jadir walked beside him. "You have to realize Ythis isn't always the cesspool it seems. I think most people would help out others without expecting payment in return if there weren't just enough scumbags to take advantage of that and make people suspicious of their neighbors."

"You're probably right," said Jadir, thinking about it. "It's too bad there *are* just enough scumbags. But thanks for offering to help. I really didn't mean—"

"Forget about it," Koral answered. "As I said, this costs me nothing, and you seem like a decent fellow."

They walked to the Iron Spike saying little else, although Jadir was glad for Koral's company. When they arrived, the thugs outside the entrance stepped forward to challenge them, but as soon as they saw Koral they stepped back and motioned for Jadir and Koral to proceed.

It seems everyone knows this guy, thought Jadir. *Who, exactly, is he?*

When they entered the common room, their presence was noticed by most of the patrons, and Jadir noted a young man darting into one of the back rooms. A moment later, Qudovo came out and waved them over.

Koral led the way and Jadir followed him into the room behind the gang leader. A simple wooden table sat in the center of the room surrounded by five chairs. Cards and coins were scattered across the table's surface, and three other men were vacating the seats as Jadir entered. The other men filed out silently and Qudovo closed the door.

Koral sat down and picked up one of the hands of cards. Jadir sat as well but kept his hands off the table. Qudovo remained standing.

"Koral, can I get someone to bring you anything?"

Koral looked at the cards, snorted, and tossed them face-down on the table.

"No. This is business."

Qudovo nodded and sat down as well. Jadir could see he was nervous.

"Jadir here needs a job," said Koral. "He's strong, he's honest, and he'll do well. I'd appreciate it if you would consider him as a candidate to join your gang. I'll vouch for him, if you need an outside opinion."

Qudovo looked from Koral to Jadir and back. He opened his

mouth and closed it again. Finally, he said "He wants to join my gang?"

"You asked me to join before," said Jadir, "and I turned you down. I understand if you aren't interested in having me anymore, but I've reconsidered, and I changed my mind. If you still have a place for me...well, I'm here."

Qudovo stared at Jadir, obviously confused. He turned back to Koral.

"And you...vouch...for him?"

Koral nodded once and said nothing.

"Okay. Well, like I said before, it would be worth your while to join us." Jadir could see Qudovo's mind working fast, trying to figure out why Jadir had suddenly agreed to join, and why Koral had gotten involved.

"We don't *need* you, of course," said Qudovo shrewdly. "But if you want to join now, I suppose I could find a place for you."

Qudovo's eyes darted to Koral, who frowned.

"You'll still have to follow gang rules and obey my orders," Qudovo blurted, as if he was trying to negotiate with Jadir and knew Jadir held all the cards. This was not how Jadir had expected this to go. He was here to ask for a job, but it was almost like it was the other way around.

"Um, of course," he answered. "You're the boss. I'm a hard worker and I'm not stupid. You won't get any trouble from me. I just...I need to know how much I get paid."

Qudovo looked at Koral, as if Koral would set the wages. But the other man was looking at the table, idly playing with the hand of cards. The gang leader took a breath and named a figure. Jadir almost laughed out loud.

He had expected that working for Qudovo would be a second job—that he would still have to continue working at the warehouse during the day. But the amount Qudovo was offering would allow Jadir to quit the warehouse entirely. It was enough money to cover what Jadir and Marilsa were *both* bringing in, plus a little bit left over.

It was by no means a fortune—their current wages didn't really add up to very much—but it did solve their money problem. As far as Jadir was concerned, it very nearly was a fortune.

"That sounds fine to me," Jadir answered. "When do you want me to start?"

"Tomorrow night?" suggested Qudovo. This was so very different from how this man had dealt with Jadir in the past.

"That's fine with me."

Koral stood slowly, and Qudovo jumped to his feet. Jadir saw a look pass between them and Qudovo seemed to relax a little bit.

"Jadir," said Koral. "I saw Phana in the other room. Why don't you get her to introduce you around to the others? Qudovo and I need to talk for a few minutes."

As Jadir stepped out into the common room, he was convinced that Qudovo worked for Koral. But Koral was pretty young to be a crime boss. Still, Qudovo had acted as if he was trying to do whatever Koral wanted without coming right out and asking him.

There was obviously more going on here than anyone was telling Jadir. He would just have to watch and listen and figure out what he could. In the meantime, he saw Phana across the room talking to another woman, and he felt almost…giddy…at the idea of seeing her every day.

He couldn't wait to tell her they were now working together.

Chapter Thirteen

PHANA WAS SURPRISED TO SEE JADIR AT THE IRON SPIKE, and worried that something had gone wrong, but he smiled at her as he approached and she forced herself to relax.

"Phana, do you have a minute to talk?"

She glanced at her companion and decided it would be better to speak privately. Excusing herself, she took Jadir's hand and led him through the kitchen and out back into the alley that ran behind the tavern.

Turning to face him, he stepped forward and slid his hands around her waist. Phana was glad to see him, and without thinking, she tilted her face up to his. But just before their lips met, an unsettling shiver ran up her spine and she pulled back and looked around nervously.

"What happened?" she asked him. "Where's Marilsa."

A guilty look flashed across his face. He had obviously forgotten all about his sister when Phana brought him back here.

"She's still with the witch. She'll be there all night."

"Can the witch help her?"

Jadir frowned and took her hands in his.

"Phana, what I'm going to tell you must remain between you and me. You're the only person I trust, and it's far too dangerous for anyone else to find out."

"What is it?" she asked, feeling a surge of anger at the nervous tremor in her voice.

Jadir looked up and down the alley, leaned in close, and whispered in her ear. "Marilsa is a witch, too."

His breath was warm and soft on her ear, but it wasn't a pleasant sensation, like it had been last night. Instead, she had to fight a nearly overwhelming urge to shove him away and wipe the side of her head. She could feel the skin on her arms raise in goosebumps, but she didn't know why she was reacting like this tonight.

And then Jadir's words cut through her own thoughts.

"Marilsa?" she whispered back. "Are you sure?"

Jadir nodded. He leaned in again to whisper in her ear, and she pulled back involuntarily.

"Is something wrong?" he asked in a low voice.

"No, I...we don't have to whisper. Just speak quietly."

He nodded again but didn't let go of her hands. She could almost feel her skin *crawling* under his touch. This was insane. Last night she would have had sex with him if Marilsa hadn't been sleeping in the same room. Now, his very touch was revolting, and she didn't understand why.

She pulled her hands out of his and surreptitiously wiped them on her pants.

"Sorry, I...we shouldn't act like this here. I don't want anyone to see that I'm involved with you. It...might not be safe."

She could see the doubt in his eyes—he wasn't sure he believed her. Tonight, it would just have to do.

"Are you sure about Marilsa?" she asked again.

"Yes. The man, the spirit...it's called an *incubo*, I think. It's the spirit that gives a witch her powers. But Marilsa has to learn to control it, or it will kill her. The witch is teaching her what she needs to know tonight, and then Marilsa will have to practice...whatever it is she needs to do...so that she can develop the skill she needs."

Phana was shocked at Jadir's news. Marilsa had seemed like such a normal, almost plain, girl.

"Is she going to stop working?"

Jadir heaved a sigh, and then a thought occurred to him and he smiled at Phana. It didn't look pleasant, it looked...hungry, as if he was sizing Phana up as a meal.

"Marilsa will have to stop working so that she can practice every day. But I've found a new job that will let me support both of us."

"Really? Where?" Jadir didn't have many skills—his strength was his best asset when trying to find employment, but common laborers didn't make much money. Phana silently cursed the timing. It would have been a perfect opportunity to recruit him into the gang.

"Here," he replied. "I just met with Qudovo, and Koral put in a good word for me. I've joined your gang. We're going to be working together."

Phana felt a pang of something she rarely experienced, fear. What was wrong with her? There was no reason to fear Jadir. She was extremely attracted to him. Or, at least, most nights she was. Tonight, something about him repelled her for some reason.

Was it Marilsa? No, she had felt it before he told her about his sister. It was *him*.

But why?

He was watching her face, waiting for her reaction, and for an instant she was terrified her expression had matched her thoughts. But Phana was well versed in remaining outwardly calm, even when her thoughts were in turmoil.

Phana smiled at him, and he grinned back. It wasn't comforting.

"That's...that's fantastic!" she said, with what she hoped was a convincing tone. Jadir stepped forward to give her a hug and she stepped back. He faltered, and then muttered "Sorry."

"It's okay," she replied. "Just not here at the Iron Spike."

He nodded once more.

"So, when do you start?"

"Tomorrow. I'm going to watch over Marilsa while she sleeps during the day until I'm sure she's safe, and then I'll go quit my old job and come here."

"Who will stay with Marilsa during the night?"

"I...I'm not sure yet. I'll have to see how things go tomorrow. Maybe she'll change her schedule so that she'll sleep during the day with me and practice her abilities at night when I'm working."

"Did Qudovo tell you who you'll be paired up with for the first while?"

"No," he replied. "I was kind of hoping he might give me over to you—to show me the ropes."

At the moment, that was the last thing Phana wanted. "He probably won't—he already thinks something is going on between us. Besides, I can't teach you everything you need to learn."

She decided she would talk to Qudovo as soon as Jadir left—make sure she suggested someone else to be his trainer until she figured out why she was so put off by his presence. Not that Jadir needed to know that.

"Okay, well, I should get back to the witch's house. I don't know how long they will take, and I want to be there when Marilsa comes out."

"Good idea," said Phana and turned and walked back into the rear entrance of the Iron Spike. She could feel Jadir behind her as he followed her into the common room, like a lurking, threatening presence at her back. She marched back to her table, turned and said "Goodnight!" in an all-too-cheery voice.

Jadir stood there for a moment, blinking at her, and then mumbled "Goodnight" as he walked to the front door and left the tavern.

Phana stared at the door after Jadir had left, and the cold dread in her stomach slowly dissipated.

"Phana!"

She nearly yelled in fright as someone shouted her name. She turned to see Qudovo standing at the door to his "office." He waved her over.

"He wants to talk to you," he explained, and then walked off into the kitchen.

Phana wanted to ask who it was, but turned and looked into the small room. Koral was standing beside the table.

"You have a minute?" Koral asked her.

Phana stepped into the room, shut the door, and practically threw herself into his arms. Koral was nearly knocked off balance as she hugged him, but he recovered quickly.

"Uh, it's nice to see you, too."

Phana held onto him, saying nothing, until she was sure she could speak without bursting into tears.

*　　　　*　　　　*

JADIR ARRIVED BACK AT THE WITCH'S HOUSE JUST AS THE door opened and Marilsa stepped out. She saw him and gave him a wan smile, though he could see she had been crying at some point during her time with the witch.

"Is everything okay?" he asked her.

She nodded, saying nothing, and gave him a hug.

"Did...did you learn everything you need to know?"

Marilsa pulled back and looked up into Jadir's face.

"She showed me how to keep the *incubo* from harming me. But there's so much more that I must learn on my own. Jadir, what are we going to do for money?"

"I've already taken care of that," he reassured her. "I'm going to be working with Phana."

He hoped mentioning their friend would ease Marilsa's concerns, but she saw right through his ploy.

"You've joined the gang? I thought you didn't want to do that. I thought it was dangerous."

Jadir put his arm around Marilsa's shoulders as they started to walk toward their home. The sky was lightening in the east, and the streets of the Warren were practically deserted at this early hour. This was the transition time, when walking in the Warren was least dangerous. The nighttime predators had retreated to their lairs, and the daytime gangs had not yet moved out onto the streets.

"Koral put in a good word for me. I won't be doing anything dangerous. And they will pay me more than you and I were earning together at both of our old jobs. And it means you'll probably get to see Phana more often, too."

Marilsa looked up at him again, and he saw something in her gaze...pity?

"What?" he asked. She blinked and it was gone, and she turned away from him to look around at the decrepit buildings lining the narrows streets of the Warren. To the northeast, a plume of black smoke was now visible rising into the lightening sky, marking the location of the new tower that had risen on the very edge of the Warren less than a week before.

"Nothing," Marilsa replied. "You're so good to me, Jadir. I love you, and you will always be my brother. Nothing will change that, okay?"

Jadir felt his throat go dry. It wasn't like Marilsa to talk like this, like she knew something terrible was going to happen.

"What happened with the old woman? I need you to tell me what she told you."

Marilsa was silent for a few minutes as they walked. Jadir didn't push her—he knew she needed time to figure out how to tell him what the witch had done while Marilsa had been alone with her. Finally, she took a deep breath.

"No."

Jadir was taken aback.

"What? Why not?"

"It's not for you to know, Jadir. You were sent away tonight so that I could learn what I needed to know, but those secrets are...well, they're secret."

"But we tell each other everything."

"Not anymore. I'm sorry, Jadir, but you have no right to know. This belongs to *me*."

Jadir wanted to argue, but held back. His little sister had gone through so much lately, and obviously the witch had frightened her even more with the knowledge she had shared with Marilsa. He knew his sister would change her mind in time, and while he was still worried, he was sure she would eventually tell him everything.

She just needed some time to come to grips with all that had happened.

In truth, he was relieved to hear that the man, the spirit, was not going to be able to hurt her anymore. He knew there was still great danger in who she was, what she still needed to learn. But they would face that together.

They stopped at one of the food vendors in the market who had opened early, bought breakfast, and returned to their room. Marilsa wolfed down her bread and cheese, though Jadir found he didn't have much of an appetite even though he had not eaten since early last night. He *was* exhausted, though.

Marilsa sat on her pallet and crossed her legs.

"Jadir, you need to sleep."

"So do you," he said, yawning.

"I will in a while. I'm not tired, and there are some things I must practice before I can let myself sleep.

There was something different about Marilsa, something in the way she spoke to him, but he couldn't put his finger on it. Maybe it was just his tired brain playing tricks on him.

"I'll need to go quit my job today."

"You need sleep first. I'll wake you around midday, and then I will sleep while you go out and take care of that stuff."

"Marilsa, my new job…I'll be away a lot during the evening and through the night."

She nodded.

"I know. It's okay, I'll usually be awake during the night, too. Don't worry; it'll be just like before, when we both had jobs. We're just changing when we sleep, and instead of leaving to go work, I'll be here, practicing and learning."

Confidence, he decided. There was a new confidence in her voice. She was taking charge, telling him how things were going to be. She was trying to reassure him, as if suddenly she were the big sister and he, her little brother.

It was a strange reversal of their relationship, and he wasn't sure how he felt about it. She was still so young, and he was worried she was trying to grow up too fast. But then—he had to admit—she had just been given a huge responsibility, one she had no choice but to accept. He hoped she would be able to cope with it.

"You know I'm still here for you, right? Even if you can't tell me everything right now, it's okay. I'll take care of both of us while you learn what you need to learn. No matter what, you'll always be my little sister."

He saw that look in her eyes again, as if she knew some truth that made her sad, but couldn't share it with him. As if he had changed, somehow, in her eyes. The thought frightened him. He had heard witches could foretell possible futures—that they saw the most likely outcome of a course of action. Had the witch told Marilsa's future? Or Jadir's?

Or had Marilsa done that herself?

If so, was something going to happen to one of them? Was there a doom hanging over their heads right now, something he might be able to avoid if only he knew what it was?

But she wasn't ready to tell him anything yet, and he knew pushing would only make the situation worse. He could only hope she decided to share it with him before it was too late to change it.

"I know, Jadir. Now go to sleep."

He lay down and almost immediately felt himself drifting off. He knew he needed a full night's rest to make up for getting so few hours over the past few nights. But he still had things to do today, and he would start his new job tonight.

Jadir didn't like the idea of not being there first thing this morning to quit his old job. Showing up partway through the day was just not like him. But his thoughts began to flit around, and he couldn't hold the thread in his mind any longer.

The last thing he heard before he lost consciousness was Marilsa's voice, chanting something softly under her breath.

Chapter Fourteen

ROTHER RELAEL OCHALLUM PUSHED THE IRON-BOUND door open and entered the small chamber. The other man was already there, he noted with some satisfaction, but the other two priests had not yet arrived. He had been concerned they might start without him—he could never trust that they would not try to usurp his position as head of this "project."

The mad were notoriously unpredictable.

As, apparently, were their two subjects. The priests had returned to the street outside the tenement last night, only to discover the young man and his sister were not there. And neither was Wilau, the spy they had set to watch over the pair. Obviously, they had gone somewhere, and Wilau had followed them, but it left Relael and his companions with nothing to do but wait.

Finally, in the early hours of the morning, they had given up and returned to the Temple. Brother Ontherim had grumbled about the waste of time but otherwise wasn't too bothered by the situation. Sister Zera had been in a cold fury. She seemed to take it as a personal slight that events had moved on without warning.

Relael hoped she wouldn't pose a problem this morning.

When he received word from Wilau that the spy was here to report on the events of the evening, Relael was glad he had set his best man on the job.

The other man stood up from the chair in which he had been reclining and bowed deeply to Relael. Wilau looked the part of someone who would blend in on the streets of Ythis, dressed as a simple tradesman, nothing to distinguish him or give cause for any witnesses to remember his presence.

"Wilau, please," Relael said, motioning for the other man to sit. "I don't require such formality."

The spy nodded and sat. Relael appreciated his professionalism. He showed no fear of Relael and his brethren, only deference. It made him even more valuable.

They were meeting in one of the small buildings near the Temple where the day-to-day administration of the Church's dealings across the breadth of the Empire was conducted. Few priests worked here—it was mostly clerks and other laypersons who needed their wits about them to perform their duties.

These buildings were all connected to the Temple and to each other through underground passages, which allowed the priests and their hirelings to move about without needing to step outside. It helped to keep their activities private and away from prying eyes.

Relael took a seat just as the door opened and Brother Ontherim Worestald and Sister Zera Xodoc entered the room. Wilau stood and bowed to each of the new arrivals. Relael remained seated.

Sister Zera gave him a cold look and sat at the opposite end of the table. Brother Ontherim seemed unaware of Relael's slight, and sat beside him. Relael again motioned for Wilau to sit so they could start the meeting.

"Wilau," he began, "why don't you update us on the activities of our two subjects."

The man cleared his throat before speaking.

"In the early evening, both the girl, Marilsa, and her brother returned home from their respective jobs. Shortly after, they left their tenement and met up with another man a few blocks away. They proceeded into the Warren, the third man obviously leading them somewhere in particular."

Relael raised his eyebrows at this. He expected he knew who they had been taken to see, though the other two priests would be surprised at the news.

"The third man took them to a small building," Wilau continued. "They were greeted by a young girl at the door. The other man waited outside while Jadir and Marilsa went in. Shortly after, Jadir came out, and he and the other man left the area."

"Where was the girl?" Brother Ontherim asked.

"She remained inside. I decided that she was unlikely to leave while her brother was away, so I followed Jadir and the third man to the tavern known as the Iron Spike. They stayed for a short time, and then Jadir left and returned to the building where his sister was."

"And the third man?" Relael prompted.

"He did not return with Jadir. I did not see him leave the Iron Spike, but he may have done so after I followed Jadir back into the Warren. Just before dawn, Marilsa came out and the two of them bought some food from a vendor in the market before returning to their room."

Sister Zera spoke up for the first time. "Who lives in the building in the Warren?"

"I haven't yet been able to confirm, though there are rumors."

Wilau looked to Relael to see if the priest wanted to hear about rumors or just wanted to stick to known facts. But just as Relael was giving a tiny shake of his head, Sister Zera grabbed Wilau's attention again.

"Well? Tell us what you've heard!"

"Some of my contacts think a witch lives there. They don't know any more than that."

Brother Ontherim scoffed. "Another witch? If you believe the inhabitants of that place, the Warren is always full of witches, isn't it? But it always turns out to be nonsense."

Relael nodded at the priest's words. He knew about the witch in the Warren, had kept tabs on her for some time, though he did not know her exact location. He had kept her existence to himself, holding onto it in case he could use her in the future. Relael hated to see the opportunity wasted after so long.

But Sister Zera latched onto Wilau's words.

"The girl is going to be a witch soon enough," she declared. "We know that for a fact, Brother Worestald. And the only way the girl is going to learn how to control her *incubo* is from another witch. That's why she spent the night in the Warren."

"We don't know that for sure, Sister Zera," replied Relael. "And our focus is on the girl. I don't want to divide our attention right now, when the situation is delicate."

"The witch must be brought to the Temple!" demanded Sister Zera. "I will not shirk my duty to the Church just to fulfill the plan you have for this girl. One witch in Ythis is too many, but I am willing to participate because she will die once she completes her part. But a second witch must not be allowed to go free. That is too much."

Relael sighed heavily. He could have manipulated Brother Ontherim to ignore the old witch, but Sister Zera was too strong-willed. She was angry at being left out in the cold last night, and had now latched onto this witch as a target on which she would take out her rage. Relael saw it as a waste of a potential resource. But he also knew there was nothing he could do.

"Very well," he said. "Tomorrow morning at dawn, we will raid that house in the Warren and take the witch into custody."

"Why tomorrow?" Sister Zera asked. "Why not now?"

"Because the witch in the Warren is not as important as making sure the situation with Marilsa goes according to plan. We need to see what she's doing, and this is out of Wilau's area of expertise. If the girl is interacting with her *incubo*, gaining control over it, we need to be there to ensure the situation turns to our advantage. This witch in the Warren has probably lived there for some time—another night won't make any difference. We'll strike at the time where there will be no interference from locals in that neighborhood, and take the witch by surprise."

Relael could see Sister Zera didn't like it, but his words made sense. Brother Ontherim nodded and muttered "I agree with Brother Ochallum."

"Sister, I need you near the tenement. You know what must be done, and we cannot waste any time."

Relael watched a struggle going on behind her eyes, but finally she gave a single, short, sharp nod.

"I'm glad we are all aligned," he concluded. "Soon, this project will be over and there will be no more witches in Ythis."

Relael stood and walked confidently out of the room. There was still much to do.

*   *   *

JADIR FUMED AS HE STRODE TOWARD THE IRON SPIKE, silently cursing his stupidity for believing his former employer would have taken his resignation in a reasonable manner. Chayesh had been furious when Jadir showed up mid-afternoon. Before Jadir could get a word in, the foreman had threatened to fire him if he ever did such a thing again.

Jadir had asked to speak to Chayesh privately, but the man had refused—he wanted the other workers to hear him berate Jadir for not showing up on time this morning. So Jadir had explained that he was quitting the job. The foreman nearly swallowed his tongue. Chayesh was angry, but the last thing he wanted was to lose his best and—generally—most reliable worker.

Chayesh had been forced to back down on his threats, which clearly made him even angrier, and told Jadir that he was still welcome to work at the warehouse. When Jadir had tried to explain that Marilsa couldn't work anymore, and so Jadir had found a job that paid better, Chayesh had decided to be petty and vindictive.

The foreman declared he was docking Jadir's pay for the trouble he had caused by not showing up for work, and so refused to pay him for the extra time Jadir had spent in the warehouse after hours a few days before.

Unfortunately for Jadir, everyone knew he would back down—he had never displayed a temper or threatened physical violence before—and so Chayesh wasn't worried about what Jadir might do. And Chayesh had been right. Jadir had left with a vague warning of "trouble," but it was a hollow threat, and everyone knew it.

The two men guarding the door to the Iron Spike saw him approach and waved him through without challenge. He was one of them, now. He entered the common room of the tavern and looked around for Phana, but she wasn't sitting at any of the tables tonight. Jadir had been looking forward to seeing her again, especially after she had acted so strangely the night before.

One of the men in the bar stood up and walked over. He wasn't a big man, a full head shorter than Jadir, but he was solidly built like a bulldog. A scar ran across his chin, and something in his eyes told Jadir this was a man who had killed before, and would do again without hesitation.

"You Jadir?" the man asked.

"Yeah. I'm looking for Phana."

"She's busy. You're with me tonight."

The man turned and began to walk toward the exit. Jadir took a step after him, but wasn't sure if he should follow or not.

"Can I ask who you are?"

The man glanced back over his shoulder as he shoved the tavern door open. "Rifain. Come on."

Rifain left the Iron Spike, and Jadir took a quick last look around before hurrying out the door after him. The other man had crossed the street and was heading toward the mouth of an alley. Jadir ran to catch up with him and Rifain stopped and turned as Jadir reached him.

"Don't run. Running calls attention to you. It makes people look, instead of looking away like they're supposed to. Running makes people remember."

"Sorry. I just…where are we going?"

"You'll see. For now, stay quiet, follow me, and do what I do."

Jadir nodded and Rifain turned and led the way into the alley. They walked for some minutes before coming to a wooden door in the wall of what looked like a warehouse. Rifain pounded on it, and the door opened a crack. The person on the other side looked at Rifain and Jadir, and then opened the door.

Rifain led Jadir into the warehouse. The man who had let them in pushed the door closed and lowered a heavy bar into place.

Jadir took a look around the warehouse. Crates of various sizes were stacked along one wall, and simple wooden dividers had been put up between the supports to create smaller rooms across one-half of the large space. Opposite the partitions there was a clear area surrounded by racks of weapons and a few benches. It was where

Rifain was heading.

Jadir followed him into the center of the cleared space and Rifain turned to face him.

"You any good in a fight?" he asked. Jadir shrugged.

"I guess so. I'm strong, really strong."

"Have you been in any fights?"

"A couple," Jadir answered. "My size keeps most troublemakers away from me."

Rifain snorted.

"The kind of people you're gonna meet won't care about your size. You don't move like a fighter. That means anyone who knows what they're doin' is gonna see you as an easy target, which you are."

Rifain spread his hands.

"Hit me," he said.

"What?"

"Come on, I need to see if you're any good. I need to see what you know. I'm some thug who's wandered into the Iron Spike and is causing trouble, and you're the only guy there. So stop me."

"You want me to...spar with you?"

"No. I want you to *fight* with me."

Jadir looked around, and saw a few men and women drifting over and taking seats on the benches.

"What if I hurt you?"

Rifain laughed. "Don't worry about that. I can take a punch."

And then Jadir saw Phana come out from around one of the wooden partitions and walk over to take a seat on one of the benches.

"Can I have a minute?" he asked Rifain.

"For what?"

"I...I just need to talk to someone for a minute." There were a few chuckles from the onlookers and Jadir glanced over to see a horrified look on Phana's face. "Please."

Rifain shrugged, grinning. "Suit yourself."

Jadir walked over to Phana, who stood as he approached.

"What are you doing?" she asked before he could say anything.

"I was hoping you and I could get a chance to talk sometime tonight. When I'm done here." He was acutely aware the others were all watching them. Phana frowned and shook her head.

"You're not here to talk to me, Jadir. You're here because you asked for a job. And your job," she pointed back at Rifain, "is right there."

He could see she was angry with him. He didn't understand the problem. It wasn't like everyone didn't already know Phana was his friend.

"Don't make me regret helping you," she said.

Jadir opened his mouth, but realized that nothing he could say would make this situation any better. The truth was he wanted to spend some time alone with Phana, but telling her that would only make her angrier. She was right. This wasn't the time or the place for them to talk about what had happened between them and what it meant.

"Okay," he said. "You're right. We'll talk when...whenever." He gave her a small smile to show he wasn't offended, but she drew back, as if she was...afraid of something. Maybe there was some kind of rule against members of the gang getting involved.

He turned and walked back to where Rifain was waiting, and could hear the whispers and chuckles from the onlookers as he returned.

"You ready?" Rifain asked. There was obvious disdain in his voice. Jadir thought that perhaps he should show them what his strength could do. He wouldn't hurt Rifain—maybe just toss him around a bit.

Suddenly, Rifain launched himself at Jadir, and Jadir found himself caught entirely by surprise. He raised his hands and tried to grab the other man's shirt, but Rifain ducked under Jadir's arms and drove his own fist into Jadir's stomach.

It was like being hit by a mallet.

The wind was driven from Jadir's lungs as Rifain stepped inside his guard and hammered Jadir in the ribs with another iron fist. As Jadir lowered his arms to block the hits to his body, Rifain curled his arm and brought his fist up under Jadir's chin.

Jadir's head snapped up and he felt the floor crash into his back. Stars swam across his vision and he lay there, trying to draw breath, fighting to hold onto consciousness.

Rifain stepped over to him and looked down into Jadir's face.

"Yeah, you don't know how to fight at all. This is gonna take some work."

Chapter Fifteen

RELAEL SAT ON THE HORSE UNEASILY. HE HATED ANIMALS, especially ones he was forced to ride. He much preferred to walk or use a carriage, but neither was an option this morning. To one side, Sister Zera sat her horse as if she was born to it, while Brother Ontherim barely managed to keep his balance in the saddle. There was no way the priest would be able to keep up with the rest of them.

Relael flicked his reigns and angled his horse toward the Imperial Guard Commander who was leading the force this morning. A contingent of twelve Guardsmen were arrayed behind him, all polished armor and gleaming weapons. Their horses stamped and snorted in the pre-dawn light.

"Commander Zopu, a word, please."

The Commander rode over to Relael and drew up beside him.

"Commander, we have a problem with Brother Ontherim. He can barely sit his horse. How fast are we going to ride?"

"Well, sir, word travels fast in the Warren. There are lookouts for the gangs on the edges of that area, and they run back to warn everyone whenever we make an incursion into the neighborhood. The only way to keep ahead of their messengers is to ride hard for our target and get there first."

Relael sighed. Carriages were useless in the narrow, winding streets of the Warren. But it was risky for Sister Zera to face the witch without another priest to back her up. Relael couldn't do it—he didn't have the abilities that came with full communion with Iathephos. The thought sent a shiver up his spine.

"Have a couple of your men tie Brother Ontherim to the saddle. It's the only way he'll still be on the horse when we arrive."

The Commander glanced sideways at the other priest. "Will he agree to that, sir?"

"I'll handle that," Relael said as he turned his horse and walked it over to Brother Ontherim.

"Brother," said Relael. "These are foul beasts, are they not?"

Brother Ontherim nodded, his lips pressed grimly together.

"Unfortunately, we have no other choice this morning. I'd like to give you some assistance with the animal, make sure you reach our target safely."

"How?"

Two Guardsmen approached, holding rope.

"I believe you should let these men secure you in the saddle. If you fall while we ride, you may injure yourself, or get trampled by the horses behind. I assume you do not want that?"

Brother Ontherim eyed the guards nervously, as they just as nervously eyed the priest. At this rate, the force would never move out.

"Brother Ontherim, please let them help you."

The other man considered Relael's suggestion for a moment, and gave a single nod. Relael motioned for the Guardsmen to approach and bind Ontherim to the saddle. He had to give them credit for their stoicism—one of the soldiers nearly retched when he caught a whiff of Brother Ontherim's scent—but they forced themselves to do the job quickly and professionally.

Relael turned and called to the Commander.

"I believe we are ready to proceed."

The horsemen formed up with two outriders in the lead, the priests in the center of the column. Relael found himself beside Sister Zera. She did not so much as glance in his direction.

The Commander gave the order and the horses began to trot along the avenue that split the dock from the Trades District. They crossed over the bridge where the East and West Rivers merged, and then the Commander barked another order and the horses lunged into a full gallop.

They entered the Warren moving at full speed, and the horsemen at the front of the column led the way along the twisting, turning streets, following the route Relael's spy had mapped out the night before. The few people on the streets at this early hour scattered out of their path, and Relael could only imagine the lookouts racing back to their gangs to warn them of an Imperial Guard contingent in their midst.

Suddenly, the column came to an abrupt halt as they reached their destination, a small stone building surrounded by broken tenements. Eight of the Guardsmen arrayed their horses in a defensive formation around the group, weapons ready and all facing outward to guard against any threat from within the Warren. The other four slid from their saddles and drew their own swords. The Commander himself cut the ropes holding Brother Ontherim in place on his saddle and helped the Priest down to the ground.

Relael stayed on his horse and watched the four soldiers lead Sister Zera and Brother Ontherim to the door of the small building. One of the soldiers kicked the wooden portal open and the Guardsmen lunged through the dark doorway, followed closely by Relael's brethren.

Moments passed, and then Sister Zera exploded out from the door, her rage a palpable presence as a strange wind rose up and swirled around her. The horses whinnied and sidestepped as she marched toward Relael, her face in a rictus of fury.

"The witch is gone!" she screamed at Relael. "It's all your fault! We should have come here immediately, and now she's gone!"

The Guardsmen were as nervous as the horses, and the Commander had to bark an order to keep them in formation. Once again, the soldiers forced themselves to swallow their fear and execute their orders. Relael sometimes wished such discipline could be found in the Church, though such a thing was simply impossible.

"Sister Zera," said Relael, keeping his voice calm. "It is unfortunate this morning's efforts were wasted, but perhaps we can discuss this back at the Temple."

If anything, his words only enraged her further.

"Your games cost us the witch! I will see you face the Disciplinary Council for this! I will have your head!"

Relael grit his teeth and forced himself to remain calm. Public displays such as this harmed the Church in ways too many to count. Discipline or not, the soldiers here today would repeat this confrontation to others, both within and without their organization. His life was dedicated to keeping the Church strong, and he wouldn't let this madwoman harm his efforts.

Brother Ontherim emerged from the building with the soldiers who had been first inside. He looked over at Sister Zera and stopped, not wanting to get involved in this situation.

"The witch is nothing," he said in a low voice, pitched only for Sister Zera to hear. Her eyes went wide at his words, as if she thought he was deliberately provoking her.

"The witch is nothing," he repeated, pointing his arm at the plume of smoke rising above the city. "Compared to *that*, I could not care less about your witch. I have been given a mission, Sister, and I will see it through. You can bring whatever charges you want. But I'm after a real threat to Ythis and the Church, not some old woman who creates charms and mends broken bodies. If you don't wish to be part of my mission, I will have you removed."

He turned to the Commander.

"It is time for us to leave the Warren, Commander. Please give the order to your soldiers."

The Commander shouted commands to the Guardsmen and, while two of them helped Brother Ontherim back onto his horse, the rest formed up into the column again.

Sister Zera stood rooted to the spot, the wind still swirling around her. Relael knew he was taking a risk. She could easily channel enough force to kill him if she lost control of herself. But he was gambling on her political ambitions. If Relael succeeded, she would reap the benefits of being part of his scheme.

The wind died down, and she said in a low voice "This isn't over, Brother."

She turned and climbed into her saddle—Relael decided she definitely had some real experience with horses—and galloped to the head of the column.

As the Guardsmen escorted the priests out of the Warren, Relael gripped the pommel of his saddle to keep his hands from shaking. Sister Zera would not bring him before the Disciplinary Council as long as he succeeded in his mission.

And that was important, for the Council would put him to the question, and he would eventually tell them all about the warning he had sent to the witch last night.

*　　　*　　　*

JADIR SWUNG HIS FIST AT HIS OPPONENT'S HEAD, BUT THE OTHER man simply ducked under the swing and charged forward. Jadir backpedaled, trying to keep Rifain from getting inside his guard, but he was too slow and once again found himself on his back, his instructor sitting on his chest.

Rifain cocked his arm back in preparation for driving his fist into Jadir's face, and Jadir covered up.

"No, no, no!" Rifain shouted as he stood up. "I pulled myself off balance, showed you what I was gonna do, and you didn't take advantage of it. You should have yanked on my other arm and thrown me to the floor."

Jadir dragged himself to his feet. "I'm sorry, I'm just not as fast as you are."

"That's not your problem. You're holding back, worried you might hurt me. In a real fight, that's going to get you beaten or killed."

"But this isn't a real fight," Jadir protested.

"So what? You hold back now, all you're doin' is practicing holding back. And in a real fight, when it's time for your instincts to kick in, you'll fall back on what you've practiced."

Rifain sat on one of the benches and wiped his arm across his brow. Jadir sat beside him, picked up the ladle from the bucket of water and drank deeply.

"You're swinging your fists like they're hammers, but that's too slow. I can see it coming long before you connect, and when you miss, you're not fast enough to recover before I'm on you."

"But if I don't swing, how can I hit you?" Jadir asked.

"You're already strong—you don't need to swing that hard. If you drive your fists instead of swinging them, it'll be harder for me to come at you even if you miss. And you'll recover faster."

Rifain jumped to his feet, but Jadir was tired from sparring since the moment he had arrived.

"Can we rest for a bit?"

"No. Fights don't wait for you to be ready."

Jadir stood up and walked back out into the center of the space and faced Rifain. He raised his fists and got ready to thrust rather than swing.

"You're droppin' your fists."

"I'm tired," Jadir replied, raising his fists to better protect his face.

"Don't care," said Rifain and began to move around, poking and prodding at Jadir's defenses. They went at it like this for a full minute before Rifain lunged and tried to get close to Jadir. Jadir saw him coming and drove his fist out, but checked the amount of force he put into the punch. Rifain sidestepped the punch and tried to close, but Jadir managed to recover and stepped back to prevent getting knocked down again.

"Good, you're learning."

Rifain tried again, and Jadir tried to punch again, but missed. His recovery was a little shaky, but he was still on his feet.

The third time Rifain tried to move in, Jadir was ready for him. He threw his fist at where he expected Rifain's head to be, but the man wasn't there. Instead, Rifain had moved to one side where Jadir's ribs were completely exposed. Jadir almost heard his ribs creak under the force of Rifain's strike, and he automatically dropped his arms to cover his side, leaving his head unprotected.

Once again, Jadir found himself on his back, blinking back stars. Pain had blossomed across the entire side of his head. He groaned and rolled over onto his unhurt side. Rifain said nothing, waiting for him to recover.

It took a few minutes for the pain to ease enough that Jadir was able to sit upright. He looked up at Rifain, who was watching him without expression.

"Do you think beating on me is going to teach me anything?" he asked the other man. "Maybe I need to practice one thing and get it down before you change it on me."

Rifain shrugged.

"This isn't a guild, or an academy. It's just me. Most people coming into this gang already know how to fight. I just teach them a few new tricks, tighten up their skills. But you've *got* no skills."

He crouched down to look Jadir in the eyes. "You have no skills, no experience, and you really don't have the killer instinct. If you weren't so big, you'd probably have been killed in some brawl before now."

"And beating me up is going to help?"

Rifain snorted and stood back up. "I'm not beating you up. If I was, you wouldn't be able to talk to me right now. You need to get used to feeling pain, Jadir, 'cuz that's what you're going to feel a lot if you find yourself in any real fights. Even if I can teach you enough to keep you alive, even if you end up walking away as the winner, you're gonna get hurt often. I don't think you'll ever be good enough to avoid that."

"So I have to be willing to kill someone to be good at fighting?" Jadir asked bitterly.

"By the Abyss, yeah!" answered Rifain. "Any time you get in a fight, there's a chance someone will die. You can kill someone by accident—it's not that hard to do. Think about it, what would make you willing to kill, either in self-defense or the defense of another person?"

Jadir considered it. "If I had to kill to save Marilsa's life, I would do it. But I'd try to find another way first."

"*Another way?*" Rifain asked in shock. "While you're trying to find another way, your sister would *die*."

Jadir stood up and faced Rifain. "I've never been in that situation, so I don't know what I'd do. Maybe I would try to talk the person down, or offer my life for hers, or maybe I'd go berserk and get us both killed. You talk like this is easy, but you've been doing it for years. It's nothing to you. But not everyone thinks life is as cheap as you do."

Rifain lunged at Jadir, and instead of recoiling, Jadir drove his fist out toward the other man's face. Rifain twisted his head at the last second, but Jadir still scored a glancing blow that knocked his opponent off balance.

Rifain's shoulder drove into Jadir's stomach, but there was no real force behind it. Jadir realized his other arm was in a perfect position to loop around Rifain's neck, and he grappled the smaller man, twisting him further off balance.

Jadir placed his free hand under Rifain's armpit and heaved, and the other man flew across the clear space, somersaulting once in mid-air, to land with a crash on his back amidst the benches.

Immediately, terror gripped Jadir—had he just killed the other man? He hadn't meant to throw him so hard, but his own anger had pushed him farther than he wanted. Jadir ran over to check on Rifain as other members of the gang came over to see what had happened.

Rifain's eyes were open, and he slowly rolled himself onto his side as Jadir knelt down beside him.

"Are you okay?"

Rifain grimaced and slowly pushed himself up to a sitting position. "Yeah, I've had worse."

"I'm sorry; I didn't mean what I said—"

Rifain held up one hand and Jadir stopped. "I pushed you on purpose. I wanted to see what you'd do if you got angry."

Jadir couldn't help but feel some pride in coming out the victor this time.

"I guess I'm not so helpless after all."

Rifain snorted. "No? By the Abyss, Jadir, you threw me. You could have choked me out, snapped my neck, or broken my back if you wanted to. But all you did was throw me."

He shook his head and snorted again. "No killer instinct at all."

"But...but I *won*," Jadir protested.

"Then that's the next thing you need to learn," answered Rifain. "When someone's life is on the line, it's not enough to just be the last man standing."

Jadir stood up and stalked across the room, furious. The other man was being ridiculous. There was more to victory than just taking someone's life.

Maybe he just wasn't cut out for this kind of work.

Chapter Sixteen

PHANA REMOVED THE WEIGHTS FROM THE SMALL SCALE and placed them back on their rack. Dozens of small strips of oilcloth wrapped around single doses of dreamleaf spread across the worktable. Someone else would tie the packages closed with string. Qudovo had asked Phana to help with measuring out the dosages because she worked quickly and was always precise. But she had other things she wanted to do tonight, and didn't feel like hanging around the warehouse.

This part of the warehouse was divided into many small rooms by the thin, wooden partitions set up between the roof supports. But the walls didn't reach all the way up to the warehouse's ceiling, which left a vast, open space above. Sound traveled easily through that space, and Phana had been dimly aware of the sounds of fighting from the training area on the other side of the warehouse.

Rifain was trying to teach Jadir how to fight, and it didn't sound like it was going too well. A moment ago, there had been a large crash. It sounded like a bunch of wood broke, and she wondered if Jadir or Rifain had been sent right through one of the wooden panels. She also wondered if Rifain noticed anything...off...about Jadir. She couldn't be the only one to feel it—a sense that Jadir was not quite right. Not quite human.

She gave her head a shake, annoyed at these thoughts. Jadir had been good to her for a long time. She had been quite attracted to him for most of that time. And the other night had been...well, the start of something she really wanted. But now she could barely stand to be within arm's reach of him.

Something about him now terrified her.

She stepped out of the room where she had been working and moved toward the "hallway" that ran the length of the warehouse. As she came around the corner, she saw Jadir at the other end, pacing back and forth. He had obviously decided to take a break from Rifain's training.

He looked up and saw her, and their eyes locked. Phana shivered, and tried to suppress her fear from showing on her face.

Jadir stalked toward her, his annoyance plain on his own face, and it was all Phana could do to remain still and not run in the other direction.

"Phana, we need to talk. Now," he growled. She took a step back, and then forced herself to remain calm. She motioned him to step into a side alcove created by the wooden partitions.

"What just happened," she asked.

"I threw Rifain across the room. He still thinks I lost."

Phana said nothing, not looking him in the eyes. She couldn't imagine how she had flirted with him for so long, couldn't imagine touching him, hugging him. She could only stand apart from him, her arms crossed protectively over her.

"I think I deserve to know what's going on," he said to her.

"I don't know what you mean," she lied. She sounded almost convincing.

"Really? You've done nothing but flirt with me, tease me, act like you wanted me for as long as I can remember. You came to my home and kissed me and we near ... well, I want to know what happened. Since that night, you've completely changed. You wanted me to join your gang, and now that I have, you act like I repel you. So what happened?"

Phana looked down at the floor and said nothing. She didn't know how to answer him.

"Is it Marilsa? You changed your attitude as soon as I told you she was a witch. Are you afraid of my sister—is that why you won't come near me?"

Phana felt a pang of pity for the poor girl. She hoped Marilsa didn't think she was driving Phana away; nothing could be further from the truth. She wasn't afraid of Marilsa being a witch. She had realized it didn't bother her at all.

Phana took a deep breath and, still looking at the floor, spoke in a low voice.

"It's not Marilsa. I'm not afraid of her."

"Then what is the problem?"

She raised her head, and tears formed in her eyes. She mentally cursed herself for showing such weakness, but she had to answer him, and she knew what it was going to do to him.

"It's you."

"What? What about me? Was it something I did the other night when—"

Phana shook her head. "No, not then. There's something…different…about you, Jadir. After you took Marilsa to see the witch in the Warren, when you came back to the Iron Spike, you…I don't know. You were different, that's all. What happened there?"

Jadir was obviously stunned, and hurt, by Phana's words. None of this made any sense.

"Where? The witch's house? Nothing. Marilsa and I talked to the witch, and then she told me to leave while she taught Marilsa what she needed to know. Koral and I walked back to the Iron Spike together, I met with Qudovo, and then saw you."

Jadir fell silent and she could almost see his mind working, coming to all the wrong conclusions.

"Did Qudovo tell you to stay away from me? Or Koral? It's obvious he wants…he's attracted to you. What did he say—"

"No," Phana interrupted, more forcefully. "It's not them, or anyone else. It's you. Jadir, there's something just wrong about you. You give off this feeling—it scares me, and you know I don't scare easily."

"This is crazy," he argued. "I'm the same person I always was. The only difference is that Marilsa now knows why that spirit was attacking her…."

He trailed off, and she knew he was thinking about the spirit.

"Do you think the spirit has been following me? Trying to harm me in some way? That would explain why I seem different to you."

Phana shrugged. She wanted to latch onto that explanation, but the truth was she didn't know what was causing this, and she was afraid to get her hopes up that it would be this simple.

"I have no idea, Jadir."

She could see he was frustrated and angry, and she agreed with him. He had finally given in to her, had finally admitted he wanted her, and now she couldn't bear to be near him.

"By the Abyss, Phana, I did everything you wanted. I joined your gang…."

He stopped, and a strange look came over his face. She could almost feel a rage building up inside him—it was almost a palpable thing, sending waves of heat out from his body.

"That's it, isn't it?" he spat at her. "All you wanted was for me to join your gang, and you were willing to do anything to convince me. Here I thought you cared about me, but you just wanted me to finally give in."

He clenched his fists, and Phana nearly flinched.

"And Koral was pretty eager to help me, too. Did you and he cook this up together? You and your boyfriend playing me for a fool?"

"Jadir, please…," Phana was shaking, and a cold sweat had broken out all over her body. "Calm down, please."

"You never wanted me! It was a trick!" He was shouting now, and Phana could hear others coming to see what was happening. She worried their presence would cause him to lash out, to do something drastic.

Jadir turned and smashed his fist right through one of the thin, wooden walls. Phana literally jumped back, her eyes darting around, looking for a way to escape. But he was blocking her way.

He won't hurt you, she told herself. But when he turned back to her, something in his eyes told her that was no longer true, if it had ever been.

"I won't stand for this! Do you understand? You won't manipulate me this way and—"

And suddenly he brought his hands up to grip the sides of his head and his eyes went wide. He sank to his knees as the others in the warehouse reached them. Phana looked into his eyes, but he was seeing something else, somewhere else.

"*MARILSA, LOOK AROUND YOU!*" he yelled. "*HE HAS A SWORD!*"

And then Jadir screamed, an inhuman sound full of pain and rage. It went on and on, and Jadir surged to his feet and his howl transformed into Marilsa's name, over and over.

A couple of the others reached out to steady him, but Jadir shoved them aside as he bolted back down the passage toward the door. Rifain stepped in front of him, but Jadir swept the other man away, sending him crashing through one of the wooden partitions. He kicked open the warehouse door, shattering the wooden beam, and ran off into the night.

Phana tried to follow, but the others held her back.

"Get your hands off me right now! Let. Me. GO!" She tore herself from their grasp and ran after Jadir. There was no question where he was headed.

Phana could only hope Marilsa was still alive when he got there.

*   *   *

JADIR HAD NO THOUGHT FOR ANYONE ELSE, NO THOUGHT FOR how he knew what he knew. All that mattered was that he get back to Marilsa right away, or what he had seen would happen. Maybe it had already happened, but somehow, he knew he wasn't too late. Not yet.

There was no hesitation, no need to get his bearings. He knew exactly where Marilsa was, and exactly how to reach her in the shortest amount of time. He bolted from the alley, across the street, and into another alley heedless of anyone or anything in his way. Bystanders leaped out of his path, his size and the no doubt crazed look on his face giving them ample warning not to impede his progress.

Jadir had never moved so fast, never run for so long without tiring, but his breathing came easy despite his exertions and he felt no fatigue gathering in his legs. If anything, the closer he got to Marilsa, the more energy he seemed to have.

Finally, he rounded a corner and saw the tenement where they lived. As he sprinted up the street toward his building, he spotted a man wearing a black cloak standing by the main door. Something about the man set off a warning in Jadir's head, and as he got closer, the man noticed Jadir and drew a long blade from under the cloak.

Jadir slowed only slightly as he neared the man, who had dropped into a warrior's stance, the blade held comfortably, point facing in Jadir's direction. Jadir had no time to think, to consider what he would do. Somehow, he knew just how to move. As Jadir came within reach, the cloaked man lunged forward to plant the sword in Jadir's chest.

Time seemed to slow and Jadir realized he could easily avoid the deadly thrust. He twisted to one side, the point passing harmlessly under his right arm. The man immediately tried to pull back, to recover, but he was moving so slowly.

Jadir stepped within the man's guard and drove his fist toward the man's face. The swordsman tried to weave away from the strike, but Jadir easily adjusted his angle and connected solidly with the man's jaw. Bone shattered under Jadir's hand and the cloaked man's head snapped backward.

With his other hand, Jadir grabbed the man's wrist and twisted, and the sword dropped to the ground as the joint snapped under the force of Jadir's attack.

The swordsman fell to the ground, choking on bits of jawbone that had been driven into his throat. Jadir raised his boot and brought it down on the man's head. The sound of the man's skull cracking sent a fresh burst of energy through Jadir's body. He spun and threw himself toward the stairs to the second floor.

A moment later, Jadir's foot sent the door to his room crashing open. Two men stood inside, one in front of Marilsa, and one just moving behind her. Jadir's sister sat on her sleeping pallet, her eyes closed, apparently completely unaware of the danger so close to her.

The assassin closest to Jadir spun and threw a knife, but Jadir easily slapped it out of the air and lunged for the man. This man was faster, more skilled than the one outside, but he still seemed to be moving in slow motion. He flicked his blade out toward Jadir's eye, but Jadir moved just enough, and the point missed by less than a finger's width.

But it was still a miss, and Jadir grabbed the man's head in both hands and twisted hard. He saw the other assassin raise his sword in preparation for striking Marilsa from behind. Jadir's vision was about to come true, and he was going to be too slow to stop it.

In desperation, he stepped forward and threw the man he was holding toward the last assassin. Jadir's target dove to one side and rolled away as the body crashed through the closed shutters and flew out of sight down to the street below.

It was enough to give Jadir a chance to protect Marilsa. The last assassin leaped to his feet and drew a knife. The man appeared to be throwing it toward Jadir, but somehow Jadir knew it was a ploy. He threw himself between Marilsa and the assassin just as the other man changed the angle of his arm and threw the blade at the girl.

Jadir watched it spin once before embedding itself in his gut. He landed heavily, but immediately pulled himself to his feet as a terrible pain took hold of his lower body. The assassin moved in, swinging his sword at Jadir's head. Jadir leaned back just enough for the point of the blade to nick him across the bridge of his nose, and then lunged at the man.

The assassin checked his swing and recovered before Jadir could fully close with him, but the room wasn't very large, and the man's sword was too big to be fully useful here. He tried to thrust at Jadir's chest, but Jadir slapped the blade to one side with his open palm and grabbed the man by the throat.

With a yell, Jadir yanked the knife from his own stomach and buried it to the hilt in the assassin's chest. Still holding the twitching man, Jadir forced the blade down, opening up the assassin's body from sternum to groin. He saw a metal disk, an amulet, hit the floor below the man's feet. Jadir dropped the body to one side and knelt beside Marilsa.

He was about to say her name when she opened her eyes and immediately focused on him.

"We can't stay here anymore," she said before he could get any words out.

"There were men, assassins—"

"Yes," she interrupted. "I knew you would protect me. You did well, Jadir, but you're wounded, and we have to find someplace else to live now."

Jadir realized he was getting dizzy, and he looked down to see the front of his shirt was soaked with blood.

"Help will be here in a few minutes. Just lie down and rest."

"No...the noise...people will come...."

"Hush, my brother. No one heard anything. I've taken care of it. We've got time to wait for help, and I need to tend to your wound."

"I'm sorry...Mar...," Jadir felt himself fall over and his sister helped him lie on his back. "I don't...think you can...fix this."

Marilsa said nothing, just pulled his shirt up and examined his wound. Jadir could not feel his legs, and his stomach was a burning agony. He tried to keep himself from crying out, tried to be brave for Marilsa.

I gave my life to save hers, he thought to himself. *But she's still in danger.*

"Go to...Phana...she'll put you...somewhere safe."

"I told you to hush."

"Bodies outside...you need to...leave now."

He heard footsteps in the hallway and terror gripped him. Was it more assassins coming for Marilsa? Was it the Watch, or others from the building? What would happen once he was no longer around to protect his sister?

He saw Marilsa look up at a figure in the doorway. Jadir was too weak to turn his head—a terrible lethargy had gripped him.

"By the Abyss," he heard someone say, a woman's voice.

"Come here, he needs you," Marilsa replied, and Jadir's eyes closed against his will. "Jadir, everything will be alright. Phana is here."

He felt someone take his hand.

At least she's able to touch me now, he thought, and then darkness swept over him and he knew nothing else.

Chapter Seventeen

K ORAL TURNED THE CORNER AND SAW RIFAIN STANDING a few doors up from the tenement where Jadir and Marilsa had their room. The other man acknowledged him with a quick nod before maintaining his lookout. Koral walked past without speaking—he knew they were under a time limit.

Three more members of Qudovo's gang were stationed around the entrance to the tenement. They all knew who Koral was, and stood aside as he passed. He jogged up the stairs and found yet another gang member outside the door to Jadir's room.

The young man guarding the door stepped back and allowed Koral to enter. As soon as he opened the door, the hairs on the back of his neck stood up as the strangest sensation washed over him, as if he was standing in a pool of water that had just been struck by lightning. He stepped into the room and pushed the door closed and then faced the others.

Jadir lay on his sleeping pallet in a pool of blood. Marilsa knelt over him, her feet on either side of his torso. She chanted words he could not fully hear, as if she were speaking from under the surface of a pool of water. The sounds didn't really seem to match the movement of her mouth.

Phana crouched on the far side of Jadir, holding one of his hands in hers. The expression on her face was a mixture of hope and fear, as if she wasn't sure if she wanted whatever Marilsa was doing to succeed or not.

Koral carefully closed the door and stood watching. Blood covered Jadir's stomach, and sweat beaded his face, but his chest rose and fell rhythmically so at least he was still alive. Marilsa continued to chant as she reached down and touched his forehead with her index finger. Jadir's body convulsed once, but he didn't open his eyes.

The feeling of electric energy in the room seemed to reach a crescendo, and then Marilsa uttered a final, strangled moan, and fell to her side. Phana grabbed her and helped her lie down on her own pallet as Koral moved over and examined Jadir.

"He's alive," he whispered to Phana as Marilsa gave another low moan, as if she was waking up from a deep sleep. Phana looked over at Jadir and then focused her attention on Marilsa again, helping the young woman to sit up and regain her balance.

"You did it," Phana said to her. "You saved your brother."

Marilsa gave a slow nod and leaned into Phana's embrace.

"We can't stay here," Marilsa said in a voice that was slow and thick. Phana stroked her hair and shushed her.

"She's right," replied Koral. "We don't have much time. The bodies outside have been removed by the gang, but someone is going to notice our presence sooner rather than later."

Phana glared at him, but Marilsa pulled away from her and nodded. "I can't keep them all asleep for much longer."

"Who, honey?" Phana asked her, but Koral understood. No one had come to investigate the battle that had happened in here—apparently all the neighbors had slept right through it. Was Marilsa somehow keeping them all unconscious?

Jadir's eyes fluttered open and he reached for his stomach. Koral tried to stop him, but Jadir pulled his hand away and felt for the knife wound. But as he smeared his hand across the blood on his belly, Koral saw that the skin was no longer broken. Marilsa had closed the wound.

Jadir turned his head slightly so he could see his sister. "Did...did you heal me?"

Marilsa nodded at him. "I can't hold on much longer, Jadir."

That seemed to energize her brother, and Jadir forced himself to sit up. Koral put out a hand to steady him, and this time Jadir accepted his help.

Once Koral was sure the other man wouldn't fall back if he let go, he left Jadir to check on the corpse that had fallen in a heap against the far wall. The man had been eviscerated, but a glint of metal on the floor in the drying pool of blood caught Koral's eye. He used the point of his dagger to drag the small disk out of the blood, and then ripped off a hunk of the dead man's cloak with which to pick it up.

It was an amulet of beaten bronze, with strange markings carved into both sides. But it was the symbol painted in the center of the amulet that turned Koral's blood cold.

"This man is a Witch Hunter," he said to the others.

Jadir looked puzzled, but Phana knew instantly what Koral was saying.

"But Witch Hunters don't work in teams," she replied.

"No. Those other men were hired muscle. Skilled men, but residents of Ythis. If a Witch Hunter thinks he or she will meet up with resistance—a witch's corrupted followers—extra bodies will be hired to help out with the fighting."

"But...but Marilsa only found out she was a witch last night," argued Jadir. "How could word have spread far enough to bring a Witch Hunter here so quickly?"

Koral was searching through the dead man's pouches and pockets for anything that might give him a clue as to how the Witch Hunter had come to be here. "I don't know. Maybe he was already in the city. Maybe he was here for someone else."

Phana's eyes widened in alarm. "The old woman in the Warren?"

Koral nodded. "I'll have word sent to her to keep a low profile for the next while."

"Jadir...," whispered Phana.

Jadir pulled himself to his feet and grimaced in pain as he did so. But he reached down and picked up his sister as if she weighed less than a sack of grain.

"We have to leave *now*," he said to Koral and Phana.

Koral stood and led them out of the room. He stopped just outside their door and spoke to the young man stationed there.

"It's time to go. Tell the others to clear out and take a roundabout route back to the warehouse."

The young man nodded once and swallowed nervously. "What

about the last one?"

"Leave him. We have to clear out of here right away."

Koral followed the young man down the stairs, with Jadir behind him and Phana coming last. He felt safer with her at his back—no one would ever sneak up on them without her noticing in plenty of time to give warning.

As Koral left the building, he looked around for any sign of someone watching, but noticed nothing out of the ordinary. Rifain came jogging over, a worried expression on his face.

"Koral, there may be witnesses."

"Who?"

"There was a black carriage stopped just down the block. I sent one of our guys to walk past it and take a look, see if it was occupied. As soon as he got close, the carriage pulled away and took off."

"Was it here the whole time?"

Rifain shrugged. "It was here when I got here. Was it here when the body came flyin' out the window? No idea."

Koral didn't like the sound of that. This wasn't the kind of neighborhood where carriages were often found parked on the street. Perhaps whoever had been in there was allied with the Witch Hunter.

That thought did little to assuage Koral's concern. The Witch Hunters were a sect within the Church. They weren't priests; they were hunters, trackers, investigators, people who could survive on their own in the wilderness, who traveled the length and breadth of the Empire looking for witches to kill. The Church paid them, fed them information, took them in when they needed healing or a place to stay.

Did the Church now know Marilsa was a witch? Would she bring not just Witch Hunters, but priests and their holy warriors, down on Qudovo's gang?

This was getting out of hand, and Koral still didn't know why the Wolf wanted Jadir and his sister protected. Until he had a chance to meet with his boss and ask the man directly, Koral was responsible for making sure they got somewhere safe.

"How far can you carry her?" he asked Jadir.

"As far as I need to," the big man replied with all seriousness.

Koral gave directions to Rifain and sent him scouting ahead, and left Phana to guard their backs. He stayed within arm's reach of Jadir and Marilsa and led them toward the safe house where they would hide until Koral could get some information from the Wolf.

He had a feeling things were going to get much worse before they got better.

*   *   *

THE CALLS OF THE HAWKERS IN THE MARKET SQUARE FLOATED up through the small window and prevented Jadir from falling asleep. Beside him, Marilsa snored softly, exhausted from the ordeal of last night. But for Jadir, sleep was elusive.

It wasn't really the noise that was keeping him awake, he had to admit. No, he couldn't let himself relax after so nearly losing his sister to the Witch Hunter's blade. He tensed at every creak on the stairs outside the door to their room, flinching at every shout from the square below.

At first, Jadir had been opposed to staying in a room near so many people. But Koral explained that the crowds would mask their presence better than any isolated hiding spot. More importantly, if anyone hostile did find Jadir and Marilsa, they'd have a better chance escaping through the crowded marketplace than standing and fighting—regardless of what Jadir had done last night.

He turned his thoughts away from that. The last thing he wanted was to relive the deaths of those three men. Not more than an hour before, he had argued with Rifain about taking lives, but in the end, he had been so quick to . . . .

Jadir rolled onto his side to face away from Marilsa and forced himself to think of something else. Unfortunately for him, his mind went right to Phana, and another problem he didn't know how to solve.

"It's you, Jadir, there's something just wrong about you. You give off this feeling—it scares me, and you know I don't scare easily."

Those had been Phana's words to him right before his vision of Marilsa. They were burned into his brain. He had kept himself apart from others, alone except for Marilsa, for so long. He had refused to let himself feel anything for anyone, had refused to get involved in any kind of romantic relationship, out of fear of how it might affect his sister.

And then, the first time he had let himself open to someone else, it had lasted all of one night. And now Phana was frightened to be near him, was repelled by him. And there was nothing he could do about it. He hadn't changed—he was the same person he had been a few days ago.

But that person was driving Phana away, right after he had finally admitted to himself how he felt about her. When she left with Koral, he had wanted to grab her, stop her from spending time with the other man.

Jadir sat up and rubbed his hands over his face. He hadn't shaved in a few days, and the stubble was rough on his palms. At least he had been able to quickly bathe himself last night before coming here—he had been covered in the blood of the men he had killed as well as his own. By now the clothes he had worn yesterday would be nothing but ashes.

His thoughts turned to Koral. The man was a puzzle. He had to admit he genuinely liked Koral. They got along well, and Koral seemed ready to help Jadir and Marilsa time and time again, with no indication he wanted anything in return. In other circumstances, he could see the two of them becoming good friends.

But when Phana was around, he wanted nothing more than for Koral to cease to exist. He knew the other man was interested in her; it had been obvious from the start. And Phana wasn't exactly pushing him away. Was Jadir going to lose her to Koral? Would he be forced to see them together, a constant reminder of what he had lost before he even had a chance to see what might have been?

Jadir should be as tired as Marilsa. After everything he had gone through last night, he should be unable to keep his eyes open. He knew members of Qudovo's gang, of *his* gang, were out there in the market, keeping an eye on this place, ready to intervene if anyone tried to come after Marilsa. He knew they were as safe as they ever could be in this city.

What was wrong with him? From the moment the old woman had told Marilsa she was a witch, something had changed.

No, it had been a different moment. The witch had looked at Jadir with her sightless eyes, and then she had reacted as if he was going to strike her. Her face, just for an instant, had been twisted in fear. She had refused to face him again for the rest of their meeting.

"Young…man. You know what I'm telling this girl is true… you feel it… You know what she has to do, what she has to become, or she will die. And you cannot let that happen, can you?"

He had felt something inside him twist at her words. Some part of him finally woke up, or perhaps it took its first breath as it was born—a part of his soul he never knew existed, but which had always been a part of him, buried deep. He had always wanted to protect Marilsa from the harshest elements of life. But at that moment in the old witch's home, he had finally *assumed* the role at which he had previously only been playing.

But what did that mean? Marilsa's *incubo* was the source of her power. She now had abilities Jadir could barely understand. And the spirit had its own gifts, which it had used against both Marilsa and Jadir in the past. But what did Jadir have?

A man's jawbone shattered under Jadir's fist.

The thought came to him unbidden and he clenched his eyes tight and tried to will it away, but it was connected to other thoughts, a web of ideas and questions and conclusions.

Jadir had taken on three armed men, skilled men, and had slain them all. He had moved with preternatural speed, had reacted with precision and deadly force. He had done things he didn't know how to do. But that hadn't stopped him, because Marilsa was in danger.

It was the role he had truly assumed in the house of the old witch.

But what did that mean for him? Why did that make him so repellent in the eyes of Phana? And why did no one else react this way toward him?

He thought about the others he had been near. Koral, Qudovo, Rifain—none of them had reacted in a fearful manner toward him. Marilsa didn't seem to have any issues.

It was only Phana.

And that brought his thoughts back around to what he had said to her, when his rage had taken over, when he had been so angry he wanted to hit her, something he would never have imagined he could possibly be capable of doing.

"All you wanted was for me to join your gang, and you were willing to do anything to convince me. Here I thought you cared about me, but you just wanted me to finally give in."

His fury had been directed at Phana, but where had it come from? It wasn't like him to act in such a manner. And it had certainly shown Phana she did have something to fear from him.

When he lay dying last night, she had come to his side, had taken his hand. But when he woke up after Marilsa had healed him, Phana was no longer willing to touch him. She had barely said two words to him before she had left.

With Koral.

Jadir needed some answers. He didn't want to put any more pressure on his sister, but he no longer felt he had any choice.

When Marilsa woke up, they would have much to talk about.

Chapter Eighteen

AS SOON AS RELAEL PUSHED OPEN THE DOOR TO the meeting room, he knew something bad had happened. The summons from High Counselor Assirra Untoleu, the woman who had created—and still led—the Hidden, was a warning in itself. But Relael immediately recognized the man in the room with her as High Counselor Vorsulroth.

He ran the organization of Witch Hunters.

Relael cursed silently as he bowed deeply to both. "Exalted Sister, Exalted Brother," he greeted them.

Assirra motioned for him to enter and take a seat. Relael could feel his heart quicken as she looked him over and he met her gaze. She was an extraordinarily beautiful woman, with pale blue eyes, flawless white skin, perfectly formed lips, and long golden hair tied back with a blood-red silken ribbon. Rumor was Assirra had already lived well over a century, but she could easily pass for someone in her early twenties. Except, perhaps, for her eyes.

He felt himself getting lost in those eyes, but then iron bars closed behind her gaze and he was almost physically shoved backward into his chair.

Turning to Vorsulroth, Relael examined this man he had never directly met before. The High Counselor of the Witch Hunters was rough where Assirra was refined. His white hair was cropped short, the lines around his eyes and mouth and his weathered skin telling the tale of someone who had spent much time outdoors—though he had obviously not been under the sun in some time.

"You are no doubt aware of why the Exalted Brother and I wished to speak to you, Brother Ochallum." Assirra's voice was smooth and throaty. Relael felt desire stirring in his belly, and suppressed it with a supreme effort.

"I am afraid not, Exalted Sister," Relael replied. "I feel I may be missing some new—"

"You are," Vorsulroth interrupted, his voice full of gravel. "That's the problem."

Relael looked from one to the other and realized there was a power struggle going on here, and he was apparently caught in the middle.

"The young girl—the witch—was found last night by one of our Exalted Brother's Witch Hunters."

Relael barely managed to control his reaction. He had heard nothing from Sister Xodoc or Brother Worestald about this. Was the girl dead? Was his plan over before it could even have started?

"They killed him," barked Vorsulroth. "The brother of that witch murdered my Hunter. And your priests were right there and did nothing but hide in their carriage."

"They are not my priests," replied Assirra smoothly. Relael could see how her calm demeanor was annoying Vorsulroth.

"The girl is still alive?" Relael asked his High Counselor. "Where are they now?"

"You should be telling us!" Vorsulroth's face darkened in his anger. "This is your situation. So *you* are responsible for what happened!"

"Brother Ochallum," Assirra said calmly. "You will meet with your brethren who were watching the young witch and find out where she and her brother have gone."

"And then you'll report their location to me so my Hunters can eliminate them," Vorsulroth interrupted again.

"High Counselor, Brother Ochallum reports to me. I understand you are angry at the death of your Witch Hunter. Such a situation is unfortunate—"

"Unfortunate?" Vorsulroth interrupted a third time, but this time Assirra simply spoke over him, and her words cut right through his anger. Relael didn't know how she did it, but the High Counselor of the Witch Hunters choked off as if his tongue had suddenly stopped working.

"Yes, unfortunate," she continued. "But the girl is not yours to kill, and neither is her brother. At this moment, their fates are in the hands of Brother Ochallum."

"Tell me why you are harboring a witch," he demanded.

The corners of Assirra's mouth turned up ever so slightly, as if she found Vorsulroth's anger amusing somehow, and yet had no intention of sharing anything with him. He glowered at her, and Relael wished he were anywhere else at this moment.

"You are not to send any more Hunters after the girl or her brother. This order comes down from our Lord High Priest himself."

"They killed one of my Hunters. They will both die for that."

"Perhaps," Assirra replied. "And perhaps it will be you and your Hunters who execute them. But not until *I* say it is time. Your little sect provides a service to the Church, but never forget who I am and what I have accomplished here."

Relael did not turn to look at Vorsulroth—the man would remember who witnessed his humiliation. And it *was* a humiliation. The truth was that of all the High Counselors, none wielded the power Assirra Untoleu could call upon within the Church.

No one knew how she prolonged her life so unnaturally, and there were rumors that she had shared the secret with the Emperor himself, that he had gained his immortality from her. She had survived the early days of the Church's overwhelming fanaticism, the later purges of those found unworthy, the schemes of the power-hungry and the mad. And she had come through it all, not just unscathed but more powerful than ever.

Relael was terrified of her, just as he desired her. He knew her power over him was beyond mere physical beauty—such things were ephemeral and ultimately for the weak. And Relael was anything but weak. But Assirra was on a whole other level above him.

"You may go," she said, and Relael nearly gaped at her audacity to dismiss another High Counselor so easily in front of him. And then he realized, despite her looking at Vorsulroth when she spoke, she was actually dismissing Relael himself.

Relael rose from his chair and bowed deeply to both High Counselors, though neither of them so much as glanced in his direction.

"Exalted Brother, Exalted Sister," he mumbled and then fled the room.

It was only when he had returned to the lower levels of the Temple did he stop and lean on the wall to regain his breath. He looked down at his hands and they were shaking. He clenched his fists and forced himself to breathe deeply and calm down.

Relael was a master at manipulating others, skilled in the political games that were needed in such an organization as the Church. He was used to dealing with people who were dangerously insane. But the thought of being the pawn in a struggle between two High Counselors filled him with dread. One misstep could lead to a rather unpleasant death, and this was a game with rules that were completely unfamiliar to him.

The girl, Marilsa, and her brother, Jadir, had survived an attack by a Witch Hunter. They had killed the man sent to execute them. What had really happened there?

Another question rose, unbidden, in Relael's mind. How did the Witch Hunter find them? Had Brother Worestald or Sister Xodoc spoken out of turn? Had one of them deliberately betrayed him? The priestess hated Relael, that much was clear. Would she sabotage this scheme just to get at him?

Relael hadn't thought to ask Vorsulroth, though he doubted he would have gotten a satisfactory answer. Perhaps Assirra already knew, though she would probably warn Relael if he was betrayed. Unless she intended to sacrifice him as part of one of her own, grander schemes.

Relael couldn't answer any of these questions yet. There were too many missing pieces of information. He would have to meet with Wilau, who was still tasked with watching the young witch and her brother at all times. Relael needed to know exactly what happened last night before he spoke with his brethren.

Only then could he determine if one of them was trying to betray him. He would have to be prepared for any contingency. Relael didn't believe for a second that other Witch Hunters wouldn't be sent after Marilsa and Jadir. Vorsulroth wanted them dead, and though he might be wary of crossing Assirra, the man was a brute with little or no subtlety.

Relael's balancing act had just become that much more difficult.

*   *   *

JADIR PACED BACK AND FORTH IN THE SMALL ROOM. ON THE other side of the thin, wooden wall, Marilsa practiced her control over her *incubo*. She had banished Jadir from their new home as soon as she was awake. He had wanted to talk to her about last night, but she said she needed to get started immediately and didn't have time for his questions.

This neighboring room had been taken by the gang so that someone could be within hearing distance of them at all times in case they were attacked again. Jadir had told the young man to clear out for the night—he wanted time to himself if he couldn't talk to Marilsa.

But Jadir couldn't relax and found himself walking in circles just to burn off some of his excess energy. His mind kept returning to what had happened last night, to his murder of those three men.

Someone tapped on the door, and Jadir turned to see who it was as the person pushed the door open.

Phana stood in the doorway.

"Jadir, can I…can I come in?"

He didn't know what to say. He was confused, embarrassed and ashamed at his behavior toward her last night before he had gone to save Marilsa. He wanted to hide from Phana, to pretend he hadn't been so terrible toward her….

But she was here to see him. Despite what she felt, her discomfort, her fear of being near him, she had come here.

He nodded to her and stepped back. Jadir realized he would be less threatening if he sat down, so he moved over to one corner and sat with his back against the two walls.

Phana stepped into the room and pushed the door closed. She saw what he was doing and looked at him with such pity in her eyes that he wanted to scream in frustration. Instead, he took a deep breath.

"Phana, I'm so sorry about yesterday. I didn't mean what I said—"

"You don't need to apologize, Jadir. None of this is your fault. I can't even imagine what you're going through, and you don't deserve any of this. I want to go to you, wrap my arms around you. I *want* to."

She looked at him and he could see tears in her eyes. "But I can't, Jadir. I don't know why, but I *can't*."

Jadir looked down at the floor. He couldn't bear to see her like this, to hear those words coming from her. She was telling him she still wanted him, but couldn't act on it. And neither of them knew why this was happening.

He wanted to march back into the other room and demand answers from his sister. Was this the work of her *incubo*? Was it trying to torture him for taking Marilsa to the witch so that she could learn what she needed to resist its power? Would she even know what he was talking about?

"Thank you for coming to see me, Phana. I know it's hard to just be in the same room with me," he said, unable to keep a wounded tone out of his voice.

"That's enough." Something in her voice caused him to raise his head, and he saw she was angry. "I know you're going through a lot, and I'm willing to forgive you for yesterday, but you don't get to needle me with this. It's not your fault, but it's not my fault either."

Jadir was astonished. A moment ago she was giving him pity. Now she was suddenly angry because of something that was done to *him*?

"I never said it was your fault." She raised her eyebrows at him, and he remembered his words from the warehouse. "Okay, that's what I said yesterday, but that was different. I...I don't know where that was coming from, that...rage. It wasn't me."

"Then who was it?" she asked, and her tone was cool, as if she didn't care how he answered.

"I don't know! These thoughts kept popping into my head, how you had manipulated me, how you were betraying me. I couldn't think straight, and I just kept getting angrier and angrier, even though I knew there was something wrong about it. I couldn't help it!"

"Jadir, like I said, you don't need to apologize, or even explain. In the same situation, I'd probably do and say the same thing. But that doesn't mean I'm going to put up with it again. Yes, it's hard being here in the same room with you. *But I'm still here.* I think that counts for something. But if you're still angry with me, if you don't want me here, just say so."

Jadir wanted to stand up, but he knew that would frighten her, and he wasn't sure the urge wasn't coming from outside him. He didn't know if he would start to lose control again if he started moving. So he forced himself to stay seated. And he tried to hear what she was saying, though her words stung.

"I don't want you to leave. I...I need you to be my friend."

He looked back up at her, but she was being guarded, keeping her face expressionless. He had seen her do this before, with others. He had hoped never to see her be this guarded with him.

"I've never killed anyone before," he blurted out. "I always thought I could avoid taking someone else's life. I've hit people a few times in fights, but I've never killed anyone. But yesterday, it was so easy. When I fought those men, I knew I was going to kill them, and it took barely any effort at all. I hardly needed to try, I just did it."

"The first time is always the hardest to deal with afterward." Her words shocked him as he realized she was talking from her own experience.

"You've killed people?"

"Of course I have, Jadir. Don't tell me you're surprised by this."

"I...I just never thought about it. I just assumed—"

"Then don't. Never assume anything about me. You'll just be disappointed."

The way she was speaking made Jadir wonder if he was dredging up terrible memories for her.

"Who were they?"

"What, the first people I ever killed? That's none of your business, Jadir. The fact is, you know very little about my life. But you know I work for a gang, and now so do you. And when you work for a gang, killing is inevitable, eventually."

He could see whatever pity she had shown him when she first came here was gone. She was right—he really knew very little about her. But what did that mean? Was she a completely different person than who he thought she was? Had he misread her from the beginning, turned her into someone he could be close to rather than really seeing her?

"I don't know if I will be able to kill again. I—"

"You will, Jadir. If you found it so easy last night, you'll find it just as easy the next time you need to do it. And it won't bother you nearly so much afterward. It'll become just a thing that was necessary at the time."

Jadir really didn't want to hear this. He didn't want to become a cold-blooded killer.

"You look down on Rifain because you think you're better than him. You think you managed to avoid killing anyone because of your strong moral character. But it was just chance, Jadir. You got lucky for many years, but yesterday your luck ran out. And now you see you're not better than everyone else. You're just a guy who does what has to be done to survive."

She turned and opened the door, and then looked at Jadir over her shoulder.

"I always saw you as this really strong person, and not just physically. If I was right, you'll deal with this and move on. If you don't, then maybe I was wrong about you all along."

Phana left and pulled the door closed behind her. Jadir sat in the corner for a long time after she was gone.

Chapter Nineteen

As SOON AS KORAL CREYSS WALKED INTO THE IRON Spike, he knew he was going to have a fight on his hands. Qudovo stood in the common room, surrounded by all the gang members who weren't on duty guarding Jadir and Marilsa. The gang leader had obviously been making a speech to his people, but everyone went silent as Koral entered.

All eyes turned to Koral, who took one long look around and then walked past Qudovo to the door that led to the room the gang leader used as his personal space. Qudovo didn't follow him.

"I want to talk to you out here," the man said. Koral turned and gave him an even look. He had dealt with this kind of situation before—the gang was balking at the orders from above. Koral suppressed a sigh. The outcome was inevitable, and he hated having to go through the motions.

Koral stepped back toward Qudovo. He kept his eyes on the gang leader, but addressed the rest of the gang.

"If you follow this man, then you trust him to deal with gang matters. If you don't think he represents you properly, then maybe he needs to be replaced."

Qudovo's eyes widened at those words.

"Wait a minute!" he said.

"No," replied Koral calmly. "I do not have time to wait for anything. If you lead this gang, then you speak for them. If they think they need to speak for themselves, then you're not doing your job."

He took another step toward Qudovo.

"*Are* you doing your job?"

The gang leader was bigger than Koral, much stronger, and had a mean temper. Yet, Koral knew he intimidated this man. Qudovo couldn't be sure he would win a physical confrontation. And if he managed to *hurt* Koral... well, he'd be unlikely to survive the week.

"This affects the whole gang, and I think they have a right to hear what you have to say."

Koral took another step toward Qudovo, but this time looked out at the crowd of gang members. He noted Phana's absence from this meeting—it was not a surprise. Qudovo looked on her as another burden.

"Let me make something clear to all of you. The only rights you have are those the Wolf chooses to give you. He is not required to explain his decisions to you, and neither am I. If you cannot work within the structure of the Wolf's organization, then you do not *belong* in the Wolf's organization."

He looked back at Qudovo. "And if you cannot lead your gang, then you do not belong in the position you hold. I will be in that room for the next five minutes, and I will speak with you there."

Koral, now standing within arm's reach of Qudovo, pointedly turned his back on the gang leader. It was a calculated risk. Either the man would follow Koral, or he would let his temper get the best of him and he would attack. It was a test of his ability to lead.

Qudovo stood there for a moment, shocked at Koral's insult. Koral reached the door to the room and walked inside, and waited for Qudovo to choose a course of action. He must know that he had just been set up to lose. If he gave in, he would be seen as weak by the rest of his gang. He would start to lose control of the others, and it would only be a matter of time before he was replaced.

But if he tried to establish his dominance, he would either be beaten by a smaller man, or—if he was victorious—would die soon after at the hands of the Wolf's best killers.

His days leading this gang were now numbered. Koral had not originally intended to set him up this way, but he saw now that Qudovo was no longer able to lead this gang. The man had gambled that the presence of all his people would make Koral nervous. He had tried to put Koral on the spot.

He had failed.

A shadow darkened the doorway, and Koral looked to see Qudovo step into the room. He closed the door carefully and turned to Koral, his hands clenched into fists.

"I should kill you for what you just did."

Koral watched the other man calmly and said nothing.

"If I don't punish you, they'll stop following me."

"Yes, you're right."

But Qudovo knew what would happen to him if he acted rashly.

"You think you're safe. That no one will touch you because you're under the Wolf's protection. His name is the only thing that might let you walk out of here alive, tonight."

And Koral knew, then, that Qudovo wouldn't try to attack him. The man was already making excuses in his mind, trying to justify "letting" Koral live after his insult.

"You gambled and lost, Qudovo. You tried to make me look weak, and it turned back on you. The consequences are yours to deal with. You're going to lose leadership of this gang—you can't stop it now. But you're alive and you still have a place in the Wolf's organization. Don't throw those away, too."

Koral could tell Qudovo wanted to attack him. He could see the man evaluating his chances. But the threat was already over. Qudovo stood there, glaring at Koral, but eventually he realized he was beaten. Koral saw it in his eyes.

"I should never have agreed to take in Jadir and his sister."

Qudovo still didn't know Marilsa was a witch. He knew assassins of some kind had come after her, and that Jadir had managed to kill them all, but none of the other gang members—with the exception of Phana—knew the truth about the girl yet.

"You weren't given a choice in the matter. You still don't have a choice. The Wolf wants them kept safe, and the job was given to you. That job hasn't changed."

"Who's trying to kill them?"

"You don't need to know."

Qudovo kicked one of the chairs against the wall. "By the Abyss, those are my people putting their lives in danger to protect outsiders! I *do* need to know!"

"It won't change the situation," argued Koral. "It won't give you any insight into how they'll attack, or when. It won't help you identify them. And it won't let you protect your people any better. You'll just get nervous and start making more mistakes."

"I want to speak to the Wolf."

Koral knew this was coming, and he shook his head slowly.

"That's not going to happen. The Wolf doesn't debate his orders with the leaders of the gangs. He tells me, and I tell you, and that's the way it works. You know this. No one is changing it just because you're unhappy."

"And what if I just tell my people to stop guarding them, huh? What if I just pull everyone away from that building and let those two fend for themselves? This is affecting my business, my real business. You know, the business that makes the Wolf all that money he takes from me?"

"Then," replied Koral, "you simply shorten the time you have left in charge of this gang."

"Maybe it'll be worth it to get back at you and your master."

Koral merely raised his eyebrows at Qudovo. He knew the man was making empty threats, now. He didn't feel like wasting any more time with Qudovo today.

"Do what you feel you have to, and deal with the consequences. You know what those are."

Koral walked over to the door and opened it.

"You have your orders Qudovo. It's your job to make those people out there follow those orders. Do that job, and there'll be something waiting for you after this. Fail me, fail the Wolf, and you'll have nothing at all."

Koral walked back into the common room, and all eyes were on him. He heard Qudovo step out behind him, but Koral knew there was no longer any danger here. If Qudovo had been stronger—or maybe stupider—he could have ordered his followers to take Koral down, and there's no way Koral would have been able to win through this many attackers. But to make such an order was a death sentence.

So Koral left the Iron Spike, and he heard voices erupt behind him as he walked out onto the street. Qudovo would start having real trouble in the gang now. He would lose control rapidly, regardless of what he did.

Koral swore under his breath. Now he had to find a new leader for the gang. As if he wasn't busy enough.

*   *   *

"MARILSA, WE NEED TO TALK."

Jadir's sister was crawling under the covers of her sleeping pallet. She had been up all night, practicing her new skills. Only after the sun had risen had she allowed him to return to their room. She looked tired, but Jadir couldn't wait any longer.

"Not now. I need to sleep."

Jadir knelt down beside Marilsa and looked her in the eyes. "I'm sorry, but I need to talk to you. I just can't wait any longer."

She looked back at him and he wondered what she was thinking. His little sister had changed so much in the three nights since she had met the old witch. Without warning, she had suddenly become the one in charge, the one who made all decisions about them. Jadir had not been ready for this sudden shift.

But he had to admit, he had fallen into his new role almost immediately. He deferred to her automatically now, without thinking. Jadir was no longer taking care of Marilsa. Now, he was almost serving her.

Three nights. It seemed like weeks ago he had taken Marilsa into the Warren to meet the old witch. So much had happened in the last three nights, Jadir found himself unable to keep up with it all.

Tonight, however, he needed to force the issue with his sister. He had to talk to her about what was happening to them, to him. He felt disconnected from Marilsa, even as he was subconsciously aware of her presence at all times, even when they were not in the same room.

Marilsa considered his request and nodded.

"What's bothering you, big brother?"

To Jadir's ear, those words seemed out of place now. But he was still her big brother. That hadn't changed.

"Marilsa, do you…have you noticed anything different about me?"

He saw it in her eyes. She knew something, and she couldn't hide it from him. But aloud, she said, "Different how?"

"I…someone told me that there's something wrong about me. I give off a feeling that makes people uncomfortable; that scares them a little."

He knew he was downplaying the effect he had on Phana, but he still had trouble accepting it himself. But the effect of his words on Marilsa was immediate. She sat up straight and stared into his eyes.

"Who said this to you, Jadir? Who feels uncomfortable around you?"

Jadir hesitated, worried now by Marilsa's intensity. But he knew he should tell her everything—it was why he had asked to talk to her now in the first place.

"It's Phana. Since we met the witch, Phana can't be near me. Just being the same room scares her. She says she feels something unnatural about me."

Marilsa's gaze never wavered from his. "Just Phana? Anyone else?"

"No, just Phana."

Marilsa just sat there for a moment, and then leaned back.

"Jadir, it's not you. It's me. My *incubo* is always near me, except when I send him away on a specific task. Some people are more sensitive to it than others. Phana must be able to feel his presence."

Jadir shook his head.

"But Phana feels it on me, not you. And it's there even when you and I are not near each other. The other night, when I was at the warehouse, Phana was terrified to be near me."

Marilsa shrugged, as if it was not anything to worry about.

"Jadir, you and I are connected. Maybe that connection means that the presence of my *incubo* near me comes across as if it's near you. Phana must be really sensitive if she's feeling anything at all."

"You don't think…could Phana be a witch, too?"

Marilsa laughed. "No, she couldn't be a witch. She is...she's just sensitive. It's something that happens to some people."

Jadir wasn't reassured by Marilsa's explanation. She didn't really know what was causing this—she was partly guessing.

"Could your *incubo* be doing...something to me—?"

"No," Marilsa interrupted him. "That is definitely not it. Jadir, are you sure Phana is telling the truth? Maybe she's just frightened that I'm a witch, and she's making excuses because she doesn't want to hurt me."

Jadir wanted to dismiss that possibility, but he forced himself to consider it. It didn't seem right to him. Phana wasn't one to fear much, if anything. Yet her reaction to Jadir seemed genuine.

"I'm sorry, Jadir. I know you like Phana, but if she can't be near you, then there's not really anything I can do. I never wanted this to happen, but it has, and I need you as much as I ever did. I like Phana—she's always been nice to me. But maybe she's not the right person for you."

Jadir watched his sister and was certain she was not telling him everything. He knew she was going to have secrets from him now that she was a witch. There were things she could never share with him.

But he couldn't just demand that she open up to him. As much as he was sure Marilsa was keeping something back, there was always the possibility he was wrong. He didn't know how to pull more out of her without sounding like he thought she was lying to him.

"I need my rest, Jadir, and you need to get out of here. Go for a walk in the sunlight, buy something to eat from the market, pretend this is just a normal morning for you. I think that's what you need more than anything."

He shook his head. "I'm not going to leave you—"

"Yes," she said, and there was steel behind her eyes. "You *are* going to leave me for a while. I need to sleep, and you disturb my rest with your tossing and turning and pacing. Others are watching over us, protecting this place, so I don't need you within arm's reach at every moment."

Jadir opened his mouth, but didn't know what to say. Marilsa was ordering him to leave their room, and he had an overwhelming urge to obey her. Without giving it another thought, he kissed her on the forehead and left the room.

It was only as he was stepping out onto the street that he realized how strange his sudden acquiescence to her demand had been. He hadn't wanted to leave her, except it had simply not occurred to him to argue with her about it.

Had she done something to make him obey her command to leave? Was she able to control his mind? He thought back to his sudden reaction to Marilsa being in danger, and wondered if she had taken control of his body to get him back to the tenement as quickly as possible.

What was she really capable of doing?

The noise from the market was too loud, and the thought of getting bumped and jostled in the crowd made him turn away from the open square and head off down a side street. But as he turned the corner, his attention was caught by a black carriage sitting at the side of the road less than half a block away.

A black carriage had been parked on the street outside their tenement the night the Witch Hunter attacked Marilsa.

Jadir looked around for any of the gang members, but didn't see anyone he recognized. He looked back at the carriage and the image seemed to burn itself into his mind's eye. He could feel his heart speeding up, and without thinking about the consequences, he suddenly ran toward the carriage.

In an instant, the driver—who Jadir couldn't see from his vantage point—whipped the horses and the carriage took off down the street. Even running at full speed, there was no way Jadir could keep up with it, and so he slowed to a jog as the carriage sped away.

Had the Witch Hunters already found their hiding place? Or was this some other threat, some new danger that Jadir would have to confront to protect his sister?

Jadir swore loudly. He'd had enough of this. Everyone seemed to know more than he did, and no one was sharing anything with him. But he wasn't going to put up with it anymore.

It was time to go see Koral and demand some answers.

Chapter Twenty

PHANA HESITATED BEFORE KNOCKING ON THE DOOR. SHE knew the bartender was watching her—he had given her a knowing grin when she asked if Koral was here. The man was always leering at her, as if he thought she would suddenly find an aging, pot-bellied tavern employee to be just what she had always been searching for.

But dealing with him was a necessary evil, and she needed to see Koral. And yet, Phana still wasn't sure what she was going to tell him. She knew only that she needed to speak to someone she trusted, someone who wouldn't judge her.

Phana raised her fist and knocked softly, almost hoping he wouldn't hear her, and she would be forced to leave without seeing him. But a couple of seconds later, the door opened, and she found herself face-to-face with the Wolf's right-hand man. His eyes widened in surprise when he saw who was at his door, and his face broke into a grin.

"Phana, were you looking for me?"

She raised her eyebrows at him and smiled back. "Would I be here for any other reason?"

Koral stepped back and motioned for her to enter. Phana deliberately walked to the far side of the table that sat in the center of the room. She wasn't sure why she wanted distance between them. Maybe she was having trouble trusting herself and her judgment lately.

"I hope nothing is wrong," Koral said to her as he sat down and crossed his forearms on the table.

Phana snorted. "Things sure aren't right, Koral. You know that as well as anyone."

His smile disappeared. There was something in his eyes, some knowledge that things were only going to get worse before they got better. He was trying to hide it, but she could read his face as if the thoughts were written across his skin.

"No, they aren't right. You're here about Qudovo, no doubt."

"Qudovo? What about him?"

Phana had heard the grumbling in the gang about having to protect Jadir and Marilsa, but she had been to neither the Iron Spike nor the warehouse since those two had been moved to their new room near the market square. She hadn't spoken to anyone since visiting Jadir yesterday afternoon.

"Koral, what's going on?"

He sighed and sat back in his chair. "You really don't know?"

She shook her head.

"Qudovo has lost control of the gang. I'm going to have to replace him very soon—I'm just evaluating my options. What he does in the next few days will determine where he goes from here."

"This is about Marilsa, isn't it?"

Now it was Koral's turn to nod. "I understand why they're all unhappy right now. This situation is preventing the gang from doing regular business, and it's costing everyone money. I know the problem, and so does the Wolf. But he wants Jadir and Marilsa to be safe, and that takes precedence."

"Until when?"

"Who knows?" he said with a laugh. "The Wolf does what the Wolf does. But those who stay with him get rewarded, and those who fight him get punished. This isn't new to anyone in your gang, including Qudovo."

Koral stood up and walked around the table and knelt down beside Phana's chair.

"But that's obviously not why you're here. Something else is wrong, and you came to me for help...."

He let his last words trail off, giving Phana the opportunity to take up the thread and tell him why she had come. But she stayed silent, staring into his face. She kept expecting him to speak, to fill the void, but he was a very patient man.

"It…it's about Jadir."

He did not visibly react to her admission, but she could feel Koral tense up.

"I'm sorry. I shouldn't have come—"

"But you did, Phana. You came here because you know I'll help you in whatever way I can."

She looked into his eyes. "Because the Wolf wants you to protect me as well."

He nodded slowly, never taking his gaze off her. "Yes. But that's not the only reason I'm always here for you."

He was telling the truth—she could see his desire for her in his eyes. And she had to admit it wasn't unwelcome, regardless of the moments she had shared with Jadir.

"I can't be near him anymore."

Koral blinked, completely taken off guard by her words. "You…I don't…."

"I think I'm the only one who feels it, Koral. There's something wrong with Jadir, something unnatural. It's as if he isn't human anymore. The Jadir I knew is just a shell around…something else."

"Do you know why you're feeling this? Could it have anything to do with his sister?"

"I have no idea," she said. "All I know is that being near him terrifies and sickens me. It's not fair to him, but I don't know what else to do."

Koral nodded and she saw the desire flicker and go out. He transformed in front of her to the man who ran the Wolf's business out on the streets of Ythis. There was a problem to be solved, and he would do whatever it took to solve it.

"I understand," he said. "There are many possibilities, but I'll have to speak to a few people. It's most likely this has to do with his sister, but it could also be something that happened when he encountered the witch in the Warren. Whatever it is, we'll find the cause so that you…you two can be together."

Koral went to stand up, but Phana grabbed his hand and pulled him back down.

"You don't understand," she said to him. "I'm not here to ask you to solve this for me. If there's trouble to be faced, I'll do it myself. I didn't come here for that."

Now Koral was thoroughly confused, and Phana took a certain perverse pleasure in his discomfort. It was good to know she could throw him off balance if she needed to.

"What—" he tried to say, but his throat had gone dry. He swallowed and tried again. "Why did you come here?"

"I wanted to see you. I wanted to talk to you. I'm not looking to be rescued, Koral. I put up with the Wolf's 'protection' because it's easy to ignore. But you know I can take care of myself."

He nodded. She stood up and he followed suit. Their faces were inches apart.

"I'm not making any commitments, here. No promises. But this is what I want."

She leaned in and kissed him, and then his arms were around her and their desire rose like a wave of heat to fill the room. Her tongue slid into his mouth as she curled her arms around his neck. She loved the feel of his hands on her waist, pulling her into him.

Phana knew she should stop. The privacy of this room was tenuous, at best. But she reached for Koral's belt and began to undo it as his hands slid up her chest and he kissed his way down her neck. To the Abyss with caution. At the moment, she just didn't care if they got caught.

She was still fumbling with Koral's belt buckle as someone pounded twice on the door. Koral jerked back from her as whoever was outside twisted the latch and shoved the door open.

Phana's back was to the doorway, but she saw the expression on Koral's face and instantly knew who stood there watching them. She slowly straightened her clothing and turned to face Jadir.

His skin was pale, his eyes wide, his mouth open. She knew he couldn't believe what he was seeing. He locked eyes with her, and she fought the urge to say something. Jadir slowly closed his mouth and looked from her to Koral.

"The Wolf, I want to see him."

Koral quickly recovered from his surprise and nodded. "I'll ask him if he's available to see you—"

"No," Jadir said slowly. "You're going to take me to see him right *now.*"

"I'm sorry, but you can't just—"

"You can either take me," Jadir interrupted again, "Or I can head over to the Wolf's Den myself and go through everyone in that place until I find him."

The look on his face told Phana that Jadir would do exactly that. And considering how easily he had overcome Marilsa's attackers when she was in danger, Phana wondered if the men in the Wolf's Den would be able to stop him.

Koral obviously had the same thought.

"Okay," he said. "I'll take you to see the Wolf. But you'll have to promise me you won't do anything rash when we get there. You may have to wait a bit before he can see you."

Jadir looked at Koral as if he wanted to grab the smaller man by the throat, but he nodded once.

"Just don't try to trick me. It's time I got some answers, and one way or another, I'll get them tonight."

Jadir looked at Phana one more time and then turned and walked out of the room. Koral gave her a look that said their problems were only getting started. But he ran his fingers lightly over her hand before he followed Jadir out of the room.

That tiny gesture told Phana that maybe she had made the right choice, after all.

*   *   *

THE WOLF HAD STARTED HIS TAKEOVER OF YTHIS' CRIMINAL underworld slowly. At the time, the city was split among almost a dozen minor crime lords, many of them leaders of their own gangs that had absorbed weaker local gangs and become forces in their areas of the city. But those kinds of criminal empires had a natural size limit.

No one leader was strong enough to topple the others. And so they battled each other over territory, drugs, rackets, and anything else that might cause friction among them. The Watch was smart enough to stay out of the gang wars, and the people most affected were powerless to do anything about it.

But as the excesses increased, it became inevitable that an accident would occur. When the son of a nobleman was killed in a minor skirmish between two gangs in the Market District, the Imperial Guard was suddenly interested in stopping the violence. Within days, members of both gangs involved in that fight swung from the gallows in front of the Imperial Fortress, and the Guard continued to hunt the leaders.

No one can say exactly how the Wolf convinced the heads of the various factions to meet. The idea seemed to originate within each of the gangs simultaneously, as if the seed was planted ahead of the Wolf's invitation. Some people believe the Wolf had worked his way into each of the criminal organizations without them realizing who he was.

However he did it, the leaders of the gangs listened to him as he explained how the violence and lack of control was going to end everything for all of them unless some changes were made. But there was too much bad blood between them to come to a real accord, and they eventually departed with nothing more than a general agreement to keep more to the shadows as they killed each other off.

The following night, one of the gangs involved in the murder of the nobleman's son was rounded up and captured by the Imperial Guard. No matter where any individual gang member happened to be, the Guard found him or her. Many died trying to escape or fight their way free. But by dawn, one entire faction was no more, and not a single member of that gang remained alive and free.

Again, the Wolf asked to meet with the remaining leaders. This time, most declined to show up, and two of them sent men to kill the Wolf. But those men disappeared, and the next night every single member of the other gang involved in the battle in the Market District was found by the Imperial Guard.

Koral still remembered those nights. He had been twelve at that time, and acted as one of the spies keeping tabs on the movements of the gang members. Though rumors had immediately sprung up that the Wolf was some kind of sorcerer or had supernatural powers, Koral knew the truth. The Wolf now employed a great many homeless young people to act as his eyes and ears.

Koral had been worried that one of the kids would spill the secret to one of the other gangs for some extra coin, but to his knowledge no one ever did. They all remained loyal to the Wolf, and in some ways *that* seemed like it might be supernatural.

Regardless, the Wolf's actions caused the remaining gang leaders to meet again—without the Wolf—to discuss the threat he posed to them all. What they did not realize was that their own people were already shifting their loyalties, individually and in small groups, away from their current leaders and toward the Wolf.

Again, just like when he had apparently planted the seeds of a meeting among the leaders of the gangs to address the problem of warfare in the streets, he now somehow planted the seeds of rebellion. Those who didn't believe he was a sorcerer thought he might be a master of disguise. Others thought the Wolf was really a small group of men working in tandem.

Of those who had apparently met him, no two described him the same way. He was thin and dark, he was old and barely able to walk, he was a bear of a man with a shaved head and a scar down his face, he was hardly out of his teens. The Wolf was a mystery to everyone, including those who knew him.

To Koral, the Wolf remained the same man he had been the night he had grabbed Koral's arm and gave him bread and cheese. Right up until the day he wasn't.

The night the remaining leaders met to discuss their problem with the Wolf, they all disappeared. This time, Koral and his fellow young people had nothing to do with it. The Wolf had given them all the night off, handing them each a few coins to do whatever they wished. The Imperial Guard didn't play any part either.

When the leaders—and what bodyguards they had taken with them to the meeting—didn't return, the gang members panicked. Those who were nominally second-in-command in the various criminal organizations tried to establish control over their people, but it was clear the Wolf was now dominant in Ythis's underworld.

The word went out among those who had switched sides, and quietly they all dispersed from their usual haunts. Those who remained on the fence, or who refused to bow to the Wolf at all, were left with depleted numbers. The city held its breath, waiting for the Wolf's next move.

A week passed nearly without crime. And then the Wolf's final message went out. Koral also remembered that particular night, as he helped spread the word across the city. And the word was *amnesty*.

The Wolf declared certain rules of engagement when it came to criminal activity in the city. Anyone who followed those rules was free to otherwise operate as they wished. Those who broke the rules would be dealt with, harshly. Those who wanted to work for the Wolf directly were welcome, but would not be forced.

At first, few could believe it. Some gang members attempted to find the Wolf so that they could extract revenge for his interference in the city's criminal enterprises. One by one, they disappeared, too. Within a month, when the Wolf's Den opened its doors for the first time, there were few who remained brave enough or foolish enough to break the Wolf's rules.

And one by one, those few disappeared as well.

At the time, Koral wondered how many new factions would spring up across the city, but within two years almost everybody worked for the Wolf in some manner. Unaffiliated gangs couldn't compete with the Wolf's resources, and they found their sources of income drying up. What's more, the Wolf took care of his people. That drove up recruitment more than anything else he could have done.

Today, the Wolf controlled nearly all crime in the capitol of the Empire, and Koral knew the organization had stretched out to other large cities as well. Koral had his own place, one he had earned with loyalty to the Wolf. He had long ago sworn an oath to serve the man, and he would never consider betrayal, no matter the price.

And still no one, including Koral, could agree on what the Wolf truly looked like.

Chapter Twenty-One

PHANA AND KORAL.

Jadir had been taken completely by surprise when he walked in on the two of them. Koral had never hidden his interest in Phana, but Jadir had been sure Phana wasn't ready to jump into the other man's arms. She wouldn't have come to see Jadir yesterday if she had completely given up on him.

But there was no mistaking what he had seen. Another few minutes, and they would have been rutting like animals on the table in that room. Jadir clenched his fists and tried not to picture Phana having sex with Koral.

He wanted to attack the smaller man, wanted to pound his fist into the other man's face over and over. He wanted to scream with rage and frustration.

He wanted answers.

Jadir and Koral walked into the Wolf's Den, the first time Jadir had been inside the building. He was surprised at the number of men and women already here despite it only being late afternoon. He had figured the place would be mostly empty.

Koral walked over to the bar and Jadir followed. A short, balding man with a perpetual scowl was standing behind the bar, looking over a bunch of papers. He looked up and saw Koral, put the papers down, and walked over.

"Nid, we need to see the Wolf, as quickly as possible."

Nid looked from Koral to Jadir and back. Then he nodded once and said, "He's in a meeting, so you'll have to wait a few."

Koral turned to Jadir.

"It won't be long. But we do have to wait."

Jadir looked around at the patrons of the Wolf's Den. He could see many of the men eying him, sizing him up in case there was a need for violence. Jadir was larger than most of the people in here, but he had no doubt most of them were tough enough to give him trouble. There was no way he'd be able to fight his way to the Wolf, if he could even find the man in the back rooms of this huge place.

He grunted his assent to Koral and crossed his arms.

"Listen," Koral said to him. "About what happened back there...."

"Don't." Jadir replied. "I don't want to hear it."

"I just want to say, she wasn't trying to hurt you—"

"Koral, you're going to stop talking before I lose what little control I have right now."

Koral frowned at Jadir, but closed his mouth.

Sooner than Jadir expected, Nid came back and motioned for Koral to follow him. He stopped just as they were about to go through a door into a back hallway, and turned back to Jadir.

"I know you're angry, but you're going to have to behave. The men who protect the Wolf won't let you threaten him, or insult him, and they damn well won't let you touch him. I know what you can do, but don't overestimate your fighting skills, or underestimate the Wolf's bodyguards. Be polite, and you'll get your answers."

Jadir said nothing, just stared a hole in Koral's forehead. The other man shook his head and followed Nid into the hallway.

Within minutes, Jadir was well and truly lost. They went from one hallway to the next, through doors, up and down stairs, and took turns that seemed to double back on themselves, but which always led to new passages. He knew now that he would never have found the Wolf if he had come here alone.

Finally, they arrived in front of an iron-bound door set into a stone wall. Nid knocked twice, and the door opened to a man who was even bigger than Jadir. He saw Nid and Koral, and stepped aside. They all filed into a large empty room, with a door on the far wall. Two more bodyguards stood in the open space, one man who seemed little more than a single huge slab of muscle, and a woman who stood so still it seemed she was made of marble.

Nid left the room, and the man who had opened the door took position behind Koral and Jadir. Only then did the other door open.

The man who stepped out was older than Jadir expected, in his late fifties at least. His skin was rough and wrinkled, his grey hair kept cropped close to his skull, and his eyes were a piercing blue that almost seemed to shine with an inner light. He walked smoothly, and Jadir could see the man kept himself in excellent shape.

"Jadir, it's good to meet you at last," the man said in a strong, deep voice. "I apologize, I should have invited you here long before this."

"Are you the Wolf?" Jadir asked.

The man nodded at him.

"I am."

"I heard you were younger."

Koral glanced sideways at Jadir, but Jadir ignored him. The man laughed.

"There are many rumors about me, and people often see what they want to see."

Jadir didn't understand what he meant, but didn't have the patience to play word games.

"I think I deserve an explanation," he said. "I want to know what's happening, why you are so interested in me and my sister. I want to know what you want from us."

The Wolf stepped closer to Jadir, and the woman moved—no, *flowed*—to take position behind him and slightly to his left. Jadir had never seen anyone move like that, as if she was made of stone one moment, and water the next.

"Jadir, I think you want to know more than that. And I guess I owe you some answers."

The Wolf looked around the room.

"I wish there were some chairs in here—I don't often meet people in this room, but this was where I was when I got Koral's message, so it'll have to do. I hope you don't mind."

"I'm fine," Jadir snapped. He could nearly feel the reaction it had on the two bodyguards in front of him. His words had almost triggered their protective response. Despite his anger, he really didn't want to know what that was like.

"I'm...sorry. I don't mean to be rude to you."

The Wolf waved off his apology. "I forgive you, Jadir. I know this can't be easy for you. But I have to tell you it's not going to get any easier. I'll answer your questions, at least the ones I'm in a position to answer. But I can tell you right now, you are not going to like what I have to say. If you think your life is turned upside down already, then you need to prepare yourself for the whole truth of the matter. It's not going to make anything better."

Jadir nodded. His mouth was dry, and a lead weight sat inside his chest. But he needed to know, regardless of how unpleasant it might be.

"Then I'll start with your sister," said the Wolf. "I need to first tell you about her, or nothing else will make sense."

What could this man tell Jadir about his sister that he didn't already know? Was this some kind of delaying tactic? Or was Marilsa's situation just the beginning?

"Your sister is a witch, yes. Her mother was also a witch, named Ineir, from the city of Jh'tira."

"You knew our mother?" Jadir blurted out. The Wolf held up a hand.

"No, I never met her, though I do know a great deal about her. She was discovered by a Witch Hunter while she was pregnant with Marilsa. She managed to escape and flee the city, but the man stayed on her trail, from town to town, village to village. She had seen she would die in childbirth, and the Witch Hunter would come and kill her servant and her daughter both."

"Where was I? And how did she know she wouldn't survive my sister's birth?"

"Well, as a witch she had the power of foresight, and apparently had seen her own death. As to your first question, I'll get to that in a moment. The witch had formed a coven—that's a group of people who serve a witch, protect her, and help her with ritual magic. The coven had been abandoned by Ineir when she fled Jh'tira, except for one woman who escaped with her. Eventually, Ineir gave birth to Marilsa, and she didn't survive the experience."

Jadir felt numb inside. He had no memories of his parents, had never had any idea who they were, or if either of them was still alive. Now he had been told his mother died many years ago, and it was like the Wolf was telling him a legend, a tale to which he had no connection.

"The servant, the last surviving member of the coven, knew the Witch Hunter would continue to hunt for her and Marilsa. But before Ineir died, she had made sure Marilsa had a protector, a companion, someone to love her and take care of her until she was able to come into her own power."

"You mean you?" asked Jadir. "You've been looking out for Marilsa all this time?"

"No, not me," the Wolf replied. He looked into Jadir's eyes and took a deep breath. "It was you."

"I don't understand," Jadir replied. "Tell me what you mean!"

"Ineir summoned a spirit and bound it into a dead body—a child who had died a few days before from an accidental fall. She repaired the child's body, and ordered the spirit to protect Marilsa, to take care of her as she would have herself."

Jadir knew he didn't want to hear the Wolf's next words, but he couldn't do anything to stop them.

"That spirit, that child, was you. You're not Marilsa's brother, Jadir. And Ineir wasn't your mother. The truth is, you're not truly human, and never were."

"You're lying."

The Wolf looked down at the floor, and then back up at Jadir's face. "For your sake, I wish what I've told you *was* a lie. But it's not, Jadir."

"If you weren't there, if you never met my mother…Ineir…then how do you know all this? Is her servant still alive?"

"No," the Wolf replied. "The woman brought you and Marilsa to Ythis and gave you into the care of the orphanage. Then she left the city, only steps ahead of the Witch Hunter. I spent some considerable resources finding out what happened to her. Once far from Ythis, she killed herself before she could be caught, so she wouldn't reveal your location under torture."

Jadir glared at the Wolf. None of this could be true. He was

Marilsa's brother. He *was*.

"Ineir kept a journal, Jadir. Everything I've told you up to her death was written by Ineir herself. She describes her flight from Jh'tira, her pregnancy with Marilsa, her…creation…of you. She knew she was going to die, and she wanted Marilsa to have something of hers. But she also knew Marilsa would end up in an orphanage, and so couldn't give it to her daughter to keep until Marilsa was old enough to use it."

He smiled, but there was no humor in it.

"And that's where I come in."

The Wolf's words were like poison to Jadir. He wanted to lash out, to strike this old man for telling such lies. He wanted to run, to leave this place and never come back. He wanted to curl up into a ball and hide. He wanted to be with his sister, in their old home, before any of this ever happened.

He could barely see the Wolf in front of him, the image distorted by the tears flowing from his eyes, running down his face.

"If you knew all this, why didn't you take us in?" he asked. "Why did you leave us in the orphanage all that time? If the woman trusted you with the journal…."

"Ineir's journal was not entrusted to me," the Wolf answered. "I stole it. Twelve years ago, I was not the man I am now. The woman probably spent only a day or two at most in Ythis, but our paths crossed, and I had an opportunity to take something that didn't belong to me. By the time I read the journal and realized what I had, the woman was long gone."

He shook his head sadly.

"I don't know who was supposed to get that journal, if the woman even knew anyone who might keep it safe. But the truth is, it could have ended up in far worse hands than mine. At the time I stole the journal, I was in no position to find you and Marilsa and take you out of the orphanage. And I eventually came to believe it would be better if I stayed away until Marilsa came into her power."

Jadir wiped his eyes clear with the backs of his hands.

"This doesn't make sense. You stole this journal, found out about us. Why did you keep it? Why did you decide to protect us? If you didn't even know Ineir, why would you help her daughter?"

"At the beginning of our discussion, I said I would answer the questions I was in a position to answer. I'm sorry, but my actions are my own, and I do not intend to discuss them at this time."

"So, what, you were just keeping tabs on us in case we might be of some use to you in the future? So you could trade us to the Witch Hunters in return for—"

"Silence!" the Wolf shouted, his face twisting with rage. "I will not tolerate your insults! Not after everything I've done for the two of you! This may not be easy for you, but don't you dare accuse me of being in league with any part of that Church. Do you understand?"

Jadir was taken aback by the Wolf's sudden reaction. He had been trying to hurt the man—paying him back for the grievous wounds his words had inflicted. He knew he wasn't being fair to the Wolf, but he didn't care.

He had heard, however, that the Wolf did not forgive insults easily. And despite what Jadir had done only two days ago to the Witch Hunter and his hirelings, Jadir wasn't confident that he would be able to defend himself if the bodyguards attacked him on the Wolf's orders.

The Wolf stood there, breathing heavily, his face red from his yelling. And Jadir could see the man's bodyguards were ready to act on the slightest indication from their boss. He wanted no part of this fight, despite what he was feeling.

Marilsa still needed him, and he would do nothing to jeopardize his ability to protect her.

Jadir nodded at the Wolf. "You're right. I'm sorry. This is just ... too much ...."

He could see the Wolf was still angry. The man turned and walked back to the far door, and Jadir thought his audience with the crime lord was over. But the Wolf opened the door and said something to someone on the other side. That person handed the Wolf a book.

Jadir watched the Wolf walk back to him, and he knew what the other man was holding. The book Ineir had written for her daughter. The journal that described who she was, who *he* was.

"This is for Marilsa," the Wolf said, and there was no longer any warmth in his voice. He reached out with the book, and Jadir moved to take it, but the Wolf stepped to one side and gave the book to Koral.

"Make sure she gets it," he said, glancing sideways at Jadir. Koral nodded.

"I think I have a right to see that," Jadir said, trying not to let his anger take over again. "It's about me, too."

"That is up to Marilsa to decide," answered the Wolf. "The journal belongs to her now."

Jadir turned to look at Koral, but the other man tucked the black, leather-bound journal into his vest. He looked up at Jadir, and there was a challenge there. Koral had been given an order by his boss, and would do whatever it took to make sure he delivered the book directly to Marilsa. If that meant fighting Jadir for it, Jadir knew the smaller man would do exactly that.

"At least let me talk to Marilsa first," Jadir said to Koral. "I need to break the truth to her gently."

Despite all that he had learned today about himself, he could not help but think of how it would affect Marilsa. He still wanted to protect her.

Or was that just what he had been created to do? Were any of his thoughts his own, or were they just reflections of the magical commands placed on him when he was bound into the dead body of a child? Where did his service end and the true Jadir begin?

"Marilsa most likely already knows," said the Wolf. "Don't be surprised if she figured it out over the last few days. She can see things none of the rest of us can."

Jadir turned to look at the Wolf. He wanted to say something, but didn't know what. He had lied about being sorry for his insult. Jadir still wanted to lash out at the man who had kept this from him all this time, only to reveal it now, when the situation was hard enough to deal with as it was.

But that wouldn't help Jadir or Marilsa. Still, Jadir should say something.

The moment was over, though, as the Wolf turned and walked back to the far door without another word. He stepped through and was gone.

The bodyguards remained ranged around the room, watching Jadir. He realized now why the meeting had taken place in this large space—there was plenty of room for the Wolf's protectors to fight if Jadir had decided to attack the man. Jadir was relieved it had not come to that.

"Come on," said Koral. "I'll lead you back out."

With nothing further to say, Jadir followed the other man back out of the Wolf's Den.

Chapter Twenty-Two

J ADIR STEPPED IN FRONT OF KORAL AND BLOCKED HIS WAY into the building.

"Give me the journal. *I* will give it to Marilsa."

Koral looked up at Jadir and frowned. "No."

"Don't make me take it from you. You've seen what I can do."

Koral sighed.

"Jadir, you don't want to do this. There is no way this ends well for you if you try to take this book from me."

Jadir stepped closer to Koral. Half of him wanted Koral to fight, so that he could beat on the smaller man. The other half just wanted the book so he could go speak to Marilsa in private.

"I don't think you're going to kill me now, not after trying to keep me safe all this time. So which of your orders are you going to obey? Do you give me the book, or do you end up hurting me to give it to Marilsa yourself? And you'll really have to hurt me to stop me from taking it from you."

Koral grinned. "I think you overestimate your own abilities, Jadir. You couldn't beat Rifain in a fight. What makes you think you'll beat me?"

Jadir clenched his fists. "Are you serious? You saw what I did to the Witch Hunter and his men."

"But I'm not a threat to you or Marilsa. I've been helping the two of you for quite some time. And you don't even know *how* you did what you did against the Witch Hunter. Do you really think you're suddenly going to be able to use those skills against me, just to grab a book?"

Koral shook his head. The man's confidence made Jadir pause. What if he was right? What if Jadir tried to fight him and was no better than he had been in all those mock combats against Rifain? Was he literally nothing without the need to protect Marilsa?

"Come on," Koral said. "Come upstairs with me. I will give Marilsa the book, and then I'll leave so the two of you can talk. I'm not your enemy."

Jadir thought of Koral and Phana together, their hands on each other...no, that was something he didn't want to imagine. Koral had pretended to be his friend, but he had betrayed Jadir by pursuing Phana even though the other man knew it was wrong. What kind of friend steals another man's woman?

He wanted to pound his fist into Koral's face for stealing Phana away from him. He wanted to hurt this man, with his cocky attitude and belief in his own superiority.

"You know, without the Wolf, you'd be nothing. The only thing that keeps you safe is the fact you work for him. You walk around as if you run this city, as if everyone works for you. But you're just the Wolf's tool, and he uses you to get stuff done without having to get his own hands dirty. One day, someone is going to end your life in some alleyway, and the Wolf is just going to replace you. You'll be forgotten so fast, nothing you've done will matter in the least."

Koral watched Jadir, not reacting, not saying anything. He just stood there and took Jadir's abuse. Jadir wanted him to get angry, to be hurt by the truth the same way Jadir had been destroyed by the Wolf's words less than an hour ago. Instead, he just absorbed what Jadir said and swallowed it down.

"Okay," Koral replied. "Let's go, then."

Koral stepped around Jadir and walked into the building. It was the last thing Jadir had expected him to do, and he stood there for a moment, unable to comprehend why Koral hadn't reacted to his insults.

He turned and followed Koral into the building and up the stairs. He had nothing more to say to the man, and apparently Koral had nothing more to say to him. Koral reached the second floor and knocked on the door to Marilsa's room. Jadir heard her tell Koral to enter.

They went inside to find Marilsa sitting cross-legged on the floor in the center of the room, two of the gang members who were supposed to be guarding her sitting on the floor in front of her. They both jumped up when Koral stepped into the room.

"What's going on here?" Koral asked in a low voice. "Why aren't you outside, watching the building?"

"I asked them to come up here," Marilsa replied, as the man and woman both looked at the floor guiltily. "I needed some help with something."

"Help with what?" asked Jadir. Marilsa ignored his question.

"Thank you both," she said to them. "If you'll excuse us, I need to speak to Koral and Jadir."

"Wait a minute," Koral said to them as they tried to step past him and leave the room. "I want to know why you left your positions. If the Witch Hunters showed up here, you'd all be dead."

Jadir had gotten used to seeing the gang members show deference to Koral due to his position in the Wolf's organization. This time, however, they turned and looked at Marilsa.

"It's okay," she said, looking at Koral but speaking to the two gang members. "You can go."

They said nothing, merely left the room. Koral looked at Marilsa and opened his mouth, but she spoke before he could say anything.

"You have something for me?"

Jadir saw the look of surprise on Koral's face and felt a measure of satisfaction at the other man's discomfort. He was getting used to the idea that Marilsa knew things she shouldn't have been able to know, but Koral hadn't been around her in the last few days.

"How did you—"

"Please," she interrupted him. "I'd like to see it."

She held out her small hand as if she was royalty and simply expected him to comply. He hesitated, but then pulled out the journal and handed it to her. She took it and ran her fingers lightly over the black leather cover. There was nothing written on the outside that Jadir could see, but Marilsa obviously knew what it was.

A single tear ran down her cheek as she caressed the book.

"You may leave," she said, still looking down at the journal in her hands. Neither Jadir nor Koral moved—they simply stood, watching her. Finally, Koral took a breath.

"Marilsa—"

She raised her head and looked at Koral, and her eyes blazed with a fierce anger. He faltered, unable to finish whatever he had been about to say.

"Do *not* make me repeat myself," she growled at him. A chill filled the room, as if an icy wind had blown through the small window, despite the heat outside. Koral quickly looked from Marilsa to Jadir and back, and then nodded once and left the room. Jadir pushed the door closed.

"We need to talk," he said to her. "I met the Wolf and he told me about our—about where we came from."

The anger in Marilsa's eyes disappeared and she stood up and ran to Jadir, wrapping her arms around him and burying her face in his chest. In an instant, she had transformed into his little sister again.

"Oh, Jadir!" she cried. "I'm so sorry. You shouldn't have found out like that—I should have told you everything. I was just afraid it would hurt you so much."

Jadir looked down at the top of Marilsa's head, stunned. Had she known he wasn't human all along? Had the old witch told her, or had she figured it out some other way?

"You'll always be my big brother, Jadir, no matter what," she said, her voice muffled by his shirt.

Jadir felt tears running down his own face. He loved Marilsa with his whole heart—it *wasn't* some magical imperative. She was his sister, and it didn't matter how he had come into this world. The two of them needed each other.

"I love you, Mar," he said.

She squeezed her arms around him even tighter, as if she would never let go.

*   *   *

PHANA STEPPED INTO THE IRON SPIKE AND LOOKED AROUND. The place was nearly empty, only a few gang members scattered around the room. The ones who were there looked at her with expressions ranging from neutral to actively unfriendly. Phana had not seen anyone from the gang since the night the Witch Hunter attacked Marilsa—she had kept mostly to herself, a not uncommon situation with her.

Stroim, one of Qudovo's biggest lackeys, stood up as soon as she entered and went to Qudovo's office. He stuck his head in and said something Phana couldn't hear.

Where is everyone else? she thought. *Only a few are guarding Marilsa and Jadir. Are they all at the warehouse?*

Qudovo stepped out of his office.

"Phana," he said, and she could tell he had been drinking heavily. "How nice of you to join us."

His sneer as he spoke told her what he thought of her most recent disappearance. "Get in here—I wanna talk to you."

He turned and retreated back into the other room. Stroim stood beside the door, eyeing Phana as if he wanted to strike her.

Phana sighed. She wasn't in the mood for this kind of trouble, but she wasn't going to turn and run away. So she walked into the room, acutely aware of Stroim's threat as she passed.

Apparently, he wasn't stupid enough to take a shot at her, so she pushed the door closed and turned to face Qudovo. He stood on the other side of the table, his long knife sitting within easy reach of his hand. This situation looked like it could get ugly fast.

"You've been busy," Qudovo said to her. "You want to tell me anything I don't already know about what you've been up to?"

"And what have I been up to?" she asked him. "What's got you so riled up this time?"

Try as she might, she couldn't keep her disdain out of her voice. It only made him angrier, something she honestly wanted to avoid. She didn't feel like getting into a fight.

"You've been a huge pain my ass over the last few years, Phana. But I always thought you were straightforward. That if you were going to come at me, at least you'd do it from the front. But I was wrong—you're just another back-stabbing woman."

Phana understood the situation instantly. Qudovo knew what was about to happen to him, and had decided to blame Phana for some reason. Maybe because of their past, because she was the only woman who had ever stood up to him. Maybe because, when she finally lost patience with his controlling ways, she had needed to show him how tough she really was to get him to back off.

Maybe because he had always been afraid of her after that night.

Ultimately, though, the reason didn't matter. What mattered was that he blamed her and was full of liquid courage tonight. She had picked the worst possible time to walk into the Iron Spike. If he was fully sober, she would have been able to remind him that attacking her would be a huge mistake. But right now, she wasn't sure if she'd be able to talk him down.

With Stroim right outside the door, Phana might be in for a real fight. Her actions might need to cause permanent harm. She didn't want that, but she also knew she would not hesitate if it came down to her life or theirs.

"Not that it will make any difference, Qudovo, but I didn't betray you. You know what I would do if I had a problem with you."

His eyes blazed. "You think you'd be able to take me by surprise a second time? No, I learn from my mistakes, Phana. You got lucky the first time. That won't happen again."

He was trying to convince himself that it had been luck that left him on the floor in a growing pool of blood. She could have let him die that night. She knew the Wolf would have forgiven her. But no, after putting him down, Phana had then decided to save his life. She had hoped he could be redeemed if he managed to survive.

She knew, now, that she had been wrong.

"I won't show you mercy a second time," she said to him. "You've got nothing to gain here, and everything to lose."

"I've already lost everything!" he yelled at her. "You turned my gang against me. You turned the Wolf's lapdog against me. You used us to protect your boyfriend and his bitch sister. What have I got left to lose?"

"This gang is going to be given to someone else to lead, yes. But the Wolf doesn't intend to get rid of you. You're just going to be moved somewhere else. You'll still have your job. By the Abyss, you'll probably just be given another gang to lead, in a different part of the city. You *haven't* lost everything, Qudovo, not even close."

He stared at her, and she hoped her words were getting through the haze created by the combination of his anger and the alcohol. There were those who would follow him down the hole he was falling into. Phana didn't care about Qudovo, but the others could still be saved from the mistake of following the wrong leader.

Qudovo put his hand on the handle of the knife. He said nothing else, just looked at her, his eyes filled with hatred. He was trying to work himself up to this fight—some part of him remembered what Phana had done to him last time, knew luck had nothing to do with it.

"What are you going to do, Qudovo? Kill me? You know I didn't betray you—it was your own mistakes that lost you this gang."

"Shut up," he said.

"And what happens if you manage to win this fight? You think that'll make everything better?"

"SHUT UP!"

"Are you ready to *die* tonight?"

Phana heard the door latch slowly turn and knew Stroim was ready. He would come charging in at the first sounds of battle. Who else was waiting on the other side of that door? Was everyone in the common room in agreement that Phana had betrayed them and had to die?

She could easily beat Qudovo, could even beat him and Stroim at the same time. But against a half-dozen? They would overwhelm her in this small room, pin her down, and she would be helpless.

Unless she unleashed something she hated to let loose. Because then everyone else in this building would die.

Qudovo's hand was shaking. If he picked up the knife, only one of them would leave this room alive. But he knew it wouldn't necessarily be him. Even if the rest of the gang helped, Qudovo might not live to see his "victory" over Phana.

"Get out," he said.

Phana wasn't sure she heard him correctly.

"If I ever see you again," he said to her, "I will carve you up into so many pieces they'll never identify your body."

Phana blinked at him. She was sure he was going to attack her. Maybe he was able to see though his drunkenness at how terrible an idea this was. She almost turned to leave, but then she realized what he was doing.

As soon as she opened the door, Stroim would try to attack her by surprise. And Qudovo would come at her from behind. He had planned this out ahead of time. He wasn't backing down, he was setting her up.

She said nothing, just stepped toward the door. Out of the corner of her eye, she saw Qudovo pick up the knife from the table.

Phana put her hand on the latch, and it was apparently the signal for Stroim. He shoved the door open, trying to hit her with it, as he lunged forward. But Phana had barely touched the latch and was already moving as Stroim acted.

She slid to one side as the door swung past her face, missing by a finger's width. Stroim's own long knife thrust toward her belly, but she had already raised her elbow and drove the point of it into his nose as she twisted to one side.

With her other hand, she grabbed Stroim's wrist and twisted while yanking him forward. This pulled him between Phana and Qudovo, who was coming around the table to stab her in the back— *how ironic*, she thought—and entirely prevented their ambush.

Before Stroim could recover, Phana stepped behind him, twisted his arm behind his back, plucked the knife from his hand, and wrapped her own arm around his throat.

Qudovo stopped in his tracks. Phana noticed there were three others outside the room, all with weapons drawn. She grimaced at them.

"You're following the wrong leader," she said to them. "He's going to get you all killed."

"Let him go and fight me!" Qudovo growled at her. He was brave now that he knew there was no way she would let go of her hostage.

"I don't think so," she replied. She walked toward the front door, still holding her knife at Stroim's throat.

"Running away tonight isn't going to save you," Qudovo said to her. "I'll find you."

"I look forward to it."

She reached the door and shoved it open. The street beyond was empty. She pulled Stroim into the doorway and then twisted suddenly, driving the side of his head into the wooden frame. Phana let go as Stroim's legs went limp and he collapsed right in the doorway.

Phana took off running. They wouldn't bother to give chase—by the time they pushed Stroim out of the doorway she would be too far ahead to make it worthwhile.

Now she had to go warn Koral.

Chapter Twenty-Three

JADIR STEPPED OUT INTO THE MARKET SQUARE AND LOOKED around. He didn't immediately spot anyone he would consider suspicious, but he knew the crowd in the square made it nearly impossible for any individual to stand out. But that was why the gang members were watching over the building where he and Marilsa were hiding.

Despite the events of yesterday, he had to admit to himself he felt better than expected. He had stayed at Marilsa's side all night while she meditated and whispered strange chants under her breath. He was grateful she had not banished him to the other room—she obviously understood what the Wolf's revelations had done to him.

He knew he still hadn't fully come to accept the truth. No doubt it would hit him when he least expected it, the realization that he wasn't even human. The thought was in his mind, but it still didn't feel real. It almost felt like nothing had really changed, though that couldn't be further from the truth.

Everything had changed.

And he still didn't really know much more than the basics. If he had been summoned into this body, what had he been before that moment? The Wolf said he was a spirit, but what kind of spirit? Was he the soul of someone who had lived long before? Or was he something else, some other, alien creature?

All through his life, he had never had the barest inkling that he was different. There were no strange dreams, no unusual thoughts, urges, or instincts. He had been just another member of humanity, with nothing to separate him from the masses who lived across the length and breadth of the Empire and beyond.

And today, despite what he now knew about himself, he still felt no different. The only event that marked him out as special was the night the Witch Hunter had tried to kill Marilsa.

And Phana....

Somehow, she had felt it. There was no other explanation for why she was so disturbed by his presence—she could feel that he wasn't normal. Except, Phana had not felt anything strange from him until the night Marilsa met the old witch. That had been the turning point. The moment when he had truly assumed the role he had been playing for so many years.

Jadir turned and walked along the edge of the market toward the area where the vendors sold foodstuffs. He glanced sideways down one of the streets that led from the market square and saw the black carriage.

The same black carriage from yesterday.

Jadir silently cursed himself. He had completely forgotten to question Koral or the Wolf about the carriage yesterday. After catching Phana and Koral...and then the Wolf's revelations, Jadir had been unable to think straight.

And now the carriage was back.

Jadir looked around again for any sign of the gang members who were watching the building, but he didn't spot them. He knew if he ran toward the carriage, it would leave again. If he was going to get near it, he would need to approach it stealthily.

The only problem was Jadir had no experience sneaking around. With his size, it was generally a pointless endeavor. But he needed to get close to the carriage without being detected.

He scanned the street and saw that one of the buildings near the carriage was only one story tall. If he could get to the roof of that building from the other side, he could approach quite close to the carriage. Jadir knew he would need to get down from that roof quickly once he was spotted—he would probably have to jump down before the carriage-driver got the vehicle moving.

But it was Jadir's only chance to find out who was in there. If the carriage was related somehow to the Witch Hunters, then he and

Marilsa would have to move again, find a new place to hide. There was always a chance, however, that some other entity was keeping tabs on them. If so, Jadir wanted to know who it was.

He jogged along the edge of the square to the next street over, and then slowed his pace as he turned down this avenue. He didn't want to call undue attention to himself, and he needed to figure out where that one-story building was on the other side. Gaps between the buildings on this street led no doubt to the alleyway that ran between the backs of the structures.

Jadir reached the spot he figured was parallel to the building he wanted and ducked into the ally's entrance. The floor of the passage was strewn with garbage and smelled like an animal had died in here recently. He picked his way to the alley and was glad to see his estimate was correct.

There was no ladder that he could use to access the roof of the building, but Jadir's height was an advantage here. With a running jump, he was sure he could gain a handhold on the lip of the roof. He knew, however, there was no way he could do it without making a racket inside the building.

If the building was occupied, anyone inside would know someone had climbed up on their roof.

There was a single door leading from the building into the back alley. Jadir considered blocking it closed, but that would, truthfully, work to his disadvantage. If anyone came out to investigate the noise, Jadir didn't want them spilling out into the street. That would surely catch the attention of the carriage driver.

Speed would be Jadir's best asset. He would need to climb up, cross the roof, and leap off before anyone inside had time to react. He was sure he could deal with the situation once he had caught the coachman to prevent him from driving off.

Jadir prepared himself and then broke into a run. He approached the building at a direct angle, and then launched himself up just before reaching the wall. He stretched up as high as he could while he was in the air, and then his body crashed into the side of the building, knocking the wind out of him.

But his hands found the edge and gripped hard to prevent having to do this a second time.

He wasn't sure at first if he could haul himself up until he recovered his breath, but the strength in his arms was up to the task, and a few seconds later he rolled onto the roof. He didn't hear any cries of alarm from below, but then he had no way of knowing how thick the walls were.

Regardless, he didn't have time to think about that. He pulled himself to his feet and moved across the roof to the front of the building.

He was just behind the carriage and saw that the blinds were pulled down over the windows. The driver sat on top, continually scanning the street for anyone who might approach his vehicle. He didn't immediately look up, however, and that gave Jadir hope for the success of his plan.

Jadir glanced down and hesitated. From up here, the ground looked farther away than he had expected. If he jumped, could he land without injuring himself? Was there any way to lower himself quickly so that the carriage driver had no time to react?

He considered his options and made his decision in only a couple of seconds. At any instant, the carriage driver might look up and spot Jadir. And he knew there was no fast way to get down without taking the risk and jumping.

He took a deep breath and then flung himself off the roof. As his feet hit the cobblestones of the street, Jadir bent his knees to absorb the impact, but he lost his balance and went sprawling forward onto the ground. His left knee connected solidly with a stone, and pain shot up his leg.

The coachman gave a yelp of surprise as Jadir hit the ground. The man stared at Jadir for a moment as Jadir lay there trying not to cry out from the pain in his knee. And then Jadir saw the look of recognition in the other man's eyes.

Jadir pushed himself to his feet as his knee screamed at him, and he saw the carriage driver spin in his seat and grab the reigns. He lunged forward as the driver whipped the horses, and Jadir managed to grab the metal bar on the back of the carriage.

The horses bolted forward and Jadir nearly lost his grip. He was yanked off balance and fell, hanging onto the bar as he was dragged down the street. His knee connected once again with the road and the pain was too much. Jadir let go of the bar and fell into the street, rolling a couple of times before coming to rest.

He lay there for a moment as he heard the carriage rolling away from him, breathing heavily and trying to feel if he had broken anything. But aside a mass of bruises, he still seemed to be in one piece.

Jadir slowly pulled himself to his feet and began to limp back to Marilsa. He knew now he couldn't do this alone. As much as he hated the idea, later today he'd have to go see Koral again, and ask the gang for help.

* * *

KORAL WAS WALKING ALONG THE STREET BACK TO THE CROWN and Coin when he spotted Jadir coming up the street from the other direction. He felt a moment of uneasiness at the appearance of the other man, but quickly pushed it away. The news that Jadir was not truly human had shocked Koral more than he wanted to admit, but he knew he must hide his reaction from Jadir and everyone else.

Koral wasn't supposed to be shocked by anything.

He stopped and waited for Jadir to approach. The big man didn't look angry like he had the day before, which immediately brought Koral's thoughts back around to Phana. Koral felt no guilt for what Jadir had seen yesterday—the man shouldn't have just walked in without permission. He understood why Jadir had been upset finding Phana with Koral, but that was Phana's decision to make, not Jadir's.

And Phana felt something was wrong with Jadir, that he was different in a way that made her terribly uncomfortable around him. She had somehow known Jadir wasn't human. Was she just more sensitive than most people, or was there something different about Phana as well? The Wolf had an interest in her just as much as he had an interest in Jadir.

What was *her* secret?

Jadir stopped a few paces from Koral.

"I want to talk to you," he said. "Privately."

Koral could feel no threat coming from the other man, so he nodded.

"We can go to the Crown and Coin—it's only a few minutes away."

Jadir shook his head and started walking the other way, waving Koral to follow. He led Koral down the street into a narrow alleyway between two buildings. There were no doors or windows opening into this area, and the noise from the street would mask their discussion from anyone trying to eavesdrop.

"How is Marilsa?" Koral asked him.

Jadir looked at him and opened his mouth, as if he wanted to say something nasty to Koral. But then he visibly wilted before Koral's eyes and looked down at the ground.

"She's fine," he muttered. "She's doing a lot better with all this than I am."

"If you need any help, I'm...well, I'll do whatever I can."

Jadir looked up sharply at Koral. "You've done enough."

"I know you're pissed off at catching Phana with me yesterday—"

"Don't," Jadir interrupted. "You don't want to go down that road with me right now."

"I'm not your enemy, Jadir," Koral persisted. "I didn't stab you in the back, and neither did Phana."

"You don't understand a thing!" Jadir hissed at him. "You have everything! You've got power in this city, even if it's only because of who you work for. You've got influence. Now you've got Phana. And when you want it, you've got *answers*. The rest of us scrape by with little bits of knowledge, but mostly ignorant of all that's going on in this city. But you, you can find out anything whenever you run up against a problem you can't immediately solve."

Jadir's fists were clenched as if he wanted to smash something, or someone. But Koral knew it wasn't really anger he was feeling. It was frustration. As much as Jadir liked Phana, Koral understood the jealousy the other man was feeling wasn't because she had chosen Koral. He realized Jadir was jealous of Koral's connections, of his access to information.

The fact was Jadir was lost. He was walking through a dark forest with a guttering candle, only getting fleeting glimpses of what was around him. And he obviously felt Koral didn't have that problem. Sure, the Wolf kept plenty of secrets. But when Koral needed to know a piece of information in order to do his job, he could find that knowledge. It really was his biggest advantage, and that's what Jadir wanted the most.

"I...I didn't know about you," he said to Jadir. "I honestly had no idea what the Wolf was going to tell you yesterday. I just want to make that clear—I wasn't keeping anything from you about you or Marilsa."

Jadir stood there, staring at Koral and breathing heavily, as if he had just been in a fight.

"I wasn't always in this position. I know what it's like to be on the outside, to have nothing, to know nothing about what's going on. I know how horrible it is. But I do want to help you. I told you before that I thought you and your sister were decent people, and I meant it. I will share what information I have, on anything that directly affects you, as long as I am able."

"And what's that supposed to mean?" Jadir replied, no longer on the verge of yelling.

"It means I cannot promise to share everything, because I do work for the Wolf, and I have to obey him. But you now know everything I know about your situation. And if I find out anything else, unless the Wolf specifically tells me not to share it with you, you have my word that I will give you what information I have."

Jadir thought about that for a minute. Finally, he asked "How do I know I can trust you?"

"You don't," answered Koral. "There's no way to know if anyone is trustworthy—your best friend can betray you after years of trust. That's life in the Empire. But the alternative keeps you on the outside. You have to decide if the risk of trusting me is worth the help I can give you."

Jadir looked down at the ground again, obviously torn between wanting to remain angry with Koral and needing his help. He had no way to know if Koral was telling him the truth, and Koral knew there was no point in trying to reassure the other man. Jadir would accept his help or not.

Finally, Jadir looked back up at Koral.

"I need your help with something," he said. "I keep seeing a black carriage on the road around the corner from the building where Marilsa and I are staying. I tried to approach it, but it left before I could get close."

Koral nodded. "There was a black carriage parked near your building on the night the Witch Hunters attacked."

"Yeah. But I'm not sure it's related to the Hunters—they would have come in force by now if they knew for sure Marilsa was staying there, especially after I killed one of them."

Koral knew Jadir was right. There was no reason for the Witch Hunters to keep the pair under surveillance.

"Do you want to move again?" he asked Jadir.

"Not yet. What I want is to find out who is in that carriage. I'm assuming it's not someone working for the Wolf..." he looked searchingly at Koral, who shook his head. "Then it seems there's another person or group who is interested in my...in Marilsa."

Koral knew Jadir had been about to say, "my sister" and had stopped himself. He couldn't imagine what Jadir was feeling right now—to not only find out he wasn't human, but to lose that connection to his only family at the same time.

"So you want to stop this carriage and find out who is inside," he said aloud. "That will take more than just you and me."

Jadir smiled, but it didn't reach his eyes. "Well, now I know Qudovo takes his orders from you. So get the gang to help us out. We surround the carriage, stop it from leaving, and I find out who is inside."

"It might not be quite as easy as that," Koral said, thinking about the trouble he was having with Qudovo. "You go back to the building and stay with Marilsa, and I'll go to the warehouse and round up whoever I can."

"What about the Iron Spike?" Jadir asked.

"Qudovo is being...uncooperative right now," he answered, trying to keep his word to tell Jadir as much as he could. "He doesn't want his gang spending all their time protecting you and Marilsa.

But I will take care of that."

"So the gang is now fighting over whether they should help us or not? I can't say I blame them."

"No, it's nothing like that. It's just an issue I've been having with Qudovo. I said I will take care of it and I will. Just go watch over Marilsa, and I'll come meet you shortly."

Jadir gave him a short nod and began to walk away. Then he stopped and looked back over his shoulder.

"Thanks," he said.

Koral stepped up and clasped Jadir on the shoulder. "Let's go," he said.

The two men left the alley and walked off in opposite directions.

Chapter Twenty-Four

JADIR JUMPED UP AS SOMEONE KNOCKED SOFTLY ON THE door. Marilsa opened her eyes and let out a small sigh. Her sleep had been interrupted again, and she needed her rest. It was taking her some time to get used to sleeping during the day and remaining awake at night. But she had said that her rituals were so much easier to practice when the sun wasn't in the sky, so she was trying to adjust to this new schedule.

"Yes?" Jadir said in a low voice to the person on the other side of the door.

"Koral is back, we're ready," one of the gang members replied.

Jadir turned back to Marilsa. "Go back to sleep. I won't be long."

Marilsa closed her eyes as Jadir opened the door and stepped out into the hallway, pulling the door closed behind him. The messenger was the same young man who had stood outside their room the night Jadir had been wounded by the Witch Hunter.

Jadir nodded at him, and the other man led him outside and across the street to another alley. Koral was waiting, along with five more gang members, Rifain among them. Jadir greeted them all.

"Okay," Koral said, taking charge. "We're in luck—the carriage is back. Jadir didn't scare them off for long."

"This doesn't make sense," Jadir said. "They know I'm watching them, just as they're watching Marilsa and me. They know I'm trying to find out who they are. But they just keep coming back."

"It does seem too obvious," Koral replied. "It's possible the carriage is just a diversion—the real watchers are stationed somewhere else around here, but you're so focused on the carriage that you'll never spot them."

"What if they're trying to get us to focus so much on the carriage so that they can send an assassin in to kill Marilsa while we're doing this?"

Koral shook his head. "The Witch Hunters don't operate that way. Remember, they're a part of the Church. If they knew you were here, they would come with whichever Hunters were in the city, backed up by a bunch of priests. There's no way you would be able to protect Marilsa against a force like that. And they would have struck before now."

"Besides," Rifain said, "We've got a few people in the building to make sure your sister doesn't get attacked while we're all out here."

Jadir was grateful for the help they were giving him. These people were putting their lives on the line for Marilsa, and Jadir had no way to pay them back for all they were doing.

Koral explained his plan to catch the black carriage, and then sent everyone on their way.

"Come on, you're with me," he said to Jadir.

Jadir followed the other man away from the street, and around in a circle to approach his building from a direction not immediately visible to the carriage. Koral and Jadir ducked into the building entrance, and Koral led him down a passage to a rear door that opened into a back alley.

"This brings us out just before the point where the carriage will have to stop."

They proceeded down the alley and waited in the darkness just inside. Neither of them could see the carriage from their vantage point, but they refrained from peeking around the corner in case the carriage driver spotted them.

They remained in the alley for almost ten minutes, and then the sound of a cracking whip came to them as the carriage driver began driving his horses to pull away from where they were parked. Jadir knew two gang members had come running around the corner to charge the carriage.

There was no way they would catch the vehicle, but that wasn't their job.

A moment later, the carriage thundered past the alley opening where Koral and Jadir waited.

"Go!" Koral shouted.

The two men shot out of the mouth of the alley just behind the carriage, which had almost reached the end of the block. But just as it was about to reach the first cross-street, a wagon heavily laden with barrels came around the corner and stopped, blocking the street.

The carriage driver heaved on the reigns, barely able to stop the horses from crashing into the wagon. He immediately began trying to turn the carriage, but the three men on the wagon leaped off and grabbed at the carriage horses' bridles, stopping the animals in their tracks.

The carriage driver tried to whip the men holding his horses, but Jadir and Koral arrived just at that moment. Jadir reached up and grabbed the driver's leg and yanked him down off the seat. The man flailed at Jadir, trying to punch him in the face, but he was no combatant, and Jadir quickly grappled the driver and pinned his arms to his sides.

We did it! Jadir thought, elated at how smoothly it had gone.

And then the door of the carriage burst open, revealing a woman in black robes.

The robes of a priestess.

Everyone froze as she stepped down from the carriage, her mouth twisted in a grimace. Jadir saw a stain spread across the pants of the young man who had come to get him from his room shortly before. The look of shock on the faces of Rifain and the other gang members mirrored his own.

The Church is here. Koral was wrong—the Church has been watching us all this time.

From behind the priestess, another black-robed figure emerged. This priest was a smaller man, aged and meek looking. Jadir knew appearances meant nothing. These two could kill everyone on this street with little effort.

The priestess raised a hand and pointed at Jadir.

"You," she said to him. "Release my driver."

Jadir reluctantly let go of the man, who scrambled away from him and put his back to the carriage.

Koral was the first to recover from his shock. He stepped forward and bowed to the priestess.

"Please accept my apologies, Sister. We thought this carriage belonged to someone else—"

"Silence!" she hissed at him. "Your lies mean nothing. You have been trying to find out who was in this carriage for days. Now you know."

She took a step closer to Koral. "Is your curiosity satisfied? Do you feel this was worth the trouble?"

Jadir could see the others were terrified, but he himself felt only relief at knowing what he was facing. He might die here today, but at least he would die protecting his sister from these murderers.

"Leave them alone," he said to the priestess. "It's me you want."

The priestess turned to Jadir and laughed in his face.

"You flatter yourself. You are nothing, boy. You play a game you do not understand, with powers beyond your comprehension."

She faced Koral again. "And you. Your master oversteps his bounds. Perhaps I should send your head back to him as a warning to keep his fingers out of other people's business."

At her words, Jadir saw a look come over Rifain's face. The man was about to do something stupid, something that might get them all killed.

She's going to kill us all, anyway.

The thought came into Jadir's head, but it didn't feel right. The priestess was enjoying their fear. She was toying with them. But Jadir couldn't convince himself that she was truly about to do anything to them.

"I know someone who wants your head," she said to Jadir. "He's hunting you, and when the time is right, his face will be the last thing you see."

She turned to Rifain, who Jadir could see was getting ready to draw a weapon and rush the priestess.

"Move your wagon before I decide to boil your blood where you stand, worm."

Rifain blinked stupidly at her, and Jadir spoke up. "Please, do as she says."

It was enough to stop Rifain from killing himself in a futile attempt to slay the priestess. He turned and climbed up into the wagon and flicked the reigns. As the wagon began to roll, the priestess turned back to the others.

"An example is needed here, I think. The rest of you...," she looked at Jadir, "...run."

The young man with the soiled trousers screamed and pitched backwards onto the road. His body convulsed as steam began to rise from his skin. The priestess was going to kill him right in the street.

Jadir took a step toward her, but felt Koral's hand on his arm. He looked down into the other man's face.

"Think of Marilsa," Koral said to him. "She's letting the rest of us go—don't die for nothing."

Jadir hesitated as the young man's screams choked off, though he continued to convulse and writhe on the ground. Koral pulled on Jadir's arm, and Jadir swore at the priestess.

She looked at him and laughed once again.

The other gang members had already fled. Jadir swore again, and turned and ran with Koral at his side.

Jadir realized he didn't even know the name of the young man who was dying because he had tried to help. But the image of his death was forever burned into Jadir's mind.

*   *   *

RELAEL SLAMMED HIS FISTS ON THE TABLE AND LEAPED TO HIS feet, snarling.

"How stupid can one person get?" he yelled at Wilau, who flinched and took a step back. Relael knew it wasn't the poor man's fault he was the bearer of such news, but Relael didn't care at the moment. His fury was so great that he was ready to kill everyone involved, no matter how tangentially.

"Where was Brother Worestald?"

Wilau swallowed before answering. "He was there, but did not speak or do anything to any of the gang members."

"He did nothing to stop Sister Xodoc, either, did he?"

Wilau shook his head.

"By the Abyss, I want to kill them both! How could they let themselves get into such a position?"

"The gang set up an ambush," explained Wilau. "They blocked the street with a wagon, and then surrounded the carriage. The boy, Jadir, had tried to approach the carriage twice before."

Relael didn't think it was possible, but his rage boiled even higher.

"They knew the boy was trying to catch the carriage, but they decided to return to the same spot, in the same carriage, regardless?"

Wilau nodded at him.

"Where is the driver now?"

"He just returned to the Temple with the priest and priestess. Sister Xodoc apparently decided to leave the area for tonight. I don't know when she intends to return."

Relael pondered for a moment. Then he yanked open the door and motioned for the guard in the hallway to come into the room. The Church was permitted to have their own soldiers for the purpose of guarding their temples and brethren. Known as the Sentinels, they were not priests, but belonged instead to a separate sect of the Church, skilled warriors with absolute and unquestioning loyalty.

The Sentinel stepped into the room and stood at attention. Relael noted Wilau lick his lips nervously and take another step back, which put his back against the wall.

He thinks I'm going to have him killed, thought Relael. *Let him worry, and let him see what I do to those who fail me.*

"Soldier, the carriage driver who just returned Sister Xodoc and Brother Worestald to the Temple—find him and arrest him. He is to be taken downstairs and given to the priests who attend our God who dwells below."

Relael heard a small whimper come from Wilau.

"If anyone questions you," he continued, "tell them to come see me."

The Sentinel saluted smartly and left the room. Relael turned back to Wilau, who was visibly trembling.

"Calm down," he ordered. "You're not going to die tonight. Not unless you suddenly decide you're too stupid to live as well."

Wilau nodded, and managed to pull himself together, but Relael could tell the man was still terrified.

"Tell me you've got someone watching the witch right now in case they decide to flee," Relael said to him, a dangerous note in his voice.

"I have two separate people watching the building from different spots. I've been rotating my people so that no one is there two days in a row."

"It's good to see you're not a moron, Wilau. But I want you back out there. I can't afford another mistake, not after what that priestess did."

Wilau nodded at him, still nervous.

"*Now*," said Relael, and the man took off out the door, almost running.

Relael followed Wilau out into the hallway, but turned in the opposite direction. He made his way to one of the passages that led under the streets to the buildings that surrounded the Temple. In the sub-levels below one of those buildings, he came to a room with an unmarked door.

Relael knocked on the door and waited. He stood there for almost five minutes before he heard a metal bolt slide back and then the portal opened a crack. A wide eye peered out at him.

"Yondos," said Relael. "It's just me. We need to talk."

The door opened wider and Relael faced a small, fat man dressed in tattered black priest robes. His bald head shone with sweat and his wide eyes rolled in his head, as if he was hearing voices from all directions at once. He stepped back and allowed Relael to enter.

The room was dimly lit with a couple of small candles on a workbench against one wall. An archway led off into darkness, but Relael could hear whimpering and the occasional deep growl from down that passage. He pushed the door closed but kept one hand on the latch.

"It has...been some time," Yondos said in his raspy voice. "I thought you...had forgotten about me."

He spoke as someone who was constantly getting interrupted by voices only he could hear. Considering what some of those voices seemed to know, Relael had never figured out if the man was simply mad, or had some unknown source of information.

"I merely wanted to leave you undisturbed to continue your work. I know how important it is to you."

"You...didn't need my help. Now you...do, again."

Relael knew he shouldn't bother trying to convince the other man of his altruism. It was pointless—their relationship was based on transactions, not friendship.

"Yes, I do," he confirmed. "I have a problem that needs to go away."

"What has she done?" Yondos asked. Relael frowned.

"What has *who* done?"

"The woman...I don't know her name, but...you want her removed."

"How do you know it's a woman, Yondos?"

"You just said so."

Relael suppressed a shudder. The voice the priest had heard hadn't been Relael's, but it didn't matter—he was correct.

"Yes," he continued. "Her name is Sister Zera Xodoc. She—"

"There is...power, there," Yondos interrupted. "She is being...watched by her superiors. That one will...advance soon."

"Not if I have anything to say about it. She's a threat to the Church, Yondos. Something must be done."

Yondos shrugged. "We are...all threats to the Church. Even you. But...it always survives anyway."

Relael started to feel frustrated. It sounded to him as if Yondos was hesitant to get involved this time. Did Sister Xodoc really have that much power? Had Relael finally made an enemy he couldn't overcome?

"Are you saying you can't help me, Yondos?"

The man's eyes continued to roll in his head, but he smiled slowly, revealing a handful of rotting teeth in blackened gums. Relael didn't react—he had seen this particular show before.

"Perhaps I can...do what you need. But I...have needs as well."

"I am prepared to pay your price, Yondos. I wouldn't be here otherwise. Same as last time?"

Yondos shook his head slowly. "The ones you brought...me last time were weak. They...didn't last long enough."

Relael smiled back at Yondos. "I could bring you someone with a great deal of power. Someone you'd never get your hands on, otherwise."

A look of desire transformed Yondos' face into a visage even more disturbing.

"But how would...you get Ontherim down here...without a fight?"

Relael hated that Yondos was seemingly able to know what he was thinking. He wondered what other secrets this man knew about him. He also wondered if anyone else was using Yondos' connections to make things happen in the Church. Relael couldn't be the only one who understood how this man could sway the right people at the right time.

Regardless, Relael felt using Yondos was the right choice here. Sister Xodoc had her own connections, and Relael couldn't remove her from his path by himself.

"Leave that to me, Yondos. I offer Brother Ontherim Worestald as payment."

Yondos nodded slowly. "I don't...need to remind you—"

"No, I know the terms of our agreement. I will deliver him to you at the appointed time."

"Good...good," the small man mumbled as he turned away from Relael and returned to his worktable.

Relael yanked open the door and stepped into the hallway. As soon as he pulled the wooden panel shut, he heard the metal bolt slide back into place—despite Yondos being on the other side of the room.

Now it was time to see how he could mitigate the immediate damage to his plans.

Chapter Twenty-Five

JADIR CROSSED HIS ARMS AND STARED AT KORAL.
"The Warren? No, I'm not keeping Marilsa in the Warren. It's too dangerous."

"The rest of the city hasn't exactly been safe for the two of you."

Jadir sighed and leaned against the damp stone wall. Marilsa sat on an old crate, resting after their rapid flight from the building where they had been staying. This basement in the bowels of a crumbling, abandoned building was a temporary rest stop while they decided where Jadir and Marilsa could hide.

"Or for any of us," noted Rifain. Jadir looked down at the floor, refusing to meet the other man's gaze. He knew Rifain blamed Jadir for the death of Flouty, the young man who had been killed by the priestess.

Jadir had felt horrible needing to ask what the boy's name had been. That was the point at which Rifain had revealed his anger toward Jadir. The gang member had almost left them, but Koral convinced him to stay for now. But it was only a matter of time before Rifain blew up again and walked out.

"The Warren is filled with the poorest, the most desperate, and the nastiest people in Ythis," Jadir argued. "I don't see how that's an improvement over hiding somewhere else in the city."

"You don't seem to get it," Koral snapped at him. "They've found you, not once, but twice. This is the Church we're talking about, Jadir. There were two of them in that carriage, and they've been watching you all this time. Think about what she said—they're playing a game here. They want something from Marilsa, and that's why the Witch Hunters haven't shown up, why the Church hasn't come for you."

"You don't know that," Jadir replied.

"By the Abyss, use your head! She knew who you were, she knew who *I* was. We took you out of your old place, and they found you again in less than a day. But they didn't attack. No, they've been watching you, waiting for…something. None of us has any idea what that is, but I'm willing to bet everything I have that it's not going to be pleasant for Marilsa."

"That's enough," Marilsa said quietly.

Jadir wasn't sure what to do. He wanted to take Marilsa and just get out of Ythis. But he knew this impulse would, in truth, be worse for them. Here they had people who were willing to help them. Out there, they would know no one. It would be only a matter of time before another Witch Hunter caught up with them. A city like this at least offered a multitude of places to hide until Marilsa was ready to choose her own path.

"Being in the Warren won't help if the Church comes for us. And if they can find us wherever we hide, then the Warren won't make a difference there, either. I think we'd be better off being where we have more options, some part of the city that's more open, where we can run when we need to. The Warren is too closed off, the streets are too narrow, there's no room."

"For those who know the Warren, it's the best place in the city to hide, or to run," countered Koral.

"But we don't know the Warren!" shouted Jadir. "You know it, but Marilsa and I don't. And as much as you've agreed to help us, if anything happens to you and we're on our own, the Warren is the worst place for us to be."

"I said enough!" Marilsa declared, standing up from the crate. Though she was the shortest one in the basement, she seemed to tower over all the others. Everyone stared at her, dumbfounded.

"Jadir," she continued, "You make good points, but Koral is right. The Warren is where we need to be."

Jadir tried to open his mouth to convince her otherwise, but he found himself unable to speak.

"Koral," she said, "I'm concerned about your people, but we need your help. If you had told me what you were going to do, I could have protected you."

She looked around the room and her gaze rested on Rifain. "*All* of you. I cannot defeat a priestess on my own in a straight confrontation, but that doesn't mean I'm a helpless child who needs protecting."

She turned back to Koral. "I'm not going to hide in some abandoned tenement. I need a place where I can sleep well during the day, and concentrate—uninterrupted—through the night. If you know of a place like that, then that's where Jadir and I will stay. Otherwise, we will find a place that suits us near the Warren, but not inside."

Koral suddenly gasped, as if he had been holding his breath while Marilsa spoke. Jadir found he still could not speak.

"Marilsa, I know of two places that fit your needs. Both of them are well hidden and provide many escape routes if you need them."

Marilsa nodded. "Whichever one is closer to the Tower of Ash is the one I want to try first."

Koral blinked at her. "*Closer* to the Tower of Ash?"

"Yes, Koral, you heard me correctly."

He nodded slowly. "Okay, if that's what you want."

"One other thing," she said. "There are a few other members of the gang who I want to stay with us for now. I will give you their names, and you will get word to them."

"I think this has reached the point that I'm going to ask for volunteers, rather than ordering anyone to stay with you."

"They will volunteer," Marilsa said with complete confidence. "You just let them know where we are."

And suddenly, all the men in the room were able to speak. But before Jadir could open his mouth, Rifain swore out loud.

"I have had enough of this!" he snarled at them. "This has gone beyond anything I signed up for. I don't care what the Wolf wants with these two, I'm not going to throw my life away to get into a fight with the Church over…whatever this girl is. You say you can protect us, but Flouty was boiled alive. That's not going to happen to me."

Koral turned to him to respond, but Marilsa spoke over him.

"I understand, and don't hold any grudge against you. You may leave."

Rifain looked at her, and then at Koral. It seemed to Jadir that Koral did not know what to say. Finally, Koral nodded at Rifain.

Rifain looked around the room, but none of the other men would meet his gaze, none except Jadir, who now looked him in the eye. The two men glared at each other, and then Rifain swore again and stalked off to the stairs leading up to the ground level.

"Marilsa," Jadir said to her. "Are you sure—"

"Of course I am," she snapped at him. "Koral, please take us to our new home."

Koral literally started when Marilsa said his name. He couldn't hide his discomfort from being near her. Jadir looked around at the others, but they all gazed at Marilsa with strange expressions on their faces, as if they were waking up from a deep sleep and seeing something wondrous.

Jadir wasn't sure what it meant, but something about it seemed wrong to him. Marilsa had power, of that there was no doubt. Her use of it, however, was beginning to concern Jadir. Controlling others, the way she had taken control of everyone in this room, was something one would expect from the Church, or the sorcerers.

It was moments like these when Jadir wondered if Marilsa was still Marilsa, or was becoming . . . something else.

*   *   *

"WHERE HAVE YOU BEEN?"

There was an edge in Phana's voice and Koral took a step back to look at her. He had been pleasantly surprised to find her waiting in his room at the Crown and Coin when he returned from getting Jadir and Marilsa settled in their new hiding place. But now he realized this was not a social call. Something was wrong.

"I was taking care of some business with our two friends. Have you been here long?"

"Koral, Qudovo has turned on us."

The news didn't surprise him, though it did disappoint him. He had hoped Qudovo would be sensible and stay with the Wolf. But sometimes people did stupid things, and then they had to face the consequences of those decisions.

"What has he done?"

"He's got a bunch of gang members who are loyal to him, and they're at the Iron Spike," she answered. "Or at least they were last night when I left there. They would have killed me, but they weren't ready yet to sacrifice one of their own people to do it. I've been looking for you since then to warn you—it's obvious he'll come after you next."

"I was at the warehouse last night, Phana. No one said anything to me about this."

"That's because they're afraid. Those who haven't sided with Qudovo are going to keep out of it—until he's no longer a threat to them."

Koral swore long and loudly. Phana waited calmly for him to finish.

"By the Abyss, Phana, I need more from them than that! If anyone had said something to me last night, I'd already have dealt with Qudovo. Instead, he's had a full night and day to cause trouble. I'll bet a more than a few throats were slit in the past twenty-four hours."

"Everyone's on edge," Phana explained. "No one has been happy with the situation since Marilsa was attacked. We've been protecting outsiders on your orders, and never mind the rest of our responsibilities. Even those who haven't thrown in their lot with Qudovo think he's partly in the right."

Koral didn't want to hear this, but he forced himself to listen. He wasn't happy about the situation either. He had known it would be a recipe for trouble—only a strong leader would take the gang through a trial like this without serious problems, and Qudovo was the wrong man for the job. But the Wolf had given Koral orders, and it was his job to make sure they were followed.

Phana took a deep breath, obviously expecting him to protest, but when he said nothing she continued.

"The Wolf expects us to make money, Koral. And so most of the members of the gang have some racket going on. But they need time to manage those things, or the money starts to dry up. It's one thing have a lean month or two, it's another when you start losing control of ventures you set up in the first place. This isn't just them losing a bit of money. Taking them away from their responsibilities means they may just have to start over when this is all done."

She looked Koral in the eyes.

"You can't just expect them to accept that without some kind of explanation. But instead, you brought Jadir into the gang and then a few days later turned us all into protectors of Marilsa. What do you expect everyone to think?"

Koral took a deep breath and let it out slowly. He had completely mishandled the situation, and now lives were going to be lost over it. Now that Qudovo had tried to attack Phana, he would have to die, and so inevitably would some of his followers.

The Wolf paid Koral to manage these situations, but Koral had to admit he had let it all get away from him, thinking he could force it back onto the right path if it went too far astray. But now it was too late for that.

Koral prided himself on his ability to learn from his mistakes, and this was a big one. He wasn't sure if the gang could be salvaged at this point—it might be better to let it dissolve and have the neighboring gangs absorb whichever members who still wanted to remain with the Wolf.

And then it occurred to him that Phana might really be telling him this because she wanted to take over the gang. It was unlikely, but she had surprised him before. But he knew such a decision would be another mistake.

"You're not thinking...?" he asked Phana, hoping she wouldn't take it the wrong way. Her eyes widened as she realized what he was asking her.

"By the Abyss, no!" she nearly shouted. "I'm a worse choice than Qudovo was. I'm no leader—I can barely stand to remain in the gang as it is. Everyone knows it, and they won't follow me."

Koral nodded. "Okay, I just wanted to make sure that's not what you had in mind, because I couldn't agree to that, regardless of how I feel about you."

He thought about his options—who else was ready and able to take over this gang and bring it back together? He knew of one person, but she was currently wanted by the Imperial Guard and would have to lay low for at least another month or two. Was there someone else ready to step up and assume control of one of the more stable gangs, freeing up a more experienced leader?

Koral was exhausted, and would find no answers tonight. It was very late—dawn would be breaking in a few hours and he had barely slept in what felt like days.

"You're right, you know," he said to Phana. "I've royally messed this whole thing up and now I've got to find some way to put it all back together. I'm sorry I got you involved in this."

Her look softened and she took a step forward and put her arms around his neck.

"It's not all your fault, Koral. You were just trying to do what your boss wanted. Speaking of which, did you take Jadir to see the Wolf?"

To Koral, it felt like that had happened weeks ago, but in reality, little more than 24 hours had passed since their meeting with the Wolf. And then it hit him, Phana didn't know the truth about Jadir yet.

He stepped back out of her embrace and took her hands in his.

"Um, Phana, we learned the truth about Jadir and Marilsa."

"What truth? I already know Marilsa's a witch."

"Not that—not *just* that. Jadir is…not really her brother."

He saw the confusion in Phana's eyes and decided he just had to tell her and stop prevaricating.

"Jadir is a…creation of Marilsa's mother. She was also a witch, a powerful one. She…put a spirit into the body of a dead boy, and created Jadir as a protector for Marilsa. He's not human, Phana. Well, his body is, but his soul is something else entirely."

Phana stepped back from Koral and sat on the edge of the table. He could see the shock on her face as his words sank in.

"So…what I felt…," she muttered.

"You must be sensitive to stuff like that. You can feel the wrong-ness from him—that's why you can't stand to be near him."

She looked up at Koral. "But I could before. I wanted him, Koral, and we almost...,"

She stopped when she saw the look on Koral's face, but then she frowned at him.

"Listen, you're not the first man in my life, and you'll just have to deal with it. I almost had sex with him because I wanted to, he didn't repel me at all. And then, as soon as he met the witch in the Warren, suddenly everything was different. And I have to wonder why that is."

Koral put his hand on the wall to steady himself and Phana saw how tired he was.

"Well, it's not something we can do anything about right now. You look dead on your feet, Koral. When was the last time you slept?"

"A real sleep?" he asked, grinning at her. "Or a catnap? I get twen-ty minutes here and there all the time."

She shook her head at him, but she was smiling, too.

"So where do you live? I assume you don't sleep here," she said.

"No, I've got a place. It's not far."

Phana stepped back into his arms and spoke softly, her lips just barely brushing his. "With Qudovo out there, we should stay to-gether...for safety."

Koral was having trouble speaking, so he just nodded dumbly. Maybe it wasn't time to go to sleep just yet.

Chapter Twenty-Six

JADIR OPENED HIS EYES AND LOOKED AROUND THE SMALL room. Dim light filtered in between the slats of the shutters—it was just after dawn. He had not expected to fall asleep, but sitting here alone in the dark had inevitably led to his losing consciousness. He sat up and groaned at the pain in his back. The rough, wooden floor had made a poor bed.

He stepped through the open doorway into a short passage that was capped on each end by a wooden door. The portal nearest him led into another small room where Marilsa had settled herself last night and then demanded privacy. The other led out to the staircase.

Jadir heard Marilsa's voice—muffled by the closed door—ask a question. She was answered by a male voice, and Jadir felt a protective rush come over him. Without thinking, he shoved the door open and surged into the room.

The two men and one woman who were in the room with Marilsa scrambled to their feet, knives appearing in their hands. Jadir grabbed one man by the arm and threw him into the wall. The man's head bounced off the wooden panel and the knife fell from nerveless fingers. Jadir turned to the others, but Marilsa's voice brought him up short.

"Jadir, stop!" she commanded, and he suddenly found himself unable to move. The effect lasted for only a second or two, but it would have been enough to let the others gut him if they had decided to attack. But instead of coming at the temporarily helpless Jadir, they crowded around Marilsa protectively.

Jadir recognized them as members of the gang. *His* gang.

He stumbled as his muscles suddenly unlocked once more.

"Jadir, that's enough," Marilsa said to him, anger in her voice. "I was not being threatened."

The other two rushed over to their fallen comrade and helped him sit up. Jadir knew the man would have a nasty bump on his head, but would otherwise be fine. Jadir realized he had felt none of the control he had the night he faced the Witch Hunter.

Consciously, Jadir had thought Marilsa was being threatened, but apparently his subconscious knew the difference. It was the only reason the man he attacked was still alive.

"I...I'm sorry. I thought—"

"I know," Marilsa interrupted him. "I had hoped your rest would do you some good. I guess I should have expected your senses to be groggy when you woke up."

Jadir wondered if Marilsa meant she had put him to sleep last night—had kept him unconscious while she met with these three people. He didn't want to think about the control she had over him, but he couldn't deny he was at her beck and call.

After all, he was hardly his own person, was he?

"What are they doing here?" he asked her, trying to assert some authority in his tone. She merely smiled at him.

"They came to visit me," she answered. "And they've been a big help with some things I was doing."

"What do you mean? How are they helping you?"

Marilsa yawned. "I really don't feel like explaining it all right now, Jadir. I'm rather tired, and I need to get some sleep."

She turned to the three gang members. The man Jadir had attacked slowly regained his feet and glared at Jadir, hatred in his eyes. Jadir opened his mouth to say something to the man, but Marilsa spoke over him.

"Thank you, all of you. I will summon you again when I need your help."

The three gang members left, saying nothing to Jadir. He turned to Marilsa.

"What do you mean 'summon' them? How did you get them to come here?"

Marilsa looked at Jadir evenly. "I *am* a witch, dear brother."

Jadir thought she sneered when she said 'brother,' but he couldn't be sure in his agitated state.

"Marilsa, we've gone to all this trouble to hide you from the Church, and you're bringing gang members straight here? We have to be careful—we can't trust everybody just because they're in the gang."

"We can trust *them*."

"And why is that?" he asked.

"Because I said so, that's why. They are no more likely to betray me than you are. And we both know that's not going to happen."

He didn't know why, but she was taunting him, getting not-so-subtle digs in. But he didn't have any idea why she was being like this. Her behavior was troubling because it was so unlike her.

"You're angry because I burst in here," he said to her, seeking an explanation.

"I'm not angry, Jadir. You'd know it if I was." The threat in her words hung in the air between them. He took a deep breath and tried to start over.

"I'm sorry I barged in here. I thought we had been found again. I thought you were in danger."

"Yes, well, that's not something you need to worry about much anymore. You're not the only one protecting me. And as helpful as you were with the Witch Hunter, things have changed since then."

" 'Since then?' That was only three nights ago!"

"It was a lifetime ago, Jadir," she growled at him, and something in her eyes told him that if she hadn't been angry before, she certainly was now. "Do I need to remind you of everything that's happened since then? Three nights ago you still thought you were human."

Jadir felt like he had been punched in the gut. He loved his sister more than anything, wanted nothing more than for her to have a happy, safe life. But now it seemed like she blamed him for what had happened.

"Please, Marilsa. Don't say that."

"Don't grovel! I hate that. You used to be strong. It was one of the reasons Phana liked you. But look at you now. I know you think I'm doing something to control you, but you're doing that yourself. You used to be more than just my summoned protector. But you've used that knowledge as an excuse to give up your own free will."

Marilsa stood up and glared into Jadir's face.

"You can be more than you are!" she yelled at him. "But instead you're just going to crawl into your role, and you're going to fail me!"

Jadir tried to speak, but he couldn't. Marilsa's words were like daggers that had sunk straight into his heart. The fact that she was right only made it worse.

He *had* been more than this before he knew his origin. Why was he letting himself get subsumed by his history, instead of being the man he knew he was? Why couldn't he fight back?

Jadir realized he was standing hunched over, shoulders slumped, and he forced himself to stand up straight. He took another breath and resolved to be stronger—to be the brother he had been all these years.

"You're right," he said, his voice held even. "I've been so worried about you I stopped being *me*. Thanks for reminding me who I am. Maybe I even needed this…this cruelty from you to realize it."

He stepped toward Marilsa and looked down into her face. "I may be your protector, or at least one of them, but I'm not your servant. That's going to change, starting now. You should get some sleep—you look exhausted."

Jadir began to leave the room, but stopped at the threshold and looked back at his sister.

"You're wrong about one thing, though. I'm *not* going to fail you."

As he pulled the door closed, she mumbled something that he didn't quite catch. It was only later, after he was sure she was asleep, that he realized she had said "You already have."

*   *   *

PHANA OPENED HER EYES INTO A SQUINT AND RAISED HER arm over her head to block the sliver of sunlight spearing through the crack in the wooden shutter. She took a moment to get her bearings, listening to the sound of Koral's even breathing behind her.

Carefully, she sat up on the edge of his sleeping pallet, so as not to disturb him.

"Something wrong?" he murmured. Of course he would wake at the slightest movement.

"No, I just woke up," she replied. "Time for me to go."

She heard him roll onto his back and stretch.

"It's still early. You didn't get much sleep."

Phana grabbed her leggings and began to pull them on. She knew Koral was watching her, but she didn't turn to look at him.

"I'm not going to sleep until Qudovo is dealt with, Koral. I'm worried about Marilsa and Jadir—if he can get a chance to do something nasty to them, he won't hesitate."

"From what I've seen lately, I think those two can take care of themselves. If Qudovo goes after them, he's the one who'll be in trouble."

Phana pulled her tunic over her head and grabbed her vest. She glanced at Koral as she stood up. He was watching her get dressed, his expression carefully neutral. She wasn't fooled.

He's wondering if I regret what happened between us. But we don't have time for insecurity.

"Koral, the rest of the gang are feeling lost. They need some direction. Qudovo wants them to join him, and he makes a good argument. It's only fear of the Wolf that's keeping more of them from switching sides. But the rest are worried—it's one thing to let Qudovo and his people face the consequences for their treason. It's another entirely to fight them directly, to kill people who used to protect your back against your enemies."

"I wish I had someone ready to step in who understood the situation as well as you," he said to her. She didn't bother to comment, but just jammed her feet into her boots and grabbed her knives.

"Don't worry," he said. "I know you don't want that. But I also have no idea what you *do* want. You didn't exactly have an easy time following Qudovo's orders, and I have to wonder how much of that was him and how much was your independence."

"If you're looking for me be a good little soldier, Koral, then you and the Wolf have sadly misjudged me. I joined the gang because

I felt like I could belong there. In truth, I like the people—most of them, at least—and I have skills that can help them out. I was never asked to do anything I wasn't willing to do. And I was given the freedom I needed."

She knelt on the edge of the pallet and looked down at Koral, who still hadn't moved.

"That's what I want. That's what I *need*. And if that's no longer possible, if this gang has seen its final days and everyone is going to be split up and absorbed into others scattered across the city, then I need to think about whether it's time for me to move on."

Koral's eyes widened. "What does that mean?"

"Ythis doesn't have to be my home. If I can't find a place to belong here, then maybe I need to keep looking somewhere else."

"But—"

Phana interrupted him by leaning down and kissing him. He tried to put his arm around her neck, but she pulled away before he could pull her down fully onto the pallet.

"You've got stuff to do," she said to him. "And so do I. I'll come by the Crown and Coin later and tell you what I've been able to find out."

"Where are you going?"

"To the warehouse," she answered. "You should stay away from there today—give me a chance to find out what's going on, who we can trust, how everyone is leaning. There's no way Qudovo is still at the Iron Spike. He knows you're going to come after him because he tried to kill me, so he'll be in hiding. You do what you have to do, and I'll help where I can."

"Be careful," Koral said to her, the look in his eyes telling her he was worried about her more than he should. "What if Qudovo goes to the warehouse?"

"He won't. Not unless the entire gang joins him, and they're not ready to do that. You need to be careful, too. You're the bigger threat to him, and if he wants to hurt the Wolf, the best way to do that is by killing you."

Koral nodded. Phana gave him a smile and left the room.

The moment Phana was out on the street, she felt as if a weight had been lifted from her. This was a typical reaction for her. She liked Koral a great deal—he was smart, attractive, had proven to be a skilled lover. But there was something missing.

There was *always* something missing.

This was not the first time she had gotten involved with someone only to find herself immediately feeling restless. She knew she had not made the wrong decision last night. And she had no intention of ending their relationship so quickly after it had begun. But she also hadn't been lying to him about possibly leaving Ythis.

She didn't belong here. At least, not like this, in this kind of life. But she had never been able to articulate what was wrong, what she was really looking for. There were moments when she could almost see it, like it was on the tip of her brain and she would understand if only she concentrated hard enough. But it always slipped away, and she was left wondering if there was something wrong with her.

Phana continually scanned her surroundings as she walked, noting doorways or alley mouths where an ambush would most likely be set, if one were waiting for her. She had to admit she enjoyed the heightened sense of danger—it made her feel alive in a way little else did. As much as an attack by Qudovo in daylight was unlikely, it paid to be aware of her surroundings.

Within the hour, she had reached the warehouse without incident. As far as she could tell, she wasn't followed. Phana wondered if Koral would be as cautious, but there was little she could do if the man decided to be careless. Like always, she would deal with whatever life sent her way.

She knocked on the door and the small slot slid back almost immediately. Whoever was guarding the door recognized her immediately and slid the bolt back and pulled the door open. It turned out to be Cheyoj, a man of few words but great muscle. She smiled at him as she entered, and he gave her a solemn nod and motioned to the open area where the combat training usually took place.

Almost the entirety of the gang was gathered in that space, arrayed on the benches around the fighting ring. In the center stood Rifain and a couple of others. Phana moved up to the rear of the crowd as Cheyoj pushed the door closed and slammed the bolt back into place.

Rifain noticed Phana and frowned at her.

"It looks like *everyone* showed up," he said, and many heads turned to stare in her direction. "Well, everyone who hasn't already joined Qudovo, or those who are on *guard duty*."

Rifain's mouth twisted in a sneer as he mockingly derided those who were protecting Jadir and Marilsa. Phana was getting a very bad feeling about this. The gang had obviously gathered to come to a consensus on Qudovo and their duty to the Wolf. She had expected them to still be holding steady, but it looked like something had pushed them to the edge.

And there was no question Rifain was not siding with Jadir and Marilsa. Did that mean he was ready to join Qudovo? He had to understand that doing so would be a death sentence.

All eyes turned back to Rifain as he began to speak again, and Phana remained silent, wondering if she had wandered into a trap.

Chapter Twenty-Seven

ONE-BY-ONE, JADIR LOOKED THE TWO MEN IN THE eyes. Neither flinched from his gaze.

"If she wakes up and asks for me, tell her I'll be back soon."

"Where are you going?" one of the men asked.

Jadir looked at him but decided not to answer directly.

"I won't be long," he said.

Jadir left the building and went out into the Warren. He was still mostly unfamiliar with this part of the city, but he thought he recognized a couple of landmarks, and there was always the pillar of smoke coming up from the sorcerer's tower on the northern edge of this neighborhood.

That was visible no matter where one went in the city.

He ended up taking a couple of wrong turns and had to double back more than once. He knew other denizens of the Warren watched him pass, and was glad his size made them hesitate to see him as prey. A person who got lost in the Warren rarely emerged unscathed.

Eventually, Jadir spotted his destination—the stone building where he and Marilsa had met the witch only six days ago.

He walked up to the door and stopped. He had not brought anything to pay her, and there was a good chance she wouldn't even meet with him. But he had to try.

Jadir knocked on the door and waited. A full minute passed with no response, so he knocked again.

"She's gone," said a child's voice to his left. He turned to see a young boy, perhaps seven years old, barefoot and covered in grime.

"The wi... the old woman who lived her? She's gone?"

The boy nodded solemnly. Jadir's heart fell.

"When? Where did she go?"

"She was gone when the soldiers came for her," the child answered. "She hasn't come back."

"Soldiers were here, in the Warren?" Jadir asked. He knelt down in front of the boy. "Do you know when this happened?"

The boy shook his head slowly. "No. Days ago, I think."

Jadir wanted to scream in frustration. No matter what he tried, it seemed as if everyone else was always one step ahead of him, constantly throwing obstacles in his path.

"Listen," said Jadir, pulling a couple of coins from his pocket. "This is important. Do you know where the old woman went? Where can I find her now?"

The boy looked over Jadir's shoulder and his eyes went wide. He spun and darted away down the alley. Jadir threw himself sideways into a roll, expecting an attack from behind. He came up ready to fight, but there was no one there.

A movement down the block caught his eye. From around a corner stepped the young girl who had answered the door the first time Jadir and Marilsa had come to see the witch. She looked directly at Jadir, and then turned and stepped back out of his sight.

He leaped up and jogged down the street, not caring about drawing attention to himself. When he reached the intersection, he looked around for the girl, but she was gone. He began walking along this street and noticed her standing in the mouth of an alley up ahead.

Jadir bolted toward the alley, but just before he reached it, the girl stepped back into the shadows. An instant later, Jadir rounded the corner, but there was no sign of the girl in the long, narrow passage.

Aware of the danger of rushing headlong into an alley in the Warren, Jadir moved cautiously forward. He had gone perhaps halfway down its length when a voice spoke from behind him.

"What do you want?"

Jadir turned and found the girl standing a few feet away. In the shadowed alley, he couldn't see her eyes. The way the girl held her head reminded him of the blind witch.

"I need to speak to the witch," he answered. "It's about my sister. Can you take me to her?"

"You bring danger with your very presence. The risk is too great. It is not just soldiers and priests, though that is bad enough."

"I'm sorry...but, the soldiers had nothing to do with us. We didn't tell anyone about the witch. It could have been anyone who knew where she lived. Please, I need the witch's help."

The girl stood there, saying nothing.

"I will pay the witch's price," he continued. "Whatever she wants, I will find a way to deliver it. But I have questions only she can answer."

"You already have your answers," the girl replied. "You blind yourself to them, but they are all right in front of you."

"What is that supposed to mean?"

"Many eyes watch you and your sister. It is difficult to remain out of their sight. Helping you would bring their full attention. There is nothing you will gain here that do you not already know."

Jadir realized his fists were clenched. His frustration was mounting. This girl was speaking as if she knew all about him. But she was just a servant.

"Listen, if the witch refuses to help me, that's her decision, not yours. All I'm asking is for you to pass on my request to see her. Let her decide if the risk is too much or if there's a price I can pay to make it worth her while. But I have questions and I don't have the answers!"

"The decision is already made. And you have your answers—you just choose not to see them. What is about to happen cannot be changed. The time for that has already passed."

"What's about to happen? What—hey!"

The girl stepped back, away from Jadir and further into the shadows. He lunged forward, hoping to grab her arm, but where he grasped in the darkness, he felt nothing but a chill. The girl's face faded into the dimness of the alley and she disappeared from his sight.

Jadir stumbled around in the alley, searching for the girl, but he knew she was gone. Had she ever even been here, so close to him, or was it all an illusion? He didn't have any way of knowing the truth.

He sank to his knees, pounding his fists on the broken and uneven cobblestones beneath him. Jadir had believed the witch would help him, would answer some of his questions. Instead, she refused to see him.

He realized now the old woman knew what he was—he remembered her reaction the night he first met her, and her cryptic words. She had seen the truth about him. And now, through the young girl, the witch was telling him he knew the truth about his sister. But he *didn't* know.

Marilsa was acting as if Jadir had somehow let her down. And now the girl who served the witch had said that what was about to happen couldn't be stopped. Was Marilsa about to do something terrible? Or was someone else about to do something terrible *to* her?

Why had the priests been watching Marilsa instead of coming in force to capture or destroy her? The Witch Hunters were part of the Church—it made no sense for them to let her be if they knew where she was hiding. And yet, they had done exactly that.

And Jadir knew the Wolf would have no further answers. This was beyond even his ability to gather information. Koral and the rest of the gang were still helping Jadir and Marilsa, protecting them from external threats. But they knew no more than Jadir did himself.

Somehow, Jadir knew he had to prepare himself for whatever was about to happen. He had to make sure nothing bad happened to Marilsa.

If he couldn't see whatever was coming, then he would just have to do it blind.

*   *   *

KORAL STEPPED AROUND THE END OF THE BAR AND MOVED up close to Munt, who tried to backpedal but had nowhere to go.

"I don't have time for games, Munt. Where are they?"

The owner of the Iron Spike was short and fat, the thin wisps of black hair on his round, sweaty head sticking out in all directions. His normally beady eyes were wide with fear as he leaned away from Koral as far as he could.

"I-I don't know—that's the truth! Qudovo never told me anything. Him and a couple others went in ta' the back room and decided what they was gonna do, and then they told everyone to leave w' them. That's all I know!"

Koral stared into the other man's eyes, saying nothing. His silence frightened Munt even more than threats would have. The tavern owner started talking again, just to say something.

"I'm loyal to the Wolf, Koral. You have to know that. What wuz I gonna do, huh? Force them all to stay here? Qudovo, he don't listen to me. He acts like this is his place."

Koral knew the man was telling the truth. As much as he wished otherwise, Munt would be no help. He stepped back and dropped his hand from the hilt of his long knife.

"Okay, Munt, I believe you."

The fat man heaved a sigh and wiped his sweaty face with a thick hand. Koral looked around the empty common room. Qudovo was gone and he wasn't going to come back here. The gang leader knew the Wolf's people would come for him, and he had no intention of making it easy.

"Qudovo said nothing to you?" he asked Munt. "Not a final farewell, not a warning, a threat of any kind? I find that hard to believe."

Munt glanced nervously sideways at Koral.

"Well, he did threaten to kill me."

"Why?"

"For nothin'! Qudovo never needed a reason to threaten anybody. He said I was no longer any use t' him, so he might as well kill me. The others, they watched and laughed as Qudovo pulled out that knife o' his and waved it front of my face. He wanted me t' beg for my life."

"And what happened?" Koral asked. Munt grimaced and looked down at the floor.

"I begged," he answered. "I didn't think he wuz really gonna kill me, but I wasn't gonna take that chance, you know?"

Koral nodded.

"You gonna kill him?" Munt asked him.

"We'll see," he said. He had no intention of sharing his plans with Munt, just in case Qudovo paid a return visit to the Iron Spike. It was even possible the gang leader was paying Munt to tell him whatever he heard. In any case, Koral wasn't going to share anything he didn't need to.

Koral turned and headed for the door. Munt said nothing until he was across the common room and about to leave.

"Koral, what about me?"

He turned and looked at the other man, still sweating, still nervous.

"The Wolf has no problem with you. Keep yourself out of it, and you've got no worries."

"From you and your boss, maybe. What about Qudovo? What if he comes back, decides to kill me after all, just to hurt the Wolf? Who's gonna protect *me*?"

Koral almost laughed, but stopped himself. If Munt was being honest, then he deserved some protection.

"I'll have a couple of guys come over to keep an eye on you. I don't have the people available to protect this place if Qudovo comes with his whole remaining gang—they'll get you out safely if it comes to that, but this building is a different story."

Munt considered Koral's words and nodded. "Whatever you can do, it's better than nothin'."

Koral left the Iron Spike and headed west along the northern edge of the Dock District. He needed to get back to the Crown and Coin and get messages out to the Wolf and the other gang leaders across the city, just in case Qudovo decided to go after anyone connected to the organization. He should also start getting reports back from those he had sent out earlier to find where Qudovo had decided to hide.

Koral had just turned up the West River Road when he spotted Qudovo on the street ahead. The gang leader was leaning against the wall of a storefront, his arms crossed, looking right in Koral's direction. He almost stopped and ducked into a side alley, but knew he had been spotted already. Qudovo was obviously waiting for him.

Koral continued to walk calmly up the street, toward where Qudovo stood seemingly relaxed. The man appeared to be alone, but Koral knew others could be waiting hidden within a merchant's shop or around a corner. The West River Road was a major thoroughfare through Ythis' Market District, and the street was thronged with people in the late afternoon sun.

If a fight broke out here, there would be many witnesses, and a fairly quick response by the City Watch.

Koral stopped a few strides away from Qudovo, who pushed himself away from the wall and turned to fully face Koral.

"You were looking for me," he said to Koral.

"I was. You've been busy."

Qudovo grinned and spat into the street.

"I guess you're coming to kill me now," Qudovo said with a sneer.

Koral shrugged.

"That depends on you. You made a mistake—a bad one—but you got lucky and no one was hurt. There are ways to resolve this that don't end with you at the bottom of the Bay."

"It's that bitch Phana who got lucky, Koral. If I had my way, I would have cut her throat from ear to ear and let her bleed out on the floor of the Iron Spike. And then I would have taken her head and sent it to the Wolf as a present."

He took a step closer to Koral.

"In fact, just because she got away once, doesn't mean I won't get another chance. And you can't protect her, boy."

"You really think she needs protecting? Funny, from what I've heard, she almost killed you once. Next time maybe she won't be so merciful."

Qudovo's hands clenched and Koral relaxed his body. It was going to come to a fight, right here in the street. Qudovo was strong, but he wasn't nearly as fast as Koral. It wouldn't be easy, but Koral was confident he would walk away from this.

Someone walking along the street looked at Koral, and then over his shoulder, and gasped. Koral was moving even before he consciously realized there was a threat. Something hit him in the back, but the combination of his movement and his leathers stopped the weapon from doing any damage.

Koral tumbled away and came up with his short sword in one hand, and his long knife in the other. One of Qudovo's gang members had tried to attack him from behind, and was now lunging at him with his own sword. People around Koral screamed and scrambled out of his way as he met his attacker in a clash of steel.

He saw Qudovo draw his own long knife and begin to circle around, trying to get behind Koral. He parried a thrust with his sword and jammed his knife into the other man's hand. His attacker yelled as he lost his thumb and the man's weapon dropped to the ground. Before he could recover, Koral reversed his grip on the knife and stabbed upward, driving the point of the blade under the man's chin.

Koral spun, letting go of the knife and blocking Qudovo's attack from behind at the last second. He noticed a second and a third gang member come out of the crowd that had formed as bystanders tried to get some distance between themselves and the melee. Koral flicked his wrist and another blade dropped into his empty hand.

Qudovo tried to hammer Koral off his feet as the man he had killed dropped to the cobblestones behind him. Koral leaped backward and Qudovo rushed forward and almost tripped over the corpse. It gave Koral the opening he needed to kill the gang leader, but he was forced to spin away to prevent getting skewered by the other two attackers.

These men were skilled knife fighters. They approached slowly, cautiously, giving no opening but forcing Koral back. Qudovo recovered and again tried to maneuver around behind Koral. There was no way Koral would be able to fight off all three men without help.

He threw himself sideways and slipped past one of the other gang members, his leathers stopping a wild slash as he tumbled away. Regaining his feet, he charged at the nearest knot of bystanders, who screamed and tried to get out of his way. Koral suddenly reversed direction and faced the three men who were charging after him.

A flick of his wrist sent his knife spinning toward the face of the first man, who flinched away. But Koral was right behind the thrown blade, and he drove his short sword into the man's side in that instant of distraction. He used the blade as leverage to yank the dying man into the path of his second attacker. Pulling his sword free of the body, Koral engaged the second man while he was still off balance.

Koral drew another knife with his empty hand while he attacked with his sword. The member of Qudovo's gang backpedaled, his face twisting in fear as he realized his shorter weapon was no match for Koral's sword and dagger combination. The man's eyes darted around, searching for Qudovo, but there was no sign of the gang leader.

In a few more seconds, Koral knocked the knife from the man's hand before driving his sword deep into the other man's chest. He drew the blade free as he spun, searching for Qudovo.

The gang leader was nowhere to be seen. He had disappeared into the crowd.

Koral quickly retrieved his other two blades and sped off down a side alley. The entire battle had taken less than two minutes, and no Watchmen had arrived yet.

Qudovo had gambled on four men being enough to kill Koral. He had been wrong. After failing with Phana, and now Koral, the gang leader was going to get desperate. Koral had to stop him before he tried something crazy.

Chapter Twenty-Eight

JADIR SAT UP AS SOMEONE KNOCKED SOFTLY ON THE DOOR to his room. He stood and stepped to one side of the door.

"Jadir?" said a low voice from the other side. "It's Phana. I need to speak to you."

Despite himself, Jadir's heart started beating faster. No matter what had happened, he couldn't make himself forget the connection that had existed between them. They had been starting something, before Marilsa became a witch and Jadir discovered he was....

He pulled open the door to find Phana standing in the hallway outside. She glanced nervously at Marilsa's door and stepped into the room with Jadir. He pushed the door closed and looked down at her. She shivered and stepped back from him.

So, I still repel you, he thought.

"What brings you here?" he asked her. "What's wrong?"

She frowned at him, but the truth was Phana wasn't likely to come see him unless there was a problem of some kind, something he needed to know.

"How much has Koral told you about Qudovo?"

"Why would he tell me anything, Phana? It's not like anyone needs a reason to keep things from me."

He watched Phana clench her jaw, but she visibly forced herself to stop and relax.

"Jadir, I understand your bitterness about what happened. But you're not going to get any sympathy from me if you keep playing the victim. Do you hear what I'm saying? I came here to give you some news, and I want to know how much you already know. Don't make this harder than it needs to be."

Jadir forced himself to take a deep breath. He walked back to his pallet and sat down.

"You're right. I'm sorry. Please, tell me what's going on."

"Qudovo was unhappy with his orders to have the gang focus on protecting you and Marilsa. He argued with Koral about it, said that it was harming business. But the Wolf gets what the Wolf wants, and Qudovo was told he didn't have a choice. So he gathered those members of the gang who felt the same way, and they split."

"Qudovo is no longer in charge of the gang? Who is?"

"At the moment, I guess Koral is in charge."

"How many joined Qudovo?"

Phana swallowed. "Nine or ten."

"That's a third of the gang!" Jadir blurted, shocked. "What is he going to do, form his own gang?"

"Not exactly. Jadir, Qudovo tried to kill me two nights ago. He's trying to start a war with the Wolf."

"What? Why would he attack you?"

"Because I'm the one who brought you into the gang, and I'm also under the protection of the Wolf. Qudovo wants to kill me, and he wants to kill Koral, because that would hurt the Wolf. But he also wants to harm you and Marilsa. He blames you for most of this."

"But I—"

"It doesn't matter," Phana interrupted. "He sees you and Marilsa as the cause of his problems, and he sees me as someone who he's never been able to control. The rest of the gang had a meeting this morning at the warehouse. There ended up being three different factions."

Jadir thought about it, but could only figure out two viewpoints.

"So there's the group that wants to follow Qudovo," Jadir reasoned. "And there's the group who wants to stay loyal to the Wolf. What does the third group want?"

"The third group is loyal to Marilsa," Phana answered. "They want to stay out of the fight between Qudovo and the Wolf. Their only concern is your sister."

This news surprised Jadir. He hadn't expected anyone to jump to Marilsa's defense unless it was out of loyalty to the Wolf. But as he considered Phana's words, he remembered the three gang members he had found in her room. He remembered how they looked at Marilsa, how they were deferent to her.

Marilsa had gained followers over the past week. But how? What were they following? She was just a young girl, newly come into her power. What could she offer them in return?

"So what does all this mean?" he asked Phana.

"For now, those who remain loyal to the Wolf are working with those who are loyal to Marilsa, because their goals are aligned. However, the Wolf's people won't lay down their lives for you or your sister. They will do what they are ordered to do, and that's it. And we have no way of knowing if any of them are really spies for Qudovo."

Jadir shook his head. He couldn't understand all of this—it was getting to be too much.

"Jadir, listen to me. Qudovo is a threat. Maybe he's not a big one, not compared to the Church or the Witch Hunters, but he still wants you dead. And there are a bunch of gang members who know you and Marilsa, who agree with him and will do what he orders. I'm pretty sure I know who most of his allies are, but not all of them."

Jadir realized what that meant. Since the gang members were protecting Jadir and Marilsa, since they had full access to this building, it would be difficult to prevent the wrong people from getting close to Marilsa. They might find themselves infiltrated without realizing it.

"What is Koral doing about this?"

"The Wolf's people are hunting Qudovo. Once he's taken, his little rebellion will crumble. And that's just a matter of time. The question is how much damage he can do before that happens."

"Okay, so what can I do?"

"Jadir," Phana said slowly. "What about Marilsa? What's happening with her? Why have a bunch of tough, street-wary thugs and cutthroats decided to pledge their loyalty to a twelve-year-old girl? Has she been doing something to them, controlling their minds or something?"

Jadir sat and considered Phana's question. Could his sister be manipulating them in some way? It was possible. But something—some feeling he had—told Jadir that wasn't it. Some people were drawn to her power. He could see it in their eyes.

"I think they're looking for answers, and they think Marilsa has those answers. For some people, that's enough."

"Answers to what?"

"Whatever questions they have about their lives. I don't think Marilsa is doing anything directly. I think they're drawn to her as a source of power, of knowledge. She's not just a young woman—she's a witch."

"Okay," Phana said. "I don't understand it, but I trust you. You need to be careful, Jadir. You can't fully trust any of them, because we have no way of knowing who might be sworn to Qudovo."

"That makes my job a lot harder. But I'll do whatever I can. What will *you* do? If Qudovo is after you as well…."

Phana smiled. "I'm hoping he comes after me himself. Then I can end it quickly."

Jadir blinked at her, at how easily she spoke of killing the man she had followed as the leader of her gang.

"You'll just kill him, just like that?"

The smile left her face as she realized Jadir was unsettled by her words.

"Jadir, I will do what needs to be done. I can't afford to be squeamish."

She opened the door and glanced into the hallway. "Take care of yourself. I'll visit again to let you know if anything changes."

As she stepped into the hall, Jadir called her name. She turned and looked back at him.

"Thanks," he said. "I appreciate you coming here to warn me."

Phana gave him a fleeting grin and then pulled the door closed and was gone. Jadir sat on his pallet for some time afterward, trying to figure out what it all meant.

*   *   *

RELAEL LOCKED THE DOOR TO HIS SMALL OFFICE AND POCKETED the key. He made for the stairs that led back up to ground level, but as he came around the corner, he nearly bumped into a man who had been heading in the opposite direction.

"Brother Ochallum," the man said in a voice that sounded as if he had gravel in his throat. "I was coming to see you."

Relael stepped back and looked the man over. He wasn't young, in his early forties at least, the blond hair in his close-cropped beard and hair hiding any grey. His eyes were pale blue and stood out against his weathered and tanned skin. The man was dressed in worn leathers painted black, and a black cloak hung from his shoulders. He carried a sword on one hip and a long knife on the other.

"I don't believe I know you," Relael replied.

"I'm Tozroth. I'm a Witch Hunter."

Relael took another step back. There was always a chance the High Counselor Vorsulroth had sent one of his lackeys to remove Relael from the situation entirely. But Tozroth just laughed.

"By the Abyss, you're a suspicious lot, aren't ye? No doubt this place breeds it into ye," said Tozroth, looking at the walls and ceiling of the passage. "But ye have no worries about me—I'm here to talk, not spill anyone's blood."

Relael didn't relax, but he smiled back at the other man. There was no need to be unfriendly.

"Caution is sometimes necessary, even here in the heart of the Empire."

Especially here, in the heart of the Empire, he wanted to add, but kept that observation to himself.

"Listen," said Tozroth. "My Exalted Brother and your Exalted Sister are at odds. I've been given a job, and been told you're standing in my way. But I like politics even less than I like witches, and so I decided to come see ye directly—find out what the real problem is. I had to ask four different priests where you were, but now we're both here, so we may as well talk."

He speaks plainly enough, but is it real or just an act? Is he trying to get me to underestimate him?

Relael wasn't going to trust the Witch Hunter, but he was convinced the man meant him no harm. At least, not yet.

"I'm more than willing to tell you what I can about the current situation. You understand, of course, that I cannot share everything, but I see no reason why we cannot come to a mutual understanding."

Tozroth's mouth twisted in a grimace as Relael spoke, as if he didn't appreciate the evasive language Relael was using. But the Witch Hunter nodded anyway.

"Okay, you got somewhere we can talk?"

"Follow me."

Relael led the Witch Hunter back down the long hallway that ran under the building. One level below was another passage that stretched the length of this street and connected directly to the Temple, less than a block away. When the two men reached the center of the long passage, Relael stopped.

"This is as good a place as any."

Tozroth looked confused.

"Don't you have anywhere private?"

"I have an office, but it's barely large enough for me, and I doubt you'd fancy me having to sit in your lap. Besides, privacy is relative. This hallway allows us to see or hear anyone coming long before they can eavesdrop on our conversation—unless you plan to yell at me, of course. I cannot guarantee my office will provide that same safety."

Tozroth looked up and down the hallway and snorted in what Relael took to be amusement.

"Okay, then," the Witch Hunter said. "Tell me what's happening, where the problem is."

"What problem is that?" Relael asked.

"The problem that's stopping me from finding that little girl and putting three feet of steel through her chest. She and her brother killed Yanan. I'm led to believe you know where in this city she's hiding, but for some reason you and your sect want her to stay alive."

"I'm afraid you've got the truth of it," replied Relael. "That's the crux of the matter. The girl is part of a bigger operation that I'm conducting, and your fellow Witch Hunter stumbled into it and got himself killed before I could warn him off. I will be more than happy to give the girl to you and your High Counselor once I'm finished with her, but the Exalted Brother wants his vengeance and does not feel like waiting."

"I don't much feel like waiting, either," said Tozroth, no longer smiling.

"I'm sorry your friend was killed—"

"Yanan was far from my friend," Tozroth interrupted. "Didn't much like him at all, really. But that's not the point. There's a witch in Ythis, and ye know where she is. She's killed one of us, but for some reason ye're protecting her. I can't help thinking ye'd be on our side if she had slaughtered a priest."

Relael understood the man's position and could sympathize with it. But he wasn't going to share his plans with anyone who didn't need to know.

"You obviously don't agree with my position, but I hope at least you understand it. What I'm doing is for the good of the Church— *all* of the Church, including your sect. You have no reason to trust me, of course. But I'm telling you the truth when I say I have no desire to keep this girl alive, except for what she's about to do. And once that is done, I will throw every resource I have behind you to help you capture and kill her as quickly as possible."

"And in the meantime, I'm just supposed to wait, is that it? She's just a tool to ye, to be used for yer own ends. But I know how dangerous that is, because I know who she really is."

"Then please enlighten me," Relael replied. "If there's information you have that could change this situation, then I encourage you to share it. High Counselor Vorsulroth shared nothing but threats."

Tozroth snorted again. "Yeah, he didn't get where he is by being friendly. Listen, we've been hunting the girl since before she was born. Her mother was a witch in Jh'tira, and too many suffered at her hands, and the hands of her coven. When the Witch Hunters finally caught up with her, she killed four of them—four! Do ye have any idea how hard that is?"

Relael shook his head.

"She was powerful, Ineir was. And her daughter would be at least as powerful, perhaps e'en more so. And the girl will end up being a nasty piece o' work, too. I know ye think ye have things under control, but you can't predict what that girl will do. Ineir sent her daughter away to be left in an orphanage in Ythis because she knew she was going to die and wouldn't be able to protect the girl."

Tozroth ran a hand over his head, his eyes wide.

"That bloodline needs to be stamped out. She's too dangerous to leave alive, even for a few more days. Once she comes fully into her power, there's no telling what she'll do. But her mother led us on a merry chase across the half the Empire. If the girl slips away...."

Relael finally understood the man's concern. Perhaps Tozroth was overstating his case, but Relael had a bad feeling the situation could too easily get out of his control. But he had gambled everything on this, and was in no position to stop now.

"Believe me when say I don't want to be your enemy, Tozroth. I intend for this girl to die. But the Church has many enemies, and I need this girl for my plans right now. I swear to you I will help you bring her down once this is over. I'm not going to give her up now, however. What I do is too important, no matter the risk."

Tozroth looked into Relael's eyes for a moment, and then shook his head slowly.

"I didn't think ye'd give her up easily. I believe ye've made a big mistake, but I can't make ye tell me what I want to know. I don't want to be yer enemy either, Brother. That doesn't mean I'm not going to keep hunting her, though. And if I get to her first, she dies, and to the Abyss with your plans."

"Then I'm going to hope I can finish what I need to do before you succeed," Relael replied. "And if I do, you'll be the first to know where she is."

Tozroth was obviously not happy, but he gave Relael a final nod and turned and strode away. Relael had known this wouldn't be easy, but now he was in a race against a sect of his own church.

Chapter Twenty-Nine

J ADIR SAT UP STRAIGHT AND STILLED HIS BREATHING, TRYING to hear the slight noises from the other room where Marilsa practiced her magic. He knew there were three members of the gang in there with his sister. When he had asked what they were doing, she brushed off his question and ordered him to stay out her room for the evening.

But Jadir was filled with dread, a feeling that had no specific source he could discern. This wasn't his normal fear of something bad happening to Marilsa. It wasn't the constant worry about the Witch Hunters or the Church or what seemed like their endlessly growing list of enemies. No, the cold lump of lead in his stomach had slowly grown over the course of the afternoon and evening, and now filled the night with a sinister air.

He knew it was more than just fear. This felt almost like some kind of warning of approaching doom. He wanted to check on Marilsa, but she was so quick to anger that he hesitated to interrupt whatever she was doing. So Jadir sat in the room, alone, exploring the feeling, trying to learn something from it, some direction perhaps.

Nothing specific was coming to him, though. He closed his eyes and focused inward, trying to let the feeling guide him, but it slowly and inexorably grew stronger as the time passed.

And then a cry broke the stillness, a girl's cry, and Jadir was on his feet without thinking and was moving toward Marilsa's room before he could fully register it wasn't his sister's voice. He yanked on the latch and shoved the door open, ready to fight.

At first, he couldn't comprehend what he was seeing. A man lay on his back, a woman on top of him. A second man was on his knees behind the woman. All three of them were completely naked, and Jadir recognized them as members of the gang. The woman threw back her head and cried out again, a sound not of alarm, but of lust.

The men—*both* men—were having sex with the woman at the same time. Jadir glanced around and saw Marilsa standing against the wall, a look of intense concentration on her face as she watched the woman writhe under the attentions of the two men.

Jadir's vision went red—how *dare* these people do this in front of his innocent sister!

Without thinking Jadir lunged forward and grabbed the crouching man by the throat and picked him up effortlessly. The man's eyes went wide and he wrapped his hands around Jadir's wrist, but Jadir slammed the man backward into the wooden wall, which cracked from the force of the blow.

The man's eyes rolled up in his head and he lost consciousness as Jadir dropped him. The woman twisted around to see Jadir coming toward her, his hand outstretched, and she opened her mouth to scream....

"Jadir, stop!"

Marilsa didn't yell, but once again her voice froze him in his tracks, as if he had just walked into a stone wall. The woman rolled off the man and scrambled away from Jadir, and the man followed her.

"Marilsa—" Jadir said in a voice that was barely audible even to him. As he looked at her, all expression drained from her face. It was like looking at someone who had just died in their sleep. Only her eyes moved, only her eyes seemed to have any spark.

"Why did you disobey me?" she asked slowly.

"What—what is going on in here? Why were they—?"

"I told you not to disturb me tonight," she replied. "But you have come in here, interrupted my work, harmed one of my...my friends. You will explain yourself to me, Jadir. *Now.*"

He blinked at her. The way she was talking to him, as if he worked for her, as if he wasn't her brother...but he *wasn't* her brother, was he? His sole purpose was to serve her.

"I heard a cry...," he mumbled, his tongue thick as if he had just woken from a deep sleep. "I thought you were in danger."

"Have I not told you I am more than capable of handling any kind of danger that'll come for me here? If I need you, I will summon you. And when I say I wish to not be disturbed, then you will *not* disturb me. If my words are not enough to get you to understand, perhaps I need to do something more...lasting."

What was she saying? Did she really consider the possibility of using her magic on him?

"Get dressed," she said, and it took a moment for Jadir to realize she was talking to the others, as her eyes never left his. He heard the man and woman gather their clothes and dress themselves.

"What about him?" the man asked, and Marilsa broke eye contact with Jadir to look at the third man, still unconscious from Jadir's attack.

She stepped past Jadir and knelt beside the naked man. Placing her small hand on his sweaty chest, she began whispering just low enough that Jadir couldn't make out her words. Suddenly, the man's eyes snapped open and he gazed up at Marilsa with an intensity that made Jadir uncomfortable.

Marilsa stood and moved back, and the man slowly pushed himself to his feet. He looked around the room as if seeing it for the first time, and then his gaze locked on Jadir. The man grimaced and his fists clenched, as if he wanted to start another fight.

But the woman walked over to him and took his arm. She turned to Marilsa.

"Thank you for healing him."

"I did not heal him," Marilsa replied. "He's too injured for that, and I cannot spend all my strength right now. If he survives the night, he might eventually be okay. Please take his body somewhere safe."

Jadir was about to ask Marilsa what she meant by "his body" but she turned to the naked man.

"Follow them and do what they tell you. When the body is safe, return to me."

The man nodded once, and the woman let go of his arm and

stepped back away from him. She looked from Marilsa to the man as comprehension dawned on her face. Marilsa merely nodded at her.

"Now you see my power at work," she said to the woman.

The other man opened the door and he and the woman led the naked man out of the room. As he turned his back to Jadir, his head wound was visible. It looked like the back of his skull had been crushed from the collision with the wall. The man left the room and closed the door behind him.

Jadir turned back to Marilsa.

"How is he able to walk? It looks like I broke his skull."

"You did. He will most likely be dead by morning because of your mistake. But his body cannot stay in my room."

"Doesn't he feel any pain?" Jadir asked. "What did you do to him?"

Marilsa stepped close to Jadir and looked up into his face.

"I asked my *incubo* to move his body for me."

Jadir felt dizzy as he realized what Marilsa had done. The man he had attacked was still unconscious—his body moving because it was possessed by Marilsa's *incubo*.

"How...?" he drifted off, not knowing what question to ask.

"My power is growing, Jadir. Faster than I was led to expect. And that means my *incubo*'s power is growing, too. Possession is very difficult—few witches can do it. But *I* can."

She smiled at him, but there was no humor or happiness in it. Her expression frightened Jadir.

"Marilsa—" he started to say, but she interrupted him again.

"You probably just killed an innocent man, Jadir. I would think you'd be remorseful, but you're not feeling anything, are you?"

And Jadir realized she was right. He didn't feel any remorse, only discomfort at what Marilsa had done.

What is happening to me?

"Good," she said to him. "It is time you came to accept what you are, what *I* am. Now leave me. I have things that I must finish tonight, and I cannot spare the time right now to punish you for your interruption. It will have to wait until tomorrow."

"Punish me?" he asked. "You don't get to order me around and declare you're going to punish me—"

"You will leave now," she said and turned away from him.

Jadir sat down on his sleeping pallet and leaned back against the wall. He knew he had wanted to do something, but all he remembered was saying goodnight to his sister and walking back to his own room. He hadn't told her about his growing feeling of dread—he didn't want to worry her, and something had distracted him when he went in to talk to her, but he couldn't put his finger on exactly what had happened.

He shook his head and then closed his eyes. It must just be exhaustion. Jadir was sure he would remember in the morning.

*   *   *

PHANA KNELT IN THE DARKNESS OF THE ALLEY. THEY WERE hunting her, and she was sure they had her surrounded. She had counted three men, but she knew there would be more. Qudovo wouldn't take any chances.

She had spotted just the one crossbow, and the rest would have knives and short swords. They would try to distract her while the crossbowman would take her by surprise. Only it wasn't a surprise anymore. They still had an advantage, but wasn't nearly as large as they expected.

"Don't bother hiding, Phana. There's no way out."

Qudovo stood in the open street, calling out to her. He didn't know exactly where she was, but had a general idea. His followers were closing in on her while he tried to keep her occupied with his taunting.

"Your boyfriend Koral thought he was quite the swordsman, but he learned the hard way not to mess with me. I wonder what the Wolf will do when Koral's head is delivered to him."

Phana knew Qudovo was bluffing. She had already heard about the fight on the street earlier in the afternoon, and from what everyone was saying, Koral had escaped unscathed after killing a couple of Qudovo's men.

She heard a slight noise behind her, and she froze in the shadows. One of the hunters was approaching slowly, checking every nook and cranny for her. There were two more on the rooftops on either side of the alley, keeping pace with the man below. One of them would have the crossbow. He was the only real threat.

Phana could hear her blood start to pound in her ears. If she was going to survive this night, she could not afford to fight fair. As much as she hated it, it was time to let go of her control. It was time to let her blood go wild.

She almost gasped aloud as ice began flowing through her veins. It was difficult not to revel in the power it gave her, though she knew she must try her best to use it sparingly and then shove it back down into the dark hole inside herself where it dwelt.

Perhaps the Wolf knew her history, too. If he had known about Marilsa and Jadir all this time, he might also know where Phana had come from, what was inside her that let her do the terrible things she sometimes did.

The hunter in the alley had nearly reached her. It wasn't time for thoughtful deliberation. It was time to turn the tide.

She stood and stepped out of the alley into the street. Qudovo didn't see her at first, but the man in the alley behind her shouted as she left the safety of the shadows. Qudovo turned as she stepped out into the middle of the street and began to walk towards him.

"How precious. Come to avenge your dead lover, Phana?"

"I let you live once before," she replied. "Tonight I fix that mistake."

She could sense the other man come out of the alley and take up a position behind her but some distance back so as not to get in the way of the crossbowman. They still thought she didn't know about man on the rooftop.

Phana concentrated and her blood grew ever colder. Qudovo strode forward until he was a dozen paces away and then stopped and drew his long knife.

"You think you're a tough bitch, don't you? You think you're just going to kill me. But it's not going to go the way you want, not anymore. I'm going to gut you, and then take your head. I was going to send it to the Wolf, but I might just keep it for my own amusement. Maybe hollow it out and use it for my chamber pot."

He was stalling, waiting for the crossbowman to get into position. Phana didn't know what kind of bolt the man was using, but she was pretty sure it would be something special. Qudovo wouldn't take any chances she might survive it. Poisoned, perhaps, or cursed in some manner. Either way, if it hit her, she would likely die.

Her blood had almost turned to ice, and she wondered if Qudovo could feel the cold coming from her. It didn't matter—the warning wouldn't save him. She knew the crossbowman was settling in, adjusting his aim, preparing to release the bolt. Phana would have to time her movements precisely.

"You were never much of a leader, Qudovo. It was only a matter of time before it all went to shit in your hands. You should have begged for whatever the Wolf would give you, but instead you doomed yourself and all those who follow you. You'll be forgotten before the year is out."

He snarled at her but didn't attack, didn't move. It was time. She opened her arms and smiled at him.

"Jadir and I laughed at you when you were forced to take him in. And Koral and I laughed at you when you thought you might be a threat to the Wolf. I'm still laughing at you, Qudovo. I don't even need to draw a weapon. You're so pathetic you'll probably stab yourself to death and I'll just stand here and keep laughing."

She stepped toward him, as if to lunge, and he lurched forward, jabbing his knife at her throat. At that instant, she let go of the frost filling her veins as the blade drove into her neck and out the other side. Qudovo's arm followed as he was thrown off balance when the blade met no resistance. Phana stepped forward, stepped *through* Qudovo as if she were no more than a spirit as he stumbled.

The impact of the crossbow bolt in his chest stopped him in his tracks. Phana turned around and mentally clamped down on the cold, pulling herself back into the world. She was behind Qudovo, and she could see the frost covering his hair, his skin, as if he had lain in a field through a winter's night in the north.

He dropped the knife as he sank to his knees and gasped for

breath.

"How...?"

Phana stepped up to him and put her foot on the hilt of the knife. He looked up at her and his eyes were wide with fear.

"I don't know," she told him. "But I warned you. You could have survived this."

He lowered his face to look down at the bolt sticking out of his chest.

"What's on it," she asked. "Poison?"

"Yeah," he said, his voice slurring. "Couldn't take any chances...."

Qudovo toppled over to one side and his ragged breathing slowed, and then stopped. Phana stood there a moment, looking down at him, and then she raised her head and found the man who had hunted her through the alleys.

"There was only one way this was going to end," she said to him. He looked from Phana to Qudovo's body and back.

"H-he was our leader. What were we supposed to do? We'd sworn to follow him...."

Phana could tell the crossbowman on the roof was trying to sneak away. He couldn't escape her sight, not when the ice was flowing through her veins.

"Run," she said, and though she spoke in a low voice, she knew all three men could hear her clearly. "If you hide, you die. But if you can keep running long enough, I may be able to get this back under control before I kill you all."

The man on the street near her began to back away, but he wasn't nearly fast enough or far enough to save himself.

"Ready or not, here I come," she said. And then the cold began to flow once more.

Chapter Thirty

JADIR WOKE UP, HIS HEAD POUNDING. THE SUN WAS JUST setting outside, and he realized he had slept through the rest of the night and the entire day. Now his skull felt as if it was about to split open from the pressure inside.

He slowly pulled himself up into a sitting position and gently rested his head in his hands. Jadir didn't remember ever being sick before. It wasn't an experience he wanted to prolong. He wondered for a moment if he should ask Marilsa if she could help him, but he felt uncomfortable bothering her.

Still, Jadir knew he couldn't stay like this. If something was really wrong with him, his sister needed to know. He pushed himself to his feet and found his balance was shaky. Opening the door to his room, he peered out into the hallway and saw that Marilsa's door was partially open.

A pool of blood was visible on the floor beyond.

Jadir's stomach lurched and he tried to focus past the pain in his head. He wanted to charge in and eliminate any threat to his sister, but something held him back from such a reckless action. Instead, he crept toward the doorway as quietly as someone his size was able to move.

Jadir listened, but could hear no sound from inside the room. He reached out and pushed the door fully open. Two bodies lay on the floor, both leaking blood from multiple wounds to their chests.

Neither of the bodies belonged to Marilsa.

Jadir looked down at the bodies and recognized the two corpses—members of the gang who had not been assigned to watch over

Jadir and his sister. What had they been doing here? Had they come to attack Marilsa? Had the other gang members slain them and then taken Marilsa away?

Something in the back of Jadir's mind tugged at him, and he looked up at the ceiling. He had an urge to head for the roof of the building, though he could not have said why. Not knowing what else to do, he let himself follow the urge, and found the ladder leading to the roof hatch. He climbed it and shoved the hatch door open.

Raising his head above the level of the roof, Jadir almost gasped aloud at the sight that greeted him.

Marilsa stood at the very edge of the rooftop, her back to him, surrounded by a dozen members of the gang. They all faced the same direction, standing motionless on the roof, while on their left the last sliver of sun disappeared from where the sky met the city's horizon. Directly in front of them, a few blocks away and much nearer than Jadir wished, a column of black smoke rose into the air from the top of the Tower of Ash.

"You should join us, Jadir," Marilsa called to him, without turning. None of the rest of the gang so much as twitched. He climbed up the rest of the way onto the roof.

"Marilsa...what are you doing?"

She raised one thin arm and pointed at the Tower.

"That," she said, "is our destination."

Jadir took a step toward her, and as one all twelve of her companions turned to face him. Marilsa still faced the Tower.

"Marilsa, you don't want to go there. The sorcerers would kill you. They hate what you are as much as the Church does."

"That is where I must go," she replied.

"Why?"

"I...," she hesitated.

"Marilsa, please."

"That is where I *must* go," she repeated. "And my travel there will become the stuff of legend."

"Marilsa, I don't understand what's happening to you, to us. Please just talk to me. Let's go back to your...to my room and talk about all this. I want to understand, I want to help."

Finally, Marilsa lowered her arm and turned to face Jadir. She didn't step away from the very edge of the rooftop, and the four-story drop yawned behind her as she stood there, looking at him.

"It's a bit late for that, my brother. Time is against me, and I do...what I must."

She stepped away from the edge, toward him, and as she did so, all the other figures on the rooftop did the same.

"I would offer for you to come with me, but I need people I can trust. And you would not approve of what is about to happen. You have already failed me, Jadir, and I cannot see any reason to give you a chance to fail me again."

"How?" he asked. "How have I failed you? I protected you, took care of you, did everything you asked of me."

She took another step, and her dozen followers stepped toward Jadir in unison. The closest were only a few paces away, now.

"There are forces at work here greater than anything you can handle, Jadir. You were summoned to protect a baby, and then a child. Your purpose was to hide me, to care for me, when no one knew who I was. It was a simple job, and you were adequate. But when the situation changed, when real threats started to appear, you thought you could still protect me."

Something in Marilsa's voice changed, as if she was growling out her words, as if someone older was using her throat to speak the words.

"You are just a simple spirit, and yet you think you are so much more. Such hubris, Jadir, and now so many others, including me, will pay the price."

She raised her arm once more, but this time, she pointed at Jadir. "Take him."

Her followers—no longer members of the gang, but now members of Marilsa's coven—surged forward. Jadir intended to fight them. He was larger than them all, and much stronger, and even in such numbers he thought he might win through to his sister.

But the pain in his head exploded and he screamed as his legs collapsed beneath him. He gripped his skull and then fists and boots rained down on him from all directions. Jadir fell to his side and curled up in a fetal position, his arms wrapped around his head, as Marilsa's coven beat on him.

Jadir could barely breathe through the pain, and his limbs felt weak. The pounding went on for what seemed like an eternity before Marilsa's voice cut through the night and ordered her coven to stop. They grabbed his arms and forced him to sit up on his knees as Marilsa came to stand before him.

"You are bound to this body, Jadir. It died once before, and it can die again. And when it does, you will be released and drawn back into the void from which you were created."

She stepped back and gestured, and the men holding Jadir's arms began to drag him toward the edge of the roof.

"Marilsa!" he screamed. "Please, Marilsa, don't do this! Let me help you!"

She said nothing as the men hauled him up to the edge. He looked down at the uneven cobblestones far below.

He felt her step up to one side, and he twisted his head to look at her. He blinked a few times before realizing, in the rapidly fading light, he could see the man standing beside her, the man who had first given her such nightmares.

Jadir could see Marilsa's *incubo*.

The creature leaned forward and appeared to be whispering into Marilsa's ear, though Jadir could not hear the words. Marilsa looked into Jadir's eyes, and the men holding him waited for her to give the final order to throw him from the roof.

"Please," he whispered.

Her *incubo* leaned even closer to her and seemed to speak more rapidly into her ear. She frowned, and then flicked her hand and the *incubo* seemed to fly apart into wisps of smoke.

"Leave him," she said, and turned away. The men flung Jadir onto his back, away from the roof's edge. He rolled over to see her return to the hatch and climb down, followed by the members of her coven.

Jadir tried to push himself upright, but he couldn't get his arms and legs to move properly. He watched the coven leave the rooftop, and then he was alone.

He did not know what had happened to Marilsa, what she had

become. All he knew was that the girl he had care for all her life was lost to him now. She had let him live, but he wasn't sure that was any act of kindness on her part. He was connected to her in ways he would never fully understand.

And yet, there was now a gulf between them that seemed un-crossable.

*   *   *

JADIR DID NOT MOVE. HE LAY ON HIS BACK, STARING UP AT THE stars above, trying to make sense of everything that had happened.

Marilsa was gone. She had become someone alien to him, a witch of great power with unknown goals, who was willing to kill.

Or was she? She had certainly been ready to have him thrown off the rooftop, and yet had changed her mind and left him here, beaten but alive. And the bodies in her room downstairs? Had she given the order for those two people to die, or had her coven protected her from an attack?

Jadir didn't know what to believe. All he knew for sure was that he had lost her. She had turned on him, blamed him for whatever was happening to her. And now she was gone…

…to the Tower of Ash.

Why? What did she want with the Tower and its inhabitant? The sorcerer would kill Marilsa—no matter how powerful his sister was, Jadir knew she was nothing compared to the power wielded by the sorcerers of Ythis. And yet his sister was convinced that was where she needed to go.

Tears made the stars blur and shift above him. Marilsa was go-ing to her death, and there was nothing he could do to stop her, to protect her from herself. All he had ever wanted was for Marilsa to be safe and happy. And he had failed.

She told him that herself. His failure was in thinking he could keep her safe from threats like the Church.

But…hadn't he done just that? When she was attacked by the Witch Hunters, he had arrived in time to save her life. When the priests came to watch her, he had managed to help her escape and hide where they couldn't find her.

And he had succeeded—the black carriage had not been seen since they came into the Warren.

With a guilty start, he remembered how hard he had argued against coming here. Koral had suggested the Warren, and Jadir had fought him every step of the way until Marilsa had declared this was where they were moving. It was Koral who had found them this place to hide, not him.

Jadir rolled over onto his left side, his muscles aching from the pounding he had taken at the hands of Marilsa's coven. He couldn't help but let out a low groan, which turned into a sob.

He was nothing. Just a spirit conjured out of—what, the Abyss?—whose sole purpose had been to keep Marilsa safe. He had never even known what he really was. And now his job was over, and his life had no further purpose. He wasn't even human.

What had the Church wanted with Marilsa? The thought kept swirling back into his mind, over and over. They could have attacked at any time, but they didn't.

"You play a game you do not understand, with powers beyond your comprehension."

Those were the words the priestess had said to him. What game was the Church playing? First, they had tried to kill Marilsa, and then they had done nothing but watch and wait.

What had they been waiting for?

Could tonight have been it? Marilsa had formed her coven, and had pushed Jadir away for good. And, for some reason unknown to Jadir, Marilsa had declared she must go to the Tower of Ash.

But the sorcerers and the Church were bitter enemies. Everyone knew they constantly worked against each other, and cared nothing for whoever got caught in the middle. They would do anything to weaken or destroy their rivals.

And they cared nothing for whoever got caught in the middle.

Why was Marilsa really going to the Tower?

"That is where I must go. And my travel there will become the stuff of legend."

What did she mean by that? It was barely a ten-minute walk to the burnt and broken ground where the Tower sat. What would she do between here and there that would be so notable it would become legendary?

And why did she feel she must go there? To the enemy of the Church, the same Church who had done nothing to harm her after that first attack by the Witch Hunter.

Maybe...maybe that one Witch Hunter had been working on his own. What if he had tried to kill Marilsa without informing the Church? What if the Church had wanted Marilsa for their own plans? The black carriage had been there the night he attacked Marilsa, and yet the priestess had not interfered, even when Jadir had arrived and started killing.

But even if the Church wanted Marilsa to go attack the sorcerer in the Tower of Ash...how did they know she would do such a thing? It was a crazy idea—there was little chance Marilsa would survive it. Did she have enough power now to truly challenge a sorcerer and win?

"You play a game you do not understand, with powers beyond your comprehension."

Maybe the priestess was right, and Jadir was guessing wildly at something he couldn't ever understand. But it felt like pieces of a puzzle were beginning to fit together, and if he was still missing a few vital bits of information, he thought he might be starting to understand the overall picture.

The Church wanted to weaken or destroy the sorcerers. Marilsa, a powerful witch, was now going to the Tower of Ash. If she fought the sorcerer, she would likely die. But what might she do to the sorcerer or the Tower before she fell?

They cared nothing for whoever got caught in the middle.

Was the Church using Marilsa to attack the Tower of Ash? Was she just a pawn, thrown against an enemy she could not possibly defeat, just to see how much damage she could inflict before she was destroyed?

No, it could not be that simple. Jadir did not understand how the priestess could get Marilsa to do what she wanted just by watching her. And the priestess could not have known they would come to the Warren to hide. It had been Koral's idea.

"Whichever one is closer to the Tower of Ash is the one I want to try first."

Marilsa had said that when they decided to hide in the Warren. Jadir had forgotten about it at the time. But Marilsa had been thinking about the Tower even then.

Somehow, Marilsa was doing the Church's bidding. She probably didn't even know it, but they had set her on a path of their choosing, and she was blindly following it to her own death.

And Jadir was powerless to stop her.

Despair swept over him in a wave. He couldn't do it, couldn't save the one person who had been family to him for so long. The very person he was created to protect. Marilsa was going to her death and he could do nothing.

No.

Jadir rolled over onto his stomach and pushed himself onto his hands and knees. A grunt of pain escaped from between his clenched teeth.

He wouldn't let Marilsa march blindly into her destruction at the hands of whatever sorcerer lived in the Tower of Ash. He wouldn't let the Church sacrifice her to play their games against each other. He was Marilsa's protector, and whether she knew it or not, she still needed him.

Jadir rose to his feet and stumbled toward the trap door. He had to reach the Tower before Marilsa, had to tell her the truth about what the Church was doing.

She had to see she was being used.

Once she knew the truth, she would see their manipulations, would understand that Jadir was still here for her, would see that he hadn't failed her, after all.

The climb down the ladder was agony, but he forced himself to move quickly. He had to catch his sister before she reached the Tower.

And time was running out.

Chapter Thirty-One

J ADIR STUMBLED AS HE STEPPED OUT ONTO THE STREET AND nearly fell to his knees. He immediately looked around to see if anyone had witnessed his weakness—he didn't have time to deal with anyone in the Warren who might see him as a victim— but the street was empty of people.

He glanced up at the column of smoke and ash rising into the air and tried to get his bearings. There were few direct routes in the Warren. Most streets twisted and turned, sometimes narrowing to alleys, sometimes simply ending at a collapsed building or other blockage. At least Jadir had a visible marker in the sky to lead him in the right direction.

He was worried about Marilsa's followers. He needed to get close enough to her to speak, but the members of her coven might attack him out of hand if they saw him. He couldn't sneak around, though, as he knew he must catch her before she reached the Tower.

Jadir forced himself into a jog as he rounded a corner and saw the street in front of him curve away from the Tower. He hoped there was another branch up ahead that would let him loop back in the direction of his destination. If not, he was losing precious time.

He did eventually find another cross-street, and he turned and began to work his way back in the direction of the Tower of Ash. The nighttime denizens of the Warren were beginning to come out, and he passed pairs and small groups who watched him with cold eyes and unfriendly expressions. He hoped his size would intimidate anyone looking for an easy mark.

A light breeze brought him the scent of burning wood, and he looked around for the source before noticing a slight haze in the air around him. He stepped around another corner and found himself facing a scene of destruction.

He stood at one end of a short street that appeared to lead toward the Tower of Ash. Where Jadir stood, the buildings were decrepit but intact, the wood scarred and pitted, yet unburnt. But these stood shoulder-to-shoulder with smoking ruins. Blackened beams and partially collapsed structures framed the far end of the street, leading to an open courtyard full of drifting smoke.

Jadir stepped forward and immediately began to cough as the foul air filled his lungs. He put his arm across his mouth and tried to filter out the worst of the smoke as he proceeded. He reached the end of the street and looked across the courtyard at the twisted, misshapen Tower of Ash that rose above the surrounding buildings.

He stumbled on the uneven ground, melted cobblestones and blackened bits of metal creating treacherous footing in the courtyard. In the smoky haze, he tried to see if any other streets led into this area. In the darkness and the drifting smoke, he thought he could make out only one other entrance to the courtyard on the north side, leading away from the Warren.

For once, something had gone his way. He knew it would be unlikely for Marilsa to approach the Tower of Ash from that direction. She would have to leave the Warren entirely to reach that particular street, and he was sure she would stay in the relative "safety" of the most dangerous part of Ythis.

And then a horrid thought struck him—Marilsa may have reached the Tower before him and was already inside. If that was the case, he had lost her for good.

He moved out into the broken courtyard, tumbled stones and burnt and blackened remnants of the buildings that had filled this area before the Tower appeared, nearly tripping him up every few paces. Jadir searched for any sign that someone had passed this way recently. The smoke continued to scratch at his throat, and his eyes watered in a continuous stream down his cheeks.

He turned and looked up at the Tower, its twisted angles and strange protrusions making his stomach queasy for no reason he could discern. A single, black iron door pierced the jumbled collection of stones that made up the walls of the tower, but no window was visible from where he stood.

Jadir moved closer to the door, and a movement to his left caught his eye. He turned to see a hunched, misshapen figure duck down behind a small pile of rubble. Another movement further left spun him around, but all he caught was a glimpse of something that only vaguely resembled a human—all flying hair and twisted limbs.

He realized he had moved within reach of the great iron door, and turning back to it he saw how massive it was, twice his own height and three times his width. It had not seemed so large from the edge of the courtyard, and he wondered if it was a trick of the smoke or some kind of sorcery.

It struck him that he was standing at the entrance to the Tower of Ash, at the entrance to a sorcerer's abode, and he threw himself away from the door and back toward the street that led to the Warren. A hand with only three thick fingers and long, ragged nails snatched at him from behind a fallen stone block as he passed, and he kept running until he was back at the far end of the street that led to this foul place.

Jadir turned and faced the entrance to the Tower's courtyard, but no other creatures were visible in the haze. It appeared the figures would not pursue him out of the cloaking smoke.

And then he screamed as a blinding pain ripped through his head, his vision going white as he dropped to his knees, his hands gripping his skull to stop it from exploding.

Two of Marilsa's coven members held a man against a wooden wall while a third pounded thick iron spikes into the man's open palms.

A woman was grabbed from behind and a knife came around to sweep across her throat. The spray of blood made strange patterns on the floor, patterns that Jadir felt he should know, patterns that hearkened back to the primal energies that formed this world.

Two children were shoved together, and they screamed as they looked into each other's eyes, while Marilsa's followers sewed their faces together with blood-red twine.

The naked, writhing bodies of the coven, covered in the blood of their victims, flashed in the light of a swinging lantern, while Marilsa stood above and sang an alien song in a voice not her own.

And just as abruptly as it had begun, the visions disappeared, and with it went the white-hot spike that had driven into his brain. He lay on his back in the street, gasping for breath. He knew he couldn't stay here—someone would come to rob him of anything of value if he didn't regain his feet quickly.

Jadir pushed himself up and looked around, clenching his fists, trying to project an aura of menace, but he was alone. Of course this street would be effectively deserted at all times. Practically no one would come near a sorcerer's tower willingly.

Except himself... and, well, Marilsa.

But Marilsa had not come straight to the Tower of Ash. No, Jadir had gotten a glimpse of her, in some building not terribly far from where he stood. He could feel her presence, but couldn't tell which direction from which the sense came.

Marilsa was conducting some sort of horrid ritual, using the in-nocent people of the Warren as sacrifices, and it was happening *right now.* And Jadir knew there was nothing he could do. While he could sense her in a general way, he didn't know how to follow that sense to wherever she was. And alone, he knew he could do little to stop her.

At best, he would be beaten and left behind again. At worst, her coven members would tear him apart. Jadir needed help. But there were only two people he trusted, only two people who might really put themselves in danger for him and his sister.

He had to find Phana and Koral.

*　　　*　　　*

RELAEL PULLED OPEN HIS OFFICE DOOR TO SEE AN ACOLYTE standing in the hall. The young man appeared sane enough, except for a slight tic at the side of his mouth—and he thrust a parch-ment into Relael's hand before darting away without saying a word. Whatever the missive was, it had been deemed important enough not to trust to a slave.

Relael stepped back into the office and closed the door. He saw the seal was that of the Office of the Oracles, and he felt his pulse quicken. Cracking the wax, he unrolled the parchment to see five written words.

The Warren. It has begun.

Relael threw the parchment onto his desk and left his office. Everything he had worked for now came down the next dozen hours. If everything went according to plan, the girl would cause a great deal of death and destruction around the Tower of Ash, and Relael would make sure she was slain while trying to stop her. The blame for this night would land at the feet of the newest sorcerer of Ythis, and the Emperor would have no choice but to demand concessions from the Six.

As he strode toward the Temple building itself, he grabbed a passing slave.

"Find the Witch Hunter named Tozroth. He'll be staying in the barracks. Tell him to meet Brother Ochallum in the Grand Hall immediately. Do you understand?"

The slave nodded, and he let go of the man's thin arm. Relael proceeded along the underground hallway to the Temple and turned towards the passage where the lesser priests had their quarters. He reached a long hallway, decorated with murals depicting the great heroes of the Church destroying demons and slaying infidels. The many doors lining this passage led to small quarters for the priests stationed in the Temple itself.

Relael was nearing Sister Xodoc's door when he saw it open. Out of habit, he ducked into an alcove and stepped behind the curtain that ringed the back wall of the display. The bust of some long-dead High Priest glared malevolently out into the hallway from the recess where Relael hid.

Booted footsteps marched past Relael, and he peeked out around the curtain to get a glimpse of Sister Xodoc's visitor. Relael almost swore out loud when he saw who it was. Though he did not know the man's name, Relael knew he was one of the underlings serving High Counselor Vorsulroth.

And why would Sister Zera Xodoc be meeting with an aid to the head of the Witch Hunters?

He stepped out of the alcove once the other man had turned the far corner and proceeded to Sister Xodoc's quarters. He rapped his knuckles on the door, and it was opened almost immediately. Relael almost couldn't hide his smile at the look of surprise on the priestess' face.

But she recovered quickly, and stepped back from the door and raised her hands, as if she was going to attack him. He realized she believed he had seen her visitor and was here to kill her for her betrayal. But as much as Relael would have loved to do exactly that, such direct confrontation wasn't his way.

Instead, he put a confused expression on his face and stepped back himself.

"What are you doing?" he demanded. Zera hesitated, her narrowed eyes trying to discern if he was bluffing or not. But Relael was a masterful liar.

"If you're still angry with me," he continued, "you'll have to kill me later. I just got a message from the Oracles. The girl has tipped over the edge."

Sister Xodoc blinked at Relael and then lowered her arms. She grabbed her cloak from the wooden peg in the wall beside the door and flung it over her shoulders.

"What is she doing now?" Zera asked.

"I can only assume she is murdering innocent citizens and making her way toward the Tower of Ash. We'll find out when we get there, but we should have some time before we intervene."

Sister Xodoc stepped out into the hallway, pulling her door closed behind her.

"Where's Brother Worestald?"

"I still have to get him," Relael replied. "And we'll have another with us, a Witch Hunter."

Zera narrowed her eyes again, wondering if Relael was going to confront her about her visitor.

"His name is Tozroth," explained Relael. "He came to see me last night to ask where the girl was hiding. I promised him I would bring him when it was time to kill her."

"Why?"

Relael shrugged. "It's politically expedient. The tension between us and the Witch Hunters is unnecessary and wasteful. I'd much rather have them as reliable allies than as vindictive enemies. I'm not going to let my personal pride weaken the Church."

He could tell Zera was seething at his words. She had taken them as he meant them—an insult to her and a reminder of her behavior in the Warren when she had wanted to kill him. He could tell she no longer believed he had seen her guest leave her quarters. She had gone back to loathing Relael, which is exactly where he wanted her.

They began to walk toward the stairs leading up to the ground floor of the Temple, but Relael turned down a side passage. Sister Xodoc stopped and called after him.

"Where are you going?"

"I need to collect Brother Worestald. I told Tozroth to meet us in the Great Hall. You go ahead and I will be there shortly. I have one other quick errand to run before we leave."

"I thought we were in a hurry," she said, and he stopped and turned around to face her.

"We have at least a few hours before there's any danger of her getting too close to the Tower. She'll try to gather as much power to herself as possible, and that means lengthy rituals and sacrifices. We've got some time—and we don't want to stop her *too* quickly. It's the damage she does that's important."

He turned and walked away, and heard Sister Xodoc depart in the other direction. Relael took the next passage that led back towards the underground tunnels. Brother Worestald could wait. Relael had more pressing matters to attend to first.

In less than ten minutes, Relael was back at Yondos' door. He reached up to knock, but heard the bolt slide back as he raised his hand. The portal swung open, and Yondos stood framed in the dim light of a lantern.

Relael said nothing, and Yondos motioned for him to enter. The door swung closed behind Relael, but he didn't bother turning to look—he knew no one would be there.

"It's time," he said to the small, chubby man.

Yondos looked Relael up and down, and then his eyes rolled in his head.

"She revels in the slaughter, and yet feels such horror at her own actions."

"Who?" Relael asked.

"The girl," Yondos replied. Relael wanted to ask how the man knew about the young witch, but he knew there would be no real answer.

"Sister Xodoc has gone too far. She needs to be removed."

"When shall I do this?"

"Immediately, if possible. If not, then as soon as you can set it in motion."

"Are you sure you don't need her? Her power could be an asset."

"No," Relael replied. "I still have Brother Worestald, and a Witch Hunter. Plus I'll be taking a contingent of Imperial Guard with me."

At the mention of the priest's name, Yondos' eyes lit up.

"Don't let anything...untoward...happen to our good Brother, Relael. You promised me—"

"I know, I know. You'll have him in your hands as soon as this is over."

Yondos smiled again, and Relael turned away from the gruesome sight.

It was time to collect his companions and send word for the Imperial Guard escort to come meet them at the Temple. Though many things could still go wrong tonight, Relael was confident all was under control.

Chapter Thirty-Two

JADIR HAD TAKEN A WRONG TURN AND FOUND HIMSELF BACK near the building where he and Marilsa had been hiding the past two days. He stopped to get his bearings and, looking around, saw his sister standing in the middle of the street, less than a dozen strides away. He blinked, unsure that what he was seeing was real, and she raised her hands towards him, palms up.

"Help me," she said, but her voice was raw and distorted. Jadir felt wetness on his feet and looked down to see the street had filled with blood. Bloated corpses floated in the crimson river, and Marilsa's voice scraped at his eardrums.

"The pull is too strong, Jadir. I will slaughter them all, and I love it. Help me!"

And then Marilsa was gone, the blood was gone, the corpses faded to nothing. Jadir rubbed his eyes and then turned to face a short building on the next block.

Marilsa was in that building.

Jadir took a few steps toward it, but then forced himself to stop. He knew he couldn't do this alone. He needed help. But getting help would take time. People were dying in that building—*right now*—and Marilsa had asked him for his help. Some part of her still wanted him to protect her, and the urge to rush to her side was nearly overwhelming.

He moved closer, keeping to the shadows of the unlit street. The sky was fully dark now, the three-quarter moon barely above the horizon. If anyone was watching from the windows of the building, it would be nearly impossible to identify Jadir in the darkness.

The building had only two stories, a wooden second floor on top of the stone walls that surrounded the ground level. It had a single entrance at the front, and the windows on the second floor—there were none on the lower level—were shuttered. A sliver of flickering light shone through the crack between them.

Jadir crossed the street and approached the door. He knew without a doubt that Marilsa was inside, upstairs with her coven and bunch of victims who most likely were already dead. She needed his help, needed him to stop her from continuing the unholy acts.

He tried the latch and found it locked, so he decided to check around the back for another door. As he stepped into the alley that ran along the side of the building, a figure lunged out of the darkness at him.

Backpedaling, Jadir tried to keep the outstretched claws from his face. He recognized his attacker as one of Marilsa's followers, but the woman no longer appeared human. Her skin was stretched over her skull, most of her hair was gone, and her fingernails had grown into talons.

Jadir had seen this woman not more than an hour earlier on the roof of the tenement. What had happened to her in such a short time? It didn't matter—she was trying to tear Jadir's throat out with those claws, and he had to stop her.

Jadir grabbed her wrists, but she was far stronger than she appeared. She drove forward and shoved him off balance, causing him to fall to the street on his back. The woman landed on his chest and he barely kept her claws from his neck.

Suddenly, she threw her arms wide and lunged at his throat with her teeth. He barely twisted away, and she tore a chunk of skin from his collarbone. Jadir tensed his muscles and shoved with all his strength. The woman was thrown to one side and Jadir rolled away and regained his feet.

But before he was fully set, she was on him again. He swung his fist and collided with the side of her head, snapping her face to one side. He planted one hand on her chest and shoved her backward and her head bounced off the wall as she fell.

When he had fought the Witch Hunters, it had been completely different. The world had moved in slow motion, and Jadir's strength had been well beyond anything he knew. But now he could do none of that. It was just him against this twisted creature.

The woman leaped to her feet, but Jadir decided to take the offensive. Before she lunged at him again, he stepped forward and drove his fist directly into her face, driving her head back into the wall again. He felt her nose shatter under his blow, and with his other hand he grabbed her neck.

The woman's claws drew long slices down his arms as Jadir held her against the wall and pounded his fist into her face again and again, until her blood, thick and dark, began to ooze from her broken skull. Eventually, her scrabbling claws slowed, and her arms dropped to her sides.

Jadir stopped beating the creature and stepped back, letting her body drop to the ground at his feet. Her face was an unrecognizable mess, and her blood dripped from his hands. He could tell he had broken one or two of his knuckles, and the wounds on his arms and chest burned as they leaked blood.

He looked around, but the few people out on the street had disappeared during his fight. He was glad he didn't have to deal with any other distractions right now. The question was whether Marilsa knew her servant had died or not. Jadir figured she was aware of the loss—whatever his sister had done to this woman had likely created some sort of link between them.

Had she been sent out here specifically to stop Jadir, or was she just a guard against unwanted intrusion? He had no way to know. He stepped into the dark alley and walked to the rear of the building.

Jadir let out a frustrated growl as he found no other entrance. If he broke through the front door, it would warn the rest of the coven that he was coming. If more of them had turned into creatures like that woman, he would be unable to face multiple attackers at the same time. He would fall under their claws, and Marilsa would never be saved.

Jadir felt trapped. He knew he should go get help, but he found it nearly impossible to just leave Marilsa in this building, not while she was so close. But he couldn't see how he could reach her and do whatever it was he needed to do to help her. There was no way the coven would let him get near her.

As much as he hated the idea, he would have to leave the Warren and find Phana and Koral, and anyone else who would help him. Jadir stepped out of the alley and found the woman's body was gone. The pools of blood marked where he had dropped her, but she was no longer there.

A sound from above caused him to look up, and he spotted her climbing over the lip of the roof, like some giant insect creeping up the side of a wall. She disappeared over the edge and was gone.

How could she have survived what he had done to her? There was no doubt in his mind he had killed her by shattering her skull. And yet she still lived somehow.

What had Marilsa turned her into?

He forced himself to turn and jog away from the building. Every instinct was calling him back there, but he knew that if he went back it would be to his death. So he ran along the street and tried to figure out the fastest way to get out of the Warren and back to the Crown and Coin.

Whatever he must do to save his sister, he would find a way to accomplish. He could do nothing less.

*　　　　*　　　　*

PHANA SAT ON THE FLOOR OF AN ALLEY, HUDDLED AGAINST THE wall. Her skin was still cool to the touch, but warmth was slowly returning to her. A shiver set her whole body to shaking, and she clenched her teeth to keep them from chattering until it had passed.

Qudovo was dead, and so were all his followers who had tried to come after her. One by one, she had slain all seven men. Though, technically, Qudovo had not died by her hand. Not that it mattered.

It had been almost two years since she had let the cold loose within her. She didn't want to think about that night—it was something she tried to forget. This time, she hadn't been nearly so desperate. No, this time, she had simply decided she'd had enough.

So much for her vow to never use that power again. She couldn't deny the thrill it gave her, a high that no drug could match. But when she used the power, it changed her. She did things she would never consider otherwise.

There was no mercy in her during those times, no compassion. Only a mad desire to destroy.

Phana stood up and brushed herself off. She needed to find Koral, to make sure he was all right. She hadn't believed Qudovo when the gang leader claimed he had taken Koral's head, but it would still be good to be in his arms again, to feel his warmth.

She turned and nearly yelped when she saw the figure standing a few paces behind her. Then she realized it was a child and Phana took a deep, but unsteady breath.

"You shouldn't sneak up on people like that, kid. I could have hurt you when I reacted."

"You won't hurt anyone until you recover," said a girl's voice. Phana couldn't see the child's face in the shadows of the alley, but the girl spoke with an adult's serious tone. "You are weak now, and you need your strength back quickly."

"What are you talking about?" Phana asked. "Who are you?"

"I am acquainted with the young lady Marilsa, and her...brother."

"Did they send you to find me? Are they in trouble?"

"I am not here to talk about them. I wish to talk about you."

"What? You're not making sense, kid. What's your name?"

"You must listen, Phana. I don't have much time. A great deal is happening tonight, and I am spread thin. But when you used your power, it called to me, and I realized I must speak with you."

Phana took a step back. How did this girl know about...? Obviously, this was no ordinary little girl. But who *was* she?

"If you are who I think you are, Ythis is the most dangerous place for you to be. The forces arrayed against Marilsa are nothing compared to what will come after you should certain parties learn of your existence."

Phana almost laughed out loud. She knew the cold inside her marked her as different, but to think she would be hunted as if she was a witch—it was difficult to believe.

"If you know so much about me, then who am I? What is this thing inside me?"

"I do not *know*. I merely have my suspicions, and sharing them with you may do more harm than good. If you want answers, then you must seek them out yourself. Jadir found his answer when he met the Wolf, but you must seek elsewhere. If I am right, the Wolf will only give you stories and lies."

The girl stepped back in the shadows and was lost to Phana's sight, but her voice drifted out one last time.

"There is more to your life than you remember, Phana, that much I know. Your power called to me, and it calls to others. Be careful what attention you bring on yourself. Be careful what you bring to Ythis...."

"Wait! I'm not done yet!"

But the girl was gone, and Phana knew she had not simply run away down the alley. Whoever had been here, Phana was sure she was far more than a little girl. But who was she, and could Phana truly trust anything the girl had said to her?

She leaned against the wall and rested her head in her hands. Jadir had gone to the Wolf and discovered he wasn't even human. What rumors might the Wolf have heard about *her*? Was Phana not really human either? Did she really want to know?

But if the girl was telling the truth, then anything the Wolf would tell her would be unreliable at best. Phana had been able to bring forth the cold within her for as long as she could remember. It had been years....

Wait, had Phana had this power as a child? She couldn't remember—most of her childhood was lost to her, her memories nothing but vague feelings with no images or sounds to accompany them. She remembered feeling cold, but not really *being* cold. She remembered the taste of fresh snow on her tongue...but she couldn't remember ever living anywhere other than Ythis, where snow never fell.

How many times had she let loose the ice in her blood? Three times? Four? She wasn't sure anymore, if she had ever been. What had she forgotten? Why couldn't she remember?

Be careful what you bring to Ythis.

So others could feel it when Phana let loose. This worried her. If the sorcerers ever felt it, they might send their demons to hunt her down and bring her to one of those Towers. And she doubted she would prevail against a demon, no matter what she could do.

For now, her choices were limited. The most she could do at the moment was resolve to keep it fully under control. And she would request a meeting with the Wolf, hear what he had to say. Even if she couldn't take his words at full value, perhaps he would say something that would jog a memory, give her a thread to follow. If she could learn more about who she was, it would be worth it.

Phana yawned—she felt completely drained. What she wanted right now was to find Koral and have a long sleep curled up beside him. With Qudovo dead, there was no immediate urgency, no problem that had to be solved tonight.

Phana left the alley and headed for the Crown and Coin. Koral may not be there, but it was usually the best place to find him. After that, she'd try his home. One way or another, she decided, she was going to see him tonight.

As she walked the streets of Ythis, she replayed the girl's words in her mind, over and over, looking for new meaning, for something she might have missed. The girl's final sentence confused, and worried, Phana.

Be careful what you bring to Ythis.

What was out there, beyond the city walls, that could feel it when she used her powers? And how could she be sure something wasn't already on its way to the city, coming here to find her?

Not that it mattered. She would have to deal with whatever problems came up the way she always did.

If Phana knew anything about herself, it was that she was a survivor.

Chapter Thirty-Three

JADIR JOGGED THROUGH THE STREETS OF YTHIS, HEADING FOR the Crown and Coin. He didn't know if Koral was there, but he hoped he could find the man quickly. He was concerned about how much time he had before Marilsa decided she was ready to approach the Tower of Ash directly.

He was glad the West River Road provided a main thoroughfare from the edge of the Warren in the southeast of Ythis all the way up to the Forgotten City—the city's vast cemetery—in the northwest. He had an almost direct path to his destination, and as the evening progressed, there were fewer and fewer people out to get in his way as he ran.

Jadir crossed into the Market District and settled into a rhythm. He knew he wouldn't be able to keep up this pace the entire distance, but at the moment he was barely breathing hard and was sure he would make good time. His gaze focused on the distance ahead, allowing him to be generally aware of anything or anyone he might need to dodge around as he approached.

Unfortunately, Jadir wasn't really looking at anyone's face, and was taken completely by surprise as a man suddenly lunged into his path and tackled Jadir, throwing him off balance and driving him into the ground. Jadir's head bounced off the cobblestones as he hit, and stars swam in front of his eyes as his assailant climbed up to sit on Jadir's chest.

Jadir blinked up at the other man and was shocked to see Rifain, a look of pure rage on his face, trying to pin Jadir's arms to the street with his knees. Jadir struggled to free himself, but Rifain, though short, was almost as strong and had the advantage of leverage. Rifain let go of one arm to pull back his fist and slam it into the side of Jadir's face.

Jadir twisted and shoved with all his strength, nearly throwing Rifain off his chest, but the man was an experienced fighter and adjusted himself enough to remain in control. He punched Jadir again, but Jadir managed to get his forearm up to block most of the blow.

"What are you doing?" he shouted at Rifain. "What's wrong with you?"

"It's all your fault!" Rifain shouted back as he continued to strike.

Jadir knew he couldn't stay like this. He extended one of his legs straight out, and then brought up his knee as hard as he could, connecting with Rifain's back. At the same instant, Jadir grabbed Rifain's shirt and yanked him forward. The combination of both the kick and the throw flung Rifain forward enough that he lost his position on Jadir's chest and freed Jadir's other arm.

Jadir shoved Rifain to one side and rolled the other way, climbing to his feet as fast as he could while Rifain did the same.

"*What* is my fault? I don't know why you're attacking me!" he shouted into Rifain's face.

Rifain raised his fists and started circling Jadir, trying to find an opening to attack. Jadir also raised his own fists and tried to remember everything Rifain had taught him. He knew the other man was a far more experienced fighter, and Jadir was in trouble. His strength alone wasn't going to be enough to beat this man.

"We were all happy," Rifain snarled at him. "We had a place where we belonged, we had friends, we had money comin' in. And you and your sister ruined it all. The gang, *my* gang, has been torn apart by you."

Rifain continued to circle around, and Jadir concentrated on the small amount he had learned from this man.

Don't swing your fists, drive them straight out. Watch where he's going and don't leave yourself open.

This was hopeless. There was no way Jadir was going to walk away from this fight.

"I never wanted any of this to happen," Jadir said to the other man.

"Like that makes a difference! Qudovo is dead, and so are most of those who followed him. A bunch of the others who didn't go with Qudovo are bein' controlled by your sister. There are only a few of us who didn't take sides—we just wanted our gang back."

Rifain lunged and Jadir threw out a punch and missed, but at least Rifain was forced to step back.

"That's not gonna happen, because of *you!*" This time, Rifain went low and tried to tackle Jadir again. Jadir tried to twist away but was caught around the waist. Rifain's shoulder drove into his side, but at least Jadir avoided getting the wind knocked out of him.

He tried to backpedal away from Rifain's push, but realized almost immediately that he had done the wrong thing. He couldn't retreat as fast as Rifain could push forward, and Jadir ended up on his back again with Rifain on top of him. Jadir took two more punches to the face before he managed to grab Rifain's wrists.

But Rifain was too canny to let that stop him. As Jadir forced his arms apart, Rifain drove his forehead into Jadir's face. Jadir felt his nose shatter and his eyes slammed shut of their own accord. The shock was enough for Jadir to loosen his grip, and Rifain pulled one of his arms free and hammered him in the ribs.

Jadir tried to open his eyes, but they were streaming tears and he could barely see. Nearly blind, he knew Rifain was going to beat him to death. Jadir would never reach the Crown and Coin to get help, would never return to the Warren, would fail to reach Marilsa and stop her from going to the Tower of Ash.

He had fought so hard, and come through so much, only to fail now. This wasn't right. He understood Rifain's pain, why the man blamed Jadir and Marilsa for everything that happened. He didn't blame Rifain for attacking him.

But he wasn't just going to roll over and die.

Rifain pushed himself upright and prepared to hit Jadir again. Jadir, desperate to stop the man, saw an opening and took it. His hand shot up and wrapped around Rifain's throat as the other man's fist slammed into Jadir's mouth. Something small and hard hit the back of Jadir's throat, and he realized Rifain had just knocked out one of his teeth.

Jadir squeezed as hard as he could. Rifain grabbed Jadir's wrist and tried to pull away, but Jadir still had the man's other wrist and he held Rifain close. Rifain's eyes bulged as Jadir's fingers dug into his neck.

Rifain let go of Jadir's wrist and punched him in the face again and again, trying desperately to break Jadir's hold, but it wasn't enough. His face red, Rifain's eyelids began to flutter, and then his eyes rolled up in his head and he went limp.

Jadir pushed the man over onto the ground but didn't let go of his throat. Rifain's arms and legs twitched a few times and then went still.

Jadir finally let go and sat back. He looked at Rifain's chest, but it didn't rise or fall. The man was dead. Jadir looked around and saw a handful of onlookers, who began to hurry away when Jadir raised his head. The Watch would come around soon, and Jadir needed to be away from here before they arrived.

He pushed himself to his feet, his body aching, his face a mass of bruises. Jadir spit out the tooth he had lost, and a massive wad of blood went with it. He gingerly felt his face and found a stream of blood from his nose covering his mouth and chin, and his lips were swelling up.

I hope they let me enter the Crown and Coin, he thought. *I look like a nightmare.*

There was no way he would be able to run the rest of the way, now. So Jadir turned and marched up the West River Road as quickly as he could, hoping he would reach his destination before anyone else caught up with him.

*   *   *

KORAL SHOOK HIS HEAD.

"That's impossible. Whoever told you that is mad."

The messenger looked down at his feet and shuffled nervously.

"If you say so," he said. "But the word is Phana turned into some kind of demon, and the way those other men died...well, she didn't do that with just her knives."

"You say you got this from people who were there when it happened," Koral replied. "I want to you go find them and bring them to me. I want to hear their story directly."

The messenger nodded and nearly ran from the room.

Koral threw himself into a chair and swore loudly. The way stories and rumors got twisted and exaggerated on the street made his job so much more difficult than it needed to be. He knew Phana would tell him the truth, but he didn't know where she was.

In truth, he was worried about her.

A soft knock on the door interrupted his thoughts, and he stood and pulled the door open. Phana stood on the other side, looking exhausted but otherwise unharmed.

Without a word, Koral pulled her into his arms, not bothering to close the door. He didn't care if anyone saw them like this—he was just glad she was safe. They stayed like that for a full minute before Phana pulled away. She closed the door and then leaned back on it.

"Qudovo is dead," she said. There was no joy in her voice.

"I know, I just heard."

A guilty look crossed her face, there and gone so quickly Koral wasn't sure he had really seen it.

"Did you…hear how he died?"

Koral snorted.

"I heard a story that rivals some old legends about how he died, Phana. Apparently, you're really a demon in disguise, and you lifted him over your head and stabbed him through the heart with your arm—which had turned into a black blade, by the way. And then you summoned ice over the entire street to stop his lackeys from getting away, and one by one you shredded them with daggers made of glowing ice."

He smiled at her.

"You know, if I knew you could do things like that, we wouldn't need the Wolf. You and I could run the criminal underworld in this city."

Phana looked uncomfortable at Koral's words.

"Don't talk like that," she said in a low voice.

"I'm kidding," he protested. "I have no desire to replace the Wolf...*at all*. Sure, power is nice, but he's got no freedom. I've got the perfect balance of both."

Koral stepped toward Phana, but she turned her face away from him.

"What's wrong?"

"It's been a rough night, Koral. I'm not exactly feeling romantic."

"Sorry," he replied. "I'm just...I'm happy you came out of this okay. I was worried about you."

She shrugged and stepped around him, lowering herself into one of the chairs. Crossing her arms on the table, she put her head down on her forearms. Koral stood there and watched her, not sure what to say or do. He didn't want to push her, but he needed to know what had happened out there. He needed to know who else was dead tonight.

"Phana, I've got to get word to the Wolf about the current situation. I know you're tired, but can you tell me what happened? Who else was there?"

Phana let her head rest for a moment more, saying nothing, and then she lifted herself up to look at Koral.

"Have a seat," she said.

Koral sat across from her and waited patiently. He could see her considering everything, and it seemed to him she was carefully choosing her words.

"Qudovo and his men found me and started chasing me. He had five others with him. I couldn't fight them all, so I ran into the alleys and tried to lose them. They managed to get past me and surround the block where I was hiding, and then a few of them came into the alleys to flush me out."

She stopped and looked down at the surface of the table.

"Qudovo was on one of the streets near me, calling my name. He didn't care about witnesses. He shouted that he had killed you earlier today and sent your head to the Wolf as a present. He was trying to get me to come to fight, but I didn't believe him."

She sighed and raised her eyes to meet Koral's gaze.

"I was content to hide, but then his men came into the alley where

I had stopped, and I had to make a choice. So, before they could reach my hiding spot, I went out into the street to face Qudovo. I knew one of his men had a crossbow, and there was no way Qudovo was going to fight me directly. He knew he couldn't beat me."

But then Koral saw Phana get a look in her eye, and her expression changed slightly. Again, he thought she looked guilty in some way. She lowered her gaze back down to the table, and kept it there as she spoke.

"So I attacked him, and let him think I had left myself open, and he lunged at me. And I...dodged around him and he took the crossbow bolt meant for me. They had poisoned it, in case they only wounded me, and so he died by the hand of one of his own people."

Phana went silent, but Koral knew there was more to the story than that.

"What about the other three? Did they attack you?"

Phana waited a moment before giving him a small shake of her head.

"I told them to run, and then I attacked the man closest to me, the only one who wasn't on a roof. He was no match for me, and I killed him. I...wasn't intending to hunt the other two; I just wanted to scare them. But when I left the open street, they came after me again. It was their mistake."

Koral knew he had heard only a part of the story. He could tell Phana was holding something back, something that might be important. But he didn't want to accuse her of lying to him, and she was obviously tired. He couldn't just let it go, though.

"There's something you're not telling me," he said.

She raised her face and looked at him, and there was anger in her eyes.

"You're right," she replied. "There's a great deal I'm not telling you. And you'll just have to learn to live with that."

"You know you can trust me, Phana."

"No, I *think* I can trust you. I don't *know*. And that doesn't matter, anyway. I will tell you things when I'm ready to talk about them, and not before. I like you Koral, but that doesn't give you any right to know everything about me, not unless I give you that right."

Koral didn't know what he had done to make her angry, but he didn't want to put more of a burden on her right now. Except that he also had a duty to the Wolf, to provide his boss with all the information he needed to run his criminal empire.

"If I examine the men's bodies, what will I find?"

Phana's lips hardened into a thin line.

"Koral, just...don't. It'll only give you more questions, and I'm not prepared to give you the answers. Qudovo is dead, and so are his closest followers. Be satisfied with that, and then decide what you're going to do with the rest."

She stared into Koral's eyes, daring him to argue. He didn't want to be in this position. Koral really cared about Phana, but as much as she could trust him, he wasn't entirely convinced he could trust her. She was still a mystery, as far as he was concerned.

The Wolf was interested in her for a reason, and Koral was in the dark about that. After learning about who...*what*...Jadir really was, Koral knew he wasn't ready for another revelation like that. Especially not when it concerned Phana.

The two of them sat there in the small room, looking at each other, neither saying a word.

Chapter Thirty-Four

JADIR STEPPED INTO THE CROWN AND COIN AND STRODE over to the bar. The bartender's eyes went wide when he saw Jadir's bloody face, and he took a step back. Jadir opened his hands to show he had no weapons.

"I need to see Koral. Is he here?"

The bartender nodded and glanced at the door leading to the back room.

"I'll tell him he has a visitor," the bartender said. "What's your name?"

Jadir turned and marched toward the door.

"I don't have time for this—I need to see him *now*."

"Stop!" the bartender ordered, and Jadir heard chairs scrape on the floor as at least two men rose to their feet behind him. He didn't care. He stepped up to the door and banged on it with his fist, before turning to face the men who were now approaching him.

The men hesitated—if Jadir was a threat to Koral, he wouldn't have knocked on the door. But their job was to make sure Koral was not only safe here, but that he could conduct business uninterrupted.

"That's not how we do things here, friend," said the bartender, and the two men facing Jadir took another step forward.

"I'm not your friend," Jadir replied. "But Koral is mine, one of the only ones I've got, and I don't care about how you do things."

The door opened behind Jadir.

"Jadir?" Koral asked behind him.

Without turning Jadir said "Koral, I need to speak with you right now. These men think I need to make an appointment or something, and I don't have time for that."

"It's all right," Koral called to the men. "Thank you."

The two men turned away and Jadir faced Koral to see Phana also sitting in the room. When they saw Jadir's bloody face, Koral's eyes went wide and Phana gasped out loud.

"That bad, huh?" he asked.

Koral motioned for Jadir to enter, and he stepped into the room and gently lowered himself into one of the chairs.

"What happened to you?" Phana asked him. "Is Marilsa okay?"

"No, Marilsa is far from okay. She has...lost control of herself. I think...I think her *incubo* has corrupted her somehow—I think it's influencing her, and she can't fight it. But my Marilsa is still in there, and she's calling me to help her."

Koral sat across from Jadir and looked him in the eyes.

"Did she do that to you?" he asked, gesturing to Jadir's face.

"No, that was Rifain."

Identical looks of surprise appeared on both Koral's and Phana's faces at the same time.

"He's dead," Jadir continued. "He attacked me in the street, and I had to kill him. He blamed me for everything that's happened to the gang. I didn't want to...."

"Jadir," said Phana. "Where is Marilsa now? What's happening to her?"

"About a dozen members of the gang have decided to follow her. They have become her coven, and do whatever she tells them to do. She almost ordered them to kill me, but she managed to fight off the *incubo's* influence long enough to leave me alive."

He looked from Phana to Koral and back.

"I think those priests did something to Marilsa. She said she is going to go to the Tower of Ash, but I don't know what she's planning on doing once she gets there. The sorcerers and the Church are enemies. I think maybe the priests put the idea in Marilsa's head—maybe they're using her to attack whoever lives in the Tower of Ash. That doesn't matter, though. I need to stop her—I *can* stop her—but I need some help. Her coven won't let me get close enough to Marilsa to talk to her. I can't do this alone."

Both Koral and Phana sat there for a moment, saying nothing. Finally, Koral leaned forward.

"Is Marilsa on her way to the Tower of Ash right now? It's not a great distance from the building where you two were staying. She'll reach the Tower long before we can get back to the Warren."

Now Jadir hesitated. He wasn't sure he wanted to tell them what Marilsa was doing, in case they decided to see her as a threat. He didn't want to lie to them, but he needed their help and wasn't sure providing the whole truth was the best approach right now.

"No, she's conducting a ritual of some kind, probably gathering power to her. I think we have time to reach the building before she heads for the Tower."

"Jadir, what do you want us to do?" Phana asked.

"I can't fight off all of Marilsa's coven members myself. I need you to help me get past them, so that I can speak to Marilsa and do whatever I can to help her break free of her *incubo's* influence."

"But aren't they under Marilsa's influence—or her *incubo's* influence—as well? Some of these people are my friends. How are we supposed to fight them without killing them? There are only three of us."

Jadir turned to Koral.

"Can't you get some of the Wolf's people to help us? If we show up in numbers, then we can restrain her coven, not kill them. If they go to the Tower of Ash—and they'll follow Marilsa wherever she goes—then they'll *all* die. We can save their lives, too."

Koral considered Jadir's words. Jadir wanted to shout at him to hurry up—time was slipping away. But he forced himself to wait for Koral to make the right decision.

"I'll need to see the Wolf," Koral said at last. "He will decide who to send and what we'll do."

"We don't have time for that!" Jadir said angrily. "You've got people in the bar out there. You can find a few more quickly. Just tell them to come with us—they all follow your orders."

"I can't do that," Koral replied. "If it was just me, I'd help you. But this is bigger than that, and it's up to the Wolf to decide what he wants me—and the rest of his people—to do."

"How long will that take?"

"The Wolf's Den is not far from here. I'll go speak to the Wolf directly. If he decides to help, I'll have my pick of people who are in the Den. It's the best way to get some real help quickly, Jadir."

Koral stood up, and so did Jadir.

"Don't take too long. Marilsa is getting farther and farther away from me. I can bring her back, but we don't have all night."

Koral nodded.

"I'll do what I can. I make no promises, Jadir. The Wolf will decide what he feels is the best course of action for him and his people, and I have to abide by that."

"Then you have to convince him to do the right thing."

Koral grimaced at Jadir, and then he left without saying anything else. Perhaps Jadir shouldn't have pushed so hard, but Marilsa's life was at stake.

The truth was Jadir didn't really care about the members of her coven. All he wanted to do was save his sister. But he understood the history Phana had with them, and he needed her help.

He turned to Phana, and she looked up into his face. He couldn't read her expression—she was keeping herself closed off from him.

"Do you think the Wolf will help me?" he asked her.

"I've never met the Wolf, Jadir. After what he told you about your life, I'm not sure I ever want to."

Jadir sat down and prepared to wait for Koral's return. He only hoped this wouldn't take too long. Eventually, Marilsa would finish what she was doing and head for the Tower of Ash. Once that happened, she would be lost to Jadir forever.

*   *   *

JADIR REALIZED HE WAS ALONE WITH PHANA, AND KORAL would be gone for a bit. Jadir had an opportunity to talk to her about... everything that had happened.

"Phana, I want to... to apologize for bringing all this to you. I want to say how sorry I am for everything that happened with your gang. I never thought anything like this could...."

He drifted off, and Phana took a deep breath.

"This isn't your fault, Jadir. Marilsa is a witch. That spirit had found her, and there was nothing you could have done to prevent that. And you couldn't have known about whatever plans the Wolf had for you."

"I still don't know why he did what he did, Phana. He held the journal for thirteen years, watched us and kept our secret, but he didn't do it for us. He had his own reasons, and I doubt our well-being was part of his consideration. And when I asked him why he did it, he refused to tell me."

"I think having a witch as an ally who owes you her life is reason enough," Phana said. "But he didn't know how this situation was going to turn out, either."

"Certainly not once the Church got involved," Jadir replied.

Phana narrowed her eyes and looked off to one side.

"Jadir, how *did* the Church get involved? That's what I'd most like to know—how they knew about Marilsa."

Jadir shrugged.

"The Witch Hunter found her. They had been searching for the daughter of Ineir since she was born."

"That's what I thought, too, at first. But that doesn't make sense. The Witch Hunter showed up and tried to kill Marilsa. The priests were there in that black carriage when I arrived with the rest of the gang, only a few minutes behind you. So they must have been there when you showed up. How come they didn't try to stop you?"

"Maybe they were afraid when they saw me easily kill the man in front of our building."

Phana shook her head.

"I doubt that. You saw how easily the priestess murdered Flouty when you caught their carriage. And she had another priest with her. I think two priests would have been able to stop you—and I think they knew that, too. But they let you go in and kill the Witch Hunter, and save Marilsa."

Jadir wasn't sure where Phana was going with this.

"I'd be willing to bet money," she continued, "that the priests were already there in the carriage when the Witch Hunter arrived. I think they were already watching you by that point. I think the Witch Hunter had nothing to do with the priests in the carriage—he had just finally caught up with Marilsa after hunting her for so many years."

Jadir nodded. "They had some kind of plan to use Marilsa to attack the Tower of Ash—that's what I think. So they didn't really want her to be killed."

Phana sat back in her chair, thinking. After a moment, she spoke up again.

"The question is how the priests knew about Marilsa. How did they find her in the first place?"

Iathephos help me.

Jadir had whispered those words the first night he had seen Marilsa's *incubo* trying to get into her dreams. And it had an immediate effect, driving off the spirit and leaving Marilsa safe for the rest of that night. Jadir had regretted invoking the name of Ythis' god afterward.

Was that how the Church had discovered them? Had Jadir called their god's attention and the priests followed some kind of trail back to Jadir and Marilsa?

Was all of this really his fault?

Jadir gasped for breath, as if his lungs had stopped working. He was sure the priests had influenced Marilsa in some way, sending her the urge to go to the Tower of Ash. And Jadir had been the one to call their attention in the first place. If it hadn't been for Jadir's mistake, would Marilsa now be in full control of her *incubo*?

"Jadir, what's wrong?"

"I...I...it was me. I did it. I'm responsible for all of this."

Jadir could feel despair welling up inside of him. All his efforts had been for nothing, because he had been the one to put Marilsa in this situation in the first place.

"What do you mean? You didn't do anything—"

"The first night, when you gave me that drug for Marilsa...I saw her *incubo* trying to get into her dreams. It was visible, hovering over her. And I said something I should never have uttered."

"What did you say, Jadir?"

He looked into Phana's eyes.

"I invoked Ythis' god. I . . . I said his name and asked for his help."

Jadir saw Phana's eyes go wide, and he knew he was right—it *was* his fault.

"Oh, Jadir," she whispered.

Tears streamed down his face and his despair was like a ball of lead in his stomach. Phana reached out and put a hand on his arm, but it was small comfort. He knew she was repelled by his presence, by the reality of what he was inside this human shell.

"Jadir, you've got to stop. It was a mistake, and one anyone could have made. You were face-to-face with a spirit that was trying to harm your sister, and there was nothing you could do. Anyone might do the same thing in your position. You can't blame yourself."

Her words rolled off him, not penetrating the doom hanging over him, the guilt, the fear.

"Jadir," she said. "You've got to stop. Marilsa still needs you. It's not too late to help her, and she needs her big brother, now more than ever. You came here for my help, and together we will stop whatever the Church has done. We'll save your sister."

"She's not my sister," he said in a low voice. "I'm not human, remember? I'm—"

"No, I don't want to hear that," Phana interrupted. "You are who you decide to be. You're not the only one with a mysterious past, or the only one the Wolf has watched over for some time. You're not alone."

Jadir took a deep breath and tried to get himself under control. It took much effort, but he eventually managed to drag himself back, to compose himself enough to speak to Phana.

"Thank you, Phana. I . . . I'm glad you're still my friend."

She gave him a small smile. "I'm definitely that. And I'll tell you the truth, Jadir. I'll always wonder what might have been between us if all this other stuff hadn't happened. I do regret—at least a little bit—whatever it is that . . . pulls me away from you."

"I don't think Koral regrets it," he replied, giving her a smile back to show he wasn't bitter about it.

"No...and I'm not going to lie to you, Jadir. I'm not with him for any other reason than I *want* to be with him. I was attracted to you both, and this is how it turned out. But it's not just who you are that meant we wouldn't end up together. It's about who I am as well."

"What do you mean?"

"I'm going to tell you something, because I know you'll understand, and I trust you to keep it in confidence. I've told no one else about this, though I bet the Wolf has at least some inkling as to the truth."

She took Jadir's hands and looked into his eyes.

"I don't think I'm fully human, either. I have something within me that, when I let it loose, turns me into...well, I don't know what I become. I've only used it a few times in my life, or at least what part of my life I can remember. Because a good chunk of my past is blank, Jadir. I know I haven't lived my whole life in Ythis, but I don't know where I came from, or what I really am."

Jadir was stunned by Phana's revelation. This was beyond anything he could have expected.

"So," she continued. "It's just as likely that whatever is inside me is the reason I can't be with you, as much as it is because of what *you* are."

Jadir opened his mouth but didn't know what to say. Finally, he decided to ask a question.

"What are you going to do? How are you going to find out about your past?"

"Well, first, I'm going to worry about that once this is over. It can wait until you and Marilsa are safe. And then maybe I'll ask to talk to the Wolf. He might give me an answer, like he did with you."

She shrugged and Jadir was amazed at how confident she was. Whatever the truth was, he knew she would handle it well, would take it in stride, and would live her life on her own terms.

"What are you able to do?" he asked her.

"Well, we've got some time, so I guess I can give you a few details. But no one else knows about this, Jadir. Not even Koral. Nothing I tell you here goes outside of this room."

Jadir nodded. "You have my word."

"Okay, then. I guess I'll start by telling you how Qudovo really died."

Andrew J. Luther

Chapter Thirty-Five

THE WOLF WAS SITTING AT HIS DESK WHEN KORAL ENTERED his boss' well-appointed office. One of the bodyguards, a big man who Koral knew was far faster than his overly-muscled body would indicate, stood beside the door. Koral didn't know the man's name, but he gave a quick nod of acknowledgement and the bodyguard returned the courtesy.

The Wolf looked up from some parchments he was reading and gestured for Koral to sit in the single chair placed in front of the large desk. Not many visitors were invited to meet the Wolf in his actual office, but Koral had been here many times and felt comfortable in the presence of the man he was sworn to serve.

"I received word the leader of the gang in the Dock District is no longer troubling us," the Wolf said by way of greeting.

"Qudovo attacked Phana, and she killed him," replied Koral. "A few of Qudovo's followers didn't get the message and attacked her as well. They're dead now, too."

The Wolf nodded slowly. "That's not why you're here, though, is it?"

Koral was always impressed at how well the Wolf seemed to read people. It was a major contributor to his success.

"No, it's not. We have a problem with Jadir and Marilsa. It appears she has lost control of her power in some manner. A number of the gang members who were tasked with watching over her have decided to become...I believe they're called her coven, now. She has taken them and is apparently planning to visit the new Tower of Ash."

"Why?" the Wolf asked.

"I don't know, sir. Jadir came to ask for my help. He's sure that he can talk Marilsa down from her…whatever it is that's going on with her. But the coven won't let him get near his sister."

"She's not really his sister, remember?"

Koral nodded. "I know, but he still calls her his sister and when I'm talking to him it's easy to forget he's not human."

"So he wants me to give you some men to accompany him to fight off these coven members, my own people who now follow the girl. Do I have that right?"

When the Wolf said it, Koral had to admit it sounded crazy. Marilsa had taken people who were supposedly loyal to the Wolf, and turned them into her own followers. And now Jadir wanted to put more of the Wolf's people in harm's way.

"This hasn't worked out quite the way I intended," the Wolf said in a low voice. "I knew Jadir would be angry with me as the bearer of bad news about who he was. But I believed Marilsa would have some measure of gratitude for keeping her safe and giving her brother a way to earn a living for the both of them. Now Jadir wants me to throw more resources at them."

Koral waited, saying nothing. The Wolf did not like to be interrupted when he was reasoning his way to a conclusion. Koral could see where his boss' mind was going, though. The Wolf was leaning towards cutting his losses and leaving Jadir and Marilsa to fend for themselves.

The truth was the trouble with Qudovo may have come regardless, but the situation with Marilsa had been the tipping point for him. She was the direct influence that led to betrayal and the deaths of multiple members of the gang. The Wolf tried to generally do right by those who worked for him, at least to a reasonable extent. He likely felt responsible for the deaths as a result of his own direct orders.

And Koral knew the Wolf wouldn't want to send more of his people to die unless he had no other choice.

"No," the Wolf said finally. "I won't be helping Jadir and Marilsa any further. The Church is still an unknown player in this game—I don't know what the priests are after. And now the witch is planning to head for the Tower of Ash? As if we needed a sorcerer to make this situation even more complicated than it was."

The Wolf sighed and ran his hand over his cropped hair. "I know I'm likely condemning Marilsa to a horrid death, but I can't risk everything to help one young woman."

Koral understood the Wolf's position, but he was surprised to himself disappointed in the older man's decision. Despite the danger, Koral realized he had been hoping the Wolf would order him to gather some able bodies and head to the Warren with Jadir. He didn't know why he felt the way he did—perhaps he couldn't help but see Jadir as a friend.

Without help, it wouldn't just be Marilsa who would die. Jadir would sacrifice himself in a desperate attempt to save his sister from what he believed was an outside influence.

"Sir, Jadir believes the Church is manipulating Marilsa in some manner—that they are the ones pushing her to focus on the Tower. He said she was trying to fight her urge to do the things she's doing, but it was too strong. Perhaps, by doing nothing, we are letting the priests get what they want."

The Wolf stood up from his desk, a signal that it was time for Koral to leave. Koral stood and watched the Wolf move over to a curtain that covered the wall opposite his desk. He pulled the curtain back to reveal the door that led to his inner chambers. Koral had never been beyond that door, and had no idea what the Wolf's private quarters looked like.

The Wolf turned back to Koral.

"Jadir may be correct. There are risks I'm willing to take, and risks I feel are weighted too heavily against me. As much I don't relish the thought of the Church achieving their goals, stopping them could have too high a price, and success is far from guaranteed."

The Wolf opened the door, but looked at Koral with his piercing blue eyes and hesitated.

"You want to go help him, don't you?" the Wolf asked. Koral nodded.

"Why?" the Wolf persisted.

"I don't really know," Koral replied. "Maybe I think Jadir deserves something better than this. All he's ever wanted was to protect his sister."

"That's the magical compulsion, Koral. He has no choice in the matter. It's the only reason he exists as he is."

"But maybe that shouldn't matter, sir. We all have reasons for what we do, and it's rare we fully understand those reasons. It wasn't magic that made me swear an oath to you, but it was a compulsion, nonetheless. I can say I had a choice in the matter, but the truth is I wouldn't have made any other choice, because that wouldn't have been me."

The Wolf said nothing, but kept watching Koral, perhaps wanting to be convinced.

"Jadir has given up everything to protect Marilsa, and maybe it was the magic that made him do it. But he's also lived a real life over the last thirteen years. Day after day, for *thirteen years*, he's been a real person who loved, and was loved by, the only family he had. If he fails now, if Marilsa dies, that life will have meant nothing."

"Every day, people die in this city, having accomplished nothing," the Wolf argued. "Their lives are empty, they have left no mark, and they have inspired no one. Why is this life different?"

"Because Jadir's life *isn't* empty, and he *has* left a mark. He's my friend. Phana cares about him, too. He's become more than he was created to be."

The Wolf considered Koral's words, and the fact that he hadn't walked away meant there was a chance he would change his mind. Koral hoped he had made the Wolf understand.

But, finally, the Wolf shook his head slowly.

"I'm not going to send more people to die, Koral. It's a sacrifice I'm not willing to make."

Koral felt the disappointment hit him again. He had tried his best, and it hadn't been good enough.

"I understand your sentiments, however," the Wolf continued. "I will not forbid you to accompany Jadir tonight and help him as much as you can. If Phana wants to help as well, Jadir will have two of the best allies he could hope for. Just come back alive, Koral.

That's an order."

And with that, the Wolf stepped through the door and closed it behind him.

*   *   *

JADIR STOPPED AT THE CORNER AND PEERED AROUND.

"Here it is," he said.

Both Koral and Phana took a quick look at the building and stepped back.

"Now what?" Phana asked.

"We try to remain unseen as long as possible. The closer we get to Marilsa before the others find us, the greater the chance of Jadir reaching her," Koral answered.

Phana looked Jadir in the eye. "We're going to have to kill some of them, aren't we?"

Jadir couldn't meet her gaze and dropped his head.

"I was hoping we'd be able to overwhelm them with numbers," said Jadir. "With only three of us, we'll have to do whatever it takes to put them down so that they can't surround us."

"Having second thoughts?" Koral asked Phana. She gave him a look that almost frightened him with its intensity.

"I've already killed people tonight who used to protect my back, people I thought I could trust. I'm not really eager to add to that body count, Koral. Are you?"

Koral raised his hands in mock surrender.

"I'm not questioning your commitment, Phana. I feel the same way you do. But the situation is what it is. If we go in there, we have to be ready to do what needs to be done. If we're not, if we hesitate, the three of us will probably die."

"There's one other thing," Jadir said. "If we fail, all of Marilsa's coven members probably won't survive tonight anyway. I can't see the residents of the Tower of Ash welcoming them in with open arms. I'm not going to kill anyone if I get another option. But we may not have a choice."

Phana paused to consider Jadir's words, and then drew a pair of long knives.

"I said I'd help you, and that means doing whatever's necessary."

"Then let's go," said Koral, and led the way across the intersection toward the building where Jadir knew Marilsa had been conducting some kind of ritual. Halfway to the front entrance, Jadir slowed and then stopped.

"Jadir!" Phana whispered.

Something wasn't right. He could still feel Marilsa's presence in the building, but he also felt a tug in the opposite direction, toward the Tower of Ash. He realized his friends had reached the front door while he stood in the middle of the street. Jadir shook his head and jogged over to Koral and Phana,

"What's wrong?" Koral asked him.

"It's weird... like Marilsa is in two places at once."

Jadir saw Phana and Koral exchange glances and he wondered how reliable his senses were tonight. Koral opened the door and peered inside, and then he motioned for Jadir to follow with Phana covering their backs.

"Where to?" Koral whispered. Jadir motioned him to go up the stairs that sat on one side of a short hallway. They proceeded up the stairs, encountering none of the coven members. Jadir could sense Marilsa behind a door on the second floor and he silently pointed it out to Koral and Phana. The three of them positioned themselves around the door.

"Okay," Koral said in a low voice. "I'll go first, Phana second. We'll try to clear a path for you, Jadir. You come behind us and make a straight line for your sister. Once you've got her, we'll try to keep the coven members off you while you do what you have to do."

Jadir nodded, trying to focus on the task at hand. But in the back of his mind, he kept wondering if this was all a mistake. Would Marilsa even listen to him? With Jadir's help, would she be able to fight off the influence of her *incubo*? What if he was wrong, and the priests had not truly done anything but watch? What if Marilsa had given in to her *incubo* willingly?

That was a thought he didn't want to consider. If Marilsa had given in on purpose, then she was lost to him forever.

He glanced at Phana and saw her gaze was locked on the closed door. She was preparing herself to fight—and to kill if necessary—the people she recently counted among her closest comrades. Back at the Crown and Coin, before Koral had returned, Jadir had asked Phana if she could use her special abilities in the fight.

You don't want me to do that, Jadir, she had said to him. *I don't have the control I need for this—I'm just as likely to attack Marilsa as I am to defend you from her coven.*

He was still amazed at the story she had told him about the cold that flowed through her veins. Jadir couldn't help but consider the possibility Phana was also some kind of spirit put into a human body. It wasn't likely to be true, he knew, but it was something he almost *wanted* to believe.

Koral drew his own short sword, grabbed the latch, and shoved the door open. Without a word, he bolted into the room, looking around for any threats. Phana entered right behind him, turning in the opposite direction to protect his flank. Jadir followed his companions and looked around for Marilsa as soon as he was across the threshold.

Jadir knew immediately that Marilsa wasn't in the room, and neither was her coven. Koral and Phana skidded to a halt to avoid crossing the sigils painted across the floor in blood. The bodies of at least five men and women lay sprawled on the floor around the perimeter of the room. Jadir noticed a couple of smaller bodies in the far corner and turned his eyes away—he remembered getting a glimpse of what the coven had done to the children and didn't want to see how it had ended.

"By the Abyss," Phana whispered. Blood covered the walls and severed limbs were nailed to the boards, integrated into the alien patterns drawn in the gore. She staggered and Jadir grabbed her arm to prevent her from crossing the outer edge of a circle inscribed on the floor.

Marilsa wasn't here, but some part of her power still was. He could almost taste it on the air, though there was something wrong with it—it didn't feel quite like something from his sister should feel.

And then Jadir realized the purpose of all the symbols. Marilsa had conducted some sort of ritual to gather more power to her. Jadir was tasting the residue of energy Marilsa hadn't quite been able to absorb.

Had she already gone to the Tower?

Jadir spun and barreled out of the room and down the stairs. He could hear Koral and Phana behind, calling his name. Only when Jadir reached the street outside did he stop and look around.

"Jadir! Don't run off without us," Phana said to him, but he shushed her. He was concentrating on the feeling he had encountered as he was entering the building.

There it is.

In the direction of the Tower of Ash, another surge of power drew his attention. For an instant, Jadir almost cried out in despair at being too late to stop Marilsa. But then he realized this new feeling was too close to be coming from the Tower itself.

He turned, scanning the buildings around him and when his eyes landed on a four-story tenement further down the street, Jadir felt a physical pull in his chest and head.

"There," he said. "She's there. Marilsa is...doing it again."

He didn't need to explain what he meant to Koral and Phana. They understood that Marilsa was murdering more innocent people to draw even greater power to her. He looked at Phana and then at Koral, and their expressions told him they were ready to put a stop to this.

"Let's go," he said, and led the way.

Chapter Thirty-Six

RELAEL STEPPED INTO THE TEMPLE'S GRAND HALL and looked around. The obsidian pillars seemed to absorb the light from the three huge chandeliers that hung from the domed ceiling, the undying flames that never consumed the thousand candles casting flickering shadows among the alcoves and walkways that lined the walls of the Hall.

His boots clicked on the blood-red flagstones as he crossed the vast space toward the pair waiting for him. Sister Zera Xodoc stood a few paces away from Tozroth, the Witch Hunter, pretending to be lost in her own thoughts. She was unaware he had spied on them before entering the chamber—he had watched their hurried conversation before they stepped apart to keep up appearances.

Relael reached them and nodded to each in turn.

"Tozroth, I'm glad you were available to join us tonight."

"Are ye going to tell me what we're about tonight?" asked the Witch Hunter.

"Absolutely," Relael replied. "I—"

"Where is Brother Ontherim?" the priestess interrupted.

"He's coming shortly. Our good brother needed to take care of one small detail before joining us."

Relael turned back to Tozroth. "The young witch has revealed her presence in the Warren. I'm afraid she has lost control of her power, and is causing a disturbance. Apparently, she was connected in some way to the Burning Crone, the sorceress who lives in the new Tower of Ash. I know not what their game is, but we will put a stop to it shortly."

Tozroth said nothing, merely watched Relael with cold eyes.

From a side passage, Relael noted a group of Sentinels led by a priest wearing red robes enter the Grand Hall and begin to approach their gathering. Relael had to fight to keep a smile off his face. He turned as the other priest reached them.

Relael bowed to the new arrival, as did both Sister Zera and Tozroth. The red robes identified this man as a Keeper, one of the priests who served in the depths of the Temple, where their god Iathephos dwelt. Keepers were somehow immune to the madness that infected those who commune with Iathephos or the other gods of the Empire. This made them ideal for handling the sacrifices and other duties that required them to step into the direct presence of their god.

But Keepers were even more than that—they were responsible for removing those priests whose time had come. Madness could be useful to the Church, but it inevitably led to destructive acts. Once a priest or priestess crossed a certain threshold, they were taken from their position in the Church hierarchy and given to their god. Some bled their life force to their divine patron to power its efforts across the Empire. Others were used as conduits for Iathephos to deliver pronouncements or directives, a fate that completely destroyed the mind, and body, of the receiver. And yet others became nothing more than food for the alien being which dwelt in the pit under the Temple.

"Sister Zera Xodoc," said the Keeper, stepping directly in front of the priestess. Relael watched her twitch slightly as her confidence began to transform into fear.

"Yes, Father," she replied.

"It is time for you to descend."

At those words, the Sentinels moved forward and Relael was forced to backpedal as they surrounded Sister Zera. The Sentinel directly behind her stepped up and slipped a bronze collar around her neck, snapping the clasp shut with a small click that Relael felt should have been a booming thunder.

Sister Zera's hand went up to touch the simple bronze collar as a tear rolled down one cheek. In an instant, she had been cut off from any powers she might summon. She was no longer a priestess—now she was nothing more than an offering to Iathephos.

"But I'm not…this must be a mistake," she said in a voice barely above a whisper.

The Keeper did not respond. He turned and marched back toward the side passage from whence he had first appeared. Two Sentinels took Sister Zera by the arms and, surrounded by the rest of the soldiers, they marched her off to her fate. The priestess never looked back, and Relael was disappointed he didn't have the opportunity to acknowledge to her his part in her downfall.

"That was your work, wasn't it?" Tozroth asked him as the priestess was led out of sight. Relael turned to the Witch Hunter and gave him a placid smile.

"Our Sister has apparently become a threat to the Church," he replied. "It is the eventual fate of all who commune with our god. It just comes sooner for some than for others."

"And what have you got planned for me, eh? A knife in the back?"

"You get the same deal I offered you a few nights back. When it is time for the young witch to be taken down, you will be offered the chance to accompany us and do the deed yourself. I know Sister Zera was feeding you information, telling you things she had no right to disclose. I don't blame you for that, so there's no reason for us to be enemies."

"I've sworn to destroy any witch I find in the Empire," Tozroth said. "But what ye have done…by the Abyss, man, didn't you realize what would happen if ye kept feeding her *incubo*, making it too strong to control?"

"Yes," replied Relael. "I did."

Tozroth took a step back, not believing how calm Relael could be about this whole situation.

"All that blood is on your hands," he finally muttered.

Relael knew that relatively innocent people had died tonight, were still dying in fact. It was a price he was willing to pay to ensure the balance of power did not shift too far toward the sorcerers of Ythis. Relael would burn the Undying Empire to the ground if it meant the Church would survive. He had long ago come to accept this part of himself, and felt no guilt, no remorse, for anything he did anymore in the name of the Church.

"Tozroth," said Relael, "I have a mission to protect the Church, and that is what I do, no matter the cost. There are greater considerations than how many inhabitants of the Warren will die tonight, considerations that affect the ongoing health of this very organization we both serve. I protected the witch, while Sister Zera and Brother Worestald conducted rituals to both feed and influence the girl's *incubo*."

He smiled at Tozroth. "To be honest, I never really believed it would work. I figured we would be unable to form a connection to the *incubo*, or the witch would detect our meddling, or something would happen to stop us. But one-by-one, the pieces fell into place. And now the final step is here."

Relael turned to see Brother Worestald approaching from the other end of the Grand Hall. He turned back to Tozroth.

"The witch has done what we needed her to do. And now she must be destroyed. I am offering you the chance to be the one who destroys her. You may accompany us into the Warren, escorted by a contingent of Imperial Guard, of course. Brother Worestald will sever her link to the *incubo*, rendering her powerless, and you can do what you've been wanting to do since before you arrived in Ythis."

"And in return I keep quiet about what you've done," Tozroth said.

"Obviously," said Relael. "This will help us maintain the balance of power in the Empire. To reveal the truth would cause no end of troubles for the Church. Not to mention, you'd make a personal enemy of me, the High Counselor Untoleu, and our Lord High Priest."

Brother Ontherim arrived and looked at Tozroth. Relael made quick introductions, and the priest gave Relael a questioning look.

"Tozroth here is now part of this mission, Brother."

"Where is Sister Zera?" Worestald asked.

"She has descended," Relael replied without expression. Worestald's eyes went wide and he looked around the Grand Hall as if he expected to see a Keeper coming for him right then and there.

"We have a witch in the Warren who is murdering innocent citizens of Ythis," Relael continued. "It's up to us to stop her. Are you both ready to eliminate this threat to the Empire?"

Relael looked at Tozroth, who considered his position for moment and then nodded solemnly. Brother Ontherim bowed slightly and said, "Of course."

Relael turned and led his companions out of the Grand Hall toward the front entrance, where their mounted Imperial Guard escort waited.

*   *   *

JADIR STOOD IN THE MOUTH OF AN ALLEY ACROSS THE STREET from the building where he was sure Marilsa was conducting another ritual. He turned back to his two companions.

"That's definitely it," he said. "She's in that building. I can feel it—there's nothing pulling me anywhere else."

Koral nodded.

"One entrance in the front, and someone's got to be watching it. I'm going to scout around the back and see if there's another way in."

Phana put her hand on his arm. "I'll come with you."

"No, you stay here with Jadir. The more of us who sneak around, the more likely they'll spot us. I'll be back in a few minutes."

"Be careful," Jadir said before Koral could step out on the street. "I was attacked earlier by one of the coven members who had been...turned into something not human. She was strong and fast, and after I shattered her skull against the stone wall, she still managed to crawl up the side of the building and escape."

"Great," Koral muttered sarcastically. He crouched down and, keeping to the shadows, made his way up the street a bit before crossing over and coming back down the other side. A moment later, he ducked into the alley that ran behind the building and was lost to sight.

Jadir saw Phana was nervous, and he knew she worried that Koral might encounter something he couldn't beat.

"He'll be okay," Jadir said to her. She looked at him evenly.

"Jadir, I'm not convinced any of us will be okay after this is done. The three of us are going to fight our way through a dozen fanatics so that you can confront a witch who has, for all intents and purposes, gone insane."

"This *will* work," he insisted. "It won't be easy, but we'll do it."

"One of us will die tonight," she said, and her voice sent a shiver down Jadir's spine.

"Don't say that...you don't know—"

"That's just it, Jadir. I *do* know. I can't say how I know, but...I can feel it. One of us isn't going to survive this night."

Jadir looked at Phana, not knowing what to say. After what she had told him about the things she could do, he wasn't about to argue with her pronouncement. They were both trapped by powers they didn't understand.

Jadir stared into her eyes and felt an ache once again for what they could have had together. He loved her; it was as simple as that. The thought that she might be killed helping him rescue Marilsa....

Then again, Phana was tough, far tougher than either Koral or himself. It was Koral who was in the most danger. Yes, he was skilled, but he was just a man. Tonight, the forces at work were greater than anything a mortal man could overcome.

Had Jadir convinced Koral to help, only to be sending him to his death? As much as he had felt such great anger toward the other man over what had happened with Phana, he realized now Koral had been his friend all along. Jadir didn't want to watch his friend die.

And if Koral didn't survive, Jadir worried that Phana would hate him forever. Jadir would be the cause of her losing the man with whom she had formed a real relationship. And he couldn't bear to have Phana hate him.

"Maybe Koral shouldn't come with us," he suggested.

Phana narrowed her eyes at Jadir.

"Why do you think it will be Koral?"

"Because you and I have abilities he just doesn't have. I think he's in the most danger of all of us."

Phana shook her head.

"Jadir, don't start guessing, and don't start changing plans. I shouldn't have said anything, but I needed to tell someone else, to share what I'm feeling. But you can't let that affect what you're going to do or none of us will walk out of that building when it's over."

She stepped forward and put one hand on his arm, just like she had done with Koral moments before.

"Koral and I knew the risks when we agreed to help you. One of us won't survive this night, and it could be any one of us, including *you*. If you hesitate, or change what you need to do to make sure one of us is safe, then you'll miss your chance to save Marilsa. *That's* why we're here."

Jadir looked down into her eyes and felt tears waiting behind his own.

"Phana, I'm so sorry...."

She looked surprised. "For what?"

"For everything. For dragging you into this situation with Marilsa in the first place. For taking my anger out on you when you couldn't be with me anymore. For saying those terrible things to you, and for blaming Koral for stealing you from me, instead of accepting that it was your choice who you wanted to be with...."

"Stop," she said. "You don't need to apologize, not now. I can only guess how hard this has been on you."

"I want you to be happy, Phana. I wish it was with me, but I understand that won't happen. But I want to know you're happy so that I can focus on what I need to do."

"I can't tell you that," she replied. Jadir was confused by her answer.

"What do you—?"

"I haven't had *time* to be happy. I haven't had time to settle into anything more than a few hours here and there with Koral. And my own life isn't exactly settled right now. I can't promise you that I'm happy, or that things will work out wonderfully between Koral and me. I can't even say I'm going to remain in Ythis much longer—I need to find out who I am, what I have inside me. It's too soon to give you any reassurances, and certainly not right before what we're about to do."

Phana sighed. "Jadir, I don't want to sound angry, but you're so very frustrating sometimes. Life is complicated, and messy, and there are no guarantees. We might succeed tonight, or we might fail, but either way our lives will change permanently after this night's work is done."

Jadir nodded at her, not wanting to say anything else that would make it worse. The truth was he didn't understand her, and probably never would. Just like he didn't really understand any of the people around him. He knew that now.

Jadir wasn't human, and couldn't feel what humans felt, or at least not the way they felt it. He was different, and would always remain so.

"Jadir," Phana whispered to him. He looked up.

Phana raised her hand from his arm to his neck as she stepped close to him. Tilting her face up, she placed her lips on his and kissed him. He could feel her shudder as she did so, though he knew she was trying to suppress it. And then she stepped back and took a deep breath.

"I'm sorry, too," she said.

Jadir figured that had been very difficult for her to do, forcing herself to overcome the repulsion she felt from him, so that she could give him one last kiss. He could not have loved her more in that moment.

"Thank you," he said, feeling a tear run down his cheek. He wiped it away and she smiled at him.

"Now enough of this sadness," she said. "We have a difficult time ahead of us, and we can't go in there full of despair. We need our energy, and we need our anger."

Jadir nodded, not sure how he could let go of what he was feeling right now. And then Koral stepped around the corner and Jadir nearly yelled in surprise. Koral saw he had startled Jadir and gave him a small smile.

"There's a back door that leads to a hallway where the stairs are. I saw no lookouts, but that doesn't mean they're not there."

Koral looked at Jadir and Phana.

"Ready?" he asked.

Phana nodded, and Jadir stepped to the mouth of the alley and looked at the building across the street.

"Yeah," Jadir replied. "I'm ready. Let's go save my sister."

Chapter Thirty-Seven

PHANA STOOD BEHIND KORAL AS HE CAREFULLY OPENED the door and peered into the dark hallway beyond. Seeing no threats, he led them down the hall to the staircase. Jadir was a large presence at Phana's back, saying nothing and letting Koral and Phana lead the way.

Koral tested the first couple of stairs, and they creaked when he put his weight on them.

"We're not getting up there without announcing our presence," he whispered. "If anyone is listening, they'll hear us coming long before we reach them."

Koral turned to Jadir. "Can you sense where Marilsa is?"

"No," Jadir whispered back. "Not exactly. I'll only really be able to tell when I reach whatever floor she's on."

"If we can't sneak, we'll have to go for speed," Phana said in a low voice. "We charge up there and try to hit them before they can prepare for us."

Jadir nodded, while Koral considered her suggestion. Finally, he too agreed.

"I don't see we have any other good option. Same approach as before...ready?"

Jadir and Phana both indicated their readiness, and then Koral bolted up the stairs. Phana charged up right behind him, and she heard Jadir following. Jadir's size worked against them, as his feet slammed into the wooden boards as he ran, the sound echoing up the stairwell.

As soon as Jadir reached the second floor, he shouted "Up!" and

Koral kept ascending. Phana could hear Jadir slowing as he started the second flight of stairs. He didn't have the endurance both Phana and Koral had, and they were forced to stop when they reached the third floor to wait a few extra seconds for Jadir to catch up with them.

Koral was ready to keep ascending, but Jadir stopped and pointed at a door to their left. Phana was the first to reach it, but as Koral moved to step beside her, the other four doors on this floor opened and Marilsa's coven poured out.

Phana spun to fight their assailants and saw familiar faces, faces belonging to people with whom she had once fought side-by-side in gang skirmishes on the streets of Ythis. This time, they were trying to kill her, and she knew her survival would depend on what she was willing to do to save herself.

Her back was to Koral and she heard his blades clanking against the long knives wielded by the attackers. She stepped to one side as a man lunged at her, and she slammed her fist into his temple, knocking him away as his eyes rolled up in his head and he lost consciousness, if only for a moment.

The second man who came at Phana was not so lucky. He was more skilled, and didn't give her an easy opening to knock him senseless. So she took the only opportunity he provided, and buried her dagger in his throat while he was trying to shove his own blade into her chest. She twisted away just in time to avoid his deadly thrust.

Jadir bellowed and grabbed one woman by the front of her shirt and flung her over the wooden railing to go tumbling down the stairs to the second floor. Phana saw another man slash his blade out and leave a gash across Jadir's ribs.

"Jadir!" Phana yelled. "Get to Marilsa, *now*!"

Phana pushed her way forward as Jadir faced her and charged at the one door that had remained closed. His body slammed into the wooden panel and ripped it off its hinges as he barreled through. And then Phana backpedaled and spun to duck through the now-open doorway while Koral protected her back, facing the four remaining attackers in the hallway.

Koral planted himself in the doorway, preventing all four of his opponents from coming at him at the same time. Phana glanced around the room to see the last four members of Marilsa's coven, three of them naked and covered in blood, holding knives that dripped with the lifeblood of their victims.

Phana had no idea what had been done to the fourth, but she no longer resembled anything human. Phana thought she could still make out who the woman had been before, but her stretched and cracking skin, long talons, and distended mouth full of ragged fangs nearly hid her original identity. The creature's head was lopsided, and Phana remembered Jadir's description of what he had done to it earlier tonight.

Marilsa hovered on the far side of the room, her feet at least an arm's length above the floor. Below her, four bodies were sprawled on the floor, pools of blood making a small lake of gore which the coven were using to draw strange symbols on the walls and floor.

Jadir stopped and faced his sister.

"Marilsa," he said in a strangled voice, and then the last four members of the coven flung themselves toward him. Phana leaped forward and cut off two of them, driving them back with her quick blade work.

From the corner of her eye, she saw Jadir avoid the claws of the horrific creature but leave himself open to the last member of the coven. The man lunged forward and buried his blade in Jadir's side.

"No!" Phana yelled, and was nearly stabbed as she let herself be distracted by Jadir's fight. She dropped below the thrusting dagger and it left a shallow cut in her scalp as she went down. But her reaction gave her the opening she needed to drive one of her own knives into the man's groin. Her second attacker kicked at Phana, but she raised her arm to block the blow, leaving her knife embedded in her opponent.

The man she had stabbed fell backward, holding his groin and howling as Phana faced her remaining assailant. She turned just in time to see Jadir swing his huge fist at the head of the man who had stabbed him in the side. There was a loud crunch as the man's neck broke under the force of the blow, and he dropped to the floor as if he was a puppet with its strings suddenly cut.

"Phana!" shouted Koral behind her. She feinted toward the woman facing her, and when the blood-covered attacker flinched back, Phana took a quick look toward where Koral was fighting the coven members in the hallway.

Koral faced two remaining men, but he had taken a wound to his right leg, and his pants were dark with his blood. The men were standing back, waiting for him to weaken, and then they would rush him and cut him down.

Phana knew she didn't have time to duel with the woman who faced her. She needed to finish her own fight right away or Koral would die under the knives of those two men. Phana was the only one still uninjured, and she knew Jadir would also need help against that corrupted creature, especially with his own severe wound.

What should she do? If she helped Jadir, then Koral would be killed. But if she went to Koral's aid and Jadir fell, then there was no way to save Marilsa. For an instant, Phana considering letting loose the cold that lived in her own blood, but that was not a real option—she couldn't guarantee she wouldn't attack Koral and Jadir herself once she had taken out the most immediate threats. Regardless of how much she tried, her control of her own actions under the influence of that power was tenuous at best.

The other woman came at Phana again, but instead of dodging or stepping back, Phana drove forward. The woman's arm was raised high, ready to bring her knife down on Phana's head, but Phana raised her own forearm to block the strike as she plunged her other knife into the woman's chest.

The woman's eyes went wide as the blade sliced into her heart. She looked into Phana's eyes, and something changed in her gaze.

"Phana?" she whispered, and then her legs collapsed, and she fell at Phana's feet, dead.

A shout from behind Phana caused her to spin around to see the men charge at Koral, who went down under their combined tackle.

On the side of the room, the creature shrieked as it leaped at Jadir.

*　　　　*　　　　*

THE WOUND IN JADIR'S SIDE WAS ON FIRE AS THE TWISTED creature came at him, her claws outstretched. He grabbed at her arms and managed to get a grip on one, yanking her off balance as she tried to open his throat with her other hand. The talons raked across his face, and he felt his flesh open up in ribbons across his cheek, mouth and nose.

He backhanded the monster, still gripping her one wrist, and her head snapped around. The back of her skull was misshapen from where he had driven her head into the wall over and over the first time they fought, only a short time earlier.

She tried to slash at him again with her free hand, but he caught her other wrist. Her talons dug into the meat of his forearms, trying to cut her way free. The pain was intense, but he couldn't let go or this... thing... would shred him to pieces.

He raised his gaze to Marilsa, who watched the battle with no expression on her face. But then her eyes met his, and something changed. He could see the little girl she had been, his younger sister, who had loved him unconditionally. She was still in there, and none of this was her fault.

No matter what, Jadir would save her, even if he had to sacrifice his own life to do so.

And suddenly, he felt a powerful surge of energy flow into him. The pain from the wound in his side, and the deep cuts in his arms, became a distant murmur as his muscles overflowed with strength.

Jadir gritted his teeth as he wrenched his arms apart, stretching the creature he held before him. He could feel his muscles straining, and sweat beaded on his forehead and ran into his eyes. And then, with a roar, he tore the corrupted creature apart.

Her body dropped to the floor with a meaty thud as her arms were ripped from her body. She raised her face to him as she writhed in the pool of blood and Jadir lifted one foot and slammed it down on her head. One, two, three times he stamped down, crushing her skull until it broke open and blackened pus exploded out, spattering his pants.

Jadir dropped the creature's arms into the gore and turned to see how his companions had fared.

Phana sat on the floor, Koral in her arms. For an instant, Jadir thought Koral had been killed, but then he saw the man weekly raise his arm and hold onto Phana. Koral was obviously wounded, possibly fatally. It seemed Phana had been right—one of them wouldn't survive the night. And Jadir had been right about which of them would die.

As much as he wanted to rush over to them, he still had to accomplish what he had set out to do. Jadir turned back to his sister.

"Marilsa, I'm here to help you. This isn't you doing this. But you're strong, far stronger than you think. You have to fight this. The priests…they did something to you, influenced you in some way. That's why you want to go to the Tower of Ash. The Church and sorcerers are always fighting, and they've put us in the middle of their war. You can't let them do this to you; you can't let them use you this way."

Jadir took a step closer to Marilsa.

"Come down to me, Marilsa. Just a few days ago, you told me you'd always be my little sister. I will do anything to help you. I'll give up my life to save you from this. But you have to fight it with me. If you need to take my strength from me to help yourself, then I give it to you willingly."

As he said this, Jadir realized the strength he had used to destroy the creature was rapidly fading. And he doubted it was because Marilsa was taking it from him. He realized she had given him the power to save himself—she had managed to take control of herself long enough to do that for him.

But now she had lost control again, and he didn't know how to reach her, how to help her. He could just make out, against the shadows behind her, the figure of her *incubo* hovering in the air beside her, whispering in her ear.

"Marilsa, tell me what I can do to help you. Anything…."

Marilsa opened her mouth and whispered something. Jadir took another step closer to her.

"I can't hear you…."

She opened her mouth and spoke in a louder voice this time.

"You…can *die*."

And with that last word, a wave of energy pulsed out from her and lifted Jadir up and flung him across the room to crash against the far wall. Phana screamed as she was flung away from Koral, who was tossed out the door into the hallway beyond.

A great weight pressed Jadir into the wooden wall, and he heard the panels cracking under the pressure. Marilsa lowered to the floor, her small feet sinking into the pool of blood. She walked slowly toward Jadir, her *incubo* hovering beside her, whispering—always whispering—into her ear.

"Jadir, my brother dear. You haven't yet realized you cannot help me. The girl I was, your little sister, is gone. She was nothing, a weak, mewling creature who didn't deserve to live. But now I am here, and I will do what needs to be done. I accept what I am, I embrace *who* I am."

She stopped a few paces from where Jadir was held against the wall, a trail of bloody footprints behind her.

"I no longer have need of you, Jadir. You were summoned for a purpose, to protect that which couldn't protect itself. But that girl is dead, and now there is only me. And I don't need protecting!"

Jadir felt a horrible wrenching feeling inside his body, and he became what he could only describe as *untethered*. It was as if his body was a suit of clothes too big for him, a garment that hung off him because he wasn't large enough to fill it up. He gasped for breath, but he couldn't get enough air into his lungs.

"I would simply banish you back to wherever my mother brought you from, but my *incubo* thinks I shouldn't leave any loose ends. We've been connected for too long, you and I, and my enemies could use you against me. You must be destroyed, my brother."

Marilsa tilted her head sideways and looked up at him with a strange expression on her face.

"I know you think I'm being manipulated by the Church, Jadir, but you're wrong. I have my own reasons for going to the Tower of Ash. I will…I…must…."

She faltered, as if she couldn't remember why she felt the urge to go to such a destination.

"Marilsa," Jadir gasped at her. "The thought isn't yours. It's been put in your head...by *him*. Fight it—I know you're strong enough."

He saw the *incubo* whisper in her ear ever more urgently. She paused, listening, and then shook her head.

"But, why...?" she asked in a low voice. The *incubo* never paused, but kept trying to influence her to kill Jadir once and for all.

Marilsa raised her arms and turned her palms toward Jadir.

"This is how it must be...big brother."

Jadir tried to close his eyes, but the lids wouldn't respond. He had no control over his body anymore. Marilsa stood there, not moving, and Jadir waited for his destruction.

"No," she whispered.

Marilsa dropped her arms to her sides, and the pressure holding Jadir to the wall dissolved, dropping him to the floor. He felt his spirit snap back into place inside his body, but it didn't feel quite right, as if the connection was tenuous at best.

"I cannot do it," she said to her *incubo*. "I cannot destroy him. Something holds me back."

She looked down at Jadir, sprawled on the floor at her feet. And then she got a look in her eye and she smiled in a way that made Jadir's blood run cold. She glanced sideways at the *incubo*.

"I can't," she repeated. "But *you* can."

Chapter Thirty-Eight

JADIR TRIED TO PUSH HIMSELF TO HIS FEET, BUT WASN'T FAST enough. He saw the *incubo* move toward him, and it seemed to grow more solid, though it never became fully flesh and blood. The spirit, still resembling the naked man Jadir had seen hovering over his sister less than a fortnight ago, grabbed Jadir by his shirt and lifted him up into the air.

Though still partially transparent, the *incubo* was able to physically attack Jadir, and the spirit flung him across the room. Jadir crashed into the wall and landed on his back, the breath knocked out of him. He rolled over onto his stomach in time to see the *incubo* fly across the room and swing its foot out in an arc.

The kick caught Jadir in the ribs—on the opposite side from the knife wound, thankfully—and lifted him off the floor. Jadir cried out in pain as he landed and felt the blood pouring from his injury.

As the spirit picked him up again, Jadir lashed out with a fist and connected with the face of the *incubo*, knocking it backward.

It's solid enough for me to hit back! he thought. He lunged up and tried to tackle the *incubo*, but the spirit twisted away and Jadir went sprawling to the floor once more. He felt the creature land on his back and grab his head in both hands.

The *incubo* began to twist Jadir's head to the side, and it was strong enough that Jadir knew if he didn't get it off his back, the spirit would break his neck. Jadir heaved and tried to roll to one side, and the spirit suddenly lifted away and landed in front of him.

Jadir slowly pushed himself to his feet. He glanced around the room and saw Marilsa had not moved and was watching the fight with narrowed eyes. On the other side of the room, Phana was slowly beginning to recover from Marilsa's wave of energy that had knocked her senseless.

And Koral... Jadir could only hope the man was still alive, as he had been tossed out of the room and was no longer visible.

The *incubo* flew at Jadir and hammered into his chest, driving him back into the wall once more. Jadir flung his fists at the creature's head and connected once, twice, and the spirit staggered back. Jadir lunged again, and this time managed to wrap his arms around the creature.

It was like grappling a pillar of mud, as his arms seemed to sink through the spirit's body. Jadir pulled back one arm and tried to beat on the *incubo's* head again, but the spirit wrapped its own hands around Jadir's throat and began to squeeze.

Jadir knew he had only seconds before he would lose consciousness. He swung with all of his strength at the *incubo's* face, and hit the creature again and again. Each time he connected, he could feel its substance give a little more.

Stars swam before Jadir's eyes and he kept swinging his fists at the spirit choking him to death. Finally, the creature became insubstantial enough that its grip loosened, and Jadir threw himself away from the fingers locked around his throat.

He gasped and coughed as he tried to suck more air into his lungs. Jadir's body wasn't responding properly—it was as if he was no longer fully in control of his own limbs. The *incubo* hovered a few arm spans away, and Jadir heard Marilsa whisper.

"Kill him," she hissed at the *incubo*.

The spirit became more substantial again and dove at Jadir. Its own fists connected with the side of Jadir's face, the same cheek that had been shredded by the claws of the twisted member of Marilsa's coven. He screamed as a white-hot pain blossomed on his face, and the floor came up to hit Jadir in the back.

Groggy, Jadir realized he had been knocked down again. The *incubo* reached out a hand, and one of the bloody daggers flew up from the floor to land in its fist. It reached out the other hand, and another dagger skittered across the floor and jumped up into his grip.

Jadir knew he was finished. The *incubo* represented everything that had gone wrong in Jadir's and Marilsa's lives. Jadir wanted nothing more than to destroy that creature, even if it meant Marilsa would lose whatever abilities she had developed over the last two weeks.

But the creature was too powerful for Jadir to defeat. And Jadir was weakened by the knife wound in his side, and the blood flowing down his face. He looked at the *incubo*, and then at the daggers, and understood he was going to die here. And then Marilsa would kill Phana, and Koral too, if he wasn't already dead.

Jadir slowly pushed himself to his feet, and the *incubo* waited, relishing this moment before it would cut him to pieces. He looked at Marilsa, but she still watched the fight with an evil smile. She was lost to him now. Only by destroying the *incubo* could Jadir possibly free his sister from its—and the Church's—influence.

And he had nearly no fight left in him.

The *incubo* was suddenly in motion, flying at Jadir with knives outstretched on either side. Jadir didn't try to dodge, but stepped forward and reached out to grab the creature as it collided with him.

Jadir felt a sharp coldness enter his side as the first knife plunged into his flesh. But he was already swinging his fist with all his might. The other knife sliced a line across his chest as he knocked the *incubo* sideways with the force of his blow.

If the creature had been fully tangible, Jadir would have shattered its neck with his second swing. As it was, he screamed as the knife was yanked from his side and the spirit fell back. But Jadir kept with it, putting everything he had had into each swing of his fists. The knives plunged into his body, or scored deep cuts across his arms and chest as he fought.

A liquid bubbling came up from his lungs as Jadir tried to breath, and he coughed a bright bubble of blood into the face of the *incubo* before slamming his hands together on either side of the spirit's head.

The creature lost its solidity once again, the knives dropping to the floor in front of Jadir. He threw himself forward, through the *incubo*, and staggered to the door. Marilsa turned to watch Jadir as he pulled himself out into the hallway and stumbled to the stairs, starting to climb as he saw back through the doorway the *incubo* beginning to solidify once again.

I can't beat him, thought Jadir. *All I can do is draw him as far away from Marilsa as possible.*

Jadir didn't really believe it would make a difference, but it was the only thing he could think to do. Perhaps if the *incubo* left Marilsa's side, his influence would weaken just enough for Marilsa to regain control of herself.

He also hoped Phana would be able to escape while the *incubo* was chasing after Jadir. And then the thought hit him that the spirit might be attacking Phana right now, finishing her off before coming after him.

She had said one of them was going to die tonight. But she hadn't said *only* one of them would die. If Jadir's last, desperate gamble didn't work, none of them would see the morning.

*   *   *

JADIR REACHED THE TOP FLOOR OF THE TENEMENT AND LOOKED around the hallway. At the far end, a ladder led up to a hatch in the ceiling. He slowly pushed himself to his feet and staggered toward the ladder.

His shirt and pants were soaked with his blood, the cuts and stab wounds burning and aching as he moved. He was starting to feel light-headed from the loss of blood, and the more he moved, the worse it became.

Jadir knew, even if he managed to free Marilsa from the influence of the *incubo*, that he was not likely to survive this night. He coughed, and another spray of blood erupted from his mouth. One of the knife thrusts had pierced a lung, and he felt like he was drowning in his own blood.

He reached the ladder, and began to drag himself up the rungs, one at a time. He released the latch and shoved the hatch open, and a patch of night sky greeted him, full of stars wheeling overhead.

Jadir pulled himself up, bit by bit, as his life leaked out the ragged holes in his body.

As he put his hands on the lip of the rooftop, he heard a whistling noise, as of a wind through a narrow gap, and he knew the *incubo* was coming for him. Jadir put on a last burst of speed and pushed himself up and onto the roof, where he lay on his back, a warm breeze blowing over him.

To his left, the Tower of Ash rose into the sky, the black cloud of smoke rising from its own roof. He looked at it and silently cursed it and the Church both.

Beside him, the *incubo* rose through the open hatch and floated above him, the bloody daggers in its hands.

"I won't let...you have...her," he said to the spirit. The man-shaped creature merely watched him, waiting. Perhaps it would simply wait for Jadir to lose enough blood that he was helpless. And then the *incubo* would finish him off easily.

Jadir could feel the malevolence coming from the *incubo*. He could feel its power. He understood, now, that drawing it away from Marilsa had made no difference at all. His final gamble had failed.

Despair took hold of Jadir. He was dying on this dirty rooftop in the Warren, his friends injured or possibly already dead. The *incubo* was still in control of Marilsa. And once Jadir was gone, his little sister would go to the Tower of Ash and confront the sorceress who lived there.

There was no question Marilsa would also fail. No witch had ever managed to defeat a sorcerer in battle. Witches were forced to hide themselves from the Church and the sorcerers, because they just didn't have the same kind of power. No, Marilsa would be destroyed.

She had told him, only a few days ago, that he had already failed her. And Jadir had promised her that he would not fail her again. But tonight, he had done exactly that.

No matter how hard he tried, Jadir had been unable to beat the *incubo*. It was too powerful—had too many tricks that Jadir couldn't counter. He had done his best, and his best simply wasn't good enough.

Jadir felt himself getting weaker. He was going to die soon, and then it would all be over. He wouldn't even be aware of whatever happened to Marilsa afterward—she would be truly alone for the first time since she had been born.

He would leave this body, that hadn't even been his....

Jadir stopped, and then repeated that last thought to himself.

This body hadn't even been his. This body, that felt as if he was wearing a suit of clothes that didn't fit right. This body, that Marilsa had almost wrenched him out of only a few minutes ago while she had him pinned to the wall.

She had said she could banish him back to wherever Ineir had summoned him from, but then decided to destroy him instead. He was a spirit who had been bound into this body, and she had already severed most of those ties.

If the body died, what would happen to the spirit? Would he be set free? Would he be drawn back to the place where he had been before Ineir had brought him forth?

No, neither of those things would happen. The *incubo* would destroy him. It was waiting for the body to die so that it could reach the spirit, and it would attack him once again.

Jadir had no memory of being a spirit, had no idea what it was like. Could he fight the *incubo* on its own terms? He didn't believe he would win such a fight—the *incubo* knew what it was, had such power at its command. Jadir didn't know what he could do. Even if he was stronger than the *incubo*, he wouldn't have any idea how to use that strength to defeat the other spirit.

Jadir rolled over and slowly pushed himself to his feet. He staggered over to the edge of the roof and looked down at the cobblestone streets below. If he threw himself off now, would it free his spirit as the body hit the ground and died? Could he perhaps flee from the *incubo*?

But that wouldn't save Marilsa, and he had sworn to do whatever was necessary to help her.

And then, looking down, Jadir saw a large group of armored men on horseback come galloping around the corner to reign up in front of the building upon which he stood. Without counting, he guessed there were around twenty riders.

Horses, here in the Warren!

And then he spotted three men in the center of the group who were different from the soldiers around them. Two were dressed in priest's black robes, and the third wore leather armor and looked like he would be more comfortable in the wilderness than in the middle of a city like Ythis.

The Church was here.

Jadir scanned the crowd below, looking for the priestess who had confronted them on the street a few days ago, but she was not among this group. Jadir knew there was only one reason why they had come into the Warren this night. They had finally come for Marilsa.

But hadn't they wanted her to go to the Tower of Ash? Hadn't they been doing...something...to manipulate Marilsa into attacking their enemy? Had Jadir been wrong about that all along?

It didn't matter, now. If they decided to capture or kill his sister, it was unlikely she would escape, or survive. Even with the power of her *incubo*, she couldn't....

Jadir gasped as the thought hit him. He turned to face the spirit, hovering only a few strides behind him. Jadir's heels were at the very edge of the roof, and the open space yawned at his back. He felt so weak, so tired. He wanted nothing more than to go to sleep, but he knew it wasn't time yet.

He had one last thing to do. He still had to save Marilsa.

Chapter Thirty-Nine

J ADIR SPREAD HIS HANDS OUT TO EITHER SIDE OF HIS BODY and confronted the *incubo*.

"Look, you...degenerate son of a...whore. Look who I...brought," he lied. He only hoped the *incubo* wouldn't be able to tell Jadir was bluffing. "The...Church is here. They've come to...stop Marilsa and...get rid of *you*."

Jadir forced himself to laugh once, and he nearly lost grip on his own body as more blood poured out of his mouth and down his chin.

"I knew I...couldn't beat you, but *they* can. You're a...weak, pathetic nothing of a...spirit. You thought you could...destroy me, but all you've done is...kill this...body. I'm leaving now, but you...you're going to be erased...from existence."

The *incubo*'s cat-eyes glowed a deep yellow, like they had the first night he had seen it, when Jadir had invoked the name of Iathephos to drive it away.

It flew at Jadir, knives outstretched. The blades entered his chest, piercing both his lungs, and Jadir didn't move, didn't try to block the thrusts.

Instead, Jadir *let go*.

With every iota of willpower he possessed, Jadir pushed himself to separate from this body that wasn't his. He focused on the feeling he had endured in the room below, of becoming untethered from the limbs he controlled, from the eyes and mouth, from the heart and stomach.

And with a final wrench, Jadir was free.

An instant later, a rush of sensation flooded Jadir's consciousness, new senses he had not experienced in thirteen years nearly overwhelming him. And with his new awareness came a torrent of memory, his existence before the summoning, before the binding.

He could feel a connection to a river far to the west and north, somewhere between here and the city of Jh'tira. He had been a part of that river, and the trees that lined its bank. He had lived in that natural setting, taking care of the forest and the river, protecting the uncountable lives that depended on that land and water.

Jadir had been torn away from his home and sent here, to this city, a festering wound that repelled nature instead of embracing it. He felt almost physical pain to be here in the center of such a malignant blight on the land, and he wanted nothing more than to return to his home.

But there was something he needed to do first.

The *incubo* hovered in the air, holding the knives embedded in the chest of the dead body Jadir had inhabited for so long. Barely an instant had passed since Jadir had let go of the flesh in which he had been trapped.

Jadir reached out with his essence and grabbed the *incubo*. And as he retreated from the body, he pulled the *incubo* forward.

He pulled it *into* the corpse still standing on the edge of the roof.

Jadir knew he couldn't bind the *incubo* into the body, not the way *he* had been bound. And death always released the spirit, regardless. But the *incubo* was taken by surprise, and Jadir used what power he possessed—power he now remembered how to use—to wrap the *incubo* in a barrier and contain it inside the now-empty flesh.

His trap would last only a minute or two, at most, and he hoped it would be enough.

Jadir floated in the air above the building and watched his body slowly topple backward. A shout from below told him the soldiers saw the falling figure and were moving out of the way. With a sickening crash, the body hit the rough, uneven cobblestones, bones shattering and blood spraying outward from the corpse.

As the soldiers dismounted and began to form a protective ring around the priests and their companion, the man in leather armor leaped off his horse and grabbed an amulet that hung around his neck.

"The witch's spirit, it's here!" the man shouted to the priests.

The older of the two priests slid off his horse and began to chant, as the man with the amulet held it over Jadir's body.

Even from up here, Jadir could feel the *incubo* struggling to get free of the corpse. But as the priest continued to chant, Jadir saw a barrier of black energy form around the body. It would not be visible to the men down below, but Jadir could see the priest's magic working to contain the *incubo*.

And then the amulet held by the other man started to glow with a fierce light that caused Jadir to recoil from the intense pain, and he heard the *incubo* screech as the light washed over it. Jadir retreated from the scene, as the *incubo* was consumed by the power of the Church's gods.

With a thought, Jadir plunged down through the rooftop and the floor below to find Marilsa unconscious in the room where they had fought. Phana stood over her, her long knife in her hand, about to slay the young girl before she could do any more damage.

No! Jadir sent the thought at Phana with all his will, and Phana grabbed her head and staggered away from Marilsa. Phana shook her head and looked around the room, and Jadir tried to communicate with her.

I saved her! he thought at Phana. *The incubo is destroyed! The Church is here, and you have to get out now!*

"Jadir?" Phana said out loud. "Jadir, is that you? I can hear you in my mind."

It's me! Jadir replied. *You have to wake Marilsa up and get her out of here! The Church is right outside the building!*

He couldn't tell how clear his thoughts were to Phana, and he knew if it had been anyone else, they wouldn't have been able to hear him at all. But Phana seemed to understand, and she sheathed her knife and knelt down beside Marilsa.

Gently shaking Marilsa's shoulder, Phana called her name a few times. Marilsa's eyes fluttered and then opened and focused on Phana's face. Phana drew back, obviously worried that Marilsa would attack her again. But Marilsa's eyes welled up in tears.

"Phana?" she whispered. "He did it, Phana. He...he saved me."

And then she sat up and wrapped her arms around Phana and sobbed. Phana hesitated, and then embraced Marilsa and soothed her as well as she was able.

"Marilsa," Phana said to her a moment later. "We have to leave. The Church is outside the building. We can't delay."

Jadir watched Phana help Marilsa regain her feet, and then he flew out of the room and searched for Koral. He found the young man sprawled on the stairs leading down to the second floor. It was where he had landed after being tossed out of the room by Marilsa's pulse of energy.

Koral was unconscious as well, but breathing regularly. Phana had managed to tie his belt around his leg just above the knife wound to slow the bleeding. Jadir could sense Koral's life-force, strong and steady. He wished he could do something to heal Koral, but they didn't have time for that.

Marilsa and Phana appeared at the top of the stairs, and Phana rushed down to check on Koral. She was able to wake him up, and he said he was okay to move.

With Phana helping Koral, they made their way down to the ground floor and along the hallway to the back door. All three slipped out into the alley and closed the door just as the soldiers burst into the building through the front.

"They'll check out here in a moment," Phana said, a note of fear in her voice. "We've got to get out of here."

"You two go ahead," said Koral in a strained voice. "You can get away, but I'm too slow with this wound. But you have to go right now!"

"I'm not leaving you to the Church," Phana argued.

"Quiet, both of you," Marilsa interrupted. They looked at her with fear in their eyes, but she merely glanced around the alley and then seemed to look directly at Jadir.

"Stay close to me, and be as quiet as you can. We're walking out of here."

And then Marilsa closed her eyes and Jadir felt power coursing through him in a channel directly into her. He watched as a cloud formed around the three figures in the alley, and realized what it was for.

"We can't just walk out in the open," said Phana.

"We can now. They cannot see us, at least for the next few minutes," Marilsa answered. "Let's go."

Jadir watched Marilsa lead them out of the alley. He worried that the priests or the man with the amulet would be able to detect their cloak of shadows, but the three men had gone inside the building to search for Marilsa, leaving only the soldiers in the street.

The door in the rear of the building burst open, and four soldiers emerged into the alley. But though they appeared to look directly at Marilsa, Phana, and Koral, they acted as if the alley was empty.

Marilsa led the trio across the street and into another alley before the cloud dispersed. Jadir stayed with them as they made their way through the Warren and found a place to rest in an abandoned building some distance from the Tower of Ash.

While Phana made Koral as comfortable as possible, Marilsa turned and looked directly at Jadir again.

"You saved me," she said simply. "I was... I was trapped inside myself, doing things I never wanted to do, and it looked like I was going to cause your death as well. But my *incubo* is gone—I felt his fear as he was destroyed. You did that, didn't you?"

Yes, he thought at his sister. *I couldn't fight him, but I tricked him. I trapped him in my body, and the priests could sense him. They did some kind of ritual and destroyed him. It delayed them long enough for us to get out before they came into the building to look for you.*

"They're going to keep hunting me," she said. "No matter where I go, they'll come after me."

With the incubo gone, how did you create the cloak to hide you from the soldiers? Jadir asked.

Marilsa smiled. "You did that for me. My *incubo* is gone, but I'm connected to you with a stronger bond than I ever had with him. I'm sorry I used you for that, but we needed to hide. I promise I won't do that again without your permission."

Jadir was amazed at her words. He had expected her to lose all her gifts once the *incubo* was destroyed. He didn't understand how she had used him.

"Marilsa," Phana called to her. Phana and Koral were looking at her with pensive expressions. They still weren't entirely sure they could trust her.

Marilsa walked over to them, and Jadir saw tears begin to run down her cheeks again.

"I…I'm so sorry for everything. I never wanted to…all those people…."

She stopped, unable to continue, and Phana reached out and put her hand on Marilsa's shoulder.

"Marilsa," she repeated. "There will be time to think about that later. But we're all still in great danger. Right now, we need to decide what we're going to do next."

Marilsa nodded and wiped her tears away. Jadir hovered over them, watching.

*   *   *

TOZROTH GRABBED RELAEL BY HIS ROBES AND SHOVED HIM UP against the wall. Relael's head bounced painfully off the rough wooden planks.

"Where is the witch?" he yelled.

Relael could see the Imperial Guardsmen watching nervously, unsure whether they should intervene or not. Relael waved them off.

"I do not know, Tozroth. She was here, obviously. And you've destroyed her *incubo*. So she cannot have gone far."

Tozroth looked into Relael's eyes, and then let go and stepped back. He spoke in a low voice, so the soldiers couldn't hear.

"Ye said you'd give up the girl to me once ye were done with her. Are ye still using her, or is she mine?"

"She's yours," Relael whispered back. "I believe I've achieved what I've wanted, and not only do I have no further use for her, it's in my best interests that she die as quickly as possible. You can have whatever help from me you need."

Tozroth swore and paced to the window, looking out into the street.

"The body, it was her brother, Jadir. Why was the *incubo* in his body? And who stabbed him?" Relael asked.

"I don't know," Tozroth snapped. "There was quite a battle in here. Someone attacked the witch's coven. But it looks like whoever else was here got away, too."

"Could it have been Jadir? Could the witch have killed him and given his body to her *incubo*?"

Tozroth turned away from the window and faced Relael.

"It's possible, though I don't know why a witch would tether the spirit to a physical body like that. And that doesn't explain why he jumped—or was pushed—off the roof."

Relael looked around the room, at the bodies, at the remains of some twisted creature that had seemingly been ripped in half, at the pools of blood covering the floor. The girl had not gotten as close to the Tower of Ash as Relael had hoped, but he was sure it would be enough to place the blame for this slaughter at the feet of the Burning Crone.

But as long as the witch was still alive, that young girl was a potential threat. If any of the sorcerers got their hands on her, Relael's plan would crumble apart. That was a situation he could ill afford.

"We have to assume not all of her coven was killed here," Relael said out loud. "Whoever remained must have helped her escape while you were destroying the *incubo*. That means she's still somewhere in the Warren, and she's not alone."

He turned to Commander Zopu, who once again led this contingent of Guardsmen.

"We need to find this girl, Commander. Even if we must search every inch of the Warren."

The commander's eyes went wide.

"I...I'm sorry, Brother, but that's not really possible. Even if we mobilize the entire Imperial Guard in Ythis, invading the Warren like that won't be easy. The inhabitants of this area will fight us every step of the way, using ambushes and hit-and-run tactics. And there's no way to ensure the girl won't slip past us in the sewers or some other underground passage. The Warren is just too big."

Relael knew the man was correct—Marilsa wasn't the first fugitive to hide in the Warren, and the Guard had never come in here in force, no matter the crime.

"I don't need the Guard's help," Tozroth said, interrupting Relael's thoughts. "They'll only get in the way. If she's in the Warren, if she's in this city, I'll find her."

The Witch Hunter stepped close to Relael again and glared into his eyes as he spoke in a low voice. "Look at what she's done, priest. Look at the bodies of those she sacrificed. This is all on you. I hope whatever it was ye were trying to do was worth it."

"It was," Relael said without hesitation. "And I'd do it again in a heartbeat."

Tozroth snorted in derision and walked out of the room. Commander Zopu turned to Relael, waiting for new orders.

"Gather your men, Commander. It's time for us to leave. The Witch Hunter will find the girl and do what he needs to do. We're no longer needed here."

The soldiers left the room and Relael took one last look around. He would report back to High Counselor Untoleu, and she would in turn spin it to look like some servant of the Burning Crone's who had caused all this destruction. The Imperial spymaster, Tyath, would use his influence to push the Emperor in the right direction.

The Six would be censured by the Emperor, and would be forced to make concessions to the Church. And it would all fall on the newest of their members, the Burning Crone.

Perhaps her brethren would destroy her outright for the problems she had caused them, Relael mused. That would be the best-case scenario, though he doubted it would come to that. Still, it was something to hope for.

Relael didn't like to rely on others to tie up loose ends. But he would have to let Tozroth do his job and eliminate the girl. He only hoped the man didn't take too long.

Relael walked down to the street and found Brother Worestald being helped up onto his horse again by two soldiers. Relael climbed onto his own mount and leaned across to the other priest.

"Brother, there is one more thing we must do when we return to the Temple."

"And what is that, Brother Ochallum?"

Relael smiled. "Another member of our order has been helping me with this mission. I need you to come with me to talk to him, give him a report of everything that's happened here. Don't worry, it won't take long."

Brother Worestald nodded. "Very well. I must admit, I will be pleased to put this all behind us. I don't believe I'm cut out for this type of work."

Relael wanted to tell the priest he wouldn't have to worry about that anymore. But he kept silent—Ontherim would realize it soon enough when he was in the clutches of Yondos.

After all, Relael had a debt to be paid. And one last loose end to tie up.

Chapter Forty

PHANA ENTERED THE ROOM AND LOOKED DOWN AT Koral, resting peacefully on the bed. A thin blanket covered him, and she could see the lump where bandages wrapped his thigh. He opened his eyes, saw her, and smiled.

"You look comfortable," she said as she came over and sat on the stool beside the bed.

"My leg hurts something fierce, but I don't often get to sleep in a real bed, so I suppose there's some good to be found."

She looked at his face and couldn't suppress the nervousness that fluttered around inside her stomach. With everything Koral had been through, she didn't want to put more of a burden on him, but she knew she couldn't wait anymore.

By the time she had managed to get Koral out of the Warren last night and find some help for him, he had barely been able to remain conscious from loss of blood. But once he had been taken into the care of the Wolf's people, she knew he would survive. And she wasn't ready to lose him yet.

It was the 'yet' that bothered her. But she knew, deep down, that they wouldn't be together for very long, no matter how much she liked being with him. Phana knew she wasn't good at long-term commitments, though her memories of previous relationships were hazy at best. She could almost picture a few faces, but names were completely lost to her.

And she needed to know why that was.

"You saved my life," Koral said to her. "I want to thank you for that."

"Did you think I was just going to leave you in the Warren to bleed to death?"

He chuckled, and then winced in pain when it caused a slight movement in his leg.

"No," he said. "I knew you wouldn't, even to save your own life."

Phana's thoughts turned back to Marilsa, and what she had done in the alley to hide them from the eyes of the soldiers. Koral was obviously thinking the same thing.

"She saved us both," he said. Phana knew he was thinking about Jadir, and how they had been unable to save their friend.

"He's not dead," Phana blurted out.

"What? Who's not dead?"

"Jadir. His body died, but he...his spirit still exists."

There hadn't been time last night for Phana or Marilsa to explain what had happened to Jadir. Koral still wasn't sure how they had survived, or how Jadir had saved his sister.

Koral looked at Phana, confusion in his eyes.

"Marilsa told me what happened while you were slipping in and out of consciousness. Jadir beat the *incubo*, and it was destroyed by the priests, but Jadir's body died. It was never really his body, though. So now he's just a spirit again, and he's with Marilsa."

Koral's eyes widened as he realized his friend hadn't been destroyed in the battle last night.

"Can...can she speak to him? Can he speak back?"

Phana nodded. "I could hear him, too, but very faintly. I was about to kill Marilsa, and he stopped me."

Phana had argued with Marilsa before they split up. She had wanted them to stay together, but Marilsa said it was time for her to leave. The Witch Hunter would keep following her, she had said, and she wouldn't put Phana or Koral in any more danger.

There had been time for Phana to give the young girl a quick hug, and then Marilsa left them. Koral hadn't had a chance to say goodbye.

"So she isn't alone, then," Koral mumbled. Phana could see he was getting sleepy again. She wanted to let him rest, but there was something she needed to say first.

"Koral, listen to me."

He opened his eyes and focused on her face.

"When you're better, I need you to take me to see the Wolf."

Koral's eyebrows drew together. "Why would you want...?"

"I need to know who I am. The Wolf was able to tell Jadir and Marilsa about their past. And I know he's had me under his protection, too. I need to know why."

Koral couldn't keep the guilty look off his face. She didn't blame him for not telling her, however. She understood his vow to the Wolf, and couldn't hold it against him. But the time for games was over.

"You may not like what you hear," Koral said to her. "Jadir wasn't any happier when he found out the truth."

She smiled at him, more to relieve him about his guilt than because of any humor.

"You may not have noticed, Koral, but I'm not Jadir."

"Oh...I've noticed," he replied. "Believe me, I've noticed. But—"

She leaned over and kissed him gently, cutting off his words. He could barely keep his eyes open.

"Get some rest. We can talk about it later."

"You know...I'm not wearing anything...under this blanket."

Phana laughed out loud and stood up.

"Don't bother," she said, grinning at him. "You'll need to be in better shape than this to make it worth my while."

Koral gave a mock sigh that turned into a real yawn. Phana turned away, and by the time she was closing the door behind her, he was already asleep.

Phana didn't know what the Wolf would tell her, or even if he would give her the truth, but it didn't matter. What mattered was knowing who she was. She had a feeling she had been running away from something for a very long time, though she had no idea what it might be.

Regardless, it was time to stop running. It was time to face her past. She knew she was strong enough to deal with whatever came her way.

And she would enjoy her time with Koral while it lasted.

*　　　　　*　　　　　*

THE CHAMBER WASN'T VERY BRIGHT, THOUGH THE BOY WAS used to the lack of illumination. The Burning Crone's very presence always caused any nearby light sources to dim, and he was near her often enough that he barely noticed the effect anymore. He seemed to have become, he reflected, the sorceress' primary servant.

The Crone stood before her guest, wisps of smoke rising from her clothing and skin as if she still smoldered from the great conflagration that had taken her youth and appearance. The guest, an old woman with milky white eyes, sat on a wooden chair in the middle of the room. A young girl stood behind the blind woman, watching the boy with a bright, inquisitive air.

"Such crude, clumsy efforts," the Burning Crone continued. "An act of desperation, nothing more."

"You are not concerned with the outcome, then," the guest said, and the boy noted the similarity in their voices, both cracked and ancient.

"The only outcome of this is the one I have already planned. I dispatched a message to the Emperor the day the young girl moved into the Warren, asking him if he'd prefer to let me handle the situation personally or leave it to the Church. His response was that the Church was already looking into it."

"So when they try to lay the blame for it at your feet—"

"They'll show their little scheme for what it was, an attempt to manipulate the Emperor. They must have thought me such a fool to remain unaware of what was happening around my own home. That priest, the one who warned you about the attempt to capture you—he's a slippery one, but not nearly as clever as he thinks he is."

"I suppose," said the blind woman, "That things will return to normal around here, then?"

The Burning Crone laughed, a dark, nasty sound with no mirth in it—only mocking sarcasm.

"There is no 'normal' anymore. The balance of power in Ythis has shifted, and the Church has no way to pull it back into equilibrium. Change is here, witch, and it will only come faster and faster."

The boy watched the old woman flinch at the word 'witch.' He had heard that witches were outlawed in the Empire, and while the Church had the Witch Hunters, the sorcerers were not above stepping in directly to eliminate a witch when one was discovered. The boy knew this witch had helped the Burning Crone in some manner, and he figured that was the only reason his master hadn't already destroyed her.

"I am free to leave, then?" the old woman asked.

The Burning Crone hesitated, turning her head to one side and regarding her guest with a cold stare. Finally, she waved one hand, as if dismissing the other woman.

"You are free to leave. You have done me a service, and earned your peace with me. Stay out of my way, and I will ignore your presence in the Warren."

The old woman let out a breath and the girl stepped around her chair and laid a hand on her shoulder.

"Thank you," the witch said.

The Burning Crone ignored her gratitude and turned to the boy.

"Sulid, show them out."

She turned and left the room, which brightened slightly in the glow of the lamp once she had departed.

Sulid hobbled forward, his ruined feet little more than dead knobs of flesh on the ends of his legs. His was hardly the worst deformity among those who served the Crone. The ones who lurked outside around the Tower of Ash were barely human.

The old woman stood, and the girl took her hand. Sulid led them back to the entry chamber. As they stepped before the large black iron door, it swung open to reveal the smoky courtyard beyond.

The boy watched the witch and her assistant leave, and the portal swung closed behind them. Then he turned and headed for the Burning Crone's chambers. As always, there was much to do.

*   *   *

MARILSA STOOD ON THE HILL AND LOOKED BACK AT YTHIS, the sprawling city that was the dark heart of the Empire.

"I'm not going to miss it," she said out loud. "I've never really been happy here."

Jadir knew that wasn't entirely true, but he could feel that Marilsa needed to tell herself that to make it easier to leave. She had been in Ythis for as long as she could remember.

But Jadir had new memories, memories of a time long before they came to Ythis. Long before he was bound into someone else's flesh. And Ythis now represented nothing to him but pain.

"I want to see where you came from," she said. "I bet it's beautiful."

It is, he said in her mind. *I can't wait to show you. But it's far from here, and we will travel for a long time before we reach my home.*

"I don't care. As long as we're together, Jadir, we'll be fine."

She didn't voice any concerns about the Witch Hunter, though Jadir knew it was on her mind. The man who had destroyed her *incubo* would not stop until he found her. They would lose him for a while, but eventually he'd pick up their trail and come after Marilsa again.

One day, he'd catch up with her. And then Marilsa would be forced to take another life, or give up her own.

Jadir could feel Marilsa's guilt like a huge wound in her soul. He knew she was barely holding herself together. She took full responsibility for the deaths of those innocent people in the Warren, and she was on the verge of weeping at any moment.

She had explained to him that her *incubo* had rapidly become too strong to control. It was as if the spirit had found a source of power that kept feeding him, allowing him to reverse their roles. Such a thing was unheard of—at least not without outside influence.

Jadir wondered if that was what the priests had been doing, if they had been feeding power to the *incubo*. Once the spirit had taken over, Marilsa had expected him to impregnate her. It was what the old witch in the Warren had told Marilsa that night they met.

But Marilsa's *incubo* had done no such thing. Instead, it drew her toward the Tower of Ash, and encouraged her to conduct sacrifices to gain even more power.

Neither Jadir nor Marilsa would ever know the truth of what happened. But Marilsa would always feel the guilt over the deaths she had caused while under the spirit's influence.

We should go. It is a long journey ahead of us.

Marilsa turned away from Ythis.

"Why are you helping me, Jadir? After what I did to you, why are you still with me? The spell that bound you has been severed. You're free to go where you want."

She was ready to burst into tears once more. Jadir sent feelings of love through the link between them.

Because you're my little sister, Marilsa. That hasn't changed, no matter where we came from, no matter what we've done. For most of your life, it has been just you and me. I wouldn't have it any other way.

Marilsa wiped her tears away and began to walk. It would be a long journey indeed.

~ *End* ~

More books in the Tales of the Undying Empire series are available in print or ebook at Amazon.

Thank you for reading The Witch's Path. If you enjoyed this book, please tell others about it. Honest reviews are also greatly appreciated and are the best way to help other readers discover new authors.

About Andrew J. Luther

Andrew J. Luther lives in Burlington, Ontario with his wife and son. He currently works as a communications professional in his day-job, but spends his spare time playing tabletop roleplaying games and writing.

You can keep up-to-date with Andew by joining his mailing list at www.andrewjluther.com or on Twitter @andrewjluther.